THE
ADVENTURES
OF
DOD

CODE OF THE KINGS

D1572237

Also by Thomas R. Williams:

The Adventures of Dod, Confronting The Dread
The Adventures of Dod, Dark Hood and the Lair

THE
ADVENTURES
OF
DOD

CODE OF THE KINGS

THOMAS R. WILLIAMS

Zettai Makeru

Publisher's Cataloging-in-Publication Data

Williams, Thomas R. (Thomas Richards), 1971-
The Adventures of Dod : Code of the Kings / by Thomas R. Williams ; illustrations by Christine Coleman.

p. : ill. ; cm.

Summary: When a strange visitor ruins Cole's Christmas on Earth with frightening news, Cole escapes to Green and discovers that while facing the wrath of The Order and their monstrous dragon, he and his Twistyard friends must race to put clues together sufficient to solve an ancient mystery regarding the Code of the Kings before evil men beat them to it.

ISBN: 978-0-9833601-3-1 (pbk.)

[1. Adventure and adventurers—Juvenile fiction. 2. Imaginary places—Juvenile fiction. 3. Magic—Juvenile fiction. 4. Schools—Juvenile fiction. 5. Adventure and adventurers—Fiction. 6. Magic—Fiction. 7. Schools—Fiction. 8. Adventure fiction. 9. Fantasy fiction.] I. Coleman, Christine, 1975- II. Title.

PZ7.W6683Ad   2013
[Fic]   2013935170

Printed in the United States of America

10   9   8   7   6   5   4   3   2   1

For my friends in Green
who have welcomed me
into their lives

TABLE OF CONTENTS

PROLOGUE

As you've been told before, this story is almost too amazing to believe, but it's true! One seemingly insignificant boy did change the future for everyone. It's a tale that is filled with intrigue and mystery, loyal friendships and dark betrayals.

Cole's most recent visit to Green had left him with as many questions as answers. Was The Dread right about Humberrone being Cole's father, and if so, why hadn't Bonboo said anything about him? And how did someone in the trailer on Earth leave a note that was clearly from The Dread? With the destinies of Green, Raul, Soosh, and Earth becoming intertwined, Cole and his friends must race to defeat The Order before it's too late.

If you dare continue to read, keep your eyes open and your lights on. Who's a friend and who's a foe? Can you discover the truth? Good luck hunting for clues. Some people will stop at nothing to get what they want.

CHAPTER ONE

THE TRUTH

"He's a liar, Son!" huffed an aging man, leaning against a giant oak. The half moon was shrouded by clouds, forcing the stars out of hiding. "Don't speak for him! He's tilted your head by his hissings. That forked-tongue of his knows plenty of tricks. Mauj or not, he's full of trouble. That's why he's staying with the Zoots tonight. Shortly, my boy, he'll get what he deserves for dosing poison into the ears of our people."

"But he's right about your father...isn't he?"

"No! Of course not!"

Three regal horses stood cloaked in darkness, wearing shadows cast by millennial trees. A young boy waited patiently aboard one steed while the other two chargers held empty saddles.

"Then why don't *you* tell me the truth?" demanded the son, his manly figure encroaching upon his father. "You must know — now tell me —"

"The truth?" scoffed the old man. "It doesn't matter what's true and what's not — not anymore. What matters is where we are today. Look around us. The Code of the Kings is a thing of the

* 1 *

past, and we're left to keep what's ours by sword and sweat. With the wind on our side, perhaps the Tillius Empire will continue to grow. But it won't come from following the ridiculous babblings of a stiff-collared tredder who claims to have come from the cities of the Mauj."

The old man moved closer to his son and added, "Don't you think it's convenient that *he's* the only one in touch with humans in Soosh. Think of it. Even our friends in Raul haven't been in contact with Mauj visitors for decades. He's a liar! Nobody goes to *their* lands."

"And what of The Lost City — here in Green?" the strong man asked of his father, digging his hands into his overcoat pockets. "The visitor spoke of it, and now I've got proof that it's real — I've gathered books." He pointed at a sack that was secured behind the young lad. "People made visits through the underground waterways — "

"Or so they say," scoffed the old man. "Just let it die, Son. Burn the books. If it's hidden from us, it's just as well if it never existed. I'd agree that Mauj guests took a short stay here in Green and gave us our portal to Raul and a few other fancy contraptions, but there's no proof of them actually living here."

"Old timers talk of The City — they say your dad destroyed it with devilish beasts and drove the Mauj back to Soosh."

"Let them talk!" barked the aged man. "Commoners' memories are often flawed, but don't worry, they end at death. Let's write a new truth and be free of the slanderous past. Protect our blood, Son."

"And hide the cages atop our fortress?"

"My father kept a fleet of flutters back when they were more plentiful — I'd say that. He was a bold thinker. The lands and castles we have today are because of him. His efforts to behave wisely the world over have paid dividends aplenty. Look at all we own and control. You can sail the seas in every direction and find yourself welcomed by clusters of our subjects. Even among the rabble of billies we have the Hook and Palm Tree Islands and their productive ports."

"It doesn't matter!" argued the younger man. "We still can't change the past. Do you really think people will forget how the Ankle Weed Desert was created? People have maps that show what once was. The three biggest cities in Green were completely destroyed! Some horrible, awful, nightmarish power of evil was in the storm that struck with violence and melted them away. Even Lake Zoots and the Twin Discommo Lakes, with their vast expanses of fishable waters, disappeared overnight. The ground is scarred forever. The toughest blade of grass can't sprout for hundreds of miles, and that, too, if anyone can stand the stench enough to venture out to plant a seed. If my grandfather was involved, as the Mauj visitor suggests, then I want to know. Tell me the truth, Dad!"

"Nothing more than a storm," assured the old man, turning to smell the night breeze that blew uphill to them. "We're just lucky High Gate, Twistyard, and Lake Mauj were spared. Kingdoms fall everyday by the twitch of nature's finger. And you must admit, horrible as the landscape may appear, that that desert is the perfect spot to put a prison. No one would survive long trying to cross the wastelands on foot. When Driaxom is completed, it'll persuade people to stay loyal to us. Mark my words, with the leverage of a decent workhouse facility into which we may incarcerate insubordinates, High Gate will flourish and become Green's most prosperous city, and we shall reign from upon our thrones at Twistyard like the kings of old."

"Well then, it sounds like you've been listening to *the liar*, too, I see. He's very much in favor of your ongoing project in the Ankle Weed Desert."

"Rocks of rubbish! Perhaps he's been eavesdropping on me. He's cunning and deserves death."

"But he's right about so many things, Dad. He knows things — things that I can see must be true — things you won't tell me. Like the portal from Green to Soosh—when I was young…remember…you brought me with you to clean up the remains of the giant portal. I helped load the strange metal parts into carts that were sent to the furnaces. The stories he tells fit perfectly—about the TCC, and the fall of the Code of the Kings, and the rise of The Order. If an army didn't storm through the portal and cause it to collapse, then what did?"

"Oh my foolish son, you are right in saying you were young. I led you to think it had once been a portal to Soosh—to make the job fun for you—but the truth you need to know is this: There has never been a portal from here to Soosh. The debris we hauled was nothing more than the skeletal framing of a broken-down machine. Trust me, Son. There's nothing there worth remembering. Let it all go. The past doesn't matter anyway, only how we portray it to the people. If we remember the good my father did, and write it down, the kingdom will grow stronger."

A battalion of strapping soldiers approached stealthily through the darkness.

"Besides," conceded the old man, patting his son on the shoulder, as if sensing their opportunity to talk was drawing to a close. "You are the last of my children, and your son is all that you have to reign in your stead. It is time for the fighting to end. With this final battle, we'll finish our work and leave the ramblings of history behind us. Let's enjoy what we have."

"Sir," whispered the first soldier who reached the duo. "All of our men are in position. On your command we can end this struggle. The Zoot stronghold will fall quickly unless they're aided by swappers."

"We've given plenty to the poor," said the old man, moving to mount his horse. "Good is on our side. Press on! Attack! Zoot tyranny must never be allowed to resurface! At last we'll silence them and their libelous library of books!"

Within seconds, a horn blew and the air was filled with flaming arrows. The sparkling assault pelted the walls surrounding the fortified city and reached beyond to the buildings within. Flames quickly took hold of the mostly-wooden complex until the inferno burned so brightly that the two confronting armies battled in full light.

Tillius forces poured from the nearby woods and fields and were met powerfully by Zoot soldiers who seemed to have been waiting. The clanking and clatter of their fighting roared like a deafening wall of noise, making it hard for the royal father and son to say much of anything to their men from atop the hill where they viewed the scene. The young lad who was with them watched silently.

"One day all of the trees will grow back," yelled the old man to the young boy as he pointed toward the burning city. "You'll live to see beauty return to the Tillius Woodlands. Stay here for now. You're too young to enter battle. We'll be back shortly."

The old man signaled and his son nudged his horse to trot beside him. Together, with swords drawn, the two men made their way down the wooded hillside to the raging fight and disappeared into the chaos.

Minutes turned to hours as the conflict continued deep into the night. The flames from the once beautiful city kept the surrounding terrain lit for the duration and filled the skies with plumes of black smoke. It wasn't until early morning that the attacking forces finished their job and let out a howling cry—eerie sounds of joy in victory and sorrow in the loss of so many fallen friends. It had been a bloody and horrible battle for the Tillius warriors, despite their triumph over the Zoots.

"I told you we would prevail," muttered the old man to the young lad as he approached, slumping in his saddle. He coughed and sputtered, as if in pain, and was helped from his horse to the ground by a dozen waiting soldiers. "Come closer, Concealio," said the man, beckoning to the boy with his hand. "Your father is gone now…he died a brave man in battle…and as your grandfather I would like to ask a dying wish."

The young lad hadn't said a word all night, and now that the battle was over, his eyes were so full of tears that he likely couldn't see.

"Please, Concealio. Listen." The man's words were urgent. "I know you're young—as young as I was when I took my father's place—but you are now the keeper of all the Tillius lands. Protect them. Protect your blood. Bring honor and glory to the mighty Tillius family, for we are heirs by inheritance of the best tredder blood."

"You'll live, Grandpa," said the boy, speaking what he seemed to hope, though his face revealed he didn't believe it. His grandfather's wounds were severe.

"Listen!" urged the old man, trying to sit up. When his efforts failed, he resorted to lying back. He held the boy's hand and squeezed it for emphasis. "Burn the books your father has gathered. If you don't, they will only cause trouble for you. No good can come of them...not for us...not for you. The Tillius family has done much good, my father included. We can't have records that would lead people to focus on the bad."

"But Grandpa—" began the boy, his throat choked with emotion.

"Books are good," insisted the old man, shaking his head. "Make sure there are lots of books—make a library of books in the castle—and tell the Tillius story. We have so much to be proud of. Do you know that my grandfather helped create the Code of the Kings? He wanted peace for everyone. His hands built the sanctuary at High Gate for their meetings...and you've read the words on the wall...KEEP EACH HIS KINGDOM STRONG FOR SUBJECTS FIRST, THEN RULERS, BY THE UNITED WILL OF ALL MANKIND."

"I've read it," said the boy, watching his grandfather's eyes grow glossy.

"And my father continued as his father, building up the Code of the Kings," insisted the old man, his voice fading. "He helped institute the three chairs for the three realms...brought order to the brotherhood for a time...but do they remember? Do they remember that?"

"Yes grandpa. I remember."

"No," mumbled the dying man, taking raspy, sparse breaths. "They talk of the TCC... and The Lost City... and The Order... and..."

CHAPTER ONE

"I remember," sobbed the boy. He felt his grandfather's grip go limp. "I'll remember. I won't forget. I promise."

The old man lay as still as the ground below him and joined ranks with the soldiers that had fallen.

Months later, Concealio Tillius rose to the full height of his stature—far from grown at twenty-one as a tredder—and held a special ceremony at High Gate where he vowed to enlarge the building that commemorated the Code of the Kings. He had sent word to Raul, and through them hoped that Soosh would also be informed, that he wished to reestablish the same system that had been had among the people hundreds of years before. At the meeting, he spoke about the need for universal peace and a resurgence of the ideals that had been embodied in the original code.

"We can't keep fighting each other and hope to find peace," he said. "We've all seen the devastating effects of war. And until we learn to be civil, to have rules that govern each area and kingdom and realm so as to prevent groups from attacking other groups, I'm determined we will remain in the dark and be blind to the secrets that could otherwise open our eyes to greater things."

The crowd grew restless at the mention of secrets, for many people sought to know what had been gathered by Concealio's father, especially as it pertained to The Lost City.

"There are mysteries to be found that would change so much around us if only we could handle the knowledge; but given our current state of disunity, let priceless keys be as ashes, the truth to dust if you will, until the three realms have representation in the matters of things hidden and their kings' scepters be joined in purpose to that end—not for war."

As a token of his true desire to reignite the feelings of brotherhood that had once been shared between groups in all three realms, he took from his family's trophy stash three objects. They were swords that had originally been made by a brilliant Mauj scientist: one for Green, one for Raul, and one for Soosh.

As the crowd gasped, Concealio continued, "These unusual swords prove that we once had good ties with the Mauj in Soosh, and that their representatives sat in this very chamber, along with eight from Raul and eight from Green. The twenty-four men passed judgment and lent support. They were a brotherhood. Of course we still had wars and conflicts, but this unusual group of people helped decide who was in the right and gave assistance accordingly."

Few people could take their eyes off the magnificent swords. Each was different, but special; one had a ruby-encrusted handle and the words *'Tillius, Freedom for All'* etched up the side in fancy writing; one had an unusual crimson blade and the words *'Chards, Knowledge for All'* written in gold; and one had a bright-white blade and the words *'Chantolli, Power for All'* imprinted in shiny black.

Many people had heard rumors of the weapons and their special capacities. The fact that they were real spoke volumes in an instant about the nature of Green's true history.

"Will the senior-most representative from Raul please come forward," called Concealio. He searched the crowd with his eyes as he held up the white sword.

From the middle of the room, a hundred-and-fifty-year-old tredder rose to his feet and looked around officiously. He swaggered his way to the front like he knew he was the best. "I'm certainly the oldest from Raul—or at least the oldest with the right blood."

A cluster of men, who had been seated near the man, laughed and looked to another portion of the room where a number of older-looking guests held their peace.

"I'm a Donefur," said the well-dressed prince. "You can give me the sword. Perhaps we can have the Chantolli name removed."

His friends roared obnoxiously.

Concealio hesitated, then chose to honor their customs. "I present this rapier to you and all of Raul on behalf of Green. May we find friendship and peace in the future as we seek *power for all*."

The prince from Raul snatched the sword, tucked it into its scabbard, and tipped his head arrogantly. Everyone clapped.

"Will the senior-most representative from Soosh please come forward," called Concealio. He waited but no one arose.

"Do we have any representation from the Mauj?" asked Concealio. The silent audience looked side to side as though they fully expected someone would eventually confess his allegiance. A handsome man near the back entrance slowly stood, hesitated, and finally worked his way forward.

"It's you!" said Concealio, eyeing the tredder suspiciously. "You escaped my grandfather's trap."

"As did you," responded the mysterious tredder, holding one hand beneath his cape. He was ready for action if Concealio's generous offer turned traitorous. "I'm sorry about your father. We were good friends. If only things had been different."

"So tell me honestly," demanded Concealio, shifting his stance. It was a sign to his soldiers, for the men guarding the doors drew their swords. "Have you really lived among the humans in Soosh?"

"I most certainly have," responded the man indignantly. "I'm as much a Mauj as any human, regardless of the obvious fact that I'm a tredder—one of noble blood!" The man glared menacingly at the prince from Raul who had just sat down. "And I'm certain I know more of these swords than anyone here."

Concealio took a step back.

The self-proclaimed Mauj visitor raised his hands in the air, showing he hadn't armed himself, and spoke up. "I'll prove I know plenty," he bragged. "On the bottom of the Chantolli sword's hilt—the one you so quickly gave to that arrogant, foolish prince of the Donefur clan—there's a tiny X inscribed. Go ahead and look."

Concealio nodded toward the man to whom he had just given the prize. A quick peek turned the noble's face red.

"Well?" asked Concealio.

"It has an X," grumbled the man with the sword. "But he could have seen it in passing."

"So true," confessed the Mauj visitor, nodding his head pleasantly. "Now grab the bottom of the hilt and give it a gentle twist to the right. You'll discover a secret compartment with tiny darts—assuming they're still there."

Concealio watched in amazement as the Donefur prince found the words to be true.

"Now then," said the Mauj visitor, pointing at the crimson blade. "May I return *that* sword to the Mauj? I'm sure they'll accept your offering as a sign that you mean to do better than your forefathers who stole it."

The audience gasped. Most of them were affiliated with the Tillius family, so slander against Concealio's blood was more than offensive.

"I'll handle this one," grunted a massive guard who left his post to approach the audacious visitor.

Quick as a flash of lightning, the Mauj tredder tripped Concealio and stripped the crimson blade from his hands as he went down. "I accept your kind offering," he gloated, spinning just in time to tap swords with the attacking guard.

CLASH, CLASH, CLANK!

"Nice moves," said the Mauj tredder. "Perhaps you know a good defense for this!" He plunged his sword toward the guard's shoulder while cleverly tripping him as he had done to Concealio. "Feel free to stay down," he added as he bolted toward the back. Though he only made it halfway when he spun around and lunged toward the Donefur prince, who immediately jumped to his feet and drew the white blade from its sheath.

Everyone hustled to clear out of their way. The makeshift seats that filled the hall were nothing more than long-board benches, so when the two began to duel, they hopped about from board to board, jabbing in and out at each other.

"You'll soon discover that the best of swordsmen come from Raul!" bellowed the Donefur prince.

"Yes, I know," said the Mauj visitor, giving blow for blow as good as he was taking. The two rivals plunged and clanked, twirling and striking with remarkable force.

Eventually, a mob of six armed guards approached the Mauj visitor from the rear at the same time as the Donefur prince pressed in. But in a twist of clever footwork, the Mauj visitor ducked and twirled his way into trading places with the Donefur prince, right as two guards drove downward with their blades, causing the prince to fall wounded to the ground.

"They did it, not me," insisted the Mauj visitor, flipping the white sword into the air with the tip of his crimson blade. He caught it and grinned.

"You'll pay!" screamed the wounded prince, his pride as beaten as were his injured legs.

"Yes, I suppose I will," said the Mauj visitor, hopping benches with his nimble feet. "I'll pay this sword to your Chantolli associates—the ones who should have rightly been given this gift."

The crowd parted to avoid getting mixed in the trouble, since most of the participants weren't armed for conflict. But just as he had said, the Mauj visitor worked his way in the direction of the older guests from Raul and slid the white sword to them before fighting his way to freedom with the crimson blade.

"What a clever man," sighed Concealio when the guards turned up empty. "It's a pity we were never properly introduced. He's the best swordsman I've ever seen."

Despite Concealio's efforts, the Code of the Kings was a thing of the past, though Concealio's influence certainly affected his grandson, Bonboo's father. As ambassadors to the Mauj, Bonboo's parents learned of democracy and brought the ideas back home, changing the Tillius Empire forever—and all of Green as well.

CHAPTER TWO

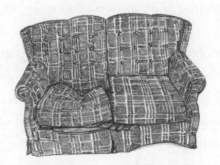

BACK HOME

"Do I get to open your present now?" asked Cole, inspecting Josh's face. Cole felt relieved to be home with his family in time for Christmas. It seemed like ages since he had seen his loved ones.

"No!" said ten-year-old Josh. "It's only Christmas Eve. You have to wait until tomorrow morning."

"Oh, right," said Cole, still hugging his mother and Alex. Cole was curious about the large, wrapped box Josh held, especially since Josh's face was bursting with a secret.

"I'm really sorry about everything," confessed Cole, looking down into his mother's teary eyes. "I shouldn't have run off like that."

In truth, Cole hadn't. He had been caught in a bind with a bunch of mean pirate-like men in the trailer where he had found his medallion—the one someone had stolen from him. And once he had made it to Green, he had taken the charm off so that time could pass on Earth, allowing him to return to an empty trailer. The plan had worked well, except it had left Cole's family thinking he had run away for a couple of days.

"You can't fool me, Cole!" blared Josh, tucking the beautiful present back under the Christmas tree. "You were off fighting with The Dread. I kept telling Mom you'd be back once the job was done."

"How did you know?" asked Cole, only half serious. Josh alone seemed to truly believe Green existed.

"I have my secrets, too," he said, grinning ear-to-ear. "If you share your stories with me, I might tell you what I know."

Two knocks hit the front door before it swung open. "I knew it was you!" burst Aunt Hilda, rushing to hug Cole. "You can't scare us like that again. Running away is one thing, but running away to *Sin City* is another! Las Vegas can be a dangerous place. You never know what kind of trouble can be lurking around the corner."

"Right—I'm sorry," said Cole. He couldn't help thinking that the worst, most frightening alley in Las Vegas, or pretty much anywhere else on Earth, couldn't possibly be as bad as where he had been: Driaxom! Just the thought of Driaxom made his ankle ache. At least the venomous weed was gone.

"Besides," continued Aunt Hilda, "you missed a caller last night—a special guest."

"Huh?" Cole was clueless.

"It was a *girl*," said Josh, dancing around the room. "A girl came to our house to talk with you."

"What? Who?" stuttered Cole. Something wasn't right. His gut felt uneasy. He had never had a girl try to visit him at home. It was a first, and it smelled fishy.

"You didn't tell me—" began Doralee.

"Well, she only stopped by for a minute," said Aunt Hilda. "And it was late. But I must say, Cole, she's quite a looker! Are you sure she's in ninth grade?"

"Who?" asked Cole.

"Your friend. She's a tall brunette. Dresses really classy. I think she said she's in one of your classes."

"Oh no!" groaned Cole. Aunt Hilda could have said that a mob of pirates had stopped by to get the medallion and it wouldn't have made him feel any worse. The girl was surely his mystery partner from his science class—the one who had likely stolen his charm while he was unconscious. And judging by her timely visit, she was connected to the brutes who had nearly mashed him while in the trailer.

"Don't be silly," insisted Aunt Hilda. "You don't need to act that way anymore about *them*. You'll be turning fifteen soon. Girls don't really have cooties."

"Yes, they do!" blared Josh. "After Ashley kissed Robbie on the playground, he got sick for three days."

Alex tugged at Cole's shirt and smiled. "What's her name?" he asked gingerly.

"I don't know," answered Cole. His mind was rushing to think of what to do next. Should he call the police? What would he say? It was really complicated. Even his own relatives wouldn't likely believe him if he explained.

"She probably wanted to give you a Christmas present," said Cole's mother. "You better help me put together a few extra plates of cookies in case more of your *classmates* come calling."

Cookies, thought Cole. *I don't need cookies, I need Boot and a few of my friends from Green, or at least a battalion of drat soldiers.*

Christmas Eve was ruined. Every knock at the door was nerve racking, and with all of the kind neighbors bringing treats, there were plenty of guests. But it wasn't until visiting hours were long over and Doralee had just finished leading a round of Silent Night that the mystery girl decided to show up.

"Can I please speak with Cole?" asked the girl, facing Aunt Hilda first.

"Come on in," said Aunt Hilda warmly, wearing an enormous smile. "Have a seat by the tree."

Cole couldn't believe it. He had searched and searched for months, trying to discover the identity of his lab partner, and now here she was, sitting in his living room.

"Hey Cole," said the girl. She flipped her straight brown hair out of her face and nervously tucked it behind her ear as she situated herself on the worn, two-cushion loveseat by the window. A regular couch wouldn't fit very well in the tiny room, especially with the meager Christmas tree consuming much of the walking space.

"I'm Doralee Richards," said Cole's mother, putting out her hand to shake. "And these are Cole's brothers, Alex and Josh."

"And I'm his aunt," added Hilda. "We met last night."

"Right," chuckled the girl uncomfortably. "I'm Ruth Gunderson."

The room went silent momentarily—an awkward, heavy kind of silence while everyone stared.

"Well then. I'll be back in the morning to see what Santa's brought for me," sighed Hilda, winking at Cole. It made him want to die.

"Santa won't be coming unless Alex and Josh head up to bed," said Doralee, taking one last proud look at her oldest son as though he had just brought home a championship trophy.

"We're going," responded Alex, tugging his brother Josh into the kitchen, leaving Cole and Ruth alone.

"Hi," choked Cole, looking away from Ruth with his milk chocolate eyes. He felt mixed up inside. The cocky, popular, couldn't-care-less girl who had ignored him in science class didn't even resemble the concerned girl who sat in his living room.

"I know you're going to think I'm crazy," began the girl, mostly staring at the floor as she whispered, "but I really, really need your help right now."

"With what?" asked Cole, cautiously moving closer so he could hear.

"Okay, first off, I'm sorry I had any part in helping Brewer steal your coin."

"I knew it!" snapped Cole.

"I thought it was just a joke."

"Huh?"

"You know," said Ruth, "I thought you guys were playing a game. Brewer lived next door to my aunt, so while I was visiting, he asked me to help him figure out where you kept your coin. He told me the two of you pretended it could take you to another world. If I helped him, he promised to pay my cell phone bill."

"You thought I was playing a game with Mr. Brewer?" scoffed Cole. He felt like the girl was telling the truth, but her story sounded stupid. "He was my science teacher. Why would I play games with him?"

"I don't know," mumbled Ruth. She was tearing up. "I guess I'm an idiot. After my mom died, everything's been crazy. My dad was hardly home before, and now that I'm alone, he moves me around with him like a suitcase—military. I hate moving!" She used the ends of her sleeves to wipe tears. "He thinks being a general is like being the president of the United States."

"Oh," said Cole. He didn't know how to handle a crying girl. But he did the boldest thing he could think of: He sat next to her.

"I don't even know where he is right now. You would think he would give me his number. He's been gone for over a month doing important training on a base in Germany...or England... or somewhere far away. I was staying with friends in Texas when I got the call."

"Well, if he's calling—" began Cole sheepishly.

Ruth looked at Cole. "Not my dad—Brewer!"

"Oh," sighed Cole. "He's not happy right now, is he?" Cole pulled the medallion out from beneath his shirt and dangled it from his hand.

"You do have it," gasped the girl, her voice drenched with relief. "How did you get it from him?"

"It wasn't easy," said Cole. "After you stole it from me in class—"

"I didn't steal it," snapped Ruth. "When you got hurt, I was the one who tried to help you. But you punched and kicked me—gave me a black eye and a bloody lip."

At last the truth was coming out.

"And then what—Mr. Brewer took it?" asked Cole.

"No. But he would've if he could've. He had people leave the room—told them to go and get help from the office. And then he asked me if I knew where your coin was. I had seen you touch your shirt when talking about going to another world, so I assumed you wore it around your neck."

"You kept helping him?" grumbled Cole. "You couldn't have thought it was a game—not with me unconscious on the floor!"

"You don't understand," sobbed Ruth, "I thought the coin-necklace thing was one of Brewer's trinkets and it was causing you to freak out—lead poisoning or something...I don't know."

"So that's when Mr. Brewer stole it?"

"No," said the girl. She cracked a weak smile through her tears. "When he tried to get it, you kicked him in the knee so hard I heard it crack. After that, two people from the office came in and his opportunity was gone."

Cole smiled.

"Anyway, he said something about getting it from you later. He must have stolen it from your house. Within a week, he moved away from my aunt's neighborhood and that was the end of him—or so I thought."

"Maybe," admitted Cole, remembering how the day after his injury he had awakened on the floor of his bedroom with a sore hand.

Ruth nodded quietly, as if building the courage to say something. "I don't know what to do or where to turn. Brewer has my Aunt Naomi. She's my favorite, Cole. I was planning on moving in with her this summer—like for good. No more moving unless I choose to move."

"He has your aunt?" asked Cole. "Where are they?"

"I don't know," said Ruth. "He called me Saturday night and told me not to tell anyone or he'd kill her. He wants that coin back and thinks I can get it from you."

"And you're sure he has her?"

"Yeah. I used the spare key to get into her house," said Ruth. "She's gone, and her purse and car are still there."

"What about the police?"

Ruth shook her head. "They'll kill her. We can't tell anyone else. Brewer gave me until Friday. He said he'll call on Thursday to tell me where to make the exchange—so that gives us a few days. But don't worry—we'll pay you for the coin. I promise. Just help me get my aunt back. Please."

"Is everything all right?" asked Doralee, entering the room. The crying had likely tipped her off.

"I'm fine," lied Ruth, faking a happier voice. "I was just getting ready to leave. Sorry I barged in on your Christmas Eve celebration."

"Are you okay, honey?"

"She's just sad about spending Christmas alone," said Cole.

"Where are your parents?" asked Doralee.

"It's fine...I'm fine," responded Ruth, standing up. "I'm seventeen. I actually graduated from high school early—last spring—so I don't mind being at my aunt's place by myself."

"Not on Christmas," insisted Doralee. "If you don't have family to share it with, you can stay next door with Hilda and celebrate Christmas with us."

Cole had mixed feelings about his mother's generous offer.

"No," said Ruth. "I'm fine. Really."

"Now where did you say your parents are?" asked Doralee, moving toward Ruth.

Cole jumped in. "Her mom's dead, her dad's away in the military, and her aunt is out of town for the holidays."

"Oh! I see why you two are friends," said Doralee. "It's been hard on Cole losing his father and grandfather."

"Mom!"

Ruth shot Cole a glance that suggested the new information had changed her opinion of him. "I really can't stay," argued Ruth.

"I insist," said Doralee, and she wrapped an arm around Ruth and escorted her to Hilda's half of the duplex. The commotion was loud enough that Cole could hear the battle going on through the wall, though with both Hilda and Doralee pressing Ruth to spend Christmas with them, Ruth didn't stand a chance.

JOSH'S GIFT

All night Cole worried about Ruth. Would she attempt to steal the medallion? Were her tears fake? Was her aunt really a hostage? So many things pointed uncomfortably toward trouble. Cole finally took his blanket and wormed his way under Alex's bed, behind piles of junk. He certainly didn't want to lose his medallion again, this time to the sticky fingers of a cute girl in distress.

In the morning, everyone was eating breakfast before Cole made his entrance.

"See, I told you he was just hiding under his blankets," said Doralee.

"No. He was gone—off fighting bad guys in Green!" protested Josh, sharing the edge of Ruth's chair. "I checked everywhere."

"Your brother's funny," said Ruth, not bothered by Josh's intrusion of her personal space. Alex was sitting in the other good chair, Hilda was balancing on the broken one, and Doralee was standing at the counter. Nobody seemed rushed to open presents since there were so few, and waiting longer in suspense helped keep the excitement of Christmas alive.

"Hot chocolate?" asked Doralee, grabbing a mug that had 'Best Mother Ever' written in pink cursive. She filled the cup, poured in a heaping pile of little marshmallows, and handed it to Cole.

"If you look out the window you'll feel like drinking it," added Hilda. "It's snowing outside. We've got at least a foot. Apparently, someone's been praying for a white Christmas." Everyone but Cole looked at Alex.

"What? I like it when it snows."

"Then *you* can do all of the shoveling," said Cole.

"I like shoveling," mumbled Josh. His mouth was full of French toast.

"I'll help," chirped Ruth. "It's been years since I've had a white Christmas. Last year I was in California, the year before—let's see—Okinawa, and the year before that I was in Hawaii."

"That must have been rough," said Cole. "You probably had to spend Christmas on the beach."

Ruth smiled. "I've done that a few times. It's not bad. But after a while, it's just another place. People are what make the holidays fun."

"Well, we're happy to have you here with us this year," said Hilda. "The more the merrier."

"Thanks."

Cole felt bad for having misjudged Ruth.

When it came time for opening presents, Josh was nearly uncontrollable. He seemed extra eager to see the looks on people's faces when they opened the presents he had wrapped for them, though he insisted that his gifts be given at the end.

Josh's Gift

Ruth went first. Josh forced a wad of tape and old crinkled assignments into her lap. "Sorry I didn't have real wrapping paper," he said. "I got up early to make you a present."

Inside, Ruth found a pair of superhero wristbands made of toilet paper tubes and a headband made of braided scraps of old socks.

"I figured you might need stuff like that since you're hanging around *him*," explained Josh, tipping his head toward Cole. "He's always catching criminals, like he caught the guy who poisoned our grandpa."

Ruth raised her eyebrows at Cole and then slipped her presents on.

"One day he's gonna bring me to Green, too," insisted Josh. "It's our destiny."

"Your destiny?" laughed Ruth. "Sounds fun. Thanks for the bracelets."

Alex followed Ruth and opened his present from Josh. He got a well-used flashlight. Next, Hilda unwrapped a homemade wreath and Doralee unwrapped a ceramic blob that was supposed to be a crocodile coin holder.

Cole got his present last. Inside the box was a shiny, golden crown. It had triangle-shaped points that circled a thick, adjustable band. In the center of the largest triangle someone had drawn in permanent black marker a circle with three smaller circles inside it. The craftsmanship of the sketch appeared to be as homemade as Hilda's wreath.

"Now you can be the king of Green," said Josh. "You deserve it."

"Thanks," responded Cole. He didn't have the heart to tell Josh that the government in Green was a democracy, not a monarchy.

"I bought it with my weeding money," added Josh proudly. "But I made a few changes. Maybe we could take turns."

"Sure," said Cole, adjusting the band so Josh could wear it first. "We can share the throne."

"Don't forget about me," burst Alex. He had been happy with his present from Josh until Cole's was unwrapped.

"We could be just like the three kings," said Josh excitedly, sticking his chest out as he marched back and forth wearing the crown. "Take me and Alex with you next time you go to Green, okay?"

"Don't you mean the three wise men?" giggled Hilda.

"No—the three kings," insisted Josh. He glanced at Cole for backup and found none. "I mean…well…I guess they are the three wise men, huh?"

Cole sensed Josh had more to say but was curiously holding back.

"That crown would be a perfect prop for the neighborhood Christmas pageant next year," said Hilda. She borrowed it and inspected the craftsmanship. "This one's a keeper. Where did you get it from?"

"Aunt Hilda!" proclaimed Josh. "It's a Christmas present!"

"Right," mumbled Hilda. Not more than a week before, Doralee had spent thirty minutes lecturing Josh and Alex on the finer points of gift receiving, since they had both broken all of the rules and asked Coach Smith how much he had paid for the gloves and hats he had brought over, and whether he had gotten them on sale, and whether they had come from the thrift store.

"Can I be the queen?" asked Ruth, situating her headband.

"I don't think so," answered Josh, looking doubtful. "Dilly and Sawny wouldn't allow it—right Cole?"

"Oh, I don't know," said Cole sheepishly. He felt uncomfortable talking about Green in front of Ruth. She didn't seem to think it was a real place. As far as she knew, the coin around Cole's neck was only valuable as a collector's item, not as a real mechanism for transporting someone to another world.

"Perhaps I could *persuade* them to change their minds," responded Ruth playfully in an ominous voice. She displayed her wristbands as she pretended to prepare for a scuffle.

"Good luck," said Josh matter-of-factly. "Dilly's about as good as they come with a sword, and those wrist shields are just pretend. They wouldn't help you in a real duel."

A groaning sound rumbled from the front yard and drew everyone to the window, which nearly knocked the Christmas tree over.

"Keep making him cookies," said Hilda, patting Doralee on the shoulder. Coach Smith had just emptied the bed of his truck and was unleashing his massive snow blower on the front walks.

"He's stealing our snow," whined Josh.

"Then you better hurry out there and help him," said Doralee. "The stairs and front porch are all yours."

"Yes!" cried Josh eagerly. He jumped three steps to the closet and proceeded to put his snow gear on over his pajamas. Alex shivered and climbed under a blanket on the loveseat.

"Wait for me," said Ruth. She stole Cole's hat, boots, coat, and gloves before following Josh out the door to help with shoveling. Cole was glad he had an excuse to not go out.

The rest of Christmas day proceeded in a relatively uneventful fashion, with Coach Smith and Bobby spending the day playing Monopoly on the floor with Alex, Ruth, and Hilda while Doralee baked in the kitchen and Cole and Josh tinkered around the small duplex.

Cole couldn't stop worrying. He was surprised that Ruth appeared to be enjoying herself. Thoughts of having to confront trouble in a few days were enough to ruin his Christmas. Ruth's solution of buying the coin wasn't an option. The medallion wasn't for sale at any price.

Wednesday flew by as quickly as Christmas had. Ruth cornered Cole for a few moments before he bolted out the door to spend the day with The Guys. She made sure Cole was willing to keep their secret. Nobody could know of her aunt's capture and Mr. Brewer's price for her safe release.

While fencing with Jack Parry, Cole did his best to pick Jack's brain for ideas without divulging too much. The best advice he got from the old man was, "Whatever it takes, be true to yourself." For Cole, that meant keeping the necklace. But it didn't answer the big question: What should he do?

When Thursday arrived, solutions were as difficult to find as they had been the moment Cole had first heard of the problem. He pushed his oatmeal around in his bowl for an hour, as though his breakfast contained the answer. And Ruth hardly touched her food. Together they sat at the kitchen table and made small talk while Josh and Alex played Checkers on the floor. Doralee was working and scheduled to be gone until late since she was pulling two shifts—one for a sick friend.

"I still don't know why we can't go sledding," complained Josh, glancing up at Ruth. She had shoveled and thrown snowballs for hours on Christmas.

"Today's an inside day," responded Cole. "It's snowing again."

"So?" said Josh "It's fun to play in the snow—huh Ruth?"

She didn't reply. Her eyes were fixed on her cell phone, dreading its ring.

"Come on. Please!"

"Not today," mumbled Ruth, flipping her hair for the hundredth time. She appeared to be processing Cole's reluctance to sell his medallion. The night before, she had asked him how much he wanted her Aunt Naomi to pay, as reimbursement, and Cole hadn't given her a price.

"Your turn," said Alex, prodding Josh to move.

"Then let's go to Green," argued Josh. "Does it snow much there?"

Cole hesitated. "In the mountains, I guess. And probably up north." He looked wistful. He had tried repeatedly to get back to Green, hoping to postpone his troubles on Earth.

Ruth glanced at Cole. "So, in your games, do you use the necklace to go to your magical world?"

Josh's eyes lit up. "Is that how you do it?" He inspected Cole's face and jumped to his feet. "No wonder! I've been trying to get there for months, but every time I go into our closet, it's just a closet."

"That's silly," said Cole defensively.

"Not really," added Ruth. "Haven't you ever read *The Lion, the Witch, and the Wardrobe*? It's a classic. They enter another world through a special closet."

"That's why you wanted your luck charm back!" shouted Josh with glee. He delighted in finally discovering the mystery. Cole's face didn't lie.

"Who gave it to you?" asked Ruth.

"He got it from our dad," said Josh, dancing around.

"No, I didn't," argued Cole.

"Yes!" insisted Josh. "Our dad gave it to our grandpa for keeping…" Josh's enthusiasm dimmed and he went quiet for a moment before adding in a more subdued tone, "Now it's Cole's."

"Dang!" said Ruth. "Sounds special." She seemed to be calculating how much more she and her aunt would be paying to get Cole to part with it. "Have you ever tried to get to Bean using a lucky rabbit's foot?" She dug into her jacket pocket and pulled out a pink rabbit's foot keychain.

Josh laughed. "It's Green, not Bean."

"Oh, right." Ruth's leg jiggled up and down nervously.

"You don't think it's a real place, do you?" asked Josh, moving in to inspect Ruth's keychain.

Ruth looked at Josh with burrowing eyes. "Yes. I think it's real. I've actually been there before." She held up her rabbit's foot. "The cool thing is…well…if you use this instead of Cole's necklace, Santa comes and gives you a ride there in his sleigh."

"He does not!" said Josh. "I don't think Santa visits people in Green, does he?" Josh looked to Cole for the answer.

"I don't know," responded Cole reluctantly. The conversation was making his stomach hurt worse.

"It works," insisted Ruth. "I've gone there many times and fought all sorts of bad people. I'm the quickest gun in Green. Nobody gets past me."

Josh looked at Cole and shook his head. "She's another doubter. Why is it so hard for people to believe that Green is real? I bet nobody in Green has a problem with you being from Earth."

Cole felt a foreboding wave of discomfort. None of the Coosings knew of his origins.

"What makes you so sure I haven't been there?" asked Ruth. She poked at Josh with her lucky keychain.

"They don't have guns in Green," snapped Alex, who unexpectedly spoke up from the floor.

"Says who?"

Josh walked past Ruth to Cole. "Show her your scar."

Cole shook his head, though he didn't physically stop Josh when he pulled at Cole's shirt, revealing the spot where The Dread had sliced Cole's shoulder.

"Huh," said Ruth, looking interested. And then her cell phone rang. The number of the caller was blocked. It startled Ruth. When she answered it, her face regained composure. It was her father, wishing her a belated merry Christmas.

Cole left his unfinished bowl of oatmeal at the table and plopped himself down on the loveseat in the living room. He watched the falling snow and wished to be in Green. He hated to hurt anyone, and the more he was around Ruth, the more he felt sorry for her. The two sides of the situation tore at him and plagued his mind ceaselessly. There had to be a way to save Ruth's aunt without giving up the necklace.

In time, the dancing flakes of snow soothed Cole's aching mind and he succumbed to the pull of three sleepless nights. He only dozed off for a moment, but in horror awoke and found Josh holding the medallion!

"What are you doing?" exploded Cole, snatching the necklace. "How long have you had it?"

"I was just looking at the markings," said Josh. "I want to draw the star." He had a piece of paper and pencil next to him on the floor.

"How long?" demanded Cole, his heart racing anxiously. It terrified him to think that someone could take it without him knowing.

"I just barely got it," said Josh.

"How long?" continued Cole. "A few minutes, seconds, what?"

"Maybe a minute," confessed Josh. "I don't know."

Cole groaned as he slipped the chain back over his head.

"I wasn't going to keep it," insisted Josh, wearing a confused, hurt look. "Honest. I promise."

Two knocks hit the door and Hilda came in with a large, grease-stained box in her hands. "Food's still warm if you're hungry," she said, hustling to the kitchen. "Sausage, bacon, eggs, hash browns, pancakes—come and get it."

"Smells great!" said Ruth, greeting her at the table. "Who were you serving this morning?"

"A half-empty room of employees at the University. I think the snow and holidays kept people from attending their annual winter planning meeting."

"Real food!" squealed Alex excitedly. "We'll be eating like kings for a week."

"Catering has its perks," admitted Hilda. She set the large box on the counter and began stuffing miscellaneous containers with leftovers until the fridge was full.

Ruth waited behind Josh and Alex for a turn to make a plate, when her phone rang again. This time her face drained.

She scurried from the room and stepped out onto the snowy porch to take the call.

Cole watched her through the front window and felt ill.

It was only a moment before Ruth reentered the living room wearing snow-speckled hair and a relieved look. "She's okay," sighed Ruth. "They let me talk with her. If we give them the coin, they'll let her go. They want us on the Vegas Strip tomorrow afternoon, by the Circus Circus casino. Brewer said he'll phone me with more instructions."

Cole didn't speak, he just nodded his head.

TRADING TROUBLES

After Ruth knew her aunt was safe and the price for her release was within reach, she floated around the duplex as though an elephant had been lifted off her shoulders. Cole didn't feel the same relief. It was as if the two tons of worry had been shifted to him. How could he let Ruth down?

"I've got to get back to Green," mumbled Cole to himself, ignoring the food in the kitchen as he made his way up to his room.

Hour after hour he tried everything to coax the medallion to work, but his efforts were fruitless. Nothing helped. Staring made his eyes hurt, and concentrating made him sleepy. Eventually he stood at the window and did his best to reenact his first launch to Green—when he had focused on a large raindrop. Unfortunately, within a few seconds he was greatly distracted by a snowball Ruth planted against the glass and calls from Josh and Alex for Cole to come out and join them in building a snow fort.

"It's impossible," moaned Cole, flopping down on his bed.

No it's not! echoed in Cole's mind, as though Jack Parry were standing in his room scolding him. *Be a doer!*

Cole pulled the coin out of his shirt and studied the ten-point star, then glanced at the top of his cluttered chest of drawers where Josh's crown sat. Regal feelings flooded over Cole as he whispered, "I'm Pap's grandson, and Humberrone's my father. It's my destiny to return to Green."

As soon as Cole said it, his surroundings changed and he was standing in the Great Hall at Twistyard, arms wrapped around nothing, in the midst of a chaotic throng of dancing couples.

Where's Sawny? he thought as his arms fell to his sides. The slower music had been replaced by a song with a strong beat that had everyone hopping and jumping.

"Look! Dod's right there," said a familiar voice.

Dod spun around and saw a concerned Sawny being guided toward him by Dilly. Sawny's light brown hair had curls that resembled the ones in her older sister's darker, brown hair, as if the girls had pressed upon the same person to help them get ready for the dance, so they would be matching. The two looked a lot alike and were both attractive, but Dod's heart was drawn to Sawny.

"I think I'm not well," confessed Sawny, putting her hand to her brow. "One moment I was dancing and the next…" Sawny shook her head in confusion. "I need to sit."

"You're feeling overwhelmed," said Dilly knowingly. "I am, too. We were looking at losing all of this, and now, thanks to Dod, everything's okay." Dilly glanced happily at Dod, who hoped his face wasn't showing the guilt he felt.

"It's more than that," confessed Sawny as Dod and Dilly walked her toward the sitting area. "It's like…well…"

CHAPTER FOUR

"I know exactly what you mean," continued Dilly. "Wow! It's more than we could have hoped for."

"No," said Sawny bleakly. "I really think I'm not well. I'm hallucinating."

"Pinch-pinch," laughed Dilly. "It's not a dream. Dod really found the pure-sight diamonds—the whole Farmer's Sackload! I'm in shock, too. Now Twistyard won't have to be sold. The Tillius legacy continues. Everything's perfect."

"I danced with you, right?" Sawny puzzled, glancing nervously at Dod as she took a seat in a relatively empty part of the hall.

"Yes," responded Dod sheepishly. It had been the best few seconds of his life.

Sawny closed her eyes and went silent except for her steady, calculated breaths.

"I'll go for juice," chirped Dilly. She bounced away, nearly manic from the euphoria of gaining her property and life back just minutes before.

Dod sat next to Sawny and watched the beautiful swirling dresses. Four songs passed without Dilly's return, then five, then six.

"Are you feeling better?" asked Dod, beginning to grow restless. The room was anything but silent, yet the lack of conversation between Dod and Sawny was becoming more than awkward.

"I don't know." said Sawny. "I can't figure out what happened."

Dod's gut ached to tell Sawny the truth—how he had disappeared because Josh had taken his medallion off—but the story was unbelievable.

"It's a crazy day full of crazy, unexplainable things," stammered Dod. Suddenly, a wave of concern washed over him. Something was wrong.

"Maybe I've been poisoned," said Sawny, her eyes still closed. "That's why I'm hallucinating."

"You're not hallucinating," responded Dod reluctantly. He searched his feelings for the source of concern. Had Sawny really been poisoned? Was something awful happening to Dilly? Perhaps Bonboo was under attack while finding a safe place to hide the Farmer's Sackload.

As the music began to play slowly, someone broke from the shuffling crowd of dancers and approached. It was Bowy. He was tall, dark, and handsome like his older brother Boot.

"You two can't hide on the seats all night," he joked.

"We're just waiting for Dilly to bring us juice," said Dod. "Sawny's feeling lightheaded."

"Really?" chuckled Bowy. "You'll be waiting a long time. I just danced with her, and now she's with Pone."

"Classic Dilly," said Sawny with her eyes still closed.

"I guess in her defense," added Bowy, "she does seem to be moving toward the refreshments; Pone is dancing as close as you can get without sitting on the tables. I think he's sneaking cookies while he dances."

"That would be Pone," sighed Sawny. She finally opened her eyes.

Bowy stuck out his hand to help Sawny to her feet. "I promised you a dance."

"Thanks, but can I catch up with you later? I haven't finished with Dod."

CHAPTER FOUR

"Ooooh," teased Bowy, giving Dod a sly eye. "I'll be watching."

Bowy picked up his pace and hustled farther down the wall of chairs to a group of girls who were resting and wasted no time in pulling one girl to her feet.

"I know this is going to sound like I'm insane," began Sawny, finally facing Dod, "but do you have something to tell me? I mean, it seemed like you disappeared right in the middle of dancing. It was like you slipped out of my arms—like you became invisible."

"Oh," said Dod, forcing himself to rise. His knees nearly buckled. "I'll try to stay with you this time." Dod stuck out his hand just as Bowy had done and hoped Sawny couldn't read how fake his confidence was.

Sawny paused in her seat and studied Dod's face.

"If you give me a second chance, I'll show you the map I found," added Dod, sweetening the deal. The moment he said it, a wave of concern washed over him again. The map! Where was his backpack? He had left it on the floor, out in the open.

Dod turned to look when Sawny took his hand. "No more tricks," she said. "Around here, the boys wait for the song to end before they leave."

"Of course," responded Dod. In the distance, Ingrid's large frame blocked his view of where he recalled putting the bag.

Dod led Sawny into the dancing crowd and, as much as he could without appearing stupid, pushed his dance steps toward Ingrid, hoping to catch a glimpse of his backpack. The moment was much less magical than his first dance with Sawny had been. Every second was filled with worry that his priceless papers and map would turn up missing, just as the TCC pack had when he had left it unattended in Green Hall.

As the song ended, Sawny smiled. "Thank you," she said. "I think I'm feeling better."

"Good," said Dod.

"Can we look at the map now?" asked Sawny, blinking her eyes. "We can leave the dance for a few minutes, right?"

"Sure. It's in my pack," said Dod, leading the way. But he hadn't gone far when he was stopped.

"Is it true that you found Bonmoob's stash of jewels?" asked Ingrid, grabbing at Dod. She poured her weight onto his shoulder and breathed heavily. Her garlic stench made his eyes water.

"I did," said Dod, trying to extract himself.

"You've saved the day again!" praised Ingrid. "You're such a smart boy. I don't know what we would do without you. The drat soldiers are pathetic—simply pathetic. It's ludicrous how they sit around doing nothing. Bonmoob ought to dismiss them."

Dod didn't respond. He was busy wiping tears from his eyes so he could see the bag.

"We've got to go," said Sawny, tugging urgently at Dod's arm.

"Bring me with," huffed Ingrid. "I can't dance anymore. I'm getting too old for these sorts of parties. Besides, I'd rather talk to you than strut and stomp."

"Sorry," responded Sawny, bristling up. "We can't talk now."

"Are you still feeling dizzy?" asked Ingrid, her eyes focusing on Sawny. "At least Dod came back. I told you he would. You're not completely loony, just breezy between the ears. Good thing you're royalty. People give plenty of exceptions to the heirs of wealth."

Sawny turned up her nose and tugged so hard on Dod's arm that she popped Dod out of Ingrid's grasp and sent them both flying into the fray of dancers.

"Your bag's gone!" said Sawny the moment she staggered close enough to Dod's ear to be heard.

"What?" gasped Dod.

"I know where it was," she continued. "I watched where you put it—but it's gone now!"

Dod blinked until his eyes cleared. To his dismay, he saw that Sawny was right. On the edge of the dancing crowd was an empty floor. Buck, Pone, and Dilly were loading up on refreshments a short distance away.

"Did anyone see where my backpack went?" exploded Dod, pushing between Pone and Buck.

"It's right there," said Buck, casually pointing over his shoulder. "Toos slid it out of the way so dancers wouldn't step on it."

"You look like you're feeling better," chirped Dilly, moving to her sister's side with three cups of juice. She handed one to Sawny and one to Dod. "I told you it was nothing."

Dod and Sawny continued to search with their eyes, only half acknowledging Dilly.

"Could you clarify where, exactly, my pack is?" asked Dod, nudging Buck.

"It's over there…" Buck began when he tilted his head and saw it was missing. "Huh? It was over there a few minutes ago. It must be around here, somewhere."

"I'd say Mercy has it," said Dilly. "If she saw it on the floor next to her food tables, she's got it now." Dilly proudly showed

Dod she was wearing the Soosh Mayler Belt around her waist, despite the fact that it didn't even slightly match her dress.

"What's in your pack?" asked Pone, his mouth stuffed with cookies. "You're not still toting that Ankle Weed, are you? Boot told me you went up the wall with it."

"No," said Dod, glancing around for Mercy. He noticed Toos slip from the Great Hall and felt his insides jump. Maybe Toos had done more than slide the bag out of the way.

Sawny elbowed Dod and handed her drink back to Dilly. "I've got to get some fresh air," she said.

Dod took the cue and escorted Sawny on a hunt for Toos.

In the open corridor, people bustled in and out of the kitchen, but beyond that, the walkway was as calm as an early morning. Toos was out of sight. Dod and Sawny hurried quietly down the empty hall, trying to catch up with Toos without running.

"Horsely didn't give up the Farmer's Sackload without a fight, did he?" whispered Sawny.

Dod didn't respond.

"You're not very good at lying," continued Sawny. "Besides, Horsely's not the only one who's been causing problems here at Twistyard today. Ascertainy stopped me on the way to the dance and asked if I knew of anyone who had visited the library this afternoon—anyone in the know."

"Huh?"

"Ascertainy has some *special* books, and they went missing a few hours ago."

"In the know?" asked Dod.

"Mostly The Greats," whispered Sawny. "But I've flipped through a few of the books. Ascertainy keeps them in her locked closet—hidden."

"Oh," said Dod.

"Let's just say those books would be helpful if someone were trying to decipher ancient maps of this area."

Dod nodded. Toos still wasn't in view.

"So, when you showed up and said that you had a map, I assumed you'd found the books, too."

"I didn't see any," said Dod. "But Horsely could have put them somewhere else."

"Not likely," responded Sawny, stopping Dod in his tracks a short distance from Green Hall. "I've read enough to know more than I should about the way things were years ago—with the TCC, and then later with Doss. If Horsely was helping Sirlonk—faking those injuries for years—there are others. It's happening again. They're rising, Dod. That's why the representatives went missing at the same time as the burnings and the trouble on the seas with the billies—and we nearly went to war with Raul over Terro's disappearance—and that's to say nothing of the mess in Soosh—Pap and Miz were killed to keep that one going."

Sawny finished spilling her mind and shivered. "It all scares me, Dod."

"Don't worry," said Dod in his manliest voice.

"Shhhh," whispered Sawny.

Suddenly, Toos flew out of Green Hall at a dead run but was tackled to the floor within a few feet of its doors by Boot.

Dod and Sawny startled.

Toos rolled over and moaned. His usual banker-slick hair was messy from the brief scuffle.

"Toos?" said Boot with great surprise. "Why were you following me?"

"I wasn't following you, Boot. I was following the guy that was tailing you."

"I didn't see anyone," said Boot.

"Exactly," coughed Toos. "I was worried about you."

Boot started laughing as he climbed off of Toos. "Thanks for watching out for me, but don't wiggle your insides on my behalf."

Boot's black ferret, Sneaker, scurried from Green Hall and pounced on Toos.

"As you can see," added Boot, "I'm well protected." He helped Toos to his feet and patted him on the back. "Do you still have your lucky rock?"

Toos's hands were shaking as he searched his pockets and produced the marble-sized white stone Boot had given him. Sneaker raced down Toos's arm to sniff it.

"Good," praised Boot. "Make sure you keep it at all times—and say, does it work with getting dances?"

"I've had pretty good luck," began Toos, wiping at his slick hair, putting the ruffled clumps back into place. Boot's demeanor seemed to ease Toos's raddled nerves.

"Why did you run?" asked Sawny, stripping Toos's confidence with her beating eyes.

"I—well—" Toos hung his head. "I think the man that was following Boot continued that way," he said, pointing farther down toward Raul Hall. "Anyway, once I knew it was only Boot in Green Hall, I didn't want him to think I was spying on him."

"Oh," said Sawny.

CHAPTER FOUR

"Next time, don't run," suggested Boot. "Guilty people run."

"Sorry," said Toos.

"It's okay," said Boot. "I'm glad you had my back. It's hard to tell who's good these days. I never would have thought Horsely was a traitor." Boot glanced at Dod.

Dilly and Buck strolled up the hall laughing.

"I guess I'll return to the dance now," said Toos, looking out of place as the only Greenling in the crowd of Coosings.

No sooner had he trotted off than Dod remembered the map.

"I forgot to ask Toos about my pack," groaned Dod, turning to follow.

"Don't bother," said Boot. "You can't go leaving things like *that* out for people to see, so I stashed it for you, along with the money you gave us. Thanks again. Are you sure it's okay if we use the coins to buy my mom a house?"

"Yes," responded Dod. He was happy to hear that the pack hadn't been stolen.

"You're the best, Dod," said Buck. "Times have been really tough on her the past few years. Mom's lived in a real dump."

"Don't forget—we invited her to join us here," argued Dilly, "but you can't force a chick to hatch."

"She's stubborn—I'll give you that," chuckled Boot, tugging at the edges of the blue blazer he had borrowed from Dod. "If Bowy remained at Twistyard, our mom would probably starve to death."

"What about your grandpa's money?" asked Sawny innocently.

Boot's face darkened like the surprise of a summer squall, and Sneaker hissed from his perch on Boot's shoulder.

"That was a long time ago," Boot huffed. "And she most certainly didn't take so much as one coin from him, even in the wake of my father's accident. Gramps was a cantankerous rat."

"Don't get Boot started," said Buck, shaking his head.

"But Miz spoke highly of him as a mayler," argued Dilly. "And Miz knew him well, since his brother worked with your grandpa on dozens of projects. To hear Miz talk, they were inseparable. Your grandpa earned his pay. You should be proud to bear his name—Boot Bellious Dolsur III."

Boot swallowed hard and stayed civil. Dilly was given more latitude than the others would have been had they said the same things. "I'd have changed my name years ago if it weren't for my father. His legacy is worth remembering. It's nothing short of a miracle that he turned out good."

"You're being too hard on your grandpa," teased Dilly, prodding Boot with her elbow. She proudly displayed her Soosh Mayler Belt and added, "We maylers deserve respect."

"Not if you obtain it the way he did!" snapped Boot. "When they assigned him to work beasts in Driaxom, they nearly got it right—the location was fitting!"

"I can't believe you still feel that way," said Dilly. "He's been dead for years."

"I never saw his body—" grumbled Boot.

Dilly broke out laughing. "You're funny," she said, patting his shoulder. Her soft brown eyes made Boot's anger fade. "You owe me a few more dances."

"How do you figure?" asked Boot.

CHAPTER FOUR

"Well," gloated Dilly, "I just spoke with Voracio in the kitchen and he's decided you can have your things back."

"Really?" muttered Buck. "You dared?"

"Now that Bonboo's back," continued Dilly, "Voracio's on a leash again. Besides, Mercy agreed that it was a good idea."

"Perhaps I owe Mercy a few dances," taunted Boot, drifting back into his regular, cheery self.

"I think *that* would be counterproductive," grinned Sawny. "One twirl with her and Voracio would change his mind in a flippy. He's sweet on Mercy."

CHAPTER FIVE

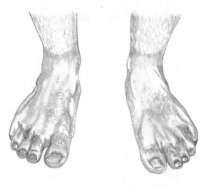

EYES OPEN

After the night of dancing, Twistyard was quieter than usual in the morning. Dod awoke suddenly with a horrible dream.

"It's nothing," mumbled Dod, trying to calm down. He knew he was lying to himself. His palms were sweaty, and his fingers ached from clenching. Dod glanced about the serene room and took comfort in Boot's hushed snores.

In the corner, perched high in the top branches of the planter box, Sneaker sat staring at Dod with a knowing look, as though he disapproved of Dod's state of denial.

"First a beast and now…well…I can't believe it," sputtered Dod.

Sneaker spun around in circles, scurried down the trunk of the biggest tree, and leaped onto Dod's bed beside him.

"A flying dragon," moaned Dod to Boot's pet. "It's just not possible."

Dod slid out of his covers and made his way to the window. The brightest stars were still faintly visible, dotting the changing

CHAPTER FIVE

sky. A quick glance at the scarred bedroom floor reminded Dod of his frightening experience with the duresser.

"You're up early," called Boot sleepily from his bed. Sneaker had made his way over and was prancing on Boot's head.

"Just looking out the window," said Dod.

"More bad dreams, huh?" asked Boot.

"What makes you say that?"

Boot sat up and held Sneaker. "My buddy is sensing trouble. So either you've set him off with a nightmare or we'd better get ready."

"Sorry," said Dod. "I didn't mean to wake you up."

"It's all right," said Boot. "Besides, it's not your fault. Sneaker was born detecting things. It's in his blood. And he's been trained well, too. Yonkston Ferrets are amazing." Boot pointed to the corner of the room and Sneaker raced back to his favorite spot atop the branches in the planter box.

"What's in our future?" asked Boot.

"I don't know," said Dod. He really wasn't sure. The dream, like so many of his nightmares, had been convoluted. And try as he did, he could only remember a few bits—a terrifying mouth of teeth plucking a flutter from the air—a tumult of noise—and a building reeling up and down as flames engulfed everything in sight.

"Come on," coached Boot. "I'm awake. Let's have it. You're not going back to Driaxom, are you?"

"No. I saw other weird stuff," confessed Dod. "But I don't think it means anything."

"Maybe," said Boot hesitantly. "You're entitled to a string of crazy dreams after what you witnessed yesterday. It must have been hard watching Horsely jump off the wall." Boot's voice whittled at Dod as his eyes indicated that he, like Sawny, didn't believe Horsely had gone down without a fight. "You know you can talk about anything with me, right Dod? I'm good at keeping secrets."

"Sure," stammered Dod. He wanted to come clean with the story of what had actually happened, but he felt mixed-up inside. Boot had been good friends with Horsely. How could Boot have not known that Horsely was playing games as a traitor?

"I'll tell you what," said Boot, quietly rising from bed. "Let's go fishing for a couple of hours—just the two of us. I know of a spot that is perfect if we hurry. We could fish while we make plans, and we'd easily be back before lunch. What do you say?"

"Okay," said Dod, recalling happy memories of fishing trips with Pap. But it didn't take long before an uncomfortable feeling crept in. "Shouldn't we ask Buck and Bowy if they want to come, too?"

"They'd probably rather sleep," whispered Boot, pulling a brown long-sleeved shirt over his head. "Bowy was out late last night, and you know Buck—he loves sleeping in."

"I love who?" mumbled Buck, buried to his nose in covers. He rolled over and snuggled his pillow.

Bowy, who as a visitor was assigned to the floor, was so deep in blankets that a tuft of hair was all that stuck out.

The room went silent. Boot tiptoed toward the exit and signaled for Dod to follow.

"Do you want to go fishing?" blurted Dod, nudging Buck's feet as he walked past. He couldn't leave without asking. It didn't feel right.

CHAPTER FIVE

Buck sat up straight and opened his eyes wide. "Wake up, Bowy!" he said excitedly. "We're going fishing! It'll be just like old times."

The two lagging brothers hurried to ready themselves and shortly joined Dod and Boot in the outer hall, where Boot was trying to teach Sneaker how to roll over on command and Dod was doing his best to forget he had awakened to the thoughts of a ghastly, monstrous dragon.

Outside the castle, the morning air was crisp and inviting. Birds chirped their wakeup songs from the large trees that surrounded the front grassy field. Boot, Buck, and Bowy joked about past fishing mishaps as they led the way to a distant barn where fishing gear and small boats were kept. The barn was closer to Lake Mauj than most of the other outbuildings, though it was still hundreds of yards farther away from the shoreline than Zerny's cottage in the forest.

Inside the musty building, gear of all shapes and sizes was organized in piles and stuffed on shelves. Hundreds of short, medium, and long fishing rods were stacked along one wall, each adorned with unusual three-fourths-loop guides for line; boxes of crude bait-casting reels sat close to the rods; a wide array of fishing hooks, lures, sinkers, and other tackle was stowed in drawers below a counter that was littered with partly-finished fix-it jobs on broken gear; and rows of small boats, crammed tightly together, stole half the space in the barn.

Boot convinced the group that they should take the largest boat, a twenty-foot-long, twelve-seat rowboat of sorts. Though once they had tipped it over and filled it with supplies, its weight was taxing to drag using the long, sturdy rope that was attached to the bow.

"The sun will rise and set before we hit the water," joked Bowy, putting his weight into the line as much as Boot. Bowy had voiced his opinion in the barn that a traditional rowboat looked plenty big enough for the group and seemed more practical to haul.

"I'll go for Shooter," offered Dod, hoping to avoid blisters. "He could move this boat to the water without breaking a sweat. Besides, I bet he'd rather be tethered in the lush grass than sitting in a stall waiting for hay."

"Sounds good to me," laughed Bowy, letting go of the rope. He flopped into the boat, covered his eyes with his hat, and blindly searched with his hands for the bag of cookies they had snatched from Pone's secret stash.

"Hurry back," called Buck, eager to get fishing but happy to labor less.

"You're all a bunch of softies," snorted Boot playfully, inching the boat forward before letting the line go limp.

Dod trotted toward the master barn and soon disappeared from his friends' view, concealed behind trees and shrubs. The big structure was on the opposite side of the row of barns and covered acres of land. Near the towering, open doors, Dod slowed at the thick hedge he and Boot had hidden in on the night they had heard the false report of Bonboo's assassination. Chills prickled his skin under his sweater. He wished Boot had accompanied him to fetch Shooter.

Once inside the barn, Dod quietly walked down the center aisle and counted horses. The deeper he ventured, the darker it got. The early morning sky was still too dim to lighten the middle section. By the time Dod passed horse ten, it was hardly visible—just a shifting blob in the stall. He began to turn,

CHAPTER FIVE

convinced that he needed to get a buster candle from the stash near the entrance, when something caught the corner of his eye. It was like the flicker of a distant firefly.

Motionless, his heart beating in his throat, Dod watched until the light flashed again. It was coming from a few stalls down, near the center of the barn, one row over.

Who could it be? thought Dod. The stillness of the morning cast an evil ambiance over the whole circumstance. Every reasonable bone in Dod's body wanted to turn and sneak away—exit the barn and run to his friends for safety. But Pap wouldn't have run. Dod knew it. He had to find out who it was.

Tiptoeing as gingerly as he could, Dod made his way toward the light that flickered intermittently. It reminded him of an anglerfish, waving its glowing bait to attract unsuspecting guppies within reach of its hungry mouth.

Someone probably left a glowing-stone necklace with the horses, thought Dod, getting closer to the light. Nevertheless, as he neared the source, he heard crackling and shuffling sounds. A person was there, one row over, carefully doing something.

The back wall of the stall was too tall to see over without climbing, but cracks between the loosely hung planks made it possible for Dod to catch glimpses of movement and light. Crouching, Dod cautiously pressed past the horse to take a look. He almost gave himself away when he narrowly missed hitting his head on a shovel.

Through a knothole near the ground, the first thing Dod saw was two large red feet, standing on a burlap bag. They weren't pink or tinged red—they were solid red. However, within moments they were stuffed into socks and plunged into handsome riding boots.

Who's changing in the barn? thought Dod, wishing he could find a decent hole higher up, though beginning to feel like a peeping tom.

"Dod?" came Buck's voice from the distant entrance to the barn. "Do you want help?"

The moment Buck called out, the neighboring stall went silent and dark.

"DOD!" shouted Buck. He lit a buster candle and entered the way Dod had come, heading for Shooter.

Not wanting to alert the hiding person beside him, Dod remained motionless, watching the bright glow of Buck's candle fill the rafters above him. Eventually Buck passed—and once he had, rustling noises ensued, as the mystery person rushed to mount his horse and ride.

"Sirlonk?" gasped Buck, encountering him by Shooter's stall. Sirlonk had trotted toward the back exit of the barn and then circled up the center aisle.

"You look surprised to see me," laughed Sirlonk.

Dod shivered as he crept to the edge of the stall for a peek.

"Everyone thinks you're dead!" stammered Buck. "The snakes ate you."

"Fool!" barked Sirlonk. "I'm *The Dread*. A couple of pond snakes can't stop me. I'm too busy to die."

Dod watched in horror as Sirlonk approached Buck on horseback with a sword in hand.

"Are you tired of being pathetic?" asked Sirlonk. "I have important things for you to do. Imagine everyone bowing to you. No more laughing behind your back. No more jokes at your expense. People would finally see you as the smart boy I know you are."

CHAPTER FIVE

From Dod's vantage, five stalls away, Buck's face wasn't visible. Sirlonk's, however, was clear. His proud smile grew broad as he spoke, as though things were going as planned.

"What?" stammered Buck, slowly stepping backward. Dod recognized Buck's posture. He was terrified.

"I'll let you live if you help me out. I have a few errands around Twistyard that need doing—the type that you seem perfectly fitted for. My other friends here at the castle could use some help now that Horsely's gone."

Buck remained silent, continuing to retreat.

"Yes, Buck, I have others. It's a shame what happened to Horsely. I liked that boy. He should have been quicker at following orders. Dod doesn't take no for an answer. He's less forgiving than I am. I guess he's young and working hard to rise in The Order."

"What are you talking about?" mumbled Buck. "Dod's not part of The Order. He's the one who returned the Farmer's Sackload to Bonboo."

"Oh. I see. You fell for that one, too," laughed Sirlonk. "Yes. We had to prop Dod up a bit...well, after the whole encounter with the diasserpentouses. Bonboo and Commendus were onto him—wondering how he magically survived the snakes while Murdore and I met our tragic deaths."

Buck continued to back up. He was now only three stalls away from Dod's hiding place.

"Dod didn't turn," said Buck timidly, his voice filled with doubt. "I would know if he had."

"You would not!" snapped Sirlonk, dark faced with anger. "You don't know the slightest thing about Dod—who he is—or *what* he is! Why do you think he was gone for so long? Not even a letter. In The Order, rules are rules. If you break them, you pay the consequences, fool! You wouldn't know if your own family members were involved unless The Order wanted you to know! Until the democracies have fallen, everyone must play his role as instructed! Do you understand?"

Sirlonk's demanding tone made it clear that his patience had run thin.

Buck said nothing.

"Do you understand!" roared Sirlonk, raising his voice. Dod hoped soldiers would hear Sirlonk and come running.

"I-I understand," stuttered Buck.

"You can't tell anyone of your loyalty to me! Am I clear?"

Buck didn't respond. He was now only two stalls away from Dod and picking up his retreating pace.

"Stop running!" ordered Sirlonk.

Buck froze momentarily, though as Sirlonk pushed closer with his sword, Buck again began to withdraw.

Sirlonk eyed Buck jeeringly, shook his head, and scoffed, "You'll never be half the man your brother is becoming; and sadly, I can't trust you enough to give you a chance. I'm wasting my breath trying. But others need a reminder from time to time; so, pathetic as you are, you can still serve me, boy—*with your death!*"

Sirlonk spurred his horse to leap forward as Buck dropped the candle, spun around, and bolted for the exit.

Without thinking, Dod reached for the shovel beside him and pounced from the stall. His timing was perfect. He swung the shovel mightily and caught Sirlonk in the hand, just as Sirlonk's sword was ready to impale Buck's spine. The sword fell to the ground, Sirlonk let out a howl, and Sirlonk's stolen horse startled into a dead run for the exit.

Dod wondered what Sirlonk was hiding when he noticed a gigantic bag tied to the frantic steed. It looked as though a hefty corpse were secured within, bouncing up and down.

"YOU'RE DEAD!" raged Sirlonk, gaining control before the horse reached the open field. He forced the beast around and prepared to attack. From his stow he drew another sword, raised it in the air with his uninjured hand, and came storming back toward Dod and Buck, who had retreated to the opposite side of the straw fire that was now raging in the middle of the row.

Sirlonk's horse slowed at the fire and refused to skirt around it, being prompted both by instinct and the agitated snorts and grunts from the neighboring corralled horses.

"Dod. What a pleasure," smiled Sirlonk, instantly ignoring Buck.

Dod raised his shovel defiantly above the flames that hungrily licked the ground. The fire raced out of control, heading toward stalls on both sides.

"Have fun buying the noble billies' loyalty now that you've lost the diamonds!" yelled Dod. "Your plans are over!"

Sirlonk lowered his weapon and forced a grin. "No, *My Little Mouse*, I'm just getting started. The noble billies will beg to follow me. I have powers of persuasion that run deeper than you know. And as for Pious, his days are numbered. He's nothing!"

"Your days are numbered!" spat Dod, feeling a rush of anger and frustration.

"Stop the act," laughed Sirlonk gleefully. "We're friends. And trust me when I say, a *criminal* like you needs my help."

Men entered from the rear of the barn and approached behind Dod and Buck. Sirlonk turned his horse around and trotted off snobbishly, as if he had no fear of being pursued.

Out of necessity, Dod and Buck hastily poured their full attention into saving the horses and extinguishing the fire. The flames, originally started by Buck's dropped candle, grew quicker than either of them would have guessed and were nearly unstoppable by the time Sirlonk had made his exit; though, thanks to the aid of a dozen farm hands, only a small portion of the barn sustained structural damage.

When Dod and Buck wearily emerged from the smoky mess, they found a crowd of people had formed at the entrance.

Voracio was first to rush to the boys, like a spider seizing a twitching moth in its web. "Look at what you've done!" he boomed, mostly spending his glares on Dod. "You could have burnt the whole barn down! This sort of behavior will not be tolerated!"

"But sir—" began Dod.

"There's no excuse!" continued Voracio. "You may think you've fooled everyone into believing you're a hero—some special treat—but we've caught on to your antics, and we have proof!"

"It's not what you think," said Buck, his shoulders rising more than Dod had seen before. "Dod just stopped The Dread! He saved me. The Dread tried to run me through with a sword and Dod sent him off with a shovel."

"What?" barked Voracio. "That's impossible! Sirlonk's dead."

The crowd gasped.

"It was him! I know what I saw," said Buck.

"He's telling the truth," confirmed Dod. "You should send soldiers after him. He couldn't have gone far."

CHAPTER FIVE

Voracio glanced solemnly at Jibb, then Youk, then back to Dod. "No more games, Dod! We've had enough!" He pulled a roll of parchment from his pocket and held it up. "These are papers for your arrest. You are hereby charged with the purposeful killing of Horsely Higgby. We have ample evidence that you stole the Farmer's Sackload and, thereafter, murdered Horsely when he threatened to expose you. Furthermore, we have great reason to believe that your crimes are treasonous, as we have some strong leads suggesting you were working in concert with The Dread to create opposition to the Democracy."

Dod stared dumbfounded by the charges. "W-working with The Dread?" he stuttered.

"That's ridiculous!" blurted Buck. "How can you believe any of that? Sirlonk nearly skewered me with his sword, and Dod saved my life. How can you be so blind as to think for one minute that Dod is friends with him?"

"Deception's a tricky game," said Youk, carefully stepping forward to inspect the boys' eyes. "Dod hasn't been tried and proven guilty, we simply have grounds sufficient to take swift action. This morning, Voracio was more than correct in pointing out that Dod does have a history of disappearing without notice."

"But murder charges?" growled Buck.

Dod gazed blearily across the crowd of unfriendly faces, especially the battalion of scowling, uppity-nosed drat soldiers, and wished to disappear. The Order was too strong and powerful to overcome. Sirlonk was right. Surely the 'evidence' being raised against him was unduly influenced by the wishes of Sirlonk's evil friends at Twistyard and elsewhere.

I can't go back to Driaxom, thought Dod, wanting to burst into tears. The whole circumstance was unfair.

"Calm yourself, Buck!" insisted Youk. "Many a wise man has been tricked by the foolish assumptions of a carefully played show. I like Dod as much as anyone; however, the facts appear peculiar to say the least."

"I can't believe it," mumbled Buck, stepping closer to Dod.

"Listen," continued Youk, waving his hand in the air for emphasis while the feather atop his fancy hat tipped in the morning breeze. "So let's say Dod and Sirlonk really did have a spat in the barn, and you were saved. I agree that sounds magnificent. Dod's a hero! But alas, what if Dod planned the whole thing, staged the fight for your benefit. Now he's won your heart and loyalty by craftiness and is one step closer to his ultimate designs—destruction of the Democracy!"

"BOOSAP!" yelled Buck. He stood like a man and looked more like Boot than Dod had ever seen. "The rest of you would still be walking around searching for *Dark Hood and his little helper*' if it weren't for Dod! He's the one who discovered that The Dread never left."

"Convenient, isn't it?" snapped Voracio, shuffling toward Dod, still tending his injured leg. He held out his hand to measure Dod's height. "I'd say Dod's short enough to be a little helper."

From the back of the crowd, Sawb's crooked smile caught Dod's eyes and spurred Dod to speak. "Jibb knows I'm not The Dread's 'little helper.' Right Jibb?" As Dod pressed, the sea of eyes turned for an answer.

"I don't know what you're talking about," stammered Jibb.

"Yes you do, the night you and your men saved my life. I was inches from death when you fought off The Dread and his helper. Remember—the night you blocked off Green Hall?"

"Oh, that," confessed Jibb. "Yes. Someone else was helping *Dark Hood*. But that's not to say you weren't involved. It's like Youk said—you could have been pretending—creating stories. Weren't you the one who just announced Sirlonk was seen at High Gate and eaten by Commendus's pond creatures? At least make your stories match."

"Sure!" blurted Buck, beyond angry. "Dod's telling stories—he's just pretending every time he stands up to Sirlonk. That's why he fought him at High Gate—nearly lost his life beside Dilly—and turned him over to the soldiers for a trip to Driaxom! Do you see how crazy your logic is?"

"Keep in mind—" began Youk, when Buck exploded.

"DOD'S NOT THE PROBLEM! You should be arresting Commendus for the '*peculiar facts*' surrounding Sirlonk's unsuccessful incarceration—and that's to say nothing of the cave full of baby duressers that Commendus was keeping in his front yard. Who's the real traitor?"

"Calm down," said Youk.

"NO!" shouted Buck. "I just told you The Dread's back and you haven't done anything! Why aren't you rushing troops?"

"We'll take action as needed," said Youk, keeping a level tone. "Don't melt on me, Buck. I understand you're mad, but nobody's suggesting Dod's guilty. We simply need to let the process proceed. There certainly is proof that one of our informants knows Dod's workings. He got it right that you were heading out early this morning to go fishing."

Boot strolled up with Bowy and pushed his way through the crowd until he stood between Voracio and Buck. "What's going on?" he asked.

"Dod's being charged with murdering Horsely," hurried Buck. "They think he's a traitor."

Boot glanced curiously at Dod and Buck, who were both holding shovels and covered with ash, then turned to face Jibb. "This again?" he asked, shaking his head scoldingly. "Leave Dod alone. So he's a Coosing and you're not. Get over it!"

"Jibb's not the arresting officer!" blasted Voracio. "I am! And if you have a problem with it, you can pack your bags and leave!"

Boot inched toward Voracio, his nostrils flaring, and spoke slowly, "I do have a problem with it, and I'm not going anywhere! Dod's innocent!"

Voracio's face reddened like a beet. "Get his lousy horse and show him from the grounds!" he commanded, signaling for Jibb to secure a soldier escort.

"Let's stay calm," begged Youk, pushing for a better outcome. "Perhaps we should discuss this further." He could see that the three Dolsur brothers weren't planning on obeying Voracio, and the tone of his voice revealed that he didn't agree with Voracio's orders.

"I see Bonboo spent all of his best blood on Dilly's line!" said Boot defiantly. "Chikada is like Bonboo—*a real man!*"

"Guards!" yelled Voracio, his fists clenched. "Take him away!"

"What?" taunted Boot. "Are you going to have them kill me the way you killed my father?"

Voracio exploded into a blind rage and unleashed his colossal fists on Boot, but Boot wasn't unprepared; he ducked out of the way and returned the assault with a booming punch that sent Voracio to the ground.

"That's for my Dad!" hissed Boot, repositioning his hands and feet like a prized boxer. "If you want more, go ahead and stand up. I've been waiting decades to have it out with you."

"You'll pay!" blared Voracio, scrambling to rise and draw his sword. "I'm a general in the royal tredder army and a chief officer in the Democracy! You *will* show me respect!"

"Or what?" sneered Boot, undeterred.

Voracio wildly plunged his sword at the ground, attempting to kill Sneaker out of spite. But by the third jab, Boot deflected the blow with a blackened shovel he'd taken from Buck.

Outraged, Voracio attacked Boot with all of his might, as though The Dread himself were standing before him. "Your blood be upon you for treason!" roared Voracio.

"And Jungo?" returned Boot heatedly, pressing furiously with the shovel until Voracio was forced to retreat toward the smoky barn. "You may hide behind your titles of power and your privilege to carry a weapon," bellowed Boot, "but the truth still stands—you're nothing but a cold-blooded murderer!"

It didn't matter that Voracio was bigger than Boot and a champion swordsman, Boot's rage was unstoppable. Eventually, Boot swung powerfully and knocked Voracio's sword from his hands, then dipped to the ground in a clever roll and rose holding the blade threateningly, backing Voracio up against the master barn.

"My father's blood requires justice!" roared Boot, pointing the sword at Voracio's throat.

"Please don't," begged Voracio, quivering.

"But my mother's forgiveness is stronger," continued Boot, plunging the rapier into the ground beside Voracio. "You're Bonboo's grandson…. Be respectable!"

Instantly, soldiers stormed Boot and Dod to haul them off, though their efforts were interrupted by Youk, who raised his voice to be heard.

"They're not going anywhere," he said. "Let's eat breakfast first and sort out the details later. As Chief Noble Tredder, Bonboo should be informed of these matters before we clutter the system with counterproductive charges. My eyes are witnesses to what just happened. Every man has a right to defend himself! Let's be fair, now, and think before we act."

"Well said," praised Bowy, starting to clap.

Jibb looked to Voracio for direction.

"Let's have Bonboo decide," growled Voracio in a winded, beaten voice. "If he wants Boot around, it's his choice. But Dod's charges stand. I've already sent a messenger to High Gate with our filings."

"It's not too late to stop him," suggested Buck. "I'll ride a quick horse with your letter."

Voracio shook his head.

Buck looked to Youk for the outcome to be better.

"If he's innocent, he shouldn't fear," said Youk. "The truth will rise. Don't worry. You must admit, Horsely's tragic death deserves our best efforts, despite any inconvenience."

And without another word, Dod was led to a guarded cell in the basement of Twistyard.

CHAPTER SIX

THE TRADE

Breakfast was cold and tasteless to Dod. Eggs and pancakes had never been as flavorless as they were in the lonely jail cell. Dod struggled to swallow them down. He couldn't believe he was accused of murder. Thinking about it made him ill. Horsely had nearly finished him off on the cliff wall; and now, as though reaching with powerful arms from beyond the grave, Horsely was positioned to condemn Dod to a living-death sentence in Driaxom. Or so Dod felt. It was horribly unfair.

The one happy thought Dod had was that Boot and his brothers were loyal to him. Without their friendship, the next logical step would be simple: Return to Earth and give up the medallion to Mr. Brewer. End of story. No more crazy people chasing him. Ruth's Aunt Naomi would be safe, and Twistyard could go back to the way it was before Dod's arrival.

Dod inspected the stone walls of his cell and the thick matrix of bars by the entrance, then hesitantly attempted to go home. But the medallion didn't take him away from the nightmare he was in.

Fear of Driaxom loomed over Dod like a giant storm cloud. Dod knew facts could easily be twisted to make him look guilty. And since he had stretched the truth when first reporting Horsely's death to everyone at the dance, the door was left wide open for attackers to destroy his credibility as a reliable witness about what had really happened. His original intent had been to allow Horsely's friends to remember Horsely as a relatively good person, but now he wished he had openly told the full, dark, horrible truth about Horsely's commitment to The Dread and The Order.

If all of Twistyard knew of Horsely's calloused role in helping The Beast eat soldiers, thought Dod, *they'd be glad he was dead.*

Just beyond Dod's cell, two guards stood watch, discussing the happenings at Twistyard. When they got around to the subject of Dod, Dod tried harder to leave for home. He couldn't stand the awful things they said—all lies. How he had befriended Bonboo's great-granddaughters in order to discover the top-secret location of the Farmer's Sackload, how he had tricked Bonboo on many occasions in different ways, thus injuring the Democracy, how he had pretended to catch Sirlonk only to personally release him days later, and how he had carefully murdered hordes of people. Even Zerny was named a casualty of Dod's murderous ways, which seemed more than unfair since Dod knew Zerny wasn't dead.

Suddenly, the soldiers' prattle ended. Dod looked to see if they had left and found Clair staring at him, wearing a sword on each hip. Clair's black wavy hair was getting long, so in the dimness of the dungeon, he seemed to have horns. His formidable frame blocked half the torchlight as he moved closer to Dod's cell.

CHAPTER SIX

"I knew you never bested Sirlonk," gloated Clair. "He's far too spectacular with weaponry."

"I never said I did," grumbled Dod. All of the bitter feelings he had toward Clair for treating him rudely at dueling practices bubbled to the surface. '*I think he hates you*,' echoed in Dod's mind, as though Dari were once more sitting beside Dod, reminding him of his first encounter with Clair. Dod couldn't help thinking he should have directed his nausea at the tournaments to the useful purpose of branding Clair across the face with sloosha-filled vomit as he sat judging the matches.

Neither person said anything for an awkward amount of time. Clair smirked at Dod through the bars, and when Dod finally looked away, Clair tauntingly banged the sheaths of his swords across the metal.

"I must admit, it's a shame you're the only one locked up for the murder. *You* certainly couldn't have done it alone. If you tell me of your connections, perhaps you could spend your life imprisoned somewhere other than Driaxom."

"Oh," sighed Dod, hating every minute he was forced to endure Clair's mocking eyes. It was like kissing Sawb's boots in front of Eluxa and her clique of friends. From his first moments at Twistyard, Clair had accused Dod of being a traitor, and now that Dod was behind bars, Clair was seemingly justified.

"Tell me who helped you murder Horsely!" pressed Clair arrogantly.

"I think it's coming to me," fibbed Dod, with only his tongue to defend himself. "Yes. The real murderer was a great swordsman. One of the best. Trained by The Dread himself. A man of respectable standing. Someone hidden beneath the cloak of military achievement. Can you guess who?"

"Do tell," said Clair. "I hate guessing games. Get on with it and I'll put in a good word for you to the council assigned to oversee the investigation. Your complete confession, and cooperation in convicting other guilty persons, may lead to a non-trial judgment. Speak up. Tell me what you know."

Dod was shocked Clair didn't see where he was going. "The real swordsman…let's see…"

Dod waited for Clair to move in, wide-eyed with anticipation.

"Out with it!" demanded Clair impatiently.

"Yes," said Dod. "The man's name is…*Clair*! You're the one who's working with The Dread!"

"Lying scum," grumbled Clair. "Ever since Tridacello explained to me about your tendency to prevaricate the truth, I've known to watch for your forked tongue. Do you really think you can waltz into a place like this and make up a past—pick your relatives like they're turnips at the market? We all know Pap wasn't your grandfather. His sons died childless!"

Dod gasped.

"And the story you told Tridacello, the one where your family was murdered at sea by the hands of billies, certainly follows you wherever Tridacello goes. You've got him convinced that you were an orphan tad, being aided by a swapper. What nonsense. And to think Tridacello's now got Bowlure believing it, too."

Dod was speechless. He didn't know where to start or what to say, not that anything he offered would change Clair's mind, anyway.

"Well," said Clair, wrapping up his chit-chatting with another round of banging the bars. "You'd never make a great swordsman like me. You lack discipline."

"I don't care," snapped Dod. He didn't know what else to say.

"Either way, it doesn't matter now," said Clair, turning to go. "Your life's headed toward *rocky days*." He laughed at his reference to smashing boulders in Driaxom and walked past the guards and out of sight. But a few moments later he reappeared, poking his head around the corner just long enough to add, "I probably won't see you again until you go before the investigators for questioning, so take time to reevaluate the truth....Oh, and I'm sure you'll enjoy this: Voracio put my name down as your personal representative to the council handling your case. Amusing, isn't it? You can sleep now, knowing that justice will be served."

Hearing that The Dread was really Santa Claus wouldn't have been any less shocking or distressing. Clair was the last person Dod would have chosen to help him accurately represent the facts to the council. Their investigation of the charges would result in an acquittal, sentencing, or trial.

Depressed and alone, knowing he was undoubtedly going straight back to the worst place imaginable, Dod flopped to the stone floor in the corner of his cell and exercised all of his mental faculties in attempting to transport to Cedar City. There was no way he was going to stick around for the guilty verdict and the welcome-back party at Driaxom. Nothing could possibly be worth the risk.

And then something strange happened. Dod noticed the letters S.R. scraped lightly at the base of the wall. "Stephen Richards," he muttered to himself. "Why was my dad locked up?"

The letters could have come from someone else, but Dod's gut assured him that they hadn't.

Momentarily sidetracked from his yearnings to escape, Dod thought about his dad. Was he really Humberrone? And if he had been a hero in Green, where had he gone? Dod wished he could speak with Bonboo and get some reliable answers.

Suddenly, images of a jungle flashed into Dod's mind. The air was hot and wet—trees, bushes, and vines were everywhere—a giant volcano stuck up in the distance—ruins of a past city peeked from the blanket of greenery like a junkyard of forgotten stone buildings and towers—and then Dod saw a face, hairy and sunburned, smiling confidently.

"My dad's alive!" burst Dod excitedly. He felt it. He knew it. In the image that Dod had seen, the man looked different than Dod remembered his father had looked—he was older and had a full beard—but the twinkle in the man's eyes confirmed that he was undeniably Stephen Richards.

"I really am Humberrone's son," said Dod with his heart beating rapidly in his chest. He had seen paintings of Humberrone and hadn't been sure, but the rush of images left no room for doubt.

"I wonder where he is? Maybe he's trapped by natives or marooned on a giant island."

"Who are you talking to?" barked one of the drat soldiers, approaching the bars. His partner stayed back and crunched on an apple.

Dod rose to his feet, full of fresh hope and confidence. After all, he hadn't been convicted yet. "I was just wondering, when do I get to speak with Bonboo?"

"Hmm," said the soldier, stroking his pointed little beard. "I'm not sure that you will. You're charged with some hefty crimes, Dod. People like Bonboo wouldn't want to associate with you. Not now that the truth is coming out."

"It's hardly the truth," responded Dod, not feeling bitter or angry as he had before. "What's your name?"

"Upton," answered the barrel-chested soldier, eyeing Dod suspiciously.

"Well, Upton," said Dod cheerfully, giving the Coosings' sign of friendship—his right arm stretched out with four fingers apart and his thumb tucked under. "It's a pleasure to meet you. I suspect Bonboo will make an exception. He'll come. He knows I've been framed. The Dread has returned to Twistyard and is angry that I successfully took the Farmer's Sackload from him—well, from one of his helpers. I was assisting Bonboo in saving Twistyard from being sold."

"Hmm," grunted Upton, looking slightly interested.

"I'm sure you think I'm awful," continued Dod. "Rumors spread fast. But if you want the truth, I've got it. I'm innocent of pretty much everything bad you've heard. Horsely was faking his injuries. When I caught him hopping around on a ledge halfway up the back wall of Twistyard, he tried to kill me for discovering his secrets."

"That's not what I heard."

"I know," said Dod, grinning. He couldn't help feeling happy. For over eight years he had thought that his father was dead and gone, but now there was reason to believe that he wasn't.

"So why should I trust you?" asked Upton.

"I don't know," said Dod, shrugging his shoulders. "I guess because it's the truth. If you want to believe lies, I can't stop you. Go on thinking I've killed Zerny if you wish. Or you can sneak down to Zerny's place and discover for yourself that he's still alive. He's just embarrassed about his beard."

"Zerny's alive?" grunted Upton.

"Yup," said Dod. "When you get a chance, go see for yourself, and then make sure you tell all your friends the truth. After all, we're on the same team. I'm fighting for you, not against you. The Beast ate soldiers and nearly ate me and Boot. That's why we killed her. If we work together, I'm sure we can root out the trouble causers here at Twistyard."

"Maybe," said Upton hesitantly, his stiff posture loosening.

Reminding the soldier of how he and Boot had recently taken care of The Beast seemed to provoke thoughts. Moments later, a bell rang and Upton rushed away.

Dod felt better after telling someone he was innocent, regardless of the fact that Upton couldn't help Dod, even if he believed him.

The two soldiers were gone for less than a minute before two more replaced them, but during the brief period where no one stood watch, a ball of paper was thrown into Dod's cell. When Dod looked up, the person who had thrown it was nowhere in sight.

Carefully, Dod pressed the sheet flat. It was a brief note.

If you're tired of trouble,
confess Sawny lent a hand.
Don't go it alone.
If Something Is Right,
Learn Of New Keys.
When Imagining Life's Lessons,
Helpers Earn Life's Pay.

CHAPTER SIX

"What in the world?" mumbled Dod to himself. The note made no sense at all. And who had given it to him?

Dod read it over and over. "Confess Sawny lent a hand in doing what?" asked Dod, thinking out loud. The only thing that came to his mind was that The Order wanted him to blame Sawny as a co-conspirator in the murder of Horsely. The rest of the note seemed like gibberish.

At lunchtime, food was delivered by a crowd of Coosings. Unfortunately, unbeknownst to Dod, Voracio had given instructions to keep Green Hall's occupants away from his prisoner, so the band of lunch-bearers was from Raul. Sawb and his pals had happily taken the assignment, knowing the fun they would have seeing Dod behind bars.

"Jail fits you," said Sawb, carrying Dod's ham, green beans, and potatoes with gravy.

"Not as much as it fits your uncle," responded Dod, trying hard to hold his ground.

"I thought you said he was dead," taunted Sawb.

"Well, I also thought you were good at swordplay," said Dod. "But clearly I'm wrong from time to time. Tonnis could have easily beaten you in the tournaments."

"He lost!" snapped Sawb, instantly prickling. Dod had struck a raw nerve.

"Oooo," taunted Eluxa, holding Dod's dessert. "That one will cost you." She smiled gleefully and began licking the frosting off the top of the large slice of blueberry cake Mercy had sent down.

When the guards didn't seem to care, Sawb broke the cake in half and took bites while ridiculing Dod.

"We all know you're working with my uncle, killing people and stealing stuff. It's coming out. You're not special, you're a footscrubber for traitors. And it's a shame. Before my father returned to Raul, he gave me this invite." Sawb held a sealed envelope in his hands and waved it back and forth. "He wanted you and your sorry bunch of losers from Green Hall to be our guests in two weeks at the annual Ghoul's Festival. All of the most important people in Raul will be there. I suppose your friends will have to go without you."

"More pie and chouyummy sticks for me," laughed Joak, his hefty frame showing he had already had plenty.

"They wouldn't even want to go," said Dod, beginning to feel bad. Sawb's father, Terro, had had his nice moments. And thinking about joining Terro in his palace for the Ghoul's Festival opened up a flood of memories. The event was three days of banquets, parties, and tournaments, with participants dressing in all sorts of unusual costumes. It was Halloween, Mardi Gras, and New Year's Eve rolled into one.

"I doubt they'll miss it," said Sawb. "My dad has never invited all of Green Hall to come to the Ghoul's Festival. It's probably been at least ten years since he's invited any of them. I think Boot's the only one who's joined us—oh, and Pone when he was doing his internship. The rest haven't seen it. Not even Dilly."

"Especially not Dilly!" griped Eluxa, rolling her eyes.

"At least she'd be wearing a costume," joked Libby, one of Eluxa's friends. Her curly hair looked as though she had spent hours getting ready for her visit to the dungeon. She kept smiling flirtatiously at Dod.

"You should tell her she can't come unless she wears a mask," whined Eluxa, poking Sawb in the shoulder.

"Right," said Sawb.

"It's too bad you'll be sitting here, instead," grunted Kwit, tugging at the bars, showing off his big muscles. "Have fun waiting for your trial."

"Yeah...months," said Doochi. "We'll see how *you* like being confined!" His scoffing tone made it clear that he believed Dod had helped Sirlonk trap him in the storage chamber, which inference Dod certainly didn't like, since he hadn't even known of Green back when Doochi was trapped. And months later, Dod had been the one who had found the collapse and instigated his rescue!

"I doubt they'll attend your dumb Raul holiday," said Dod, watching sadly as the last of his cake disappeared into Sawb's big mouth. "Even if I could go, I wouldn't!" lied Dod.

"Shame, shame," chortled Sawb. "My father will be disappointed to hear it. The only reason he's arranging papers for your useless associates to enter Raul is because of your friendship with him. He's confused enough to think you're special. It will break his heart to hear you *hate* him."

"I never said I hated him," fought Dod. "I like your father."

"What? I can't hear you?" mocked Sawb. He motioned and the mob from Raul Hall followed Sawb away laughing.

Dinner's company was only slightly better. Dari came alone and brought Dod his food. She meant well and tried to cheer him up, though the things she said had a tendency of souring his spirits, particularly when she spent twenty minutes relating the rumors that she had heard swirling around the halls of Twistyard.

"If I were you," concluded Dari honestly, "I would hope to suffocate in my sleep so I wouldn't be forced into knowing what everyone's saying."

"Thanks," said Dod, pushing his half-finished plate of food under the bars, back to Dari. He wasn't hungry once he had endured her report.

"No. I'm totally serious," said Dari. "It would be better to have rats chew your ears off tonight, when it gets pitch black down here, than to have people thinking—"

"Right, thanks," responded Dod.

"Or if one of these nice guards could just lop your head off—"

"Okay, thanks for the visit," interrupted Dod. He had heard enough.

"I'm just saying," blared Dari, continuing on like a broken record. "I wish things would work out for you, but they won't. Not unless you happen to slip on your own spit and you break your neck—or something like that—that would be lucky for you—much, much, much better than—"

"I get it!" shouted Dod, losing his temper.

"Wow!" huffed Dari, carefully retrieving Dod's plate from the floor, as though she were concerned that he would grow tentacles and pull her under the bars. The waiting guards approached Youk's daughter, ensuring her safety.

"I'm sorry," offered Dod as he watched Dari storm away.

The day had passed with no word from Bonboo, and Dari hadn't mentioned anything about Boot or his brothers, or Dilly, or any of the people that Dod had thought cared. They hadn't seemingly spent two seconds considering his predicament. The most pleasant thing Dari had said was that Ingrid had offered to sing with Bowlure and Rot in their trio, but had changed her mind when she had heard that it didn't pay well.

As Dod lay on the stone floor of the jail cell, still covered in soot from the morning's fire, he did his best to think things through. How could everyone have forgotten all of the good he had done for Twistyard? Why weren't they still talking about his spectacular part in helping Green Hall to miraculously win the Golden Swot? And who were his real friends, anyway? Youk had mentioned an informant—someone who had provided evidence against him in the murder of Horsely and had also told them that he was leaving to go fishing. Who but the Dolsur brothers had known of his plans for the day?

When the guards on night shift arrived, they brought a dim candle and withdrew farther from the cell, leaving Dod in near blackness. The atmosphere quickly summoned horrible memories of Driaxom. Thoughts of his father kept him fixed in Green with a determination to discover the truth, despite a string of dreadful nightmares that plagued his sleep.

In his dreams, he saw more glimpses of a massive, dragon-like creature, more flames, and more shouting and clanking. This time, however, he also heard something he hadn't heard before. It was Boot's voice, calling orders in a fight, telling men to kill Dod.

The experience would have been extremely upsetting if it hadn't been joined with a wide range of unexplainable and illogical things, like Dod warning Buck to beware of worms, and Sawny declaring that she loved rats, and Dilly proposing that she be in charge of hauling trash. Even Pone appeared in Dod's mishmash of delirium, adamantly insisting that he pass on two trays of cookies. If Dod were seeing glimpses of the future, it seemed to be one that would happen in an alternate universe where everyone behaved exactly opposite of the way they did in Green.

By the end of the night, Dod was ready to face reality. He had dreamed enough confusing things to prefer Dari bringing him breakfast over more sleep. But it wasn't until after dinner that he finally saw someone he recognized.

"Boot!" exclaimed Dod, the moment Boot rounded the corner. Dilly, Sawny, and Buck followed close on his heels.

"How's life in jail?" asked Boot, handing something to the guards.

"Not bad," fibbed Dod.

"Oh," added Boot. "Before I forget, Bowy wanted you to know, he's thinking of you, too. He'd have come with us today if he hadn't already left for our home up north."

Dod nodded.

"Sorry it's taken us this long to come visit," offered Buck. "You probably thought we'd forgotten about you."

"That's okay," said Dod, acting like a martyr. "I'm sure you guys were busy with your own problems."

"Hardly," said Dilly, prodding one of the guards to find his keys. "We've been working nonstop on getting these ridiculous charges dropped. I can't believe Voracio! He's gone too far this time! Someone needs to put him in his place!"

Dod started laughing. "I think Boot already did, didn't he?"

Buck and Boot both smiled.

"What do you mean?" asked Dilly.

"You didn't tell them?" burst Dod. He couldn't believe Boot, Buck, and Bowy had stayed silent about Boot's triumph over Voracio.

"Tell us what?" pressed Sawny, becoming very interested.

The two guards busied themselves in reviewing the paper Boot had handed to them while Dod went on to explain how Boot had fought with Voracio.

CHAPTER SIX

"We promised Bonboo that we wouldn't go around bragging about it if he let us remain at Twistyard," said Boot, quickly answering Dilly's mad eyes. It was clear that she didn't like anything being kept from her.

"I guess your luck continues," grumbled one of the guards as he unlocked Dod's cell. "You've been granted a temporary release by the highest authority, Commendus, with the strongest guarantor I've ever heard of."

"My great-grandpa's bet his life on you," said Dilly, moving in to give Dod a hug. "Don't do anything crazy."

"And don't be running off without telling people!" insisted Sawny with a concerned look. "If you turned up missing, our great-grandpa would face the consequences of the council's judgment regarding you—and they'd be thinking guilty for sure."

"Oh," said Dod nervously.

"Like you're one to be talking!" scolded Dilly, reminding her sister that they had feared the worst about her, a few days before at Commendus's palace, because she hadn't told anyone that she was stepping outside to stargaze with Doctor Shelderhig.

"He won't run," assured Boot, nudging Sawny and pointing at himself. "His best friend's right here. Besides, I'll have Sneaker keep an eye on him. My ferret's always watching."

"Where's he now?" asked Sawny.

"He's protecting our bedroom," said Boot proudly.

"You mean he's taking another nap in that fancy planter box," mocked Sawny. Her worried eyes kept gravitating to Dod, as though she were deciding whether to trust him or not.

"Thanks for helping me, guys," said Dod, still trying to figure out what exactly had happened.

As the group of friends made their way out of the secluded part of the basement, Dilly explained to Dod how they had rushed off to High Gate the day before, barely arriving in time to enter at the dropping of the triblot barrier; and how Bonboo had petitioned Commendus with regard to Dod's case and been granted the rare circumstance of allowing Dod to go free, so long as Bonboo accepted complete liability for all of the charges if Dod weren't available for punishment.

"So, if the council sentenced me to Driaxom…" began Dod.

"Then Bonboo would be locked in Driaxom if you went missing!" rushed Sawny firmly. "You must stay with us at all times! No games!"

"Right," mumbled Dod, disappointed. He had hoped that Bonboo, as Chief Noble Tredder, would have been able to get the charges dismissed altogether.

"Buck offered to be your guarantor," added Dilly, "but they laughed at him. When murder charges are levied, it's nearly impossible to strike a deal where the accused is set at liberty. You're lucky Bonboo's arrangement was accepted."

"You offered to take my place?" said Dod, looking at Buck. He was feeling bad for having doubted his friends.

"I owe you," Buck responded sincerely. "Sirlonk would have skewered me in the barn. You saved me."

"No, I doubt it," lied Dod. "He wasn't that close. I think you probably would have outrun him if I hadn't interrupted."

"You're being modest," said Dilly, leading the way into the main corridor. "It's a trait we both have." She glanced at Dod with a chuckle-eye, recognizing she wasn't always unpretentious, before calling it straight. "Seriously," she said, stopping the group to focus on Dod. "We all owe you our loyalty. You've saved me and Buck from Sirlonk, and Boot from his stupid triblot barrier experience, and now all of Twistyard from being sold. You're amazing! No matter what anyone says you've done, we know enough to trust you."

Dod felt his face flush hot, thinking of the little things he would need to eventually clarify.

"He's saved Boot twice—at least!" corrected Sawny, finally appearing to have settled on a verdict: Dod was innocent.

"What?" choked Boot jokingly.

"Don't you remember nearly dying in the back of the wagon with Bonboo?" asked Sawny. "The two of you were locked in what almost became your coffin."

"Oh. That time," said Boot, smiling. He puffed his chest like a marine at a flag ceremony. "I was planning on escaping at the last minute. I was just testing Dod."

"Well, stop testing!" insisted Dilly. "I'm too invested in you to watch you die again."

CHAPTER SEVEN

SIRLONK'S TRICKS

Returning to Green Hall was wonderful for Dod after spending two days and a night in the dungeon. The Coosings and Greenlings greeted Dod like a hero. Not everyone at Twistyard was as forgetful as Dari had led Dod to believe.

Pone, Voo, and Sham all knuckled Dod's hair and chanted his praise as he passed their bedroom. They were still flying high on their big Bollirse win over the Lairrington Longs, and they weren't oblivious to the fact that Dod had stopped The Dread yet again. It was as though none of them had walked the halls and heard the trash that was circulating. The only proof in Green Hall that Twistyard at large wasn't sharing their same views about Dod was the scrapes and dings a few of the boys wore from scuffles they had fallen into while defending Dod's name.

Two Greenling boys, Toby and Hermit, had matching shiners over their right eyes. They had confronted a couple of Raulings who were busy at lunch convincing Pots that Dod was a traitor. The Greenlings hadn't bought the rumors, especially

Hermit, and had done their best to forcefully sell a different story.

"Ten days of dishes is noth'n," said Hermit, responding to Boot's jab about Voracio's punishments. "Besides, Mercy's paying me and Toby in cookies and cake for clonking those Raulings. She's stirred like a dust storm over Dod being charged with murder."

"Murder?" said Pone heartily. "That's not Dod's biggest offense!" He smiled and pushed his way toward Dod, who had nearly made it through the masses to Boot's room. "They locked him up for stealing cookies from me!" Pone nodded his head admonishingly to the Greenlings and younger Coosings, adding, "Let this be a lesson to you all. Don't go lifting my stash. I'm not sane without my crumble-topped raspberries or my brown sugar delights."

"We just borrowed them," grinned Boot. "And if you're bent on sticking to a tight return policy, I suppose I can assign you to spend a week of closely monitoring the receptacles into which I anticipate their speedy return."

"Boot! That's gross!" scolded Dilly.

"I'll pass," said Pone, slipping back toward his room. "It's like I always say, 'Once you've eaten the cookie, it's yours.' Besides, access to Mercy's freshest batch is never more than a compliment away."

"And a half-hour of listening per cookie," added Voo, chuckling. "If you ate any more cookies, Pone, they'd have to put a bed in the kitchen so you could get your eight hours of beauty sleep while serving time."

"Quick, have them install the bed!" teased Sham, eyeing Pone up and down for show. "He's clearly decades short of sleep if it's supposed to make him handsome."

Dod laughed. A slam on Pone's looks was a slam on Sham, too. He and Voo looked so much like Pone, it was no wonder people often called them The Triplets.

"I think he's cute," said Donshi, momentarily taking her puppy dog eyes off Dod to stick up for Pone. Sawny took note and looked away.

"That's because you think everyone's cute," said Toos, patting his slick hair.

"You're not," teased Donshi, flipping her golden ringlets while showing a rare moment of cruelty. But her twelve-year-old-like face quickly softened in Toos's direction, which led to a speedy apology.

Dod loved the atmosphere of Green Hall. He could finally breathe freely. Hearing his friends tease each other nearly made him forget about the steep charges that had been filed against him.

The next day at breakfast, Green Hall's Coosings and Greenlings surrounded Dod like a swarm of bees protecting their queen. Anyone who wanted to ask Dod questions had to venture deep into their territory.

Mercy personally brought Dod breakfast and looked him over, then patted his shoulder. "I'm sure the council will find you innocent," she said, tugging at her graying brown curls. "You're such a good boy. Poor Voracio is beside himself with frustration. He's beginning to hate his role as Chief Security Officer at Twistyard. When someone brought information to his attention, he had no choice but to file charges and render to the investigation officials at High Gate an honest report of the information. I'm sure you understand that he certainly didn't want to cause such trouble for you, Dod. You were just in the wrong place at the wrong time."

Dod smiled and nodded, though he didn't believe any of it.

"Boosap!" coughed Boot. Buck and Pone rattled their silverware in agreement.

"Why, just the other day," continued Mercy, oblivious to the opposition, "poor Voracio was going about his duties when someone tried to escape him, and the man's horse kicked him in the face. You should see the bruise he's tending. He said it was the worst blow he's ever taken."

"Perhaps he should consider writing books," said Boot, glancing at Dod and Buck as he rubbed his knuckles. "He's got a great imagination. If he didn't make people angry, he wouldn't get hurt."

"Oh, I agree with you there," huffed Mercy. She picked at a splotch of food on her apron with vengeance. "He needs to do something else! He's really a nice person when he's not busy being in charge. I dare say, there are times when I can't stand the man—of course I adore him. You know what I mean. I just think he'd be better off if he could stop worrying about everyone else. But here we are again without Bonboo for who knows how long. I wish he hadn't gone—"

Dod's ears perked up. He hadn't been told that Bonboo was still away.

Mercy caught herself and glanced down at Dod anxiously. "No one is happier than I am that Bonboo was able to free you. You know I didn't mean things the way they came out, right?"

"Oh, I know," said Dod.

"I certainly wanted you extricated from the dungeon," continued Mercy. "The moment I heard of your dilemma, I told Voracio, 'You let that boy out! You know he's innocent! The tattler is a mistaken and unfortunate soul indeed to produce anything incriminating against Dod!'"

Of course, poor Voracio agreed fully, but his hands were tied. The law is the law. I just wish Bonboo weren't constrained to remain at High Gate as part of the agreement. He's desperately needed here at Twistyard. And the longer he's gone, the crazier things get."

"I certainly agree," said Dod, nodding his head. "Who's the mistaken soul?"

"Who?" asked Mercy.

"The rat who's lying about Dod!" said Boot agitatedly. Everyone at the table knew Boot loved Mercy like an aunt but hated that she adored Voracio.

"Oh. I don't know," responded Mercy, gazing blankly into the air. "Voracio wouldn't tell me something like that. The spineless individual is claiming his protective rights. He plans on remaining anonymous."

"Sawb!" grunted Toos quickly, stabbing at his ham for emphasis. "I knew he would do something like this. After we won the Golden Swot, he promised we'd have *bad luck* in the future. Remember, Boot?"

"Maybe," said Boot. His answer sounded more like 'no.'

From three tables over, Sawb turned to look. His ears were good enough to catch wind of his name. He smiled wickedly and tipped his head at Dod.

"Who's to say it's a boy," offered Sawny, watching Eluxa flirt with a crowd of Raul Coosings and flaunt an expensive necklace her family had sent. "If you want to find a truly vengeful, spineless rat, you're searching in the wrong gender. *'Scorn a woman and you'll watch the lightning roll out for months.'* That's what my grandma used to say."

"She's a smart woman," agreed Mercy, hurrying off to answer cries for help that bellowed from the kitchen; in the distance, two Sooshling boys stood at the entrance, covered in something brown.

"I haven't scorned any women," assured Dod, finding the very idea laughable. After all, he was *hopeless Cole*!

"You wouldn't know," said Dilly, glancing at Pone who nearly dripped pudding down his shirt—Eluxa's giggling held his gaze.

"Boys are all alike, thick between the ears when it comes to relationships," continued Dilly, shaking her head. "A common pond guppy fares better at reading signs and following cues. Who knows what Pot may have pined for you only to have had her moment at the dance ruined when you turned up late and left early."

"Oh," said Dod, remembering Boot's and Buck's advice about how seriously the girls took their dances.

"No," disagreed Buck, watching Sawb approach with his usual sidekicks. "Murder charges are a bit hefty for that kind of thing. Dod's got a full-fledged enemy—a real traitor who's been bought off by Sirlonk. Someone from Raul sounds likely to me."

"Could be," said Boot in a distracted voice. His mind appeared to be elsewhere.

Sawb strode past the outer wall of Greenlings to the center of Green Hall's breakfast club and tapped Boot on the shoulder. "I have this for you," he said smugly, looking beyond Boot at Dod.

"Is it your confession?" growled Buck from across the table. Since his near-death experience with Sirlonk, his backbone had stiffened substantially, and it seemed as though he had aged twenty years.

"Of course!" said Sawb sarcastically, tipping his nose at Buck. "I can't live with myself. How could I have joined forces with my evil uncle? I think I'll give you my stolen treasures, climb the back wall of Twistyard, and throw myself off."

Dod gulped hard as food lodged in his throat. He hated that everyone was filling Twistyard with embellished versions of his original story, the one where Horsely had confessed remorse and given up the Farmer's Sackload. It did sound stupid and unbelievable.

Boot took the envelope and opened it up as Joak and Kwit took turns making tough-guy faces at The Triplets. Pone responded with his own humorous tough-guy look—two sausages sticking out the sides of his mouth like walrus tusks and his eyebrows raised.

"Your dad's inviting all of Green Hall to the Ghoul's Festival?" said Boot, his jaw dropping. He set his eyes on the crowd from Raul with astonishment.

The table of Greenlings and Coosings warmed quickly at the prospects of getting the chance to see the wondrous event. Few people from Green had ever been invited. Pone's grin popped one of the sausages out, leaving him a goofy mess of excitement.

"You're formally requested," said Sawb. "My father is hoping you'll make time. And don't worry about the costumes, we've got plenty to share."

"The Ghoul's Festival," whispered Coosings and Greenlings alike.

"What's the catch?" asked Boot cautiously.

"There isn't one," responded Sawb, glancing at Dod with a smirk behind his eyes. "I do hope *all* of you will be able to come. It would be a shame if Dod's troubles kept him stranded here, awaiting a verdict."

"Okay," said Boot slowly, rising to his feet. He flashed the Coosings' sign of friendship and postured diplomatically. As the rivals stood face-to-face, their demeanor reminded Dod of two world leaders coming to an agreement. These Coosings were living proof that Bonboo's dream for Twistyard was being accomplished—boys and girls from all three realms were developing skills that would help them be successful ambassadors for peace.

"You can tell your father we're anxious to join him," said Boot in a polite voice. "It's a generous offer. And he can plan on *all* of us attending."

Sawb strode away arrogantly, met up with Clair near the front doors, and exited.

"What do you think he's hiding?" asked Dilly.

"I don't know," responded Dod. "But if it involves Clair, I don't want any part of it." Dod shivered as he recalled his last confrontation with Clair.

Dilly looked at Dod and smiled.

"Let's just say, he still hates me," added Dod. "If Sawb's hanging out with Clair, it can't be good."

"With or without Mr. Clair, it's fine by me," said Pone happily. "Sawb just invited us to the Ghoul's Festival! I certainly don't want to miss it!"

Dod felt a knot forming in his stomach.

"I'm worried about Sawb's motives," said Dilly, "but not Mr. Clair's. You have to admit, he's a great swordsman. We're lucky he's agreed to temporarily help us improve our skills. Pious could call him back to service in the war effort any day."

"But Clair's got it out for me!" complained Dod.

"Military life makes 'em rough," said Hermit, putting on an apron he had brought with him to breakfast. He and Toby had just finished eating and were preparing to get on with their dishes duty. "I don't think Mr. Clair hates you. He's just jealous."

"Yeah," agreed Toby. "At sword practice yesterday he said you were the youngest boy he'd ever seen swing a blade."

"Really?" choked Dod.

"Not exactly," said Hermit, shaking his head of messy hair. "He said you were proof that evil forces were even recruiting the youngest of helpers with promising sword skills."

"Oh," sighed Dod.

The conversation stopped abruptly when Juck entered the Great Hall running. He approached Boot with an urgent message, his young eyes full of excitement. "He's here! He just arrived!"

"Who?" asked Toos, turning to his fellow Greenling.

"Traygof," said Boot casually, stealing Juck's thunder.

"How did you know?" stammered Juck, his spiky hair wilting in amazement. Everyone looked at Boot, who cracked a clever grin.

"I'm turning psychic like Dod," he began, and then he shook his head and admitted, "Just kidding. Last night I heard that Traygof made port at Fisher a couple of days ago."

"Traygof," said Donshi admiringly.

Within moments, everyone had finished breakfast and was standing in the front grassy field, rubbing shoulders with hundreds of people who had gathered to catch a glimpse of the legendary Traygof.

Dod had a few memories of the reported hero. Traygof had fought alongside many famous men, including Donis and Bollath. In the celebrated tale of Drake's defeat at Rocky Ridge, Donis and Bollath had stormed the pole tower in company with Traygof and taken back the city.

"There he is," said Dilly, directing Dod's eyes to a graying, bushy-bearded man. He sat relaxed in his saddle, atop a healthy stallion, and had eight other tredders with him, each showing signs of rough character.

"Now you can meet the man who saved your horse," said Sawny. "He took Shooter from the people at Rocky Ridge and shipped him to Pious."

"Right," said Dod, trying to pull memories.

Boot's big frame pushed forward through the crowd until Dod had a good view of the scene. Clair and Voracio stood before the horsemen, explaining something to Traygof.

"We had no choice but to lock him up," argued Clair. "We are civilized, educated, and law abiding!"

Voracio nodded.

"Are you suggesting I'm not?" laughed Traygof. "Just because I'm lacking the formal title of general doesn't mean I'm uneducated or any less civilized. Furthermore, laws are created with the sole purpose of helping people possess freedom; so, in a very real sense, everywhere I go—the world over—*I am the law!*"

Traygof had a swagger of confidence that set him apart from everyone else. His daring eyes prodded at Clair and Voracio, as though he could do as he pleased, wherever he pleased. Dod hadn't seen anyone but Sirlonk possess such a brazen display of self-assurance. He would have quickly been concerned about Traygof and his little band of ruffians if the man hadn't also carried a sizable reputation for doing good.

"I'm sure you're educated," conceded Clair, "at least in the way things were done years ago. However, times have changed. Your vigilante justice needs to be retired. Mainland society requires different protocol. Perhaps you can use your name and call the shots among the billies or out in the open seas—far away from the buzz of civilization—but there's a reason you don't bear the title of general: You're simply a pirate."

Voracio stood a little taller next to Clair.

"I agree," laughed Traygof, not rattled at all. His joviality made him a crowd favorite. Strat smiled broadly from a few paces behind Clair and whispered back and forth with Tinja. They appeared to be enjoying the showdown of sorts.

Clair continued pushing to have his voice heard. "You can't run from fight to fight at will, like a whimsical bully, and then hope your gifts to superiors will buy their praise. You lack regulation, Traygof! If only you'd have taken the time to gain real skills, your life of cheerleading would have been better served as a member of the army. Who knows, maybe you'd have been appointed the rank of general like me and Voracio. Important people such as Pious and Commendus choose leaders based on merit, not over-inflated reputations."

"Wow! Now you're claiming I'm all talk!" smiled Traygof, raising his wild eyebrows in playful disgust. "I'd think you would be kinder to your elders. Some of us here were crushing the flanks of Dreadluceous's forces while your mommy was wiping your nose. I'm sure I could teach you a few moves. Contract soldiers are better with swords than you give credit. Just because we choose our battles doesn't mean we're weak."

Clair stiffened like an angry brick.

"I think you've got your own issues," continued Traygof. "Clearly you dislike this Dod fellow. If he's stopped The Dread once, I would think you would cut him some slack. Let him join me and my men. We've got plenty of room—"

"He's welcome to do as he pleases," interrupted Voracio, "just as soon as he's cleared—"

"That's the trouble," snapped Traygof. He prodded his horse to move closer. "I've seen enough to know that the hands of justice are all too often the very instigators of injustice."

"Bly was an exception!" puffed Voracio, knowing right where the blow was intended. "The investigators welcomed your help."

Traygof laughed in disagreement. "Regardless," he persisted, "Dod's earned a pass, don't you think? Let him come with me and bring a friend or two. The seas are full of trouble right now. Noble billies are rising. They'll be joining Dreaderious any day. Mark my words. Pious could use all the help we can give him."

Dod was shocked to hear Traygof was fighting with Clair over him. There wasn't a Coosing at Twistyard that wouldn't happily take a spell with Traygof aboard his famed ship, *The Avenger*. Toos's eyes turned green with jealously, and he wasn't alone. Even Dilly and Sawny looked as if they wished Traygof were seeking their help.

Clair and Voracio both shook their heads.

"Let me speak with Bonboo," requested Traygof, preparing to dismount.

"He's staying with Commendus at High Gate," responded Clair, resting his hands upon the hilts of his two swords.

"That works," said Traygof briskly. "We're having dinner with Commendus tonight. He sent word for me months ago."

The crowd parted and the celebrity of the seas rode away with his men, headed for High Gate.

"Whoa," said Toos, scooting closer to Dod. "Take me with you."

"I'm not going anywhere," mumbled Dod, feeling uncomfortable inside. It was nice that a living legend had just swapped scowls with Clair over his predicament, but the whole setting was troubling in light of the note that Dod kept in his pocket—the one he had been given anonymously while in jail.

"If anyone's joining Dod," burst Dilly, "it would be me."

"No," corrected Boot, "Dod would take his *best* friend."

"Well actually," said Dod, working hard to find a smile. "I think I'll take Ingrid. She makes the best pirate stews."

"She's gone," shot Pone, eagerly joining the conversation. "She's off checking on Higga's holdings. You'll have to take me instead. Everyone knows I'm good with food."

"The eating part," said Toos, giving Pone a shove.

"Stop!" insisted Sawny, her tone dampening the fun. "Don't tease Dod with the idea that he can run off. No matter who comes calling his name, Bonboo's given his pledge!"

"She's right," agreed Boot, half serious. "Dod can't choose his shipmates until after Traygof's gotten the investigation dismissed."

"It'll never happen," said Sawny sternly. "If it were possible, my great-grandpa would have done it."

"I wouldn't say never," fought Toos. "Traygof's known for doing the impossible. Things looked bleak for Bly until he stepped in. And remember when he convinced the natives on the Zoot Islands to give up an entire island for Pious to use as a military base? No one thought he'd be able to do it."

"That's different," said Sawny. "A lot of people say Humberrone did the heavy lifting and Traygof swooped in for the credit."

"What about the two-year peace pact he obtained from Dreaderious. It worked for over a year."

"Once again, verification of who did what is shady," said Sawny. "Mr. Clair's right in challenging Traygof's history. A lot of his accomplishments are held in question."

"Well," huffed Toos, looking stunned that anyone would say ill of the unstoppable Traygof. "It's undisputed that he went into battle beside Donis and Bollath to save Commendus. That should prove he's more than a rumor. And it was their last stand together. Dozens of Red Devils died in that fight, along with Donis and Bollath. But did he? No. He fought his way through and personally escorted Commendus to freedom. Not to mention, he wasn't even aided by swappers as Donis and Bollath were! No matter what you say, Traygof's a hero! Everyone knows it! He's nearly Humberrone!"

"I haven't seen his picture on the wall in the Hall of The Greats," taunted Sawny. At this point, she grinned from the corner of her mouth, recognizing how seriously Toos was taking his hero worship.

"SAWNY!" raged Toos in an exasperated voice, his fists clenched, when Boot put a big arm around him.

"She's a lady," said Boot, eyeing him down. "Give her respect."

"But she's a stupid one!" spat Toos.

Boot gripped Toos tightly and knuckled his hair into a flopping mess before releasing him.

"Thanks," mumbled Toos, running his hand across the top of his head as he disappeared into the crowd.

"I'll take his place on the ship," said Pone the moment he noticed Sawny's look of guilt.

"No one's going anywhere," assured Dilly.

Once inside the castle, Boot caught a glimpse of the time and rushed Dilly, Sawny, Dod, and Buck to hurry with him. He had scheduled with the drat soldiers to open the room that contained his burnt belongings.

When they arrived, they were greeted by a few young guards who had gathered in front of Green Hall with large garbage cans.

"We've come to help you clean out the smoky conference room," said Jibb's cousin Dolrus, fiddling with his small, pointed beard. He looked like a teenage version of Jibb. "Find what you want and we'll haul the rest off. I doubt there's much worth saving."

Boot entered first, his eyes searching the mess sadly. "Take a look at the remains of thirty years," he lamented.

Dilly tried to cheer him up. "Most of your clothes were overdue for a burning anyway," she said, tapping her foot against a charred purple-and-green shirt.

"They're just things," said Buck, glancing the room over with a dreamlike gaze.

Boot approached one pile and raised the burnt remains of a book. The pages were blackened. "Here's my journal," Boot confessed.

"Oh no!" groaned Dilly. "That's dreadful."

"Not really," chuckled Buck.

Boot began to grin.

"The only thing he ever wrote in it," said Buck, "was a poem about you."

"How sweet," sighed Dilly.

"Once again, not really," insisted Buck, beginning to laugh.

"Don't tell her," begged Boot.

"Do tell," said Sawny, still wearing a guilt-riddled face. It clearly bothered her to have clashed with Toos.

"Boot wrote the poem after you told Bonboo about his day of helping a fresh batch of Pots in the library. The poor guests had been scared to death. I think half the girls in that group left the next day."

Dilly searched the air.

"The snakes—" began Buck.

"Oh! I remember that one," laughed Dilly. "What is it with you boys and snakes?"

"I hate them!" said Buck. "But Boot doesn't, so in his journal, you're the mean pig with spider legs."

"I'm the what?" huffed Dilly. She bolted around piles of soot and reached for the blackened book that Boot playfully held high in the air.

"Dilly!" exclaimed Sawny. "Look what he kept!" Sawny bent down and pulled a circular braid of dried weeds from the ashes. "It's the crown you made for him, the summer we visited. I was probably only ten or fifteen. Remember how you asked him to be your king?"

"I was just being nice," defended Dilly.

"You were not!" said Sawny. "You liked him from the moment he greeted us at the carriage. All summer you couldn't stop talking about *Boot, the cutest Greenling*."

Boot blushed a rare pink in his cheeks and smiled as he handed Dilly the book, though she didn't seem interested in searching its pages anymore. Her attention had shifted to Sawny's findings and Boot's reactions.

Sawny carefully handed the weeds to Dilly, who tossed the ruined journal and inspected the crown with a deep, sentimental eye. She glanced cautiously at Boot two or three times before lifting the ring up toward Boot's head.

Boot took a step back, his face torn with conflicting signals. "I'm hardly a king fit for you, Dilly Tillius," he whispered, a frog caught in his throat.

"You're perfect," said Dilly, struggling to control her emotions. "I don't care about money or blood. You have a noble heart and are worthy of my faith."

Boot studied the room over pensively, then sheepishly glanced at Dod. "But I have snakes in my shoes," he finally confessed before awkwardly wiping a tear from the corner of his eye.

Sawny was nearly at the door, racing Buck and Dod to exit the private conversation, when she stumbled over something unusual.

"Whose is this?" she asked, more to Dod and Buck than to Boot or Dilly.

Dod's eyes seized the item with eagerness, his gut prompting him to look closer.

Buck reached for the blackened remains of what looked like a backpack and drew a spent piece of fabric from its center. As he held it up, most of the fragile threads crumbled.

"It's Sirlonk's!" gasped Dod. His eyes were aided by flashes of memories. The burnt cloth was the cloak Dark Hood had worn the night Dod had faced him in Green Hall.

"Are you sure?" asked Sawny.

"Could be," said Buck. "I don't recognize it."

"It is," insisted Dod. "It's proof of Sirlonk's trick." He suddenly knew how the two villains had escaped the locked fortress; and surprisingly, they hadn't used Boot's secret passage!

OLD BLOOD

"That's how Sirlonk escaped," muttered Dod. "How?" asked Buck, looking skeptically at the scanty remains of the black cloak.

"Sirlonk brought the pack with him," explained Dod. "He must have had it loaded with supplies to dress the part of a drat soldier—a fake beard and everything. In the morning when the guards broke through, it seems likely that Sirlonk and his helper joined the hunt without being recognized. That's how he did it. And it wouldn't have been too difficult for him to conceal his stolen prize—Dilly's Soosh Mayler Belt."

"No," said Sawny. "Jibb or Tridacello would have noticed, don't you think?"

"Hmm," added Dilly, approaching the burnt pack. She and Boot had tabled their conversation for later.

Boot ripped into the ashes. "I don't recognize the bag," he said, sifting through the charred contents until he produced a second piece of cloth. This time it was a charcoal gray.

CHAPTER EIGHT

"See!" exclaimed Dod. "That's from Dark Hood's little helper."

"You mean Horsely?" asked Dilly.

"Probably," said Dod. He went quiet when three guards entered the room.

"Have you found anything worth keeping?" asked Dolrus, wearing a curious look.

Boot quickly shoved the burnt fabric back into the mess and rose to his feet. "You can take it all," he responded. "I think we've seen enough of what's become of our stuff. It's all ruined."

"Don't you want your rock collection?" asked a scrawny drat guard who stood beside Dolrus. His beard was shaggy and his nose didn't tip up.

"I'm fine without it," said Boot. He took a few steps back and retrieved the crown of weeds from a protruding nail he had hung it on. "We're done with everything in here. Go ahead and haul it away."

"We could give you more time if you'd like," offered Dolrus.

"No. We're done," said Boot, nodding his head. "Thanks for letting us look it over." Boot slid Buck a knowing glance.

"Yeah, thanks," agreed Buck. He could tell Boot was up to something.

Dilly and Sawny read Boot's face and followed the boys back to Boot's room.

"What was that?" asked Dilly once the door was shut.

Boot walked to the planter box and hung the weed crown from a branch. "Things are getting complicated," he said.

No kidding! thought Dod, who was constantly plagued with anxiety over his trumped-up murder charges.

Dilly reached into her lowest pants pocket and produced her red leather-bound notebook. She flipped it open and prepared to write. "Begin with the facts," she said calmly, taking a seat on Buck's bed.

"That's the problem," confessed Boot. "I'm not sure what's true anymore." He studied Dod and then shook his head.

Dod's heart began to pound uncomfortably. He didn't know where to start, but wanted to tell them everything.

"What do you mean?" asked Sawny. She flopped down next to Dilly.

Boot sighed long and loud. "Back there—our burnt stuff—it could be a trap of sorts. Maybe that pack came from Sirlonk, or maybe not. Either way, I'll feel better when it's gone. Someone could be planting fake evidence against us—or at least against Dod. If the soldiers measured what we just saw, they'd probably say it was proof we were involved with Sirlonk."

Dod groaned. He hadn't even considered that the burnt cloaks could look incriminating against him.

"It's like what Sawny said on the way back from High Gate," continued Boot, "about The Order."

Dod's ears perked up.

Boot looked a little guilty as he dug his hands into his pockets and produced a crinkled paper. "Someone slipped me this while we were at the dance."

"Another note?" pounced Dilly. She rushed to inspect it.

"Why didn't you say anything?" asked Buck, appearing hurt.

"Because I felt stupid," responded Boot. "People keep slipping messages into my pockets without me noticing. If it were anyone else getting the notes, I'd be suspecting them of trouble. Besides, this one's—well…"

"Voracio killed your dad on purpose?" choked Dilly, reading the letter. "Who would write such things? We all know he didn't."

Images Dod had seen before of Boot's father's accident again raced through his mind.

"Can we be honest?" said Boot in a serious voice. "I've always suspected Voracio knew what he was doing when he ordered the soldiers to fire into the range—though I've never told anyone before now—I couldn't—not with how hard my mother worked to push forgiveness."

"Do you really think he did it on purpose?" asked Dilly. Her face revealed she was considering the possibility for the first time.

"I don't know," confessed Boot. "Maybe he was following orders."

"Whose?"

"I don't know," said Boot. "It's always been a gut feeling. And once it came out that Sirlonk was The Dread, it made more sense—like maybe people knew his sons were involved in trouble—stuff they didn't want public—so they charged Voracio with the task of taking them out. My dad was just in the way."

Dod was nodding his head.

"Who would have ordered it?" asked Dilly.

"Military people—high ups—I don't know—people who do *secret stuff*."

Dilly raised her eyebrows.

"The fifteenth floor isn't blocked off for nothing," argued Boot, glancing at Dod. "There's a lot more to our freedom than we know—things people never speak of—I'm sure of that. Anyway, getting this note tipped me sideways toward Voracio."

Buck approached Boot and glanced at the letter. "You've never liked Voracio."

"I know," agreed Boot, "but seeing my own suspicions in print confirmed everything I've always thought about him. Question is, who slipped me the tip?" Boot's eyes settled on Dod.

"And why?" added Dilly. "Even if someone knew the truth, assuming there's a horrific story in Voracio's past, why would that person wait until now to let you know. It doesn't make sense."

"Maybe X sent the letter," suggested Sawny. "He slipped you the note about The Beast."

"It's The Order," said Dod. "They're recruiting. Sirlonk said so in the barn when he tried to get Buck to join them."

"You can't trust *anything* Sirlonk says!" snapped Boot.

Dod recoiled a few feet and looked sheepishly at Boot. "I know. I'm just saying, you would be a prize to turn—"

"When I'm cold and buried I'll still be facing away from them!" fought Boot defensively.

"We know," said Dilly, patting Boot on the shoulder.

Dod mustered his courage to speak. "They got you mad enough to fight Voracio, which nearly landed you in jail."

"You're hardly one to talk!" huffed Boot. "None of us thinks Horsely handed you the jewels and threw himself off the back wall. We discussed the matter in great detail while trotting to and from High Gate trying to exonerate you."

Sawny and Buck traded awkward glances as Boot approached Dod. "We know Horsely had the Ankle Weed stuck to his arm. Sawny overheard Youk relaying the information to Clair."

"He grabbed for it—" groaned Dod, wanting to throw up.

"Look," said Boot, "my brothers and I really appreciate what you've done for us—giving us money for my mom—but you've got to come clean about everything—and I mean *everything*, regardless of how deep it goes! No more secrets." Boot's eyes seized Dod with a death grip.

"Boot!" chided Dilly. "He saved Twistyard!"

"I know," said Boot, his eyes still fixed on Dod. "It does seem that way, but there are too many unexplainable things. Who told Youk we were going fishing—"

"Not me," begged Dod.

"Well it wasn't me or Buck or Bowy. Who else does that leave?"

"Whoever saw us exiting," responded Dod.

Boot didn't let up. "The place was silent….And you—you insisted Buck come along. Why?"

"I didn't choose the big boat, and I didn't tell Buck to join me in the barn, either—if you're implying I'm the reason Buck faced Sirlonk. Think back. Who did *those things*?"

Buck answered the question with his eyes that turned on Boot, while Boot scooped the letter from Dilly and posted it squarely in Dod's face. "Do you recognize that?" Boot pointed at a strange symbol. "Tell the truth."

Dod nodded.

"Even Sawny won't be acquainted with it," said Boot.

Sawny, Dilly, and Buck hurried to inspect the squiggly insignia at the bottom of the note. All of them drew blank faces.

"What is it?" asked Sawny.

"It's a death mark," said Boot. "Dod's seen plenty of them, haven't you?"

"Well, of course. I was locked in Driaxom!"

"You're the *only* one around here that's seen them!" snapped Boot, glaring at Dod with confused, angry eyes. "Why the note?

What's your angle? Are you working with Sirlonk? Are you X, too?"

"Why would you even ask that?" fought Dod, feeling as though his best friend had just punched him repeatedly in the gut, leaving him winded.

"ARE YOU?" demanded Boot, grabbing Dod's shoulder.

"Stop!" yelled Sawny, her whole face wincing. She clearly hated the fighting.

"Tell the truth!" pressed Boot. "I saw your journal from Pap in the bag with the cloaks. If Sirlonk would have wanted it, he would have taken it with him. But there it was, sitting there... like you left your signature on your things—"

"Boot!"

"THE TRUTH!" blared Boot angrily, beginning to shake Dod. "Have you joined The Order? Did you kill Horsely on purpose?"

"No!" said Dod, stunned by the accusations.

Boot didn't let go.

"Look what's happening," interrupted Sawny, grabbing Boot's arm. "There's a logical explanation for everything, and it doesn't have to include anyone being a traitor! Dilly and I talked about this last night. We all need to stick together. Dod's innocent, and the council will figure it out soon enough."

Boot released Dod, looked at his own trembling hand, backed up, and flopped on his bed. "For your information, Dod, I stood up to Voracio because of *you*, not my dad."

Dod didn't respond.

"It's just...well." Boot sprawled out and searched the ceiling for answers. "I know people are sometimes driven to do dumb things and are stuck thinking there's no way out." Boot clenched his fists. "But they're wrong. You can always choose—every moment…every day…every minute. No one can force you to do anything you don't want to do. And we're your friends. We'll stand by you. We just need to know what's up. That's all."

Dod stretched nervously. "If you want the whole story, I'll tell you everything—all the details—but you have to believe me."

Boot sat up and slowly nodded.

"Here's how it happened," began Dod. He started with the night he had faced Sirlonk and Murdore in the pump house below the waterfall at Commendus's estate, and how he had watched a silent helper stand idly by, and how he had narrowly escaped being eaten by the swarm of baby duressers and then the two hungry diasserpentouses. From there he explained his climb up the back wall of the castle, including how he had intended on showing Abbot the Ankle Weed, and how he had come upon Horsely jumping about, and how Horsely had heard Dod and spun around.

By the time Dod got to the part where he was hanging desperately from the end of the palsarflex with Horsely rooting through his pack, Boot and the others were ready to hear Dod's miraculous triumph over Horsely. The details that flowed from Dod's lips were too specific and convincing to be invented on the fly. His words rang true.

The only subject that Dod left untouched was that he, his father, and his grandfather were from Earth, and as such, were capable of stopping time by moving from one world to the other. Since he wasn't ready to divulge that part, he withheld how Sirlonk had said he was Humberrone's son and how Horsely had been tricked by Sirlonk because he hadn't understood Pap's mishap with the medallion. Nearly everything else came out just as it had happened, including that The Order supposedly wanted him for some reason. The retelling was like dumping a swimming pool of water over his friends' heads when they had expected a light sprinkle.

"No wonder Horsely dared jump in the water off Fisher's Point," said Buck, recalling the incident. "He had to hide the Farmer's Sackload before we entered the cavern."

"*We?*" chuckled Boot, teasing Buck about having been too afraid to leave his horse. Boot had lightened up, back to his cheery self, after hearing Dod's lengthy explanations.

Sawny and Dilly both began assuring Dod everything was going to be fine when Dod remembered the note he had received.

"I got this while locked up," he said, pulling the crinkled paper from his pocket. "Someone threw it into my cell when I wasn't looking."

Boot popped to his feet and snatched the letter from Dod. "You're getting notes, too?" he said eagerly. He cleared his throat and read aloud.

> *"If you're tired of trouble, confess Sawny lent a hand.*
> *Don't go it alone. If Something Is Right,*
> *Learn Of New Keys. When Imagining Life's Lessons,*
> *Helpers Earn Life's Pay."*

Buck shook his head. "Maybe one of the guards was playing a prank on you. It sounds like twaddle to me."

"Confess Sawny lent a hand," whispered Sawny, looking uneasily over Boot's shoulder at the note. "Oh, look. A code." Sawny's eyes brightened with excitement.

CHAPTER EIGHT

Dilly, Buck, and Dod joined Sawny and Boot in studying the message, though only Sawny seemed to see the real meaning.

"That rat!" mumbled Sawny.

"Who?" asked Dilly. The suspense appeared to be killing her.

"You know who!" said Sawny. She pointed methodically with her finger, helping the others to notice the pattern. "If you're tired of trouble, confess Sawny lent a hand. Don't go it alone. I, Sirlonk, will help."

"How did you catch that?" asked Dod, amazed with Sawny's skills.

"How did you miss it?" responded Sawny. "Once the sentences shifted to having all of the first letters of each word capitalized, you had to have known it was a code."

"Oh, right," said Dod.

"That's The Order for you," said Boot assertively. "They like to put a price on their help—make you first prove your loyalty—"

Dilly glanced at Boot with concerned eyes.

"Horsely offered Dod a deal on the ledge," rushed Boot. "That's what you said, right Dod?" he added, turning quickly to Dod.

"If you can call it a deal," stammered Dod, rubbing his left hand. Thinking of them chopping two of his fingers off made him shiver.

"And that's exactly what Sirlonk's doing now," continued Boot. "He's asking Dod to sacrifice Sawny before he's willing to come to Dod's rescue—whatever that would be."

"I don't want *his* help!" scoffed Dod. He turned in time to see a patch of morning sunlight glide across Sawny's curls as she paced in front of the window. "Don't worry, Sawny," he offered sincerely, "I'd rather die in Driaxom than lie about you. Besides, your great-grandpa's already freed me from the dungeon."

"And Traygof's gonna get this whole thing settled," added Boot.

"Wouldn't that be nice," sighed Buck. "We could all sail with Traygof."

"Or at least attend the Ghoul's Festival," said Dilly. "Speaking of which, I think we should get started helping Commendus with the preparations he mentioned. Our service may sway the council into allowing Dod to go with us to Raul."

Boot and Buck raised their eyebrows.

"Were Sawny and I the only ones listening to him at breakfast yesterday?" asked Dilly.

"Sorry," chuckled Boot. "You have to admit, Sabbella's food-tasting finches were quite distracting. One kept darting at me."

"She had six of them," remarked Buck to Dod. "They were hopping around the table and up her arm the whole meal."

Sawny smiled. "She's eccentric, for sure."

"What do you expect?" pushed Dilly. "She's Neadrou's daughter. Anyway, I told Commendus we would be happy volunteering our time at the Code of the Kings Monument. He's planning on hosting a special meeting there in a few months and was hoping I'd oversee the shine-up."

"Scrubbing?" groaned Buck.

"Perhaps some," admitted Dilly. "Though as I understand it, our job will be checking to see that the edifice is returned to its prior glory—as it was back in the days of Concealio. Commendus has offered to lend skilled laborers from the Capitol site for a time if we need them. Our job is authenticating the building as my great, great, great somebody had it."

"Concealio isn't that remote," corrected Sawny. "He's Bonboo's great-grandfather, much like Bonboo is ours."

"Really?" remarked Dilly. "When you put it that way, he sounds close."

"Yes, though we have the advantage of knowing our great-grandfather. Bonboo never knew his."

"Bonboo's definitely the oldest living tredder on record," said Boot, wearing a grin. "Three hundred and thirty-three years is really old. Are you sure he's not one of those humans from the Mauj."

"Positive," insisted Dilly. "We just have good blood."

"Old blood," coughed Buck.

"Some of that, too," responded Dilly with a smile. She wasn't ashamed that she came from royal descent.

Two knocks at the door were followed by Pone's muffled voice. "You've got a visitor, Boot," he said while crunching on something.

Dilly unlatched and opened the door, revealing Tonnis standing in the middle of The Triplets with a crowd of Green Hall boys behind them. Sham had one hand on Tonnis's shoulder, as though ready to manhandle him back the way he had come.

"Easy boys," said Dilly, greeting the crowd. She smiled at Tonnis, who casually flipped his long bangs out of his face and apologized for intruding.

"Come on in," said Boot. "What brings you here?"

"I need a favor," sighed Tonnis. "While at High Gate watching you jilt the boockards out of the Lairrington Longs, Sawb bought a special ferret—you know, he's always trying to be as cool as you, Boot."

Hearing his praise, Boot glowed.

"He can keep trying!" heckled Toos from the pack of Greenlings that filled the hall.

"Yeah," said Tonnis, raising his fist in the air as he looked over his shoulder at the crowd of boys. "He's a pathetic, gold-rimmed pansy, isn't he?"

The boys went wild, whooping and cheering. Tonnis didn't seem the least bit concerned about upholding Sawb's name; to the contrary, he was fine with disparaging it.

"I saw him toting his white ferret in a cage at Commendus's palace," said Dilly. "Didn't he name it Thunder?"

"Yeah," chuckled Tonnis, looking at the ground. "Funny, huh? It looks more like a Snowball." He flipped his hair again and turned back to Boot. "The blibbin' thing ran off, and Doochi's claiming I took it. Is there any way you could bring Sneaker over to sniff out where it is? I bet the ferret's hiding in his room—maybe in his closet. If Sawb gets any more worked up over me, he'll demote my tail right out of Raul Hall."

"You could stay with your mommy!" called Toos. Three or four boys whistled in support of the jab.

"Show's over," said Boot, stepping to the exit. He waved his hand and dismissed the band of spectators before shutting the door. "I'll help you," he said. "It would be a shame to have one of the best swordsmen at Twistyard stuck bunking with the Pots."

"Dilly's better," smiled Tonnis. "I just have longer legs."

"Spider legs," giggled Sawny. She and Dilly laughed.

Tonnis snapped his hand against his hip a few times, a Raul thing, and nodded appreciatively at Boot. "I'd rather not go back with the Pots—not now. They'd suffocate me in my sleep for having a crazy father."

"You're always welcome here," suggested Sawny happily.

"To visit," said Boot curtly, drawing a distinct line. He clicked twice and Sneaker raced down the biggest tree in the planter box and jumped onto Boot's shoulder. "Let's go," he said.

Buck and Dod followed, while Sawny and Dilly watched them leave.

Raul Hall greeted the three Green Coosings as favorably as Green Hall had greeted Tonnis. Joak and Kwit plopped their double-wide bodies in front of Boot and Tonnis, insisting Sawb come to the double doors and give his permission before entry into Raul Hall; and once they were cleared, the crew that followed them filled the air with rumblings, especially about Dod and his criminal behavior. And even Tonnis wouldn't have been permitted to enter Sawb's room at all if it hadn't been for the clever play of words he used to tie Sawb's logic in knots.

"Go ahead and let Boot's pet sniff my floor if it makes you feel better," conceded Sawb, finally giving in to Tonnis. "Your game's just about up. Doochi already saw you slipping out this morning with Thunder."

"I didn't take your ferret," assured Tonnis, maintaining a submissive posture. It made Dod sick to see it. After the way Tonnis had handled himself at the tournaments, he should have been returned to the status of Coosing, or at least boosted in his standing enough to hold his head up straight.

"You did, too," boomed Doochi. "I saw you bolting out of here with it under your blanket."

Tonnis played deaf.

Boot approached Thunder's empty cage and sent Sneaker tracking. Around and around Sneaker darted, investigating the piles of things in Sawb's room. Much like Boot's, Sawb's bunking quarters were at the end of the hall and spacious, but he didn't share with anyone else.

Dod gawked. Sawb had spent a fortune on possessions that filled the room—perhaps piles of gold. He had a collection of ornately engraved swots, a glass cabinet brimming with all sorts of relics and ancient artifacts, a waist-high treelike carving that held a swarm of jeweled rings, a giant stuffed lion above the door, a display of ropes and whips, a set of masterfully crafted lounge chairs, a ten-foot cage made of gold-plated and jewel-encrusted horns and antlers and tusks, a couple of matching chests of drawers with snake carvings across the fronts, a man-sized crystal pot with a mushroom-shaped lid, a dozen bleached skulls of unusual creatures, and a million other fancy items that looked expensive. The place was a well-ordered museum. Even Sawb's bed appeared to be on display, wearing the most stunning spread Dod had ever seen.

Sneaker slowed his pace in front of a towering bookshelf that was sunken into the wall. He sniffed at the ground.

"If your pet's looking for a place to relieve himself—" began Sawb, scowling at his guests.

"He's not," assured Boot. "He's onto something."

Sneaker eventually tottered onto his hind legs, leaned against the row of ancient, three-inch thick leather-bound books that snuggly filled the bottom shelf, and squeezed himself into the narrow space between the top of the books and the oak slat that supported the next level.

"Where's he going?" barked Sawb. "If he ruins my collection of books, I'll turn him into a duster."

"Since when did you take up reading?" asked Buck boldly.

"*Some* books are worth reviewing," sneered Sawb, peering down his nose at Buck. "These are the caliber your eyes can't afford."

Boot bent down, and when he couldn't see Sneaker, he moved in. "What's behind your collection?" he asked, sticking his hand in as far as it would go. His fleshy, thick arm wedged, blocking him from feeling the back of the bookshelf.

"The wall," responded Sawb, joining Boot on the floor. "The case is inlaid. It was already here when I arrived." For one moment in time, Sawb's curiosity dimmed the pride on his face and replaced it with boyish excitement—Boot's ferret had gone farther back than either of them would have thought possible.

Carefully, Sawb and Boot began to pull the books out and stack them in piles on the floor until it became apparent that Sneaker had disappeared.

"How'd he do it?" marveled Joak, edging Eluxa out of the way to get a better look.

The back of the bookshelf was made of dark wood, and it rose up from the floor all the way to the next level. Not a hole in sight.

"It's impossible," mumbled Sawb. He glanced around the room as though expecting to see Sneaker dodging between people's legs, having slipped out unnoticed.

Boot scratched his head, too, and then whistled for Sneaker. Nothing happened.

Boot whistled again. This time, the room went so silent that Dod could hear Kwit breathing from ten feet away.

SETTING THE TRAP

Within seconds, Sneaker appeared at the far back of the bookshelf, as if descending out of the oak plank that held the second row of books. Shortly thereafter, Thunder followed. The two ferrets ran around in circles playfully, black chasing white and white chasing black.

"Where'd they come from?" asked Joak, craning his neck to see past Boot and Sawb.

"There must be a hole," said Boot. He stuck his head all the way to the back of the deep, bottom shelf, sending the ferrets racing into the room, and peered upward. "Yup. Here it is," he muttered, feeling the top corner. "The back wall has separated along its seam and this lower segment has warped, buckling rearward a little—just enough to leave a crack. While I'm down here, do you want me to stuff something in it so Thunder won't get stuck behind the bookshelf again?"

"He wasn't stuck," assured Sawb. "My ferret's quite capable of finding his way around. He's brilliant."

"Fine," said Boot, conceding gently. "All the same, if you have an old towel or rug, I'd be happy to block the breach so your books won't continue receiving a dumping of dust."

Sawb glanced at his priceless volumes and ordered Joak to go and find a spare towel from the common linens, since his were hand embroidered and shipped from halfway around the world.

While waiting for Joak to return, Boot stayed on his back, chest deep, and prodded the crevice. Everyone else watched the two ferrets play.

"I thought you said your ferret was bigger than others," said Eluxa, nudging Sawb with her shiny black boot.

"It is," grumbled Sawb. "All of the books say that Terrus Ferrets are the largest and smartest in Green. That's why Thunder cost more than your whole wardrobe. He's extremely rare."

"Then you paid too much," laughed Eluxa. "Boot's is bigger and faster. Look!"

Thunder attempted to follow Sneaker off the top of a bronze dragon statue, but came up two feet short of Sneaker's jump and, therefore, didn't make it to the chest of drawers. Instead, he plummeted into a pile of papers and sent them flying everywhere.

Sawb's face reddened.

"Mine's not from Green," called Boot. Dod could hear the smile in Boot's voice.

"Maybe Thunder's still young," offered one of Eluxa's twiggy-thin friends, batting her eyes at Sawb.

"He's done growing, Libby," responded Kwit dimly. "The mayler at High Gate said so."

Sawb grimaced, holding his venom for later.

After Boot filled the gap with a towel, he helped Sawb reposition the books. "We're looking forward to joining you at the Ghoul's Festival," he said. "Make sure you let your father know how honored we feel."

The best Sawb could do at the moment was nod.

All the way to Green Hall, Boot proudly strutted with Sneaker perched atop his shoulder.

"Back so soon?" asked Dilly. She and Sawny hadn't left his bedroom yet. They had found themselves glued to the window, entranced with watching a mock battle going on in the field below. The drat soldiers were having their skills honed by following Clair's detailed orders.

"From up here he looks deceptively helpful," commented Dod, noticing how Clair and his assistants made their rounds through the troops.

"If you'd just give him a chance," said Dilly, "he's actually quite nice. Mr. Clair's a great swordsman, even if his teaching techniques are a bit harsh."

"A *bit* harsh?" disagreed Dod. "Have you seen his assistants' arms? They make the roughest of noble billies' arms look smooth and scar free—Clair enjoys hurting people." Looking out the window at Clair made Dod anxious, even from a bird's-eye view, so he pulled back. "Did I tell you he's assigned to represent me?"

"You mentioned it," said Buck, drawn to the call of his comfy bed.

"Four times, to be exact," added Sawny flatly, inspecting the ornate planter box that had been added to Boot's room during the renovations. She seemed melancholy.

"He plans on sending me to Driaxom," complained Dod.

"Behold Sneaker!" boomed Boot, jiggling Buck's bed until Buck consented to gaze admiringly at the ferret. Boot held him up like a trophy.

"You win," said Buck.

"I'm off to Driaxom," remarked Dod glumly. "Clair's sending me there unless, of course, I divulge my associates that helped me commit *murder*. Then he's kindly agreed to seek my imprisonment elsewhere."

"He wants names?" asked Sawny.

"Yeah," huffed Dod, directing his grievances at Sawny once she had shown interest. "He's almost certainly working with Sirlonk. I bet he's the one who delivered *the note*!"

Sawny snapped. "Why me? What did I ever do to Sirlonk? I was always nice to him!"

Boot sailed back and forth in front of Dod and Sawny, showing off Sneaker. "He's bigger and better than Sawb's runt," gloated Boot. "And to think Sawb calls his pet, *Thunder*..." Boot laughed. "Maybe *Crackle* would be more fitting."

"He's using two swords," reported Dilly, her face still pressed against the glass. "I know Mr. Clair got those moves from Sirlonk. Why did Sirlonk teach them to him and not me?"

"So, nobody cares that I'm heading to Driaxom because of Clair?" puffed Dod.

"Sirlonk could have asked for Buck," whined Sawny, shoving Dod's shoulder. "Why didn't he recommend you throw Buck under the carriage? Suggesting Buck's the traitor would make more sense, especially after Sirlonk's recent barn experience."

"Thanks," said Buck sleepily from his bed.

"Tada!" blared Boot, hopping up and down, nudging his way between Sawny and Dod with Sneaker on his head. The ferret stood tall with his chest out and held his balance like a cat.

"You guys should come and see this," said Dilly enviously. Even the tips of her ears were turning green. "Mr. Clair's dueling against his two assistants and three drat soldiers...make that four...no five! He's facing seven men! This is incredible! Mr. Clair's pushing Sirlonk's double sword moves like a maniac. Why didn't Sirlonk teach them to me? I'd be unstoppable!"

"If Clair's so strong," grumbled Dod, "why doesn't *he* go and crush rocks in Driaxom? I didn't kill anyone, and he's probably killed loads of people."

"I shouldn't feel so tired," sighed Buck. He flopped his arm over his closed eyes.

"And he's done it!" popped Dilly. "They've all thrown their swords to the ground!"

Sawny pushed hair out of her face and tipped her head to see around Boot, who still continued hopping, showing off how well his ferret could keep its balance. "Now that I've thought about it, Dod, the most logical choice would have been *Boot*. Why didn't he solicit you to incriminate Boot? Why does he hate me?"

Boot stopped leaping. "Do you really want the truth?" he asked Sawny, his face cheery but firm. He scooped Sneaker out of his hair and cradled him in his arms. "Sirlonk pressed Dod to sacrifice you because he knows Dod—" Boot glanced at Dod, then turned back to Sawny. "Dod's sweet on you....You're the last person Dod would hurt. If he'd trade you for his freedom, he'd stay loyal to them forever."

Sawny carefully stole a peek at Dod's face that was quickly turning red.

"And Dilly," Boot continued, spinning to see her, "Sirlonk's always recognized you as a threat—you'd never join him, and you're a Tillius—so, certainly he's kept his best swordplay away from you. You're too good....Not just skilled—*good*! And good is dangerous to him."

"She is good," mumbled Dod, trying to act casual, like he hadn't just had his secret crush revealed to the world.

"Oh, and don't worry about Clair," added Boot, shifting back to Dod. He gave him a pat on the shoulder. "Contrary to what you may think, I do care what happens to you! Trust me, Driaxom's not in your future."

Near silence followed, with the only sound being Sneaker's clicking as he nibbled at one of his claws. Boot's words were wise and thought provoking. They instantly reminded Dod that Boot wasn't seventeen or eighteen, as he looked and often acted: He was a tredder in his fifties.

Eventually Buck spoke up in an exhausted voice. "That was beautiful," he teased, breaking the hush that had followed Boot's declarations.

"You're just saying that because you went and ate a second plate of bacon and sausages—didn't you?" responded Boot. "I warned you they'd settle deep in your gut and render you unconscious."

"Guilty as charged," moaned Buck, sounding sorry he had eaten too much.

"It's nearly lunchtime," said Dilly. "How could you still be full?"

"I just am," responded Buck.

"Well," said Boot. "I happen to know the perfect cure."

"A late-morning nap?" offered Buck, flopping his other arm across his first. His eyes were now well protected against the dreaded daylight.

"Not what I was thinking," said Boot. "We've got way too much to do. Dilly has signed us up for service at High Gate, and we've got traps to set and villains to catch, and don't forget about the treasure map Dod's hoping we'll help him decipher."

"Treasure map?" said Dilly excitedly.

"Whatever," said Buck, no longer sounding tired, but still resting his eyes.

"It's an ancient piece of work," taunted Boot, approaching Buck's bed. "It shows the location of...*The Lost City!*"

"Are you serious?" asked Dilly.

Dod studied Boot's face. He could tell Boot had already been doing his own deciphering without the others.

"You're a lost cause if you think I'm falling for that one," returned Buck. "Go tease Toos while I take a nap. You'll have him hooked if you mention The Lost City."

"He's actually telling the truth this time," confessed Dod. "Horsely had it stowed next to the Farmer's Sackload."

"Oh," said Buck eagerly, straining to sit up. "Let's see it."

"In time," replied Boot. "I have a plan that may catch a few fish with the same hook."

"No more fishing for a while," teased Buck, raising an eyebrow. "I think I'm good."

"Not literally," said Boot. "Figuratively."

"A trap," nodded Dilly, following Boot's logic. "Sounds fun."

Boot tiptoed to the door and swung it open suspiciously.

"Expecting someone?" mocked Sawny, peering past Boot at the empty hall.

"Yes," he said crisply, reentering the room. He bolted the door behind him and proceeded to pace the floor in brainstorming mode.

"Who are we trapping?" asked Dilly.

Boot lowered his voice to a discrete level and took a seat on the edge of the planter box. "I've got it," he said. "We can pack our supplies and tell the others in Green Hall that we're secretly going to stay with Iris tonight—because we want his help with a map we've found."

"Okay," said Dilly.

"Naturally, we'll swear them to keep quiet," continued Boot, "and then we'll be on our way—but not to Iris's. Instead, we'll race our horses into the thickets and head to the hills above The Goose Egg. Nobody ever camps up there since fires are strictly forbidden near the monument."

"So…your big plan is to go camping?" asked Sawny in a waning voice. She wasn't a fan of the outdoors and looked a little hurt that Dod hadn't shown her the map first.

"Not exactly." Boot shook his head. "Only kind of….In my plan, we'll spend this evening studying the map and discussing things while surrounded by the beautiful ambiance of the Hook Mountains, and then early in the morning, we'll trot down to the wooded hill above Iris's place to watch for activity."

"Sounds like camping," said Sawny.

"We've got to," insisted Boot. "The way I see it, there's a leaky hose in Green Hall—someone's feeding information—and Voracio's not the only one hearing it. I think Sirlonk's connected to the flow, too."

"A traitor that close?" stammered Dilly. "Are you sure?"

"Unfortunately, there must be," said Boot. "Dod's probably right. Someone heard us talking about going fishing and straightway passed the news along to who knows who. Anyway, Iris's place is off the main road—anyone hanging around it, looking for us, would be the direct result of our experiment."

"I see," said Sawny, her voice laced with skepticism.

"It's worth a try," said Dilly, chomping at the bit to do something adventurous. Watching Clair swordfight had charged her up. "Who knows, we might catch the rat-faced informant that's lying about Dod."

"Improbable," noted Sawny, slightly deflating Dilly's hopes for action. "The weasel won't show his face."

"We were planning on returning to High Gate tomorrow anyway, weren't we?" asked Boot. He was presenting his case to Sawny and Buck who both seemed only moderately interested. "Iris lives just a skip up the mountain from High Gate. We'd play our trap tomorrow morning and still have time to easily make the dropping of the triblot barrier."

"I wasn't planning on going anywhere," admitted Buck, his brow wrinkled. "Haven't we spent enough time trotting back and forth? Can't we make up our minds and stay put in one place? I'm getting sore from riding."

"That's the bacon talking," said Boot.

Buck rolled his eyes.

"Besides," insisted Boot, "Dilly's volunteered us to help Commendus."

Dilly smiled and nodded.

"And it'll make Dod look respectable to the council," he added. "We owe Dod, remember—especially you."

Buck cracked a grin. "You're a word-twisting wizard, you know that?"

"I have to be or you'd lie around napping in here while our day awaits us out there." Boot pointed toward his wall of windows. "The sky's spread out bluer than Saluci's turquoise lamp table, and the sun's singing more brilliantly than the High Gate Regal Choir. We can't stay inside."

"Somebody's cheered up," said Sawny. "You need to visit Raul Hall more often."

"His ferret's bigger and smarter than Sawb's," explained Buck, laughing. "You should have seen Sawb's face when Eluxa noticed the difference. I'll keep that look framed in my mind forever."

"Who cares, anyway?" asked Dilly. "They're just pets."

"Sawb cares, that's who," said Dod happily. "He told Eluxa he'd spent more money buying Thunder than she'd spent on her whole wardrobe. Can you believe it?"

"I can," said Sawny. "I'd rather have Sawb's ferret than all of Eluxa's trashy outfits."

"Don't knock 'em," joked Boot. "You'd have looked good in the one she was wearing today. Isn't black leather your thing?"

Sawny smoked Boot with her eyes and browned Dod and Buck as well before taking Dilly by the arm. "Let's pack," she said. "These boys clearly want a project to occupy their time—I hope the Code of the Kings Monument needs some hard scrubbing."

"Pack light," called Boot. "No tents. For this to work best, most of Twistyard will have to ignore us."

OVERLOOKING THE OBVIOUS

In the master barn, Dod and Buck helped Dilly carry her extra bags, since all they had brought was a blanket each. Boot, on the other hand, hefted what looked like a fluffy bedspread, though really, the center was stuffed with five swords and sheaths he had grabbed from his secret stash in Green Hall's storage closet.

"Try not to start any more fires," teased Dilly, ribbing Buck and Dod the moment they entered the barn. A smoky draft prickled Dod's skin, sparking memories in his mind.

Sawny looked over her shoulder.

As they walked up the main aisle, Dod had an unusual feeling. It was like tasting a salty breeze and knowing an ocean was near. But strangely, he couldn't decide what he was sensing.

Slowly, as though beginning to regain the use of a numb leg, Dod became more and more aware of life in the barn. Each horse looked different—or more accurately—felt different.

"You know I'm only kidding, right Dod," assured Dilly, bumping shoulders with him as they walked.

"I know," said Dod. The weird feeling continued. He sensed a bird close by, so he turned his head and immediately knew right where to look to find an owl roosting high up on a rafter, in the shadow of a giant beam.

"That's odd," mumbled Dod. He began to feel the mice hiding beneath the straw and the snakes hunting them. The whole barn was brimming with life. Even flies left an impression that announced their presence.

"Remember, just a day ride," whispered Boot, leading in front as the group approached others in the barn.

"Can I help you, Boot?" asked Jim, wearing beads of sweat across his brow. He and some of the Soosh Coosings and Sooshlings were filling shifts in the barn to help out at Twistyard, since most of their families back in Soosh couldn't afford to donate toward the cause. They had accepted the responsibility once they were sure The Beast was dead.

"We're fine, but thanks," responded Boot, flaunting Sneaker on his shoulder.

After Boot had passed him, Jim stared at Dod. He seemed to be searching for the right thing to say.

"It's good to see you, Jim," called Dod. He knew what Jim was thinking. He could see it in his eyes. Jim was assessing whether Dod was good or bad.

"Thanks," said Jim tentatively.

"Are any of the rumors true?" barked a head that popped out of a neighboring stall.

"Your name's—let's see—Hal, right?" said Dod, trying to smile, which was hard to do with the frowns and cross looks he was receiving in return. "You're Toolor's brother, aren't you?"

The boy grinned briefly, as though surprised Dod had remembered so much from their short greeting at Carsigo.

"What do *you* think about the rumors?" asked Dilly, spinning the question back to Hal.

Sawny and Buck continued on, following Boot, while Dilly and Dod lingered by Hal and Jim.

"I don't know," said Hal, holding a shovel. His face tightened for a fight. "People are saying he's joined The Dread—" and then looking squarely at Dod, he pressed, "Have you?"

"Would he be standing next to me if the rumors were true?" responded Dilly. "Besides, Dod's the one who sent him to Driaxom. It's not his fault someone else set him free."

Hal looked irritated. He wasn't buying it. And Jim stood by, a short distance away, glowering.

"Don't forget, Dod's grandpa was poisoned with your brother," snapped Dilly defensively. "The Dread's taken plenty away from him, too. You guys aren't the only ones who despise Sirlonk."

Hal sized Dod up and down. "Did you kill Horsely?"

"No!" said Dod. "Horsely fell off the back wall."

Jim grumbled something under his breath, clearly agitated.

"Then why did they lock you up?" snapped Hal, keeping his line of questions tight. For such a young-looking boy, he mustered an intimidating presence. "Innocent people sleep in their own beds, not dungeons."

"Voracio made a mistake," countered Dod.

"Huh," grunted Hal, not seeming convinced. He and Jim turned their backs on Dod and began shoveling.

Dod felt bad. He knew everyone in Raul Hall hated him, and he suspected that most of the Pots at Twistyard didn't know him well enough to dismiss the rumors as false, but he had hoped that the friendly boys from Soosh would have been on his side, the way Green Hall had rallied behind him. After all, he had stood up to Sawb for Jim on his first day at Twistyard; and Hal had been part of the presenting group that had awarded him the Redy-Alert-Band—the very gift they had given him to show Soosh's appreciation for Dod catching The Dread. Now, based on Jim's cool stance and Hal's questions, it was apparent that the two boys were done being his friend.

"People are fickle, aren't they?" whispered Dilly, once she and Dod were deeper in the barn and out of hearing range.

"You can say that again," responded Dod, noticing the bracelet around Dilly's wrist (it was presently a light pink). Dilly wore the Redy-Alert-Band everywhere she went. The woven-leather contraption was as permanent a part of her as the bones in her hand.

A few minutes later, Grubber and Song were pawing at the ground in front of Shooter's stall. "Are you about done?" rushed Dilly. "Buck and Sawny are coming up the row now."

"I've almost got it," said Dod. His rigging skills were improving, but still slow.

Dilly groaned.

"What?" asked Boot.

"They're here," said Dilly.

Dod looked up the center aisle and saw Ascertainy entering the barn, her waist-length hair swirled up in a bun on top of her head. She was accompanied by Youk and Voracio.

"So what?" pushed Boot. "Just act casual. It's not like we're robbing Central Bank."

Overlooking the Obvious

"No," said Dilly in a distressed voice. "You don't understand. Ascertainy wants me and Sawny to help her and Youk with a… well…a *special* project. I said we'd do it when we got time."

"Tell her you don't have any right now," said Boot matter-of-factly. "Problem solved."

"Not so easy," insisted Dilly.

"Yikes," gasped Sawny as her horse stopped alongside of Dilly's. "We can't go, can we? Ascertainy never leaves the castle! If they've come this far to fetch you, they're serious about getting their suspicions resolved today, not later."

Voracio pointed and said something to Youk and Ascertainy.

"I'll tell them you're too busy," offered Boot, nudging his horse.

"Wait!" cried Dilly, wearing a guilty face. "The truth is, they want to investigate Sawny for theft—some special books went missing."

"What?" burst Sawny.

"Mercy may have mentioned something about it to me while I was picking up food," confessed Dilly.

All of the blood in Sawny's face instantly drained with the shocking news. "I thought you said they wanted my help because they suspected *you* of trouble!"

Dilly cringed. "Well, if they're planning on investigating you, they must be looking at me, too, right? Besides, I figured you'd feel sick if you thought they were coming for you, so I skipped that part."

Sawny struggled to breathe.

"I was planning on telling you later," added Dilly. "I just wanted to get you to High Gate, so Gramps could help settle things. You know he'd set them straight in a hurry. The books were technically his, anyway."

Dilly rambled through her explanations; however, they didn't stop Sawny from looking as if she were going to pass out, and they didn't stop The Greats from approaching.

Dod felt his heart beating in his throat as he listened to Dilly and finished rigging his horse. Too many things were unfair. Sirlonk was surely pulling the strings. Poor Sawny hadn't done anything wrong, he knew it. Suddenly, a thought found its way to the front of Dod's mind: *Approach Song.*

No sooner had he dashed from Shooter's side and planted himself between Boot's horse and Dilly's than the life in the barn tingled his senses again, especially the mice.

MOVE! thought Dod, almost instinctively. He was calling the mice to approach Ascertainy.

Nothing happened at first, though the feeling inside Dod continued. It was like he was summoning the powers to wiggle his ears or raise the hair on the back of his neck. He could feel the mice. They were everywhere—in the cracks of the walls, under piles of straw, down shallow holes.

MOVE! pressed Dod in his mind. His fingers twitched anxiously as he begged them to fill the path between his friends and the approaching trouble.

Nothing happened.

"Get on your horse," said Boot in a hushed tone, nudging Dod with his foot. "We've got to slip out the back."

"It's not an option," said Dilly. "They've shut and locked the rear entrance. People are painting the exterior of the barn today."

MOVE! thought Dod desperately. The somber threesome was making speedy tracks in their direction and was halfway to them. Another few steps and Dod knew Voracio and Youk would look up from their conversation and call out. The chase would be over unless he and his friends resorted to fleeing like common fugitives, which didn't sound like a wise idea for him personally as a man accused of murder.

And worse still, since they suspected Sawny of theft, they would likely search the group and find the pile of swords Boot had tied to the back of Grubber and the map Dilly had stashed in her vest.

Dilly slid off her horse and bumped Dod. "I guess it's over," she said.

MOVE NOW! ordered Dod with his mind. The command was accompanied with a rush that felt like electricity. Instantly, something fell from the rafters and landed on Ascertainy, making her scream. It was a mouse—and it wasn't the last to fall! Sixteen more plummeted from the rafters like rain upon Ascertainy, Youk, and Voracio, causing them to yell and jump around. To hear their distress, you'd think they were being fed to a tank of starving sharks.

Dod could feel the mice coming. *MOVE!* he thought, continuing to push with all his might.

Mice began to scurry from the stalls toward the ranting, hopping threesome.

"What in the blazing—" said Boot, staring dumbfounded at the spectacle.

Dod continued to summon the mice using every ounce of strength he had. It was like lifting a weight heavier than he had ever lifted or pushing his body harder than he had ever pushed it. *MOVE!* thought Dod. *DRIVE THEM OUT!*

Another string of mice dropped from the rafters, this time sending the threesome running from the barn screaming.

"I guess that's our cue," said Boot. "Let's make a fuss, too, as we exit."

Dod smiled through his exhaustion and mounted Shooter.

"Aaaaa," screamed Boot, leading in the front, pushing Grubber to gallop. "HELP! Mice are attacking!" he shrieked, waving his arms in the air, making as much of a show as he could.

Buck followed right behind him doing the same, and Dod, Dilly, and Sawny did their best to act distressed as well. It would have drawn unwanted attention if Youk, Voracio, and Ascertainy hadn't just started the parade and were still running from the barn when the equestrian part of the spectacle began. But unlike The Greats who hurried toward the soldiers for safety, Boot and his crew headed around back, yelling to the painters, "Mice are raining from the rafters. We're under attack. Run!"

After a sufficiently large crowd was on its way to the entrance of the barn for a good view of the vermin, Boot led his cavalry out through the rear foliage, past the Bollirse field, and into the safety of the quiet woods.

"That was crazy," said Buck, once the thick pines hid their progress away from Twistyard.

"It couldn't have been timed any better," laughed Boot happily, keeping the troop at a trot. "Who would have guessed that one of Sirlonk's wild antics would collide perfectly with our need for a massive distraction?"

"How do you figure?" asked Dilly, pushing Song to speed up so she could better join Boot's conversation.

"Someone must have soaked Ascertainy's clothes in that stuff," said Boot. "You know—the stuff that made the rodents go nuts on the soldiers' tents."

"Oh, yeah," sparked Dilly, her face lighting up. "Right."

"That's why most of the mice seemed to favor Ascertainy," said Buck. "It makes sense. Sirlonk was probably getting her back for ruining his fun with the drats. It just shows, being smart can get you into trouble." Buck glanced over his shoulder at Sawny, who ignored him. The reality of her dilemma was still sinking in.

"If I were Ascertainy," added Dilly, shuttering, "I'd be burning that outfit. I hate mice and rats. They're so gross."

From farther back, trailing at the end, Dod could hear the others, but didn't shout his way into their conversation. *It's just as well they believe The Dread did it*, he thought. Hearing The Beast's intentions hadn't won him any coolness points. And he had already been afraid to tell of his experience with controlling the baby duressers, since he hadn't wanted his friends to have unrealistic expectations of him. After all, at times he was still struggling to get his own horse to go straight. It made no sense. Not to mention, the power he had felt in the barn was now completely gone, regardless of the fact that he was riding through the woods, a place crawling with wildlife.

Up ahead, the forest narrowed into a small wedge, separating two of Bonboo's large wheat fields.

"Single file," called Boot, keeping a quick pace. "We don't want to dip into the grain or we might be seen…not that we've done anything wrong." He looked at Sawny with a comforting smile. "Sometimes the best way to handle conflict is to sneak off and let the smoke clear. I'd hate to punch Voracio again."

Sawny nodded slowly as Buck heckled Boot with a round of 'Boosap' coughs.

"And Dilly's right," advanced Boot a few moments later, "if Voracio—or anyone else—wants to ask you questions concerning Bonboo's missing books, they should ask them with Bonboo sitting next to you. He'd certainly be able to fix the mess, even if an idiot's lying to them about you."

"I hate liars," grumbled Sawny, emerging from shock. She had never before been accused of anything bad.

"Besides," added Dilly cheerfully, flushed with adrenaline from the thrill of the escape, "maybe Mercy got it wrong. Who knows what Ascertainy would have asked you if she hadn't been rained upon by mice?"

For the next few hours, every wooded trail between Twistyard and High Gate was employed to stealthily travel to the backside of The Goose Egg. It took much longer than the regular roads, leaving the sun fading before they reached their destination, but their efforts were rewarded with never having to face anyone or answer questions.

Once the horses were loosely tethered in a grassy spot, Boot led the others to a wooded lookout point and panned the horizon. "I promised you views," he said. "Behold the world."

"It's beautiful," pronounced Dilly. "Why haven't you ever brought me here before?"

"You've never asked," said Boot.

From their lofty vantage, The Goose Egg laid just below them in the shade of the Hook Mountains, jutting hundreds of feet out of the ground like a giant, half buried egg. Its gray crystal glimmered softly.

"Crystalious Megaspheric Splendorium!" announced Sawny. "Up here it looks bigger than it does down below, don't you think?"

"I'd say," agreed Dilly. "And High Gate looks bigger, too."

From the mountainside, they could see the rolling hills and sprawl of the nearby city, with its lakes and streams and countless buildings, all the way to its distant boundary on the east, and beyond Lake Charms to the barrenness of the Ankle Weed Dessert. To the south, fields and forests eventually gave way to the massiveness of Lake Mauj.

"Map time," rushed Buck excitedly.

Dilly dug into her vest and carefully pulled the old roll of leather out. It was tied together in the center and on the ends with tassels that attached to the back of the scroll.

"I promised Sawny she'd be the first to take a look," said Dod, scooping the relic from Dilly before Buck could get to it. "Here you go. Sorry it's taken so long."

Sawny smiled coyly. While riding, she had been told enough times that Bonboo would fix things for her that she seemed to have forgotten her horrible morning. "Thanks," she said, gently untying the knots.

Everyone huddled around Sawny.

"The TCC," said Dilly, reading the letters that were penned at the top.

"This is really ancient," announced Sawny, wearing signs of surprise on her brow. "Look at the numbers!" Sawny ran her finger across a string of jumbled lines, which didn't look anything like digits to Dod.

"So you think it's authentic?" pressed Buck excitedly.

"It's definitely old," insisted Sawny. "Some of these words haven't been used for at least six or seven hundred years—" She mumbled a strange pronunciation of the phrase '*Versitclusum Repeatic Key Vor Purgoldis*' and shook her head. "I can't believe it."

"What?" pressed Dod, enjoying the look on Sawny's face. Her excitement for the brain-twisting challenge was inspiring, and Dod found it highly attractive.

"The trick to understanding this map," said Sawny, "is the advice it gives right here." She pointed at the words she had rattled off. "That's probably why it's written within this key-shaped squiggle."

"Ah," sighed Boot. "I thought that was a ship…maybe a small sailboat."

"No, it's a key," insisted Sawny. She drew Boot's attention to the one word in the phrase that was clearly legible: '*Key*.'

"What does it all mean?" asked Dilly excitedly.

"Well, translated literally, it reads, 'Flexible clues repeated key to the great treasure,' but it would be interpreted more accurately, 'The key to the great treasure is found by repeatedly using the same clues in different ways,' or so I think."

Buck stuck his finger out and plopped it on the center of the map. "Who cares about clues? That says, 'The Lost City,' doesn't it?"

"It does," nodded Sawny. "However, you'll notice it's placed right here, wedged between this mountain symbol and this little head of the long snake."

"So what?" said Buck. "If we can find the snake thing, we'll find the city and its gold. We don't need all the gibberish writings."

Sawny grinned and looked out across the horizon. "There's your snake, Buck," she said, tipping her head. "The Blue River is the snake, and Lake Charms is the head." Sawny ran her hand across the leather. "See. Right here on the map is Lake Mauj, and this is the edge of the Gulf of Blue, and along here is a strip of the Hook Mountains. That means your serpent has got to be the Blue River."

"No," said Buck. "What about these three lakes, over here, and these cities? This can't be near. Lake Mauj is the only large body of water east of the Hook Mountains for hundreds and hundreds of miles."

"Yes it is," persisted Sawny. "At least the way things are now. But this map is really old. It shows how things used to be before the Ankle Weed Desert was created."

"Huh?" mumbled Dod. The map was suddenly more interesting. "All of this was destroyed?" he asked, sliding his hand across the eastern half of the map.

"Yup," said Sawny. "We don't talk about it anymore, and good luck finding anything written down. This is actually the best record I've ever seen of the historical lay of the land—assuming it's genuine." She pointed at the marked cities that sat beside the three large lakes. "These were gone overnight by the hand of a massive storm."

"What kind of storm wipes the Earth clean of its lakes?" choked Dod, horrified by the hundreds of miles of destruction.

"The Earth?" said Sawny. She turned as if she had misheard him.

Oops, thought Dod. They didn't know of Earth. "Did the storm have mushroom-shaped clouds?" asked Dod, thinking of a different kind of disaster—one made by men.

Boot looked toward Lake Mauj and said, "I see a dog in that one."

"You boys are weird," confessed Sawny. "It's a map, not a painting of an evening stroll."

Buck sighed heavily. "The Lost City is right in front of us, isn't it?" he said in a deflated voice, pointing at High Gate.

"Probably," said Sawny, nodding her head. "But once again, that's why they've given us all of these clues and instructions.

Words are important, too. If we crack the meanings, we might be able to pinpoint where it used to be."

"I like the pictures," chimed Boot. "They've drawn six or seven keys across the side. I'd imagine it's quite a treasure to need that many locks."

"Those are boats," corrected Sawny, chuckling. "*Descendus Vesselium*," she read. "Which literally means, 'the below ships.' Strange phraseology. Perhaps they're indicating the boats in the water."

"Where else would the boats be?" complained Buck, beginning to lose interest in the map. He had gotten his hopes up high of following a simple line to the famed city of untold wealth and instead had come to the realization that it was probably long gone.

"Maybe it's stipulating the difference between the finished boats in the water and the unfinished boats on land," explained Sawny excitedly. "I don't really know. That's what makes this so fascinating. It's a puzzle! And look at these words and numbers over here. They're captivating, aren't they? I'd need to do some research before I'll have the slightest clue as to their meanings."

"Keep at it," encouraged Boot. "You're a genius. I know you'll put it all together."

"It could be hidden right under our noses," said Dilly, staring off into the distance at the charred site of the future Capitol building and surrounding structures. From where she stood, the blocks of destruction and chaos looked small, though the group knew firsthand the massive digging and hauling that was going on next to Commendus's estate.

"In all likelihood," admitted Sawny, "The Lost City was probably ransacked hundreds of years ago—its gold looted and buildings taken apart to create new ones."

"Or it's still buried," said Dod. "Sometimes you just get a feeling—the kind of nudge that keeps you going—the kind of hint that says, 'just open your eyes and you'll discover it.' I think The Order knows it's close to this area and needs to find it—so we have to beat them to it."

"That's the spirit," praised Boot. "We just have to put the clues together—the ones others have stood over and not seen." Boot smirked slyly.

"Let's have it," said Dilly, reading his face.

"Well…don't tell anyone—" he began, pausing for their nods of agreement.

"Like we would say anything," said Buck. "Dod's sharing his ancient map to The Lost City! What could you possibly have that would compare?"

"I guess so," laughed Boot. "This morning I discovered something—Sawb's got a secret stash of stuff behind his wall, and he doesn't even know it—or at least he didn't. At one point I sensed he was curious."

"Really?" said Sawny, her nose still buried in the map.

"Yes. Sneaker and Thunder were running around in it—"

"In the wall," corrected Buck.

"I'm hoping Sawb keeps thinking that," said Boot. "But look at this." He pulled a short chain from his pocket. "I fished it out of the crack. And I'm telling you, there was a bit of a draft coming down—not the kind you'd expect from an inner wall."

"That's why you helped Sawb fix the problem!" smiled Buck. "I couldn't figure it out before. You were so eager, like you hoped Sawb would let you scrub his toilets, too."

"You may have found one of the hidden rooms," said Dilly, her eyes widening. "When I was little, my father used to tell stories about the castle's mysterious chambers and their secret purposes. It made me wish to live at Twistyard."

Sawny looked up. "Our relative who expanded the castle—built the bulk of it—was certainly peculiar, wasn't he?"

Dilly shot Sawny mixed signals.

"It's no secret that he had great hopes of power and glory," said Sawny.

"Is he the one who kept the zoo?" asked Dod.

"I wouldn't say that *that* story's true—" began Dilly.

"We've seen cages," said Dod. "Up on the roof. Huh, Boot?"

"Something was kept up there," admitted Boot sheepishly.

"You should bring me next time," said Dilly, looking jealous.

"And me too," chimed Buck. "I want to see Dilly's face when she realizes who she's descended from."

"Not this again," said Dilly. "I'll concede my blood has fostered an aggressive man or two—perhaps the type that pushed their conquests more than many—but don't get your sights fogged into thinking that the fabled tales of the Crazy King are true." Dilly shifted. "It's been eight or nine hundred years. How will people remember you a thousand years from now?"

"They most likely won't," said Sawny, tapping the facts first. "We'll all be long forgotten. Of course, if I crack these riddles and lead us to The Lost City—" Sawny smiled. "Perhaps then we'd make a place for ourselves in the history books."

Buck shrugged his shoulders. "It wouldn't do us any good," he joked, carefully eyeing Dilly as he prepared to land the punch line. "Right Dilly? Someone would probably come along and burn our names out of history."

"That's it!" said Dilly. "I'm eating your pie tonight."

OVERLOOKING THE OBVIOUS

"Funny you mention Concealio," said Sawny. "We'll be studying his work shortly. He's the one who enlarged and beautified the Code of the Kings Monument. If he really hated history and burned the books as people commonly report, why did he work so hard to preserve it? There are over a dozen museums that he originated and many more that he strengthened."

"He didn't hate history," said Boot smugly, "he just had a finicky taste for it."

"If he didn't like it, it didn't happen," laughed Buck.

"Too bad," huffed Dilly in Buck's direction, "Blueberry's your favorite."

"If we're omitted from the books, you can bet it'll be one of Dilly's kids that smudges our names out," added Boot, shoving Buck and Dod playfully. "She seems to have gotten more than her fair share of the feisty blood, don't you think?"

"For sure," agreed Dod, trying to be cool.

"The whole pie's mine!" said Dilly with a stomp, leaving for the horses.

Sawny rolled the map and followed Dilly, though she paused long enough to thank Dod for the gift.

"She's becoming more like Dilly everyday," whined Dod, watching his map go the way of his Redy-Alert-Band.

"It happens," said Boot. "Buck's following, too."

"What makes you think I'm becoming like you," he pressed. "Just because you're the oldest doesn't mean you're the best. Bowy's incredible."

"I know," said Boot, struggling to hold back a smile. "I meant you were becoming more like *Dilly*!"

Buck tackled Boot to the ground and had a thirty-second run before Boot pinned him firmly.

CHAPTER TEN

"Keep trying," said Boot. "Maybe one day you'll catch me off guard."

As the sun continued to sink, its rays raced across the eastern horizon until the sky began to speckle with stars. Something foreboding haunted Dod as he lay under the pines beside his friends. He recalled his encounter with Sirlonk in the pump house and remembered how concerned Sirlonk had been about finding The Lost City—enough that he had instructed Murdore to prepare the noble billies to burn all of High Gate to the ground in search of it.

With such conviction to the cause, Dod knew The Order wanted the map back—probably even more than they wanted the Farmer's Sackload. It made Dod wish Boot hadn't 'set the trap' and 'filled the leaky pipeline' with the knowledge that they were running around with it. And before morning, Dod's fears were justified!

CHAPTER ELEVEN

SHADOWS AND MADNESS

Below an eerie full moon, Dod and his friends slept in the shade of towering pines—Dilly and Sawny in a tent they had smuggled and the boys just outside of it. Their horses were tethered a stone's throw away, eating knee-high grass by moonlight in a small opening in the forest.

Dod struggled to fall asleep once he had started worrying about The Order's intense desire to find The Lost City. *What could possibly be worth more than ten High Gates filled with gold?* thought Dod, recalling Sirlonk's words to Murdore. *If they're not searching for gold, what are they searching for?*

Dod mulled things over in his mind as he watched the branches above him sway. Directly beside him, Boot seemed to have had no trouble in finding dreamland: Within a few minutes of saying goodnight, he had begun snoring quietly, leaving Sneaker on watch up the closest tree. Buck had drifted off soon after, making his own variety of stuffed-nose noises. The girls in the tent had lasted a little longer than the Dolsur brothers, but were now getting their beauty sleep as well.

Dod, on the other hand, couldn't. He felt tired, and his brain hurt from thinking, but his heavy eyelids wouldn't give in—they really, truly couldn't shut. He wouldn't let them, not with The Order seeking the map, and Sirlonk on the loose, and the woods filled with creepy, dancing shadows. Every new sound set his nerves on edge.

Suddenly, the sky darkened and the crickets stopped chirping. Something was coming. Dod could feel it. He rolled over slowly and peeked off in the distance, but saw nothing. And then instantly, as though growing out of the shadows, a giant figure appeared and pounced in Dod's direction, pinning him firmly to the ground. Its large, hairy face blocked his view of the trees. It was a tremendous beast with long, sharp teeth and horrible breath. Dod struggled mightily to free himself—to grab the sword that he'd stashed to the side of his blanket, but it was hopeless: The creature was too powerful. Its weight began to press upon Dod's chest, crushing him.

"Boot!" called Dod. "Save me!"

But Boot didn't come, and he didn't say a word.

"Buck! Wake up! Help!" pleaded Dod.

But Buck didn't come, and he didn't say a word.

The monster stank like The Beast had. Shadowed by the trees, the creature's features were mostly hidden, though its long black hair and bulging eyes left no doubt: It was another full-grown duresser!

"Quick!" screamed Dilly from her tent. "We're under attack. Come! Now!"

"Help!" cried Sawny in agony. "It's got my arm, Dilly. It's eating my hand. Please! Help me! Anybody!"

Dod could hear the girls' sobs. They stirred within him a rage of frustration. "I'm Humberrone's son!" he shouted, feeling his fists tighten. "You'll pay for this!"

But his voice failed to leave his throat. A suffocating, thick wall of wet, putrid fur blocked his nose and mouth.

I can't die, thought Dod, feeling his oxygen slip away. *I won't let it happen. I have power. I can change this. MOVE! MOVE! MOVE!*

"No you can't!" laughed Sirlonk, reading Dod's thoughts. He stood close by, just out of view. His evil voice broke through the night air like the shrill screech of two colliding cars. "Join The Order or die!"

Dod's insides ached for air and his head felt dizzy. It was like the roof of a cave had collapsed on his chest and face, ensuring his lungs would never rise again.

"I won't join!" thought Dod, fading from consciousness. "You lose, Sirlonk!"

"Foolish boy!" rang in Dod's ears.

The creature resituated, momentarily lifting its body just enough for Dod to steal three quick breaths before its weight settled back on him.

"Don't give up!" said a voice Dod hadn't heard in years. It was his father's.

MOVE! thought Dod, focusing intensely on getting the duresser to respond. He hoped it would follow his commands as the mice had, but it didn't. The massive beast continued to press its weight on Dod, nearly crushing the life out of him, as though its ears were deaf to Dod's wishes.

CHAPTER ELEVEN

"The only way to help your friends is to join The Order," taunted Sirlonk. "Don't be stubborn. You'd be surprised how wonderful it is."

"Help!" begged Sawny, her voice fading into the darkness.

Dod saw glimpses in his mind of Sawny being carried away by a ghastly, bearish creature. The sight of her beaten, injured body, with one arm broken and dangling was infuriating.

"Do you want to see Dilly, too?" teased Sirlonk.

More images flashed through Dod's mind. Dilly was frantically trying to climb a tree—her sword was shattered in pieces at the base—her fingers kept slipping on the bark—then a second creature dove from the sky and plucked her off the trunk like a magpie collecting moths.

MOVE! thought Dod, feeling the heavy beast suffocating him. If he could just reach his sword, he'd slay the creature and bring Sirlonk to his knees.

Lightning flashed and thunder rumbled close by, causing the ground to shake. The monster shifted, once more allowing Dod to gulp air.

Images of Pap swirled in his mind—Pap was strong, happy, smiling—and then a snake rose out of the ground, slithered into Commendus's house, and struck Pap, delivering a fatal dose of poison. Strangely, before the glimpse ended, the snake turned toward Dod's view and his wicked, glossy-eyed face became Sirlonk's.

"Stop fighting me, Dod!" hissed Sirlonk. The duresser shifted again, this time releasing one of Dod's arms. Dod's hand hungrily explored the ground around him until it found what it was hunting for: the hilt of his sword.

"We're already friends, you just don't see it," said Sirlonk, pushing his way up to the duresser. He tipped his head inches above Dod's and smiled. "Do you recognize me? Look closely."

Dod clutched his weapon tightly and prepared to plunge it into Sirlonk's heart when the sky flashed again and a bolt of lightning violently struck the ground.

Dod blinked. He couldn't believe it! Right before his eyes, Sirlonk's face melted into a new one.

"Are you okay?" asked Boot, leaning over Dod. "Sorry I woke you up. I forgot to warn you about my rolling habits."

"What?" stammered Dod, clinging to the sword beneath his blanket. His blood was racing and his eyes were searching the moonlit surroundings for Sirlonk and the creature that had nearly crushed him.

"I may have smashed you a little," confessed Boot. "I thought I had a rock in my back and awoke to find it was your face. Sorry about that."

"Oh," shivered Dod. "Don't do that again." He let go of his sword and took deep breaths. A tsunami-sized wave of relief washed over him. It was just a dream! No monsters, no half-eaten friends, and no Sirlonk.

"We may have rain," said Boot, removing his blanket from overlapping Dod's. "Sawny's gonna kill me if we get wet."

The wind had begun to blow and heavy storm clouds were rolling in. Dod looked heavenward and saw the moon had moved halfway across the sky; hours had passed since he had drifted off to sleep.

"That was a bad dream," mumbled Dod.

Clouds in the distance flickered.

"Did you see our future?" asked Boot, snuggling into his blanket.

"I sure hope not!" said Dod emphatically. "It didn't feel like that kind." Dod thought back and tried to trace what he had seen. "Maybe I was just worried about The Order," he concluded. "It was on my mind when I fell asleep."

"That can happen," agreed Boot. "That's why I always think of at least six happy thoughts before I close my eyes each night.... You should try it. Maybe you'd sleep better."

"Nice trick," said Dod. His heart was finally leaving his throat and returning to his chest.

"I learned it from Pap," said Boot. "He was the best. I wish he were my grandpa. What a legacy!"

Dod shuddered. "He was in my dream."

"And it was a nightmare?" prodded Boot, sounding surprised.

"Definitely! I saw a snake kill him—it stuck its poisonous fangs into his back when he wasn't looking, while at Commendus's house."

"Strange," said Boot.

"And that's not the weirdest part," added Dod, sitting up. He could only see half of Boot's face in the shadows. "I looked at the snake's head and it turned into Sirlonk's!"

Boot stayed quiet.

"The next thing I knew, I was grabbing for my sword—and your face replaced his."

"My face, huh? What do you think of that?"

"I don't know," said Dod, straining to see the horses that were tethered just past Dilly's tent. It was comforting to count all five of them.

Boot coughed and cleared his throat. "I promise I won't turn into Sirlonk, regardless of what the shadows reveal, just don't pull a sword on me in the dark, okay?"

"I won't," agreed Dod stiffly, having a sudden panic attack. Realizing he had come seconds away from stabbing his own friend was beyond terrifying. It made him wonder what he was capable of doing in his sleep.

The wind blew harder and colder as the night progressed, though no rain fell. Hours seemed to pass with Dod lying awake, watching the trees bend. Boot went back to snoring, albeit farther away from Dod than he previously had been. He had slid his blanket toward Buck for good measure, and Dod had migrated in the opposite direction as a precaution, making the gap between them even wider. Neither of them wanted another episode in the saga that had played out before.

Dod nearly gave up his sword to Boot for safekeeping—feeling uncomfortable in his own sleeping skin—but the darting shadows played tricks on his eyes, leaving him frazzled to the core. He couldn't part with his weapon. Not now. Especially since something wasn't right. The world around him felt troubled, and it was more than the billowing storm. Ten feet up, Sneaker kept stirring from his curled position, trotting to the branch's edge, and sniffing the wind cautiously. He, too, sensed danger approaching. Dod could read the signs. They both felt it.

Eventually, Dod resorted to sitting up against a tree, his blanket wrapped around him, so he could better watch the surrounding forest. It was a maddening experience. The clouds kept taking turns covering the moon, dimming and brightening the patches of light; and all the while, the wind blew the trees and bushes, causing the whole woods to come alive.

CHAPTER ELEVEN

At one point, feeling lonely, wishing to sleep but not daring, Dod clicked in Sneaker's direction and called him with his hands. The black ferret disappeared into the darkness and reappeared at Dod's side. "You understand, don't you?" said Dod, whispering to Sneaker. "Evil forces are moving tonight, aren't they?"

The ferret spoke with its eyes, agreeing with Dod so long as he rubbed its head. "We have to watch, don't we?"

Dod muttered questions to Sneaker for half an hour, keeping himself company. It was like he was a guard assigned the nightshift. Meanwhile, his friends slept soundly, seemingly unbothered by the growing feeling of concern that whittled at Dod's insides.

And then it happened. Without warning, Sneaker rose up on his hind legs, still in Dod's lap, and sniffed the air anxiously. Something had roused him. He circled around and around.

"I know," whispered Dod, drawing his sword. It was as if the duresser from his nightmare was coming.

In the distance, Dod saw a figure dashing quickly from shadow to shadow, moving through the forest toward him. It wasn't large, but it wasn't small, either. Possibly a wolf or cougar.

"Boot, wakeup," called Dod, popping from his blanket. Sneaker scampered over and pulled at Boot's hair.

"Huh?" grumbled Boot, still half asleep. "What is it?"

"Something's coming," said Dod. "Look!"

Boot tipped his head to see and caught a glimpse of Dod standing with his sword in hand. "You're charged up tonight, aren't you?" He blinked and rubbed his eyes. "It's probably a deer. Don't worry about it. No one knows we're up here. And snakes can't really turn into The Dread."

"No! It's not a deer," insisted Dod. He saw it dart through a lighted patch of waist-high bushes and enter another blackened strip of shade, still heading right for him.

"Don't worry," mumbled Boot sleepily, pulling his covers up, "around here, animals never attack humans. The vicious ones are deeper in the mountains. This hillside is practically a park, and High Gate's a tumble away."

"But Boot," persisted Dod. He no longer saw any more patches of light between himself and the shade the creature had entered. "My gut's aching. Something's not right. Please look."

Boot sighed and pushed up on one arm. "Where is it?"

Dod pointed into the darkness.

"Yeah, I think it's a deer—" began Boot when a tremendous bolt of lightning shot sideways across the sky and momentarily illuminated the shadowed spots, revealing something mysterious: An unknown creature was indeed racing toward them, only fifty feet out.

"Oh!" startled Boot, seeing Dod had a point. He dug both hands under his blanket and clumsily drew his weapon with the sheath still attached. Dod backed up and prepared to strike.

"Don't," wheezed a feeble voice a few seconds later. Shrouded by darkness, a scrawny, bent human figure came into view, emerging from the nearest clump of bushes.

"Abbot?" gasped Dod. "What are *you* doing here?"

The old, hunching man staggered and fell at Dod's feet, huffing uncontrollably. His shirt and pants were tattered and hanging on his frail frame like a wet, draped bed sheet upon a standalone coat rack.

"I'm sorry," he sobbed in between gasps.

"Sorry for what?" demanded Boot, approaching the crouching man.

"Please don't beat me, Sir Boot," begged the man, his winded cries taking the last of his strength. He threw his hands over his head and cowered.

Sneaker scurried to Abbot for a friendly sniff.

"We won't," said Dod, dropping his sword. He bent down and attempted to draw the man out of hiding.

"Sir Boot will beat me," mumbled Abbot, beginning to twitch. "He'll beat me, he'll beat me, he'll beat me."

"No, he won't," said Dod. "No one's going to hurt you. We're friends, remember? I'm Pap's grandson." Dod rushed a string of comforting words hoping to halt Abbot's spiral into insanity. Now wasn't the time. Abbot had a reason for coming, but if he fell into chanting and shaking, he would be the most useless messenger ever sent.

"I'm sorry, sir," heaved Abbot. "It's my fault Sawny's in trouble."

Buck stirred. "Is it already time to get up?"

"We've got company," said Boot, turning to set his sword on top of his blanket. He looked at Abbot's pitiable state and shook his head. "No shoes?" he muttered to himself.

"I borrowed the books, sir," whispered Abbot cautiously to Dod, his face still covered. "I thought I could get them back before anyone noticed." Abbot peeked between his fingers. "I don't want trouble for Sawny."

"It's okay," assured Dod, carefully resting his hand on Abbot's shoulder. It felt bony and cold. "Why did you take them?"

"I like to read," confessed Abbot, still catching his breath. He straightened his neck and nearly smiled. "The library's my favorite room in the castle. I borrow books."

"Really?" chuckled Dod, imagining Abbot strolling past the crowds of Pots and Greenlings to have Ascertainy help him find a title.

"Just at night," added Abbot. "The library's nice when it's dark."

"Oh!" said Dod, suddenly connecting dots. He remembered the time he had run from something in the library, thinking it was The Beast. "Have you ever seen me there?"

"Once, sir," responded Abbot sheepishly. "But you didn't get anything. I'm sorry if I scared you. I'm sorry about Sawny." Abbot began to shake. "It's my fault. It's my fault. It's my fault."

"That's fine," said Dod. "We'll just sneak the books back once Sawny's arrived at High Gate. It'll clear her name."

"Oh, sir," sobbed Abbot. "They're gone! I left them! I was scared to see him dead. I didn't do it. I didn't do it. I didn't do it."

"Who?" asked Dod.

"I didn't do it," mumbled Abbot. "They wouldn't believe me."

Boot slid up next to Dod and listened.

"Who was dead?" pressed Dod gently.

Abbot glanced at Boot and hid his head again.

"I'm going to check on the horses," said Boot in an irritated voice. As he rose, a bolt of lighting streaked across the sky, making the world as light as day for a couple of seconds. Dod and Boot both noticed Abbot's naked feet: They were bloody and swollen.

"Maybe Dilly's got something for those," added Boot in a kinder tone, but raising his voice to be heard over the wind that suddenly blew harder. "I'll search the bags she's latched to Song and Grubber."

"She put one on the back of Shooter, too," hollered Dod, feeling squeamish. He hated seeing blood.

Once Boot had left and Buck had followed after him, Dod bent down next to Abbot's covered head. "What did you see?" he asked.

"My friend was dead," mumbled Abbot quietly. Dod strained to hear. "I climbed down to show him the books he wanted—but he wasn't resting. He was dead."

"Horsely?" asked Dod.

Abbot nodded and shivered. "He was dead. He was dead. He was dead."

No wonder! thought Dod, remembering how Abbot had arranged for Dod's transportation to Driaxom. *Taking a favor from Horsely was as good as taking one from Sirlonk himself,* he reasoned. *That's why I got such a warm welcome from the waiting guards at the prison!*

"Dead. Dead. Dead," continued Abbot, his whole body beginning to convulse.

"It's okay," assured Dod, rubbing Abbot's shaking back. "Everything's going to be okay. I'm your friend. Boot's your friend. You still have friends."

Sneaker raced around beside Dod and sniffed the breeze.

Abbot slowly recovered. "When the man yelled at me, I left the books and ran. I didn't do it."

"Oh," said Dod. "You set the books down next to Horsely?" Abbot nodded.

The news became a bit of a puzzle. If the man Abbot was referring to had been part of the security crew Dod had sent from the dance to the docks to find Horsely's body, then Voracio and Youk would have already recovered the books and would have logically thought Horsely had taken them. And if the man hadn't been part of the security crew, why had he responded first and not said anything? Either way, it was strange that The Greats suspected Sawny of having taken the books.

"I'm only trouble!" burst Abbot. His weak arms continued to palsy.

"No you're not," said Dod. "You helped Boot save my life!" Abbot's brow furrowed.

"You told Boot how to remove the Ankle Weed," said Dod, speaking loud enough to be heard over the wind. He drew closer for Abbot's answer.

"Ankle Weed?" stammered Abbot. "I don't know anything about removing an Ankle Weed. Only Pap knows things like that."

"But you had one," pressed Dod, reminding him. "I've seen your scar. It's the same as mine. I know you spent time in Driaxom."

"I didn't do it," mumbled Abbot. "I didn't do it. I didn't do it."

"I know," assured Dod. "You're innocent. Pap knew it! I know it!"

Abbot settled. "Pap took the weed off while I was unconscious. I don't remember a thing. He freed me and saved my life."

Dod looked toward the moonlit field and saw Boot and Buck returning to the shadows.

"So, you didn't tell Boot how to remove the Ankle Weed from my leg?" rushed Dod, suddenly feeling nervous.

"No," said Abbot, having a rare moment of clarity. "If he said I did, he was lying to you." And then Abbot whispered anxiously, "Watch out for Sir Boot. Tooshi-wanna, Tooshi-wanna, Tooshi-wanna."

Dod barely heard his words.

Buck and Boot strolled up chuckling. "Abbot's in luck, Dod," boomed Boot. "Dilly's packed half her room in those bags." Boot pulled two glowing-stone necklaces out of his pocket and smiled. They were dim, but better than nothing. "Now we can see to fix him up," he said, putting one light around his neck and one around Buck's.

Buck stood by holding a spare blanket, a ball of string, and a small container of fluid. "These should help," he said.

Boot bent down and began rubbing the liquid contents on Abbot's feet, cleaning them off thoroughly. The cleanser smelled like alcohol.

Abbot squirmed and shook and began to chant loudly.

Sneaker climbed up Boot's back and perched on his shoulder. He stuck his nose in the breeze and tugged at Boot's hair.

"Come on, boy," said Boot, pushing Sneaker down. "Abbot's a friend."

After Boot had finished scrubbing the mud and blood off, he ripped part of Dilly's spare blanket into strips and tied them around Abbot's swollen feet. "That'll do for now," said Boot, attempting to ignore Abbot's fit of madness and Sneaker's tugging and nipping.

Turning to Dod, Boot raised his voice. "Did he tell you how he found us?"

"No," said Dod.

Sneaker pulled Boot's hair again.

"I've got to get Sneaker away from his ranting," said Boot. "It's driving him loony."

"What's going on?" yelled Dilly, sticking her head out of her tent that was tipping sideways in the gale. The storm had decided to double its efforts and was presently blowing harder than it had all night.

Abbot was deep in his fit of psychotic behavior, doomed to be gone for hours. His raging mantra of gibberish competed with the howling wind; it seemed as if this time he had snapped too far to ever regain sanity.

"I hate camping!" shouted Sawny from within the collapsing tent.

"Who's that?" hollered Dilly, looking beyond the boys at Abbot.

Boot and Buck strode over to the girls to explain, taking the lights with them and leaving Dod and Abbot in the dark. Strangely, Abbot's voice quieted the moment the glowing rocks were gone.

"You're going to be okay," said Dod, sharing his blanket with Abbot, trying to comfort him. His eyes hadn't adjusted enough to see whether Abbot had returned to his mind or not. At least he had quieted.

For several minutes, Dod sat close to the old man and watched the storm rumble in. The mountain peaks farther up the draw were getting pounded with lightning, and as a result, the air was constantly bombarded with booming sounds, as though the rocks were being crushed by the electric storm.

Fearing that their tent would soon break, Dilly and Sawny exited with their things and had Boot and Buck disassemble it. Dod watched. It was one of the worst campouts he could remember. The only one that compared was a winter scout camp where a surprise blizzard had brought the tents down in the middle of the night, leaving a dozen cold boys stuffed into two SUVs.

"Dod?" said Abbot. He was back.

"Yes, I'm right here," responded Dod, turning to look at his face.

"I forgot," said Abbot, his dark eyes wide and bulging. "You're all in danger! They're coming! We must leave!"

"Who's coming?" asked Dod, nearly speaking right into Abbot's ear so the wind wouldn't steal his words.

"They're coming!" he repeated, trying to rise to his feet.

"Wait!" yelled Dod, holding him down. "Please, Abbot. Who's coming? How did you find us?"

"I saw you leave this morning—I was watching from the rooftop—you rode off—you escaped Voracio out the back—"

"Voracio's coming?" pressed Dod. A foreboding feeling within him answered his own question before Abbot spoke.

"No" mumbled Abbot. "I followed your tracks through the woods—so long as you stayed on the trails—but you lost me in the grass below the crystal."

Dod was surprised with how clear Abbot's mind had become.

"I searched the woods. I'm sorry I got Sawny in trouble. I wanted to tell you. I wanted to make things better. And then when I couldn't find you, I found them. They were hiding in the thickets below the crystal, waiting for someone to return with dogs. They didn't see me, but I heard them."

"Who?" asked Dod. "Who are they?"

"They knew you were up here," continued Abbot, his voice getting louder "—they said you would be camping tonight—they said they were just waiting for the dogs and the dark—so they could find you—so they could get the map—so they could take Sawny with them!"

"WHO?" yelled Dod.

"They want the map! They want Sawny!"

It was as if Abbot could recall what he had heard, but couldn't process the information for himself.

"Did you recognize them?" begged Dod. "Are the men from Twistyard?"

Abbot shook his head. "They're coming! They're on horses! They're noble billies!"

"BOOT!" yelled Dod, trying to get his attention. Dod left Abbot with the blanket and searched the ground for his sword, and Boot's, and Buck's, and Dilly's, and Sawny's.

On the blowing wind, Dod could now hear distant barking sounds, like a pack of baying hounds chasing a raccoon. He wondered why he hadn't heard them before.

"BOOT!" shouted Dod, rushing toward the horses. He caught up with Boot and Buck in the field and handed them their swords. "We've got a problem. Abbot said billies are coming to take the map and Sawny, and they've got dogs tracking us!"

Boot glanced at the girls who were securing their tent to the back of Song. "No wonder Sneaker's been gnawing my ear off."

"How'd they find us?" asked Buck, his concerned face cringing in the moonlight as he fastened his sheath to his belt.

"No time for talking!" ordered Boot, hustling Dod and Buck over to Dilly and Sawny. "Trouble's headed our way," he said to the girls, nudging Dod to give them their swords. "Billies are coming up the draw with dogs. We've got to race to the second saddle and zigzag our way down into the rolling hills above High

Gate. If we can get to the soldiers stationed outside of High Gate, we can let them deal with the billies."

"But Boot," said Sawny. "No one ever goes down that side. It's too steep."

A bright flash of lightning was quickly followed by a thunderous boom.

"Exactly," responded Boot, yelling above the raging storm. "Stay in the pines as much as possible, be as quiet as possible, move as quickly as possible, and no lights!" Boot pulled the dim glowing stone from his neck and shoved it in his pocket. Buck did the same.

"I don't know if my horse can make it," whined Sawny nervously. She looked younger than Dod had seen her since before The Games at Carsigo.

"If you need to, ride double with Dilly," ordered Boot. "Leave your horse in the pastures up top. Song can handle the slope. Now go!"

Dilly nodded and stepped toward where they had camped, to retrieve her blankets and bag, when Boot shouted, "Get on your horse, Dilly! You and Sawny need to lead us in the front—as fast as you can go! There's no time for cleanup! Listen to the dogs coming!"

The howling wind carried the unfriendly sounds of many dogs working their way through the forest. They were getting close. Only a few minutes away.

Boot helped Dilly and Sawny into their saddles while Buck untied their horses. "Do you have the map?" asked Boot.

Sawny nodded.

"We'll all be okay," he said, giving her a pulled smile. "I'll race you to the soldiers!"

Without another word, he hit the back of Sawny's horse and waved them off. Once they had begun galloping up the hill into the thick pines, Boot turned to Buck and Dod. "If the billies catch up, Buck and I will hold them off, and you, Dod, will keep going with the girls to protect them in the rear. Fair enough?"

Buck and Dod nodded, though neither of them looked ready for battle.

In a rush, the boys mounted their horses and readied their swords, but as they started off, Dod remembered Abbot.

"Don't worry about him!" yelled Boot, handing Sneaker to Buck. "You two hurry after the girls and I'll go get Abbot. My horse is faster, anyway."

Boot spun Grubber around and had just started downhill when he noticed Dod and Buck halting.

"Don't stop for anything!" scolded Boot, racing back toward them like a ferocious lion. "If I catch up to either of you and you're not with the girls, I'll whip you senseless tomorrow! Now get going! I already said I'd meet you by the guards in front of High Gate!"

Dod and Buck obeyed, though when Dod looked back toward where Abbot had been, he felt sick. Abbot was running in the wrong direction, out in the open moonlit meadow, heading right for the baying hounds—and Boot was dutifully riding after him.

LOSING A FRIEND

A short distance up the mountain, Dod pulled on Shooter's reins and waited in the trees. He couldn't go any farther or he would lose sight of the meadow below.

"Come on!" yelled Buck, noticing Dod had stopped. "Boot's really serious tonight. If you don't hurry, he'll let us have it."

"I've got to see," insisted Dod, nervously watching Boot ride toward Abbot. "Idiot!" mumbled Dod. He was frustrated that the crazy man was nearing the lower edge of the grassy field and hadn't even noticed Boot.

Buck retraced a few paces and guided his horse beside Dod's. "We've got to go!" he rushed, his horse pawing at the ground. "The moment Boot scoops Abbot, he's gonna be heading right for us, and his horse does well in this rocky terrain."

"No!" said Dod. "Think about it. Boot's not planning on following us."

"What are you talking about?" asked Buck.

"Look!"

Dod pointed at Boot, who had slowed beside Abbot, but hadn't picked him up.

"He's getting him," said Buck. "Hurry! Let's get out of here!"

"No he's not!" said Dod defiantly. A horrible knot of dread was forming in his stomach. "He's planning on facing the billies himself."

"That's ridiculous," scoffed Buck, turning his eyes expectantly on Boot, who was far below them in the draw.

"See!" shouted Dod. Abbot was now running sideways toward the closest clump of pines and Boot was staying put. The distant edge of the forest was coming to life. Massive dogs burst from the shadows and raced toward Boot and Grubber.

"What is he doing?" groaned Buck. His voice revealed that he, too, was feeling sick.

"I knew it!" said Dod. "Once Boot handed you his ferret—"

Both Dod and Buck went silent. From their lofty view, a few football fields away, they could easily hear the snarling dogs approaching Boot and, worse still, they could see the wall of billies emerging from the pines on horseback.

"They're gonna kill him," said Buck in a trembling voice. "There are at least twenty men."

Dod frantically strained his brain to think of something—anything! But nothing came, just fear, dread, and frustration. The whole situation was awful. Dod wanted to help Boot, however, seeing the mob of night riders terrified him. And it was unlikely Boot's efforts would stop them for long. Any minute they would be pushing their dogs up the draw.

"Maybe Abbot got it wrong," said Buck in a strained, hopeful sort of voice. "Boot's talking to the people. They could be a search party from Twistyard."

CHAPTER TWELVE

"I don't think so," said Dod. His head was telling him to flee. "The men don't have torches, and they're circling him."

"Oh!" groaned Buck, reaching to his side, jiggling his sword in its sheath. Dod looked at Buck's face and saw something he knew he would never forget: It was real courage! Buck was scared—truly terrified—but he wasn't going to let his fears stop him from helping his brother.

"I'm heading down," he said, mustering his manliest voice. "You probably should get out of here. Boot was right. You need to track the girls over the top—make sure they make it to the soldiers." And away he flew, galloping his horse through the pine forest as fast as he could.

Dod only paused a few seconds before following Buck. With the wind in his face, he hung onto Shooter's reins tightly as the powerful stallion charged into the dark night. Trees and bushes came and went so quickly in the shadows that Dod tucked his head down and trusted Shooter's ability to find his way.

It was only moments before he and Buck were no more than a hundred feet from the chaos that was ensuing in the meadow. Boot's voice could be heard above the howling wind and barking dogs, "It's your last chance! It's a trap! Turn and go back, now!"

"Err what?" snapped a hulking billie. Abbot was right about the mob being a formidable clan of rough men. In the moonlight, their colossal bodies and full beards reminded Dod of Murdore.

Buck and Dod watched from their hiding spot in the trees, waiting to see where things would lead.

"Or you'll all die!" said Boot.

"We'll die if we don't get the map and the girl!" roared one man.

"Aye!" yelled another. "We have our charge!"

"It's the map er your life!" barked yet another, raising his sword into the air. "We've heard enough!"

"AYE!" rumbled the mob of thirty. Buck had counted low from atop the ridge.

"Then go into the rocks and get them," said Boot, pointing due west toward a steep, clifflike embankment up into the Hook Mountains. "It's your lives—do what you will!"

"If the dogs say you're right, you get to keep breathing," rumbled the leader, only a few feet from Boot. "Where's our mayler?"

One of the rearmost men hollered that he was waiting in the trees and went to fetch him. Dod and Buck watched. When the man returned alone from the darkened forest, he called to the crowd, "This one here's Boot. Our mayler says he's a liar, an' he's protecting his friends. He says the dogs are pointing up the draw, so the girl's in the pines."

"Too bad for you, *Boot!*" yelled the leader, waving his sword. "Get him, men!"

As the mob pressed in at Boot, Buck kicked his horse into the meadow at a sudden dead run, leaving Dod staring at the nightmarish scene from the shadowed forest. Swords began clanking. Boot was fighting for his life. He deflected blows as he attempted to use his powerful horse to force his way out of the center.

Buck raced toward the conflict with his sword drawn and Sneaker riding atop his shoulder. Seemingly surprised to see Buck appear out of nowhere, the billies responded by turning most of their attention toward him, as though they thought a battalion of High Gate's soldiers were attacking.

The trick worked. As Buck rushed at the billies, screaming loudly, he drew enough attention that Boot was able to fight his way out of the depths of the mob, leaving him with only one battlefront to face rather than being surrounded. But Boot's freedom came at a horrible cost.

As Buck drew near, he tried to spin his horse and bolt away, having already accomplished his goal of providing Boot a temporary distraction. Unfortunately, from the midst of the riotous mob, a giant spear emerged and struck Buck's horse in the chest. The dastardly deed was instantly effective, sending Buck's horse toppling to the ground. Buck and Sneaker flew headlong over the horse and landed in a crumpled position against a rock, some twenty feet off. They looked dead.

No! thought Dod. Things were going wrong. He wanted to rush to Buck, but feared his sword skills would be of little use in opposition to the writhing band of pirates. There were too many of them. A dozen well-trained tredder soldiers from Pious's best battalion would struggle to fight them off. The seas had made the men hearty and heartless. What could one boy do against all of them?

Dod blinked his eyes, hoping to wake up.

Buck's horse lay on the ground dying, its legs weakly kicking at the air. It snorted aimlessly and tried to lift its head. Meanwhile, the crowd of billies sat comfortably in their saddles, appearing to enjoy the wind and the sight. Like a jovial club of mates taking in a show, they laughed and pointed. Since no more than one boy had emerged from the woods, they paused to relish the despicable pleasure of watching death. It was in their evil blood to make sport out of pain.

Boot continued to be assaulted by three riders who kept darting in at him, though while contending, he was strategically moving his horse between the billies and Buck. And it was fortunate he did. One dog broke from the pack which surrounded the dying horse and made a beeline for Buck, but was intercepted by Grubber's trampling feet.

Buck lay motionless on the ground, despite Boot's calls to him. "Come on, Buck! Get up!" pleaded Boot. "Hop on! We'll ride out of here!" Boot's sword flashed in the moonlight as it deterred the pressing men who'd been assigned to finish him off.

Dod felt tears streaming down his face. He knew Buck wasn't okay, and watching Boot discover it was heart wrenching.

"Come on, Buck!" begged Boot. He was struggling to hold the men back. It was his window of opportunity to have Buck join him. Perhaps they could outrun the billies. Grubber was a strong horse, and Boot was a skilled rider.

"Get up!" yelled Boot.

Dod was quietly pleading, too. "Please be alive," whispered Dod.

Only the wind heard his hopes; it took his words and blew them high into the cloudy sky, where they joined a terrific bolt of lightning that exploded east to west.

"Just move," mumbled Dod, fixed on the heap of twisted arms and legs in the field.

Suddenly, it seemed as if Buck waved ever so slightly. Dod stared and held his breath. From the pile on the ground, Sneaker shot out and made a tremendous leap to Boot's leg, then scurried to his shoulder.

"Buck!" shouted Boot in a discouraged voice. His chance to attempt an escape was nearly over. The pack of dogs had moved in on the dying horse like wolves. One monstrous, beastly hound with the jaws of a male lion had latched onto the stallion's throat up high, crushing its windpipe, ensuring its end was near. And with the final, futile gasps of the horse, the crowd of billies began to lose interest in the sight and, one by one, returned to the task of eliminating Boot.

"Why is he still breathing?" barked the leader, once more drawing his sword. "The girl is escaping with the map. Hurry!"

"Buck!" yelled Boot, turning his head to where his brother lay motionless. "Get up!"

Three more dogs made a lunge at Buck. Grubber trampled one, and the second and third slipped past and grabbed hold of Buck's legs. Almost instantly, Boot jumped from his horse to his brother's aid.

Dod couldn't watch. Boot sent the dogs whimpering away from Buck's body, but now faced thirty men on horseback, and Grubber had startled into trotting toward the distant trees.

"Remember, you drew this fight!" roared Boot, rising from his brother's side, holding Buck's sword in one hand and his own in the other. The first advancing horse was met with Boot's anger and stumbled backward into the mob, hobbling from a blow to one of its front legs. The billie riding it never got close enough to attempt a strike.

Another horseman advanced and was similarly repelled. A third and fourth dashed together, thinking they could run him down, but to their surprise, not only did Boot strike their steeds, he made a swipe at the billie aboard one and severed the key strap that kept his saddle in place, causing the rider to fall off when the horse bucked furiously from its injury.

"Get him on foot!" yelled the lead billie. "We need the horses alive!"

No one jumped to be first.

"I've ordered you to get him!" boomed the hefty leader, his bushy beard blowing in the wind as he pointed at a few of his men. "Or I'll pass the word along that you've disgraced your clans."

The six closest riders at once slipped from their saddles and formed a formidable row of muscle that could have easily bested the most capable of NFL defensive lines, and that without their drawn swords. Before they could approach Boot, however, Boot raced to meet them, as if he welcomed their attack and was eager to be avenged of the wrongs they had done to his brother.

"It's not your fault," whispered Dod, thinking of Boot. He feared Boot's rash actions were his way of punishing himself for causing Buck's injuries and possible death.

But if Boot were trying to die, he wasn't doing a very good job of it. With his two swords flying, he rushed through a masterful routine of moves that would have left the judges at Twistyard's sword-fighting tournaments on their feet with amazement. The billies' hulking arms and forceful blows couldn't match Boot's rage. He drove them backward, into the mob of horsemen, and let out a thunderous cry, "GET OUT OF HERE!"

Nevertheless, within moments, a fresh batch of men slid from their horses and joined the others in marching against Boot. Thirteen against one was more than unfair. Dod knew the outcome. He could see it in his mind. They would press upon Boot from all sides and, regardless of their injuries, prevail over Boot like a wave of ants taking down a praying mantis.

What would Pap do? thought Dod. *If Humberrone were here, he wouldn't let Boot die!*

Dod took a deep breath and patted his horse. "If only I could get Boot to join me," he muttered, "we could race out of here." Though Dod knew Boot wouldn't hop aboard Shooter and ride off so long as Buck was lying on the ground, and with the billies swarming the area, quickly retrieving Buck's body wasn't an option.

And then a burst of inspiration filled Dod with hope. He dug his hands into Dilly's bag and drew something out. It was possibly his only chance to save Boot. Without another thought, Dod rolled the item, stuffed it in his shirt, and nudged Shooter to leave the shadows.

"There you are!" yelled Dod to the cussing band of billies. Near where Buck lay, Boot stood breathing heavily, preparing to face the approaching men. He looked in Dod's direction as though trying to read his face.

"Another one?" grumbled the lead billie.

"What's taking you so long?" continued Dod, approaching casually, fighting the impulse to make Shooter run for High Gate. He was playing a role, as Boot had. "I've been waiting for hours—and finally was forced to take care of business myself."

The band of billies looked confused.

Dod worried they couldn't hear him above the storm, so he yelled even louder. "Sirlonk promised you'd help me get the map and break free! Where have you been? It's nearly light! Have you lost your freshy-minds? We've got to get out of here before the sun rises. High Gate's crawling with soldiers, and they've got my name on their swords."

"Who's he?" shouted one of the billies. Everyone stopped what they were doing and stared at Dod, except Boot—he took the moment of diversion to study Buck, seemingly assessing injuries.

"Didn't Murdore tell you about me?" asked Dod.

No one spoke, though the lead billie looked intrigued that someone from the mainland knew Murdore by name.

"I killed Horsely for disobeying the rules," shouted Dod. "In The Order, we don't have room for mistakes. Who's in charge of this sorry bunch of shippies?"

"I am," said the lead billie, pushing his horse to approach Dod. The man's frame was intimidating. His shoulders looked like they had been plucked off the front of an ox, and his scarred face appeared to have seen plenty of battles. The only thing going for Dod was that Shooter was a larger breed of horse, even bigger than Grubber, which boosted Dod higher up, giving him the advantage of looking down on the billie.

"Who are you, and what do you know of the map?" grumbled the man.

"I'm Dod, and I have the map to The Lost City—it's right here," he said, patting his puffy shirt. "We've got a long ride to Fisher. Let's get out of here."

"We're not headed to Fisher," said the man in a stern voice. The moonlight shined on his ugly face, revealing he doubted Dod's story and was preparing to use his weapon.

"So, you're not even going to escort me?" asked Dod, holding steady. "If the Farmer's Sackload doesn't reach Fisher by tomorrow, we'll all be answering to Sirlonk. He intends on paying your friends with the diamonds—all fifteen islands of men—a hundred dashers, isn't it?"

Dod strained to remember the little things he had heard Sirlonk and Murdore say in the pump house.

"I thought the diamonds were taken," stuttered the billie. As he drew closer, Dod noticed the man's massive hands. He could probably pop Dod's head off with one squeeze.

"They were," rushed Dod. "Why do you think I had to kill Horsely? He let the diamonds slip, and Sirlonk and I had to work hard to get them back."

"You're lying!" yelled a billie from the rear of the crowd. "Our mayler says you're tight with Bonboo, and you'd never join The Order!"

Boot glanced at Dod nervously and rose to his feet.

"Then have your mayler come and face me!" shouted Dod in defiance, drawing his sword. "This is just the kind of trouble Sirlonk is tired of having. It's like he can't trust any of you to get your jobs done! You're probably the bumbling bunch that let Dungo's relatives go, along with the other captives—you can't even watch prisoners! Simply pathetic!"

Dod poured into his voice as much of Sirlonk's vanity and pride as he could fake, attempting to sound the part of a true follower, all the while dying inside, wishing to race as far away from trouble as he could. The billies weren't buying his story, and the mysterious mayler was feeding too much information to the men.

"Go get him!" demanded Dod in an ornery voice, hoping inside that the cantankerous leader of the billies wouldn't run him through with the sword he kept waving in the air.

"Show us the map first!" ordered the lead billie.

Dod glared as he sheathed his sword. "Here!" he said sternly, unbuttoning his shirt halfway. He pulled at a rolled clump of leather and drew it out, keeping it carefully hidden in the shadows near his chest, and then pushed it back slowly. "Now bring me your fork-tongued mayler! I need to know who Sirlonk has to thank for your incompetence tonight."

The lead billie began to nod. He couldn't hear, but within, Dod was sighing heavily, grateful that Dilly's leather shorts had somehow tricked the man's eyes in the dim light and passed the test.

"Get our mayler!" huffed the large man. "Let these two talk it out and we'll decide who's true north."

"Aye!" rumbled a few men.

Dod held his breath. What would he say to the mayler, and worse still, what if the mayler were Sirlonk himself?

The clouds lit up with a sudden bolt of lightning, and rain began falling; large drops flew on the wind and beat upon the men.

"He's gone!" came a sudden response. "Our mayler's up and vanished!"

"He's a traitor!" yelled Dod. "Quick! Let's get after him!"

"AYE!" roared the mob. The men on foot abandoned their plans to fight Boot and rushed to their horses. "Kill the traitor!" they raged.

"Ride in the front where we can see you," said the commanding billie to Dod. He still seemed to hold doubts and wasn't planning on letting Dod or the map out of his sight.

"Obviously I'll be leading this crew!" snapped Dod, forcing a snobbish grunt. "I'm an expert at tracking!" He nudged Shooter and started off, while carefully stealing a last glance at Boot. The Dolsur brothers were a sad sight—Boot kneeling on the ground beside his younger brother's limp body, desperately trying to revive him as the rain poured down.

Dod wanted to cry. He had seen Buck face his fears and stand like a man, and now he beheld the price. But regardless of the sorrow Dod felt, he knew he had to stay focused in order to deceive the men into leaving or he would lose Boot and the girls as well.

CHAPTER TWELVE

"I think he's gone this way," hollered Dod, pressing right through the middle of the mob to the front, directing the billies into the thickest part of the forest below the meadow. He occasionally pointed at the ground and claimed to see tracks, though with the arrival of the heavier clouds and torrential rain, the moon had decided to hide, leaving Dod and his captors in near darkness.

"Get the dogs on these!" he yelled from time to time, trying to sound as cantankerous as he could. "We've got a traitor to catch! Hurry men! Keep up!"

But as the night wore on, the dogs seemed more and more prone to follow Dod than to lead him, which combined with the absence of proof to create tension in the group. The terrain was difficult, especially in the rain. Dod could feel the men's frustrations. He had to do something. The trick was coming to an end, and he certainly didn't want to be around when the billies discovered reality.

A large deer startled out of the thickets in front of the dogs and headed toward a treacherously steep drop. At the moment, the storm had slowed and the moon had peeked halfway out, filling the woods with just enough light to see a short distance.

"There he goes!" yelled Dod. The vicious pack of dogs was barking and beginning to chase, giving credibility to his claims.

"You've got to keep up!" he added over his shoulder, noticing how the billies had become lax in their pace and were struggling to follow. They were worn down from a night without sleep, and their natural abilities were in sailing the oceans, not riding the mountains. And their common horses were tiring from carrying such heavy men across the sloped landscape.

LOSING A FRIEND

"Don't let him get away!" grumbled the lead billie. "We hate traitors and liars!"

"AYE!" shouted Dod, feeling like a lame pirate. The words didn't sound right coming from him.

As Dod neared the drop he had seen the deer go over, he watched the dogs rush the steep slope. "I can do this," he whispered quietly to himself, mustering his courage. "Shooter's no ordinary horse."

Down the hill Dod went, prodding Shooter to race into the night. As he had before, Dod tucked his head behind the horse's, trusting Shooter's ability to find his way. The trees flew by so quickly that Dod sometimes thought he was falling, not riding. And shortly, Shooter passed the pack of dogs and continued on, picking up speed, leaving the straggling billies and barking canines far behind. It was a terrifying ride. Dod braced himself for a life-ending crash and did his best to keep breathing. The hill seemed to go on forever.

At the bottom, Dod crossed two trails and sunk deep into another forest. He prodded Shooter to continue running, fleeing from the demons at an extraordinary speed. 'We hate traitors and liars' kept creeping through his head as he pressed farther and farther away.

Eventually, Dod circled back up toward High Gate, always keeping his ears attentive to the sounds around him. It seemed he couldn't get the barking dogs to go silent. They were in the distance somewhere, perhaps tracking him, or maybe just in his mind. Regardless, as the sun took its place in the distant east, Dod found himself worn and bedraggled, wet and paranoid, and above all, sick beyond measure about what had just happened.

The night of nightmares wasn't over and felt like it would never end. Daylight couldn't bring back what had been taken.

Still, deep within, Dod was at peace. He had survived a terrifying conflict and had followed Buck's noble example of real courage! And he could be proud of how he had used his knowledge of The Order to trick the billies into riding away from Boot and Buck, and Abbot, and Dilly and Sawny, most likely saving their lives.

As Dod neared High Gate, he cut across a field of grain and finally entered a main road. The little farms and cottages that dotted the landscape were beginning to bustle with activity. Cows were being milked, horses were being fed, chickens were scratching the ground for grain, and kids were leaving for school, calling happily to one another about nothing at all. For everyone else, life went on as though the dark night hadn't happened.

CLAIR'S WRATH

Dod smelled the air and tried to appreciate that it wasn't raining, but it was hard since within him it still was. He couldn't erase from his mind the dismal sight of Boot kneeling beside Buck's lifeless body. It haunted him. It stole his appetite. It filled him with dread about everything. Yet he prodded Shooter to trot the thoroughfare toward High Gate's southwest entrance. He hoped Dilly and Sawny would be there, a short distance from the pavilion, eating breakfast with the soldiers. And he wondered whether Boot had made the journey yet, bearing his sad cargo.

"Aren't you Dod?" hollered a young tredder boy, pushing and poking his two companions as they strolled the lane. The three boys looked interested to hear his response.

"Yeah," said Dod, pausing beside them.

"I knew it!" said the boy excitedly. "You're the best at Bollirse! I can't wait to see you play next year! Can you scratch my bag?" The boy rooted through his things until he had found a slender black stick. "Here," he said, reaching way up to hand Dod his pack and stick. Shooter was tall enough to make the boy stretch.

CHAPTER THIRTEEN

An autograph, thought Dod. It was weird. He scribbled 'DOD' and stared. What was his last name, anyway? He couldn't put Richards, and for the life of him he couldn't remember what Pap's name had been, or Humberrone's. And both of them had had different ones. Dod knew that much. Pap had entered into Green, and Humberrone had come from Soosh.

"Here you go," said Dod, finally handing the bag down.

"Thanks!" stammered the boy reverently, admiring the signature.

It was just three letters. It looked more like an acronym than a name. *Department of Defense*, thought Dod sleepily, riding away from the boys. He didn't feel like much of a defense.

As Shooter trotted up the road, Dod found himself drifting deep into thought. Why did he have moments of clarity, where he recognized so much of Green and even the people, and other moments of dismal stupor? And why had he felt connected to the animals in the barn at Twistyard—enough to summon the mice from hiding—yet usually found himself as numb-witted with pets as anyone could be.

He certainly would have liked to have made the billies' dogs and horses move at his command. That would have been useful.

In the distance, High Gate's uppermost hill stuck out above the trees. It made Dod's heart pound. It was beautiful. Somehow, after having stood near the statue of Bonboo's parents—the one that overlooked High Gate—and after having heard Dilly's explanation of how it stood for democracy, seeing even a glimpse of the city brought tears to his eyes. "Freedom's not free," he mumbled, thinking of Boot and Buck. "Democracy's expensive."

When Dod reached the southwest entrance to High Gate, the pavilion sat empty. It would still be a few hours before the bustling crowds would gather to await the dropping of the barrier.

Dod looked around. A short distance off, half-concealed by the beauty of a well-manicured forest, there were a number of stone buildings.

"That must be it," sighed Dod. Butterflies filled his stomach. Were Dilly and Sawny okay? Had Boot made it? What about Buck? Dod couldn't stand the thought of seeing Buck's dead body. It was bad enough having seen what he'd seen in the moonlight. And daylight was worse in some ways—it was more definite. So long as Dod didn't know for sure, he could keep hoping, or pretend that he'd just had a bad dream.

Slowly, Dod nudged Shooter toward the complex. Upon entering, Dilly's voice was the first thing he recognized.

"You're alive!" she screamed. Dod turned and saw her running from a crowd of tables, followed closely by Sawny. It was evident from their faces that they hadn't slept much, either. "We thought for sure the billies had taken you with them—"

"Or killed you!" added Sawny. Both girls cut across the stone courtyard and raced to him.

For being an encampment of soldiers, the place looked quiet. Only a few men dotted the tables that Sawny and Dilly had come from.

"Did you see Boot?" asked Dilly.

Dod paused to think of what to say first. In truth, hearing Boot hadn't returned yet was enough to render him speechless with grief. Had some of the billies circled back?

Dod strained to think. He had led them for at least an hour or two before dashing away, and as far as he had seen, the whole group of men had followed him up to that point. Why hadn't Boot returned? It had been four or five hours since Dod had left him. That was plenty of time, especially since Boot had been given the easy route to High Gate, while the billies were off chasing deer miles away, tromping through the wet and treacherous foothills of the Hook Mountains.

Maybe Grubber had been the problem. Had he been spooked so bad that he had run off and Boot hadn't been able to find him? Or Buck. It was Buck! Boot hadn't been able to come to terms with what had happened. He was probably sitting in the same field, replaying the horrible nightmare over and over, wishing he could go back and try a different plan.

Dod didn't say anything. His mind was jumbled with thoughts.

Dilly and Sawny peered past Dod as though expecting Boot and Buck to come riding up behind him.

"What happened?"

"Everything," said Dod in a deflated, shaky voice. He slid off Shooter and struggled to walk. His legs felt like he had been doing sprints for hours, and all of his muscles hurt from tensing up.

Three large tredder soldiers came over and eyed Dod, then took Shooter's reigns without saying a word. They had helpful smiles on their faces.

"Come and sit down," said Dilly. "You look washed."

"I feel washed," stammered Dod, fighting the urge to start sobbing. He was exhausted beyond speech, his nerves were frazzled, and he couldn't think straight. Though he only took a few steps before he came to himself and called out to the soldiers. "Don't take Shooter. I need to go—and I need men to come with me."

"You need to rest," said Dilly.

"And think of poor Shooter," added Sawny. "He's been running all night, hasn't he?"

Dod's eyes opened to the mud that was caked all over his valiant horse and the way it stooped its head when it walked. "I guess I could ride a different one, if someone has a horse I could borrow."

One of the soldiers came back, resting his hand on the hilt of his sword. "Do you know where the billies went?" he asked.

"Not exactly," said Dod, blinking his eyes.

"Where did you see them last?"

"It was still dark—maybe an hour before dawn," began Dod, feeling lightheaded. "I was up in the thick pines—and there was this really steep hill—and I pointed Shooter down it and he ran—we just kept running—the dogs were barking and chasing."

"And you haven't seen them since?" asked the soldier. His voice was soothing.

"No," said Dod. "We just kept running."

"Then go rest," responded the soldier, returning to the other two. "We'll take care of things from here."

"But Boot's still out there—" protested Dod, his lip quivering. How could the soldiers walk away without hearing the rest of the story?

"Boot will probably be back soon," said Dilly, too cheerful for how she looked.

"No he won't!" said Dod. "Boot's with Buck, and he's sitting somewhere stranded, because Grubber ran off—"

"Oh!" burst Dilly. "Sorry we didn't tell you. I thought you knew. Boot's already been here this morning. He and Buck beat us by a few minutes, and then Boot took off with two hundred soldiers in search of you and the billies."

"What?" gasped Dod.

"Yeah," said Sawny. "The guards at this station were ready for something like this. They've been training for weeks. Commendus increased their numbers a while back and has had them watching for billies." Sawny leaned in closer and whispered, "And word has it, you're not the first one they've taken."

"Huh?" mumbled Dod. "What about Buck? Is he dead?" Dod winced, awaiting the answer.

"No," said Dilly. "He's got a big bump, though—"

Dod blinked in complete shock.

"And the billies killed his horse," rushed Sawny. "They're barbaric! Poor Buck's had him for years. It'll take him a while to get over that loss. It's not easy saying goodbye to a dear friend."

"But is Buck really okay?" asked Dod eagerly, tears welling up in his eyes. He couldn't believe his ears. Perhaps he was in a state of delirium and his subconscious was giving him the ending he wanted to hear.

"Yeah, he's fine," said Dilly. "He's napping."

Dod staggered, full of emotion, and leaned on Dilly to steady himself. "Are you sure?" he asked, trembling, holding back a sob. He still couldn't believe it. Buck hadn't looked fine in the field. It seemed far more than Dod could hope for that Buck had miraculously survived.

Dilly and Sawny both smiled.

"Are you all right?" asked Sawny. As far as they had seen, Dod was overreacting, since Buck was only slightly injured.

"It's just—" began Dod, unable to explain. He wiped tears from his eyes and attempted to grasp the joyous news. Buck was alive! He had survived the horrible night! He wasn't dead in a field with Boot crying over his body!

"They were worried about *you*!" said Dilly, laughing. She turned to Sawny and noted, "Boys are weird. If they're going to act like this, they should stop saying we're the weepy ones!"

"Right," agreed Sawny.

Dod quickly cleared his face and took a few deep breaths.

"Boot was convinced you were the one in trouble," said Dilly. "Once the billies took you prisoner—" Dilly's eyes fell on Dod's chest as her voice faded. "What's that?" She pointed at the lump in Dod's shirt.

Dod undid his top three buttons and pulled her leather shorts out. "Here you go," he said, struggling to speak without cracking, but wearing the first grin he'd had since the night before. Sawny and Dilly both stared at him like he had lost his mind.

"I shouldn't even ask," said Sawny, raising her eyebrows.

"It's a map," said Dod hazily.

"No. They're my pants," corrected Dilly.

"Maybe to you," said Dod, taking a few more deep breaths. "But to a bunch of dimwitted billies, it's a map. Trust me."

The ground began to rumble as horses approached. Dod and the girls turned in time to see Boot roll around the corner in the midst of a hundred soldiers. He was easy to spot since the others wore matching uniforms. The men trotted their steeds past the row of stone buildings and continued beyond view, heading in the same direction that Shooter had just gone. Boot didn't continue with the soldiers; instead, he broke away to greet Dod.

"You made it back!" exclaimed Boot, eyeing Dod with happy but curious looks.

"And you, too!" responded Dod, overjoyed to see Boot looking well.

"Thanks to you," praised Boot quickly. "I thought those billies were going to flatten me deader than dirt. Did you see the size of their paws? Those boys were massive!"

"I know," said Dod. "Pretty scary, huh?"

"But they're gone, now," said Boot, his face suddenly growing solemn. "We caught up with them, and our soldiers stood their ground."

"They fought?" asked Dilly.

"Sure did!" huffed Boot. "The billies ambushed us—"

Dilly's eyes widened.

"Well," corrected Boot, "they jumped *the soldiers* in the forest—of course, I was well protected in the back."

Dilly sighed nervously, clearly not convinced that Boot had been safe and certainly not believing he had been anywhere near the back of the battalion. It wasn't in Boot's nature.

"Anyway," continued Boot, "our men retreated and let the archers send the billies a greeting, then the swordsmen followed up. A few of the soldiers will need time to mend, but no string of years will fix the billies after the whomping they got."

Boot shot Dod a stern eye. "Serving The Order doesn't pay well, it gets you killed!"

"I'd say!" agreed Dod heartily. There was a split second where Boot's glance had pushed a lesson at Dod, as if Boot weren't completely convinced that the role Dod had played in front of the billies was entirely a hoax.

"General Gratis is currently directing troops at the site on cleanup." Boot's eyes widened. "They even put down that beast of a dog."

"Beast?" mumbled Dilly, seeming a little jealous that she had missed all the excitement.

"It was huge!" said Dod, smiling uncomfortably. What he really wanted to discuss was his innocence.

"It was the biggest dog I've ever seen," nodded Boot. "It must have been twice the size of the rest of them."

"Right," said Dod. He glanced around and saw that their conversation was now becoming relatively private, since the slowest soldiers had finally passed. It was his chance to speak openly with his friends.

"You know, Boot," he began anxiously, "everything I said to the billies was just to get them to believe that I was part of The Order—none of it's true."

Dilly and Sawny looked shocked, and Boot hopped off his horse to bring the conversation in closer.

"How did you know the billie's name?" whispered Boot. "Mur-somebody."

"Murdore," said Dod.

"You had the billies think you were part of The Order?" clarified Sawny sheepishly.

"It was the only thing I could think of," responded Dod. "I've heard things, you know. When I was in the pump house, following Sirlonk and Horsely, I heard Sirlonk speaking with Murdore, head of the billies—at least head of the ones following The Order. That's how I knew his name."

"Oh, yeah," said Boot. "Well, I must say, you had me going for a minute or two. You should consider a job in acting."

"Honestly, did you really trick the billies into thinking you were on their side?" asked Dilly with a skeptical face.

Dod nodded.

"He had them tethered like a donkey!" said Boot, now sounding proud of Dod. "The billies ate his story and followed him on a purple-turtle hunt in the middle of the night. It was epic. His timing was perfect, too. The billies had just set their sights on Buck and me when he came strolling in like Sirlonk's right-hand man, yelling orders and everything."

"That's why you had Dilly's shorts in your shirt!" said Sawny, "I get it. You told them you had the map."

"Yup," smiled Dod.

Boot began laughing. "I was wondering what you were holding."

Dilly spun her eyes at Boot pressingly. "Why did you say they took him captive? It sounds like he had them."

Boot sobered a notch and looked around. "It's not the best thing to go selling *that* story. Think about it. Dod's on trial for murder. We don't want people getting confused. It's the last thing he needs right now."

"Oh, right," agreed Dilly.

"And it's not like he wanted to go with them," added Sawny. "They'd have cut his hands off if they'd have found he was lying about the map—you know billies. So, in a way, he was their hostage."

"Definitely!" said Dod, beyond relieved that he was free of them. "When I bolted, I knew for sure they'd hunt me down and kill me."

"They were trying!" said Boot. "If you hadn't been riding Shooter, we probably wouldn't be having this conversation right now. Shooter's quite a horse!"

"You should have had me along," said Dilly, pushing Dod. "I was ready to duel last night. I was even wearing my lucky belt—just in case we ran into the rat that's been lying about you."

"Trust me," assured Boot. "Your lucky belt wouldn't have been lucky enough! Noble billies don't play fair, they just come at you growling—like a pack of mean dogs."

"And they had those, too," added Dod. "Boot's right. It wasn't your kind of fight."

"Besides," said Boot, smiling at Dilly. "You had the most important job: getting Sawny and the *real map* to a safer place!"

Dod yawned and followed the girls to a quiet room full of empty beds, while Boot took his horse to pasture. Dod glanced around in the dim light and soon saw why they had brought him there.

"He is alive," whispered Dod after a long sigh, feeling the tears returning to his eyes. Buck had a large wrap around his forehead and another around one of his hands, and Sneaker sat perched a short distance away, keeping watch. The scene was surreal. Buck's snores sounded exactly the way they always had back in Green Hall.

Without another word from the girls, Dod nodded his thanks and carefully sprawled out on a neighboring bed, and within moments he was sound asleep.

Shortly before noon, Dod and Buck were roused from their naps and escorted out by Sawny. Boot and Dilly were waiting with the horses. The bells around High Gate were ringing, preparing the watchtowers to drop the triblot barrier.

Buck seemed as relieved to see Dod as Dod had been to see him. "I thought you were a goner!" said Buck. "Boot told me you ran a distraction, and they rode off with you."

"Something like that," said Dod, covering a yawn. "It's just good to see you're alive."

"Yeah," sighed Buck. "It was a wild night." He looked at the horses and turned a few shades whiter with melancholy.

"Ride double with me," insisted Dilly. She slid forward in her saddle, as though it made more room for Buck to fit behind her.

"Or you could ride with me," offered Dod. The soldiers had cleaned Shooter off and fed and watered him.

"I don't think so," rumbled Boot. "We Dolsur brothers ride together, right Buck?"

Buck looked at his friends and offered thanks before taking his place behind Boot. Blood trumped everything else.

At the entrance to High Gate, Dod spotted Clair in the distance. He and his two assistants pushed their way forward and proceeded to cross over the wide road the moment the barrier was dropped. Clair seemed more than a little upset. The back of his neck and ears were so red that even from a hundred feet away, they shined like the polished paint of a new car. It appeared he couldn't wait to rush the city with his grudges in hand. And Dod didn't need psychic abilities to guess the likely causes of Clair's anger.

"We should hold back," suggested Dod, pointing at the reddened swordsman.

"It's Mr. Clair!" said Dilly happily. "Come on. Let's see what's brought him to High Gate. Hurry! We can catch up."

"Let's not!" said Sawny, cowering a little and slowing her horse. "He may have been sent by Youk and Voracio about the books."

"I vote with Sawny," added Buck, nudging Boot to slow down. "Our exit yesterday may have ruffled a few feathers."

"Or he's mad he didn't find us at Iris's," said Boot.

"Not Mr. Clair!" assured Dilly. "He wouldn't have been connected—"

"Don't be so sure," said Boot. "If I were involved in any way with the billies' success last night, I'd be mad, too. They failed miserably."

Buck raised his fist shoulder high in support.

"No!" said Dilly. "Stop. Not Mr. Clair."

Boot directed his horse to the side, as did the others, and let a string of wagons and carriages pass by. "Someone from Twistyard knew about us and our whereabouts," he said quietly. "Look around. Who else do you recognize?"

"But wouldn't that someone have been waiting for us at Iris's house?" asked Sawny.

"Good point," said Boot. "Huh. Who could have known where we were really going?"

"Did you mention anything to Mercy?" asked Dod.

Dilly once more looked shocked. "No! And how could you think that Mercy—of all the people in the world—would rat us out to The Dread's legion of scum. Besides, *Abbot* was the one watching us."

"And he warned us," added Boot.

"What happened to Abbot?" asked Dod. He had been so tired, the old man hadn't even crossed his mind.

"I don't know," said Boot. "By the time I had attended to Buck here and chased down Grubber, he had slipped away. I hope he makes it back to Twistyard. The poor old man."

"Or crazy, evil man," said Dilly. "If you're looking for a link, you've got one right there. He's loony enough to have an evil double inside—one warns you of the trouble that the other's gotten you into."

Boot shook his head and looked back toward the pavilion. "We've got more candidates," he whispered. He cleared his throat and pointed in the opposite direction, as if they had stopped to see some sight. Nearly all of them turned their heads, hiding their faces from view.

Jibb and Skap were coming up the lane, sitting on the front buckboard of a nice-looking carriage, calling orders to six horses that pulled the rig. The carriage windows were draped so that the people within were concealed. They almost passed by without a glance.

"Hi, Jibb," called Dilly happily, drawing their attention. "What brings the two of you to High Gate today?"

So much for going unnoticed, thought Dod.

Jibb pulled on the reins and slowed the carriage. "Business," he said gruffly, tipping his uppity drat nose as he glanced at Buck's head bandage. It looked like Buck was trying to start a new style.

"What ya doin' sittin' middle ground?" asked Skap, wearing a curious grin. "When the buzz comes up, this isn't where ya wanna be."

"I was just checking for our papers," fibbed Dilly, leaning forward to pat her lowest pants pocket, which on the pair she was wearing was nearly at her ankle.

"Awe, yeah, I know what ya mean," said Skap, all smiles. He wiped his sweaty brow with his dirty hand and left a smudge across his forehead. "They once turned me back for not hav'n the right stuff. The blibbin' papers only last 'bout a year or so, right Jibb?"

"Sometimes two," he responded curtly. Jibb looked past Dilly at Sawny, then over to Dod. "Voracio and Youk aren't happy about yesterday. You should head back to Twistyard."

Sawny went pale.

"That was some pull, I heard," laughed Skap. "How'd ya do it?"

"We didn't do anything," said Dilly defensively. "Someone else was behind the mice." Dilly eyed Skap and Jibb, adding, "You're the maylers, not us."

"I couldn' do nothin' like that," said Skap, still grinning. "My dad—well—maybe he could've. I dunno."

"Where's Joop?" asked Boot. "Have they kept him shoveling manure or is he hiding in there?" Boot pointed at the carriage.

"Naw. He's off helping Ingrid with her stuff," said Skap. "And the way he's gonna smell when he gets back, I'd take a gunnysack o' manure over him in the same room."

"She likes her garlic," grinned Buck, poking Boot in the back. Sneaker, who sat perched in his regular spot, turned to scowl at Buck.

Jibb didn't soften. "Go on. Head back to Twistyard."

"It's not in our plans," responded Boot sternly, moving Grubber between the carriage and Dilly. "If Voracio's got a problem, he can come up here and find us. We'll be staying with Commendus."

"I told you to head back!" scowled Jibb.

"That's nice," said Boot, undeterred. His eyes confidently pushed at Jibb. "Your shiny badge only works at Twistyard. Besides, Dilly's been commissioned by Commendus to prepare for a special event here at High Gate. It's just not in our schedule to return now."

Jibb fumed in his seat. And the more he fumed, the more Boot got hot under the collar.

"These are Bonboo's great-granddaughters!" added Boot, pointing at Dilly and Sawny. "If you can't remember to show them respect, you've forgotten your place!" Boot glared at Jibb's gloved hands and back up to his face. "Twistyard is theirs—and everything in it!"

The lane had become empty. The people entering High Gate had already passed the guards, and those leaving were beyond the pavilion, heading away.

"Let's get going," said Buck, nudging Grubber in the flanks. He appeared fearful that his brother was racing toward a fight, and he wasn't the only one seeing it.

"We've got to hurry," said Dilly, refusing to look at Jibb. She led out and the others followed, with Boot bringing up the rear, still looking over his shoulder at Jibb and Skap.

"I can't stand the way Jibb's been acting," complained Boot once they had passed the guards and entered High Gate. "Ever since they appointed him to help with security at Twistyard, he's lost his freshy-mind. It's like he's forgotten who owns the place."

"That's a common trend," lamented Buck. "Voracio's certain Twistyard's more his than Bonboo's anymore. I guess if you're tight with him, you feel important, too."

"And don't forget about the army of drat guards," added Dod. "They seem to think Jibb's toward the top."

Boot shook his head. "I never thought I'd say this, but I wish Zerny would come out of hiding. Beard or no, he's twice as decent as Jibb—at least toward the Tillius's."

CLAIRS'S WRATH

As the group approached the Discommo Estate, none of them could help noticing how much ground had been removed from around the remains of the burnt buildings. The charred wood from the structures was already gone, leaving blackened stone walls and foundations. Massive elephants, five times the size of a regular bull elephant, pulled giant digging blades that shoveled the dirt and debris up into house-sized wagons for moving elsewhere. Some of the pits they had dug were more than six stories deep.

"No Lost City," said Buck sadly, peering into a gaping hole as they passed.

Surprisingly, in just the short number of days since Dod's last visit to High Gate for the big Bollirse game, a city of tents had been pitched, sprawling out over much of the destroyed landscape. Tredder soldiers bustled about, making it clear that the newly-grown community was theirs.

"They've moved Fort Castle!" joked Dod gawkingly. "Why are there so many soldiers?" The tents could hold thousands.

"Look ahead," said Dilly.

Beyond the entrance to Commendus's estate, his lake was visible. Hundreds of men surrounded the water, standing as though on guard against it.

"He wasn't kidding," mumbled Dod.

"Of course not," said Dilly. "When Commendus promised the community that duressers wouldn't escape, he meant it. High Gate's filled with lakes and streams. If even a few baby duressers found their way out, it would be disastrous."

"Oh," said Dod. "I guess so."

Upon arriving at the front of the castle, a loud commotion met them. Traygof had just descended the stairs and was rushed by Clair, who was fighting mad. He had left his horse standing a few paces back, his men still sitting in their saddles, watching.

"I knew this would happen!" raged Clair. "Where have you hidden them?"

"Hidden who?" asked Traygof casually, not ruffled at all. A few of his sailors were enjoying a stroll on the porch above and began to gather at its edge to watch.

"You know who!" yelled Clair. "I told you he couldn't go, and you disregarded me completely! Do I look like a fool to you?"

"Yes," said Traygof bluntly. Behind his bushy beard, a smile was hidden.

"WHERE IS HE?" demanded Clair, instantly exploding. "I told you he couldn't join you! Not now! Not ever! He's headed to Driaxom, and there's nothing you can do about it! Do you understand?"

"No," laughed Traygof. "But if you keep spitting on me, I'm going to have to leave without hearing."

What happened next was shocking. When push came to shove, reality was revealed.

SEEING STARS

"**P**IRATE!" yelled Clair, lunging at Traygof. He positioned himself inches from the living legend and displayed his muscular frame, which looked bigger and stronger than Traygof's. "You'll give me respect or I'll take it!" raged Clair.

"He's gone mad," said Buck as the group approached. They stopped short of Clair's assistants.

Traygof stood nearly as tall as Clair, though he was older and his midsection looked squishy.

"Respect is something you earn, fool!" responded Traygof, flipping his beard at him.

Clair said nothing. He stood his ground like a menacing statue.

Dilly shifted in her saddle and leaned over to Dod. "You've got them fighting again," she whispered.

"Let's get out of here," said Dod. He was grateful nobody had noticed him yet.

"No!" insisted Dilly. "Mr. Clair just wants to know where you are."

"He wants to know I'm locked in Driaxom!" Dod whispered loudly, straining his throat. "Didn't you hear him? He's the worst representative a person could ask for." The whole depressing conversation he'd had with Clair while in prison came rushing back.

"YOU'RE A *FRAUD* AND A *FAKE*!" shouted Clair, shaking with rage. Clearly, intimidation tactics usually worked for him, and since they hadn't with Traygof, his frustration was surpassing his ability to control himself.

"You've got something on your teeth," said Traygof calmly, stepping sideways. "Perhaps it's your pride." He then turned and began to ascend the stairs.

"DON'T WALK AWAY FROM ME!" exploded Clair, his voice echoing off the castle. Up above, Bonboo and Commendus appeared on the far side of the patio; they looked over the rail with astonished faces.

Traygof kept walking, though his steps were slow—tauntingly slow.

Clair drew his two swords and galloped after him. "TELL THEM YOU'RE A FRAUD!" he pushed angrily. "YOUR MEN RARELY SEE YOU! I KNOW—I HAVE SOURCES! YOU HAVEN'T BEEN OUT AT SEA AND AROUND! YOU'RE NOTHING BUT A SILK-TONGUED LIAR!"

Traygof spun in his tracks and faced the rapiers, his own hand to his waist. "You're misinformed!" he said in a coarse voice. The jovial man who made light of everything was now gone.

"You probably can't even use a sword!" said Clair, dropping his voice a few notches. He waved his weapons, calling a challenge.

"I accept," said Traygof.

By the time the two men had made their way down the stairs and had prepared to duel in the courtyard, the patio railing was packed with spectators, and Dod and his friends were suddenly surrounded by dozens of people who came running from all over, on foot and horseback.

"Word spreads quickly," whined Buck, finding his view was being taken by newcomers. "Move up."

"I can't believe it," said Dilly. "They're really going to duel."

"Come on, Traygof!" said Boot, wearing a nervous smile. He obviously hoped Traygof would win, but his face revealed his best guess was with Clair.

"He hasn't got a chance," said Dilly. "Maybe in his prime, but Mr. Clair's as good with a sword as I've ever seen. The other day he flattened seven men. Traygof should walk now while he can. He's talented at sailing—isn't that good enough?"

Commendus left Bonboo on the patio and jogged down to the men, trailing Turly, his Chief Security Officer.

"I must object," said Commendus, gasping for air. The two rivals were just beginning to circle around each other with their swords drawn. Commendus raised his arms in the air and stepped between them. "I won't have this, Clair! Traygof's my guest."

"He's a fraud!" shoved Clair. "I know it. He hasn't done *any* of the things he's purported to have done. He hasn't been sailing the seas with his men. I have a contact—someone that must remain nameless—and he's spent the past ten years aboard *The Avenger*. He says Traygof's a sham."

"Another anonymous witness—how convenient," mocked Traygof. "Your snitches are liars for money!"

"They are not!" yelled Clair.

CHAPTER FOURTEEN

"Please, he's my guest!" insisted Commendus, glaring at Clair. "When I was in trouble and taken hostage, he came to my rescue! What does your contact have to say about that?"

Clair paused, still scowling. "A little sugar and the rest sand," he concluded.

Traygof puffed his chest and held his weapon up. "I was fighting with a sword, turning trouble upstream, when you were still working on the basics of spoon dipping. You're just jealous of me, jealous of my men, jealous of my ship, and even jealous of Dod! Pathetic! You're simply pathetic!"

"Prove it!" spat Clair, waving his swords.

Commendus raised his arms again in the air, trying to calm things, when Traygof met his pleas. "It's fine by me if I go rounds," he said. "Step back and watch. It'll be a show."

At Traygof's word, Commendus and Turly backed up, leaving the two rivals to battle.

Clair lunged at Traygof the first chance he got, slipping both swords inward. The crowd gasped. But Traygof cleverly sent the blades sideways, deflecting the blows seemingly with ease.

"You could hurt someone with a move like that," said Traygof. "Keep it friendly like *this*!" He whacked at Clair's right arm, only to hit metal.

Back and forth the men pressed. Clair floated about, striking here and there, however, never touching the legend. Similarly, Traygof pressed inward time and again, only to be repelled. The two were evenly matched.

The crowd buzzed with conversations as the men dueled. People were surprised to watch a rumor prove true: Traygof was the real thing! And he had a sense of humor, too. It wasn't long before he began using his tongue as much as his sword.

CLASH, CLANK, CLANK.

"Is that what they teach these days?" teased Traygof.

CLASH, CLANK, CLANK.

"You can do better than that. Be a sport and try harder."

CLANK! CLANK! SWIPE! CLASH! CLANK!

"Come now, I'm not a little girl."

CLINK! SWIPETY-SWIPE! CLASH! CLANK! CLANK!

Clair's intensity rose to an aggressive level where the surrounding crowd had to step back and give the men more space or risk being injured in the fray. Clair was mostly on attack, while Traygof held a rock-solid defense.

"He's amazing!" said Buck. "Look at those moves!"

"We could have used him this morning," said Boot. "No wonder the billies fear his name."

"Do you still think I'm a fraud?" asked Traygof, his beard moving with his smile.

Clair didn't respond.

"Recant your claims," pressed Traygof.

CLASH! CLANKETY-CLANK! SWIPE! SWIPE! SWIPE!

Clair only huffed.

"Aren't you ready to apologize?" continued Traygof.

CLANK! CLANK!!!

The men locked swords, Clair's two and Traygof's one. They struggled for position. And then Clair whispered something that lit Traygof on fire.

"What'd he say?" complained Buck, who kept tipping his head side-to-side for a better view. When the neighboring people weren't a problem, Sneaker seemed to enjoy flipping his tail and rear in Buck's face.

CHAPTER FOURTEEN

With a sudden jolt, Traygof pulled a move that no one had ever seen before. He let go of his sword and ducked sideways while grabbing the hilts of Clair's and tripping him to the ground, followed by a heel to the nose. And in a flash, he flipped his own sword from the ground up into his hands.

"I've got three, do you still want to fight?" growled Traygof.

Clair lay on the ground, seemingly dazed, holding a cloth to his bloody nose.

"Traygof's the winner!" roared Turly, quickly rushing in with his hands clapping. He appeared eager to see the scuffle end before someone got killed.

"Well done!" praised Commendus.

The crowd went wild with cheers as Traygof took a pleasant bow.

"Choose me!" begged Dilly to Dod. "I've got to sail with that man!"

"Dilly!" said Sawny.

"You can come, too," she added, "so long as you don't get in the way of my dueling lessons."

"We'll see," sighed Dod, clapping fiercely. It felt good watching someone beat Clair, as if the man's mean comments and attitudes had been defeated as well.

Traygof bent down and handed Clair his swords, then pointed into the crowd. "There's Dod, you fool! I told you I didn't hide him."

Dod waved slowly at the two men and felt strange. It was an unusual honor to be somebody Traygof recognized.

"Good throw, boss!" shouted a scruffy man, taking three stairs at a time and jumping the last six to land inches from Traygof. "You've still got your gentle touch!" He rapped Traygof on the back heartily. "I'd have cut the man's tongue out for spewing trash on your boots." He glared at Clair challengingly. "What's this talk of a peeping yellow-tongue on our ship?"

Clair looked at the two men, rose to his feet still holding the bloody cloth to his nose, and marched to his horse.

"Lunch is ready, I'm sure," announced Commendus, waving his hand for Traygof to follow. "You've fueled your hunger, now come and feast. I insist all of your men join me at my table."

"This isn't over, Dod!" said Clair in a cold, grumpy voice as he passed him to leave. "I've seen the evidence against you, and trust me, popular friends won't be able to save you from it."

Dod glanced at Dilly with 'I-told-you-so' eyes.

"He's got it out for you," said Sawny. "You should get a new representative."

"Can I?"

"I think," said Sawny. "With everything he's said, your situation appears clearly inequitable. And now that he's openly shown his bias in front of so many people," Sawny looked around, "it's a straight cut."

"I hope," groaned Dod, watching Clair and his two faithful subordinates ride away.

"At least *they* won't be staying here tonight," said Boot impatiently, waiting for the crowd to thin enough to lead the horses to the barn.

"Why the numbers?" asked Buck. He looked to Dilly since she often knew of Commendus's social itinerary.

"This week's the Global Business Convention, isn't it?" responded Dilly.

Sawny nodded. "Commendus always invites the most important chiefs of industry to stay here with him. I bet your dear friend Bly is among the many." Sawny giggled as Dilly rolled her eyes.

At the barn, Doctor Shelderhig was busily shoveling manure alongside a few other men. He smiled and approached Dilly the moment the group stopped to hand off their horses.

"I wouldn't have expected to see you working the stables," said Dilly, glancing at the scuffs of horse dung on his pants and shoes. She slid off of Song and held the reigns in his direction.

"I'm gathering droppings for my Hazula project," he said eagerly. "My business colleague is pleased with the progress I've made and interested in the opportunities it presents."

"Oh. Of course," said Dilly, pulling her hand back.

"Really?" laughed Sawny. "I thought you said that that venture was as pointless as spreading jam on the soles of your feet."

"Apparently not," responded Doctor Shelderhig happily. "My altered Hazula plants are proving useful in context with mining. Their capacity to rapidly produce oxygen, when fueled by high concentrations of waste excretions—and that, too, amazingly in total darkness—is receiving shining reviews."

"Fascinating!" said Sawny.

Doctor Shelderhig glanced at Buck, as if just becoming aware of his wrapped head, and noted, "I see I'm not the only one trying to ignore the noise. Businessmen like hearing themselves talk more than any other subset of the population. Odd, isn't it? You'd think they'd all be deaf by now and give up on trying to communicate with others in their same condition."

"It's not that," said Dilly, snipping Buck off from answering. "He's got a serious injury from our unfortunate encounter with a crowd of noble billies just outside of High Gate."

"Billies?" stammered Doctor Shelderhig with concern. "They're marching on us?"

Sneaker sniffed at the breeze cautiously.

"We squelched their ambitions," said Boot, squaring his shoulders and handing Grubber's reigns to a barn hand. "When the billies attacked, we hit back hard."

"So Newmi was right," groaned Doctor Shelderhig. "Billies are bringing their anger to land now."

"Only thirty or so," said Boot. "It's not like the seas are heaving them shoreward."

"Not yet," added Dod.

Doctor Shelderhig ran his hands through his sweaty gray hair. "Ever since her disappearance, I've dreaded billies."

"Is Newmi gone?" asked Dilly.

"No," said Doctor Shelderhig, looking caught. He checked over his shoulder and made his way out into the open. "You didn't hear it from me," he began quietly. "Yarni went missing months ago—she was taken and killed by billies—or that's what the buzz has been around the back corridors of the castle. That's why Commendus hired Newmi. She advises him and Turly on how to deal with them."

"Really?" said Dilly sadly. "I thought his wife went back to Soosh. Everyone's been saying she left him heartbroken and pining for her."

"I think Commendus started that rumor," whispered Doctor Shelderhig. "He's doing his best to hide her death since she was reportedly snatched from the castle. That's a big mark against his security, and after the horrendous poisoning—" Doctor Shelderhig looked at Dod. "He just didn't want people to lose total faith in his ability to be a good host."

"She's the one the soldiers were talking about this morning!" said Sawny.

The old man nodded. "He's posted guards everywhere and warned the troops to be vigilant, but the recent fires here at High Gate suggest billies are sneakier than we give them credit. Years of work burned to the ground in a matter of hours."

"It's not just billies," said Dod. "Sirlonk's behind the trouble."

Doctor Shelderhig's brow furrowed.

"He didn't die," said Dod. "He's still alive, and he's using the billies to get what he wants."

"Are you sure?" asked the doctor. "Everyone's praising the snakes for having eaten him—well—and of course, you for your part." He gave Dod a pat on the shoulder.

"We're positive," said Buck, moving in. "Dod and I saw Sirlonk in the master barn at Twistyard. He's alive and well."

"That's disturbing," said Doctor Shelderhig. "It's like he's a phantom. Nothing can harm him. He's unstoppable!"

"Go ahead and try to tell that to Traygof," laughed Buck. "I'd love to see the two of them duel. Traygof would pull some clever move and put plenty of dread in The Dread."

"He's incredible," sighed Dilly.

"Then we're in luck," said Doctor Shelderhig, perking up a few notches, nearly to his normal, proceed-forward-with-gusto self. He smiled like he couldn't wait to announce something exciting. "Traygof is in town, and he's staying here. You'll have to catch a glimpse of him before he leaves. I've heard he's counseling Commendus on how to deal with billies and offering support in the effort."

"Oh. Thanks," said Dilly, not wanting to spoil his excitement by admitting that they had just seen him in glorious action.

"Stop by the garden sometime," called the old man as the group headed for the castle.

At lunch, Dod quickly saw what Buck and Boot meant when they had said that Sabbella's food-tasting finches were distracting. The green-and-yellow birds darted around her table, stealing bits of her meal in between inspecting the neighboring guests. One bird seemed to hate the burly seaman who sat just across from Sabbella and spent the entire meal tormenting him.

"See," said Boot, pointing at the unfortunate victim who relentlessly bobbed his head and waved his arms to avoid being pecked on the face. "Last time we were here, that's where I sat."

"Now you know it's not you," said Buck, grateful they were situated a few tables away from Commendus and Sabbella.

The room was overflowing with well-dressed guests, a majority of whom were tredders, though there were some drats, bobwits, and humans; and the doctor was right about the crowd of visitors: Dod had never heard such a deafening jumble of conversations at the same time. He had to nearly yell to be heard by his friends.

"Where's Bonboo?" he asked, surprised to see that he wasn't at Commendus's table.

Dilly glanced around. "He must have already eaten. With the numbers Commendus is hosting right now, people are being served in shifts."

A cold feeling swept over Dod.

"It's a pleasure to see you've returned so quickly," said Con to Dilly, coming up behind Boot. "You couldn't stay away from me, could you?"

Dilly's eyes widened.

Con's towering frame was gigantic, surpassing his father in both height and width. "I'm sure you won't be surprised to learn that Traygof is pressing me to join him aboard *The Avenger*," he continued, glancing smugly at Buck and Dod, then down upon Boot. "He desperately wants me to sail with him and his men for a spell, since he's heard plenty of tales about my great successes at sea."

Dod started laughing. Dilly was pulling a 'please-gag-me' look and Sawny couldn't help the things her honest eyes were telling.

"Do you have a problem with me?" shot Con, pelting Dod with a string of toxic glares.

"No," said Dod uneasily, wishing he had held his laughter in.

"I've killed people, too," he gloated, showing off his billboard-sized chest. "But mine were all legal."

"Says who?" snapped Boot. "Your daddy?"

Buck chuckled.

Con breathed in deeply. He looked like he was either searching for a good comeback line or trying to figure out how he could punch Boot without anyone noticing.

"Thanks for finding space for us," rushed Dilly, grabbing at Con's attention with her eyes. "We really appreciate your family's hospitality. I keep telling everyone how lucky we are to have you and your father helping all of us through these troubled times."

"Right," said Con doubtfully. He wasn't buying it, and his glare was all but burning a hole through Boot's skull.

"Really, Con," continued Dilly, desperate to extinguish his rage. "I've heard people throwing your name around as a likely candidate for the rank of general." Dilly cringed as she fibbed. It was quite a stretch.

"Well," said Con, finally looking back at Dilly. "When you've experienced the world as I have, it makes you a prime target for praise. People can't help wanting me to lead them."

"Or leave them," coughed Buck.

Con's anger reignited.

"There you are!" called Commendus, waving to his son as he waltzed over with Sabbella on his arm. He wore a fancy deep-blue suit, and Sabbella looked the part of a queen. "I was just telling Traygof how you and Dod are great pals. It's hand-in-glove to find you talking with him."

Con smirked coolly.

"Oh, right," said Dod with a picture-perfect smile.

"Great!" said Commendus, nodding his head. "Hopefully we'll be able to get things expedited for you. It's a shame to bring charges at all, but the law's the law. I'm sure you understand. That Horuph or Horus fellow up and died—and with you involved—well, we hope the best for you—"

Dod wasn't sure what exactly Commendus was saying behind his words, or whether he meant anything at all, though what he said next seemed to clarify a little.

"If this nightmare could just blow over *gently*," continued Commendus, sounding reminiscent of Coach Smith pushing a used car, "it would be great if Con could join you and Traygof out to sea. Wouldn't that be nice, Dod—wouldn't you like that—you and Con sailing with Traygof?"

"It'd be a little better than Driaxom," said Dod, feeling the words slip out of his mouth before he'd had time to think.

Sabbella laughed, launching two birds off her shoulder, while Boot and Buck tapped their silverware lightly against the table.

"I would certainly hope so!" said Commendus, looking affronted.

Sawny turned and smiled sweet as a kitten, but opened her mouth like a lion. "If you want things to blow over for Dod, so he can pick your son to go sailing, you've got to help him get a new representative."

Commendus blinked.

"The one he's got now is horribly biased against him—no offense to Mr. Clair—but Dod needs a representative that can see Dod's innocence. We all know Dod didn't kill *Horsely*."

"Of course…I'm sure," stuttered Commendus, glancing around to see who was watching.

"Can you get that fixed for him?" asked Sawny pointedly.

"You know I would love to help," offered Commendus, "however, I have to follow the rules, too." He glanced around again.

"I know," said Sawny, "but as the highest ranking political official in Yorkum, you have the capacity to make that adjustment if you deem it necessary."

"Young lady!" huffed Commendus arrogantly. "I'm the highest official in all of Green!"

"I recognize that, sir," agreed Sawny. "I'm just noting what I've read. The highest political official in each province is given the power, among so many other things, to override the selection of a judicial representative in his area. In Dod's case, it seems more than necessary, considering dozens of people just heard Mr. Clair on your front steps telling Dod he was headed to Driaxom."

"I'll do what I can," said Commendus, leading Sabbella away quickly. Con tipped his head uncomfortably and followed after his father.

"You go for the throat, don't you?" laughed Boot, clenching his fist like the snap of teeth digging into prey.

Sawny smiled.

"We've got to talk," groaned Dilly. "You can't treat nobles like that, especially not Commendus. Who are you, anyway? Dari?"

"She can and did!" chuckled Buck. "That was great. Slam! You called him on his request for a favor and then schooled him on his duties as a politician. I've never seen Commendus hurry off like that before. I think you flustered him."

"Someone needs to speak up for Dod," said Sawny. "And if Commendus is going to be so brazen as to lay a plan for Dod to follow, it seems only fair to return the envelope with Dod's wish list."

"She's a Tillius!" grinned Boot, nodding at Dod teasingly until Dod blushed.

CHAPTER FIFTEEN

CONCEALIO'S LEGACY

Before Dod had even finished lunch, a long-nosed waiter in a black suit and bowtie came and pressed Dod and his friends to follow him out.

"See what happens when you offend the powers that be," chided Dilly to her sister. "We've never been asked to exit, much less without tasting dessert!"

"Speak for yourself," laughed Boot and Buck in unison. They had both gulped down their cream-covered blueberry tarts and had been looking longingly at the trays that passed, wondering whether they could go a second round, perhaps this time with peach crumbles or caramel wedges.

"I'm sorry," offered Sawny, following closely on her sister's heels. "He made me mad."

"That's no excuse," responded Dilly, venting as they walked. "In the future, consider things cautiously before you open your mouth. Consequences follow. That's why I'm *always* careful. Think twice, speak once."

Dilly suddenly froze, seemingly mortified, then glanced desperately for an alternate route. Seeing none, she took a deep breath, changed faces, and approached a table they were directed to pass. "It's a pleasure to see you, Bly," she said sweetly, glowing like she had just been given an award for housing orphans.

"Is it?" Bly asked gruffly, wearing a crooked grin that increased the wrinkles on his sunburned face. His well-trimmed, red beard separated him from the other clean-shaven men at the table and was a striking contrast to the shiny black hair that adorned his head. "So, you're still okay with me *here* instead of *farther east?*"

Bly's associates raised their eyebrows and awaited an explanation.

Dilly shuddered as though she would die if things didn't quickly improve. Sawny beamed a satisfied smirk standing right beside Dilly, knowing the trouble she had just stirred with Commendus was a mere pebble compared to the boulder-sized social disaster that Dilly still carried on her record because of things she had said about Bly. Dod and the Dolsur brothers waited a few steps back, smiling, watching the humorous scene unfold. It was only too befitting to have Dilly run into her worst verbal blunder while bragging to her sister that she never misspoke.

"I'm—well—very pleased you're here and not—uh, *there*—" began Dilly, struggling to communicate, which condition rarely happened to her. She always had plenty of clever things to say, but not at the moment. She paused and stuttered. "You're so busy—I'm sure—as the most celebrated man—uh, inventor and business—uh, person of our time—"

CHAPTER FIFTEEN

Bly's barrel-chested laughter broke her concentration and left her silent, mouth still open, staring like a doe in the headlights.

"Do I scare you, Dilly?" chuckled Bly.

Dilly was speechless, and her face was turning red with embarrassment.

"What brings you to High Gate? Are you dabbling in entrepreneurial activities?"

"No," stammered Dilly. An awkward pause followed.

"We're commissioned by Commendus to oversee the restoration of the Code of the Kings Monument," said Sawny, coming to her sister's rescue. "Dilly's always volunteering us to take an active role in the community. We try to do our best, even if we occasionally get things wrong."

"You're fine—at least *now*," said Bly. He shook his head and spoke to the men at his table who were now terribly curious. "This is Dilly Tillius and her sister—"

"Sawny," said Sawny, helping him when he came up blank.

"Back when I was charged as a war criminal, this young lady—" Bly pointed at Dilly and led the table's eyes in her direction, "told the investigating council that she personally knew of my guilt, and she insisted in the strongest words she could muster that I should be confined to the lowest, most miserable quarters in Driaxom."

"No!" blurted one man, saying what all of the others were clearly thinking.

"Most of her opinions, naturally, were from the rubbish she'd read in the papers—and at the time, I was the biggest sensational story in all of High Gate! You can imagine: A big money businessman—from Soosh of all places—emerging as a real contributor here in the Big City, and it's *discovered* that I was really a horrible monster back home."

"How terrible," said a heavy-set man who was seated beside Bly, filling his chair and some of the space beyond. He glanced at Dilly as if seeing a ghastly, gruesome sight.

"And she's Bonboo's great-granddaughter!" added Bly, drawing gasps from his whole table and a few neighboring people whose ears were tuned in. "The royal connection, certainly, made her words like thunder."

Dod looked over and noticed Boot's neck turning red. The humor of the setting had worn off.

"Her youthfulness made the story sound disastrously convincing," said Bly. "If Traygof hadn't produced some real proof, and if Commendus hadn't opened his ears to reason, I'd be sitting in Driaxom, watching a weed grow from my leg."

"They really do that?" gasped a beanpole-thin human, shamelessly wearing a tag that advertised he sold musical instruments in bulk to specialty stores.

"They don't call it the Ankle Weed Desert for nothing!" said Bly, building the story with his tone and eyes as much as his words. "This young lady pled with the council to give me a living-death sentence. I was nearly shackled with a plant that turns men mad."

Boot couldn't stand back any longer. "She was young, and it was one testimony. Get over it!" He pushed his way in front of Dilly and seared the men with his eyes.

"But from news reports—" began a squat man who wore rings with marble-sized jewels and had food smudges across his chin.

"It wasn't just what she'd read," added Boot boldly. "Dilly visited Soosh as a child and was persuaded to come forward because of the things she'd heard firsthand: Two separate girls spoke out against him." Boot pointed at Bly. "So, go ahead and blame *his* hometown crowd—they're the ones who put slanderous words in her ears. Dilly was just doing what any good, respectable citizen would do: She reported what she knew."

Bly sat up straight and showed off his muscular physique as his face tilted slightly back and forth from angry to composed. "It was a long time ago," he finally said. "I've forgiven and forgotten. As far as I'm concerned, Dilly's a friend, now."

"Marvelous!" exclaimed a heavy woman who was seated at a nearby table. She dug through her things and produced a delicate, lace cloth that she used to dab at her eyes, as though soaking tears. "Bly, you're truly amazing!" she insisted, leaving her place to embrace him.

Boot's fists relaxed and his shoulders dropped an inch. "For what it's worth," said Boot in a civil voice, "we all appreciate the support you give to Twistyard."

"Just doing my part," said Bly.

"Marvelous!" burst the neighboring woman, her voice turning more theatrical than it had been before. Dod looked her over and wondered what product she was hoping to sell.

"Besides," added Bly, shrugging casually. "I made good on the odds at the Bollirse game the other day. You kids really pulled moves on the Lairrington Longs. Strat was right to push me toward a heavier wager. I'm glad I listened." Bly smiled. "With a win like that, Strat's probably still somewhere in outer space, isn't he?"

Dilly finally found her tongue. "He's proud of us, and grateful for your friendship, Bly. We all appreciate you."

"And we like your inventions, too," added Sawny. "Dilly and I regularly use glowing-stone necklaces. They're so convenient—no flames and completely portable."

"Good," praised Bly, leaning back in his seat. "Good, good. That reminds me of the first time I glimpsed how useful they could be." He chuckled pleasantly and collected the men at the table with his eyes. "I was in the deep jungles of Soosh," he began, when the bowtie-clad waiter came back and tapped Boot and Dilly on the shoulder, drawing them away from Bly's next story.

Out in the hall, the waiter pointed to a room a short distance off and said someone was waiting to speak with them.

Oh no! thought Dod, *Commendus is kicking us out!* But to his surprise, Traygof and his men were seated within.

"Dod," called Traygof, rising to his feet. "I'm glad you've come. I'd like to ask you to join me and my men for a short season aboard my ship."

Dod didn't know what to say. He was now the speechless one.

"Not too far—just a jaunt through the Carsalean Sea."

"We hear you're lucky," said the only clean-shaven man in the group.

"Psychic," blurted another.

"I'm not really," said Dod in a humble voice.

"You can bring a few of your friends, too, if you'd like," offered Traygof. "We have a difficult mission ahead of us—one we can't say much about—but I suspect your abilities would be useful—you'd be a consultant of sorts."

"I can't," said Dod, catching a glimpse of Sawny's eyes. "You know—I'm charged with...a crime."

"Murder—right," huffed Traygof, moving closer to Dod. "What if I could get Commendus to figure things out—at least give you leave for a few weeks, would you come?"

Dod looked at Boot and Buck, who were both struggling to keep from jumping up and down with the answer 'yes.'

"The Democracy is depending on us," said Traygof. "Commendus needs a favor, and he's hoping we'll be able to deliver. It won't take more than a month."

"I don't know," said Dod, giving a heavy sigh. "Bonboo's secured my freedom. If something happens, he'd face the consequences."

"Sounds like you're set with a great cloak!" snapped the roughest-looking man in the bunch. His tredder ring was covered with tattoos and resembled a poisonous snake.

"I'll bargain it out," said Traygof. "Don't worry. I really need you. With Humberrone trapped up and all, you're a good second pick—or so I've been told."

Trapped? thought Dod. He stood stunned. No one had ever said Humberrone was still alive. He looked at Dilly with shocked eyes, expecting to hear her jabber on with questions. But instead, his friends were so captivated by Traygof's offer, they didn't seem one bit interested in Humberrone.

"If it's for the Democracy, Dod," said Dilly, sounding giddy with excitement, "we should probably do it."

Traygof smiled. "Think about it, Dod. You've got a few weeks before we leave port."

"Three weeks from tomorrow," said a burly man who pulled from his vest a contraption that resembled a pocket-watch. He inspected it carefully as he turned the edges. "Three weeks and sixteen hours to be exact," he announced, peering at Traygof through thick spectacles. "We'll leave with the tide. Be there, or be left behind."

Traygof nodded at the man and turned back toward Dod. "Acor's training to be a captain someday. He's starting to sound like one, isn't he?"

Dod caught Dilly envying Acor for his gadget and grinned. She hadn't been formally named to the crew and yet was already seeking to command the vessel.

Traygof cleared his throat and awaited Dod's full attention. "We'll be conducting business here at High Gate until two days prior to our departure. You can leave word with Commendus or be waiting here." Traygof's eyes prodded at Dod; they were deep and penetrating—like Bonboo's, they seemed to be hiding a world of secrets. "If you'd prefer, you can meet us at Fisher. My ship's the biggest one docked in the bay."

"I think you can count on us," said Dilly eagerly, "so long as you're able to get things worked out with Commendus and Dod's investigation council."

Dod and Sawny shot each other concerned glances, right past the faces of Boot, Buck, and Dilly, who were popping with joy over being chosen as shipmates. In truth, however, the mention of Humberrone sent Dod's mind racing through a portfolio of images of his father, and it stiffened his resolve to find a way onto *The Avenger*. If Traygof knew about Humberrone, Dod wanted to hear everything.

"Yes, I'm ready to head out!" said Dilly. "You can definitely count on us!"

"Ladies aboard our vessel?" grunted a gangly man who'd stood back, inspecting paintings on the wall. "It's been years, hasn't it?"

CHAPTER FIFTEEN

"Not for want of my tries," responded Traygof. "I've known a few women who have considered me top notch," he bragged, putting his thumbs under his lapels proudly. "But when I mention the chore of cooking for my men, they all seem to find other offers more appealing. If only there were a woman—any two-legged specimen of the female gender—who loved the sea like I do and didn't mind brewing a meal every now and then—why, I'd proffer a dowry of jewels that would set a dark room aglow from the sparkle it would give."

Sawny and Dilly both looked away as Traygof raised his eyebrows in their direction.

"Do you know of any such woman?"

"I do," said Dod, doing his best to hold back laughter. The renewed hope of his father being alive lifted his spirits. "She's a bit stout, though—maybe you'd see her as plumpish—but she loves adventure and finds an unusual sort of pleasure in cooking stews for large crowds."

"Bring her along," called Traygof, working his way to the door. Instantly, all of his men hopped to follow, lining up behind Acor.

"Ingrid?" chuckled Dilly.

"Why not?" said Traygof. "I'm not getting any younger. If she's still breathing and finds me tolerable, I'd be happy to wed at sea. I think I could even settle for a one-legged woman so long as she's polished her peg—I don't want slivers in the night."

"Are you serious?" asked Dod.

Traygof paused while he stroked his beard. "Behind my jokes, Dod, I'm just as committed to my goals as you'll ever find in a man. Bring the woman if you can. I'd love to meet her. And what better way to see a person's metal than at sea? She can bunk with your two lady friends in the queen's suite."

"All right—I'll try," said Dod, watching Traygof and his men swagger away. The whole circumstance was sounding more and more like a cruise, not a top-secret mission.

The moment the men were gone, Boot chuckled, "Ingrid and Traygof? Now that would be an interesting match! I'd like to see how that would work."

"Who cares?" said Dilly. "With or without her, we're really going to sail the seas aboard *The Avenger*! Can you believe it?"

"And their schedule's perfect!" said Boot, sauntering around the room with his feet nearly off the floor. "We'll first hit the Ghoul's Festival, and then make it back just in time to *launch with the tide*!"

"Hoi! Hoi! Hoi!" chanted Buck, waving his fist in the air. "Make the wind fill my sails, men, or I'll be sending you all to the lowers for a stern round of plogging!"

"Plogging?" said Sawny flatly, raising her eyebrows at Buck. "They're not billies. I doubt they even have a barrel of snakes in their lowers, much less a crib and hitch."

"You wish!" blared Buck, tauntingly, strutting his stuff as best as he could to appear like Traygof. "We tredder seamen like the use of torture as much as billies—at least every now and again. There's nothing quite like the sting of a dozen fangs to motivate top performance."

Sawny groaned. "What kind of mission would they want Dod for? It doesn't make sense."

"Probably one that involves intense sword fighting," offered Buck, pretending to jab in and out. His headband waved back and forth as he hopped around shadow fighting.

CHAPTER FIFTEEN

"What did *he* eat for lunch?" asked Sawny, rolling her eyes.

"Can't you tell?" said Boot, waving his hand toward Buck. "Look at me shipmate. He's been feasting on the briny breeze! We sailors need little else to keep us fit as these timbers that post our sails proudly."

"Hoi and up with the anchor, lads!" bellowed Dilly in her gruffest voice, storming up to Boot and Buck like a captain. "I need the islands in view yesterday! Pull the lines taut, secure the riggings, and let our rags fly stiff!"

"Out 'n' away!" cried Boot.

Buck pretended to tug at a line in rhythm as he chanted, as though with a chorus of men, "Steady pull and—HO! Steady pull and—HO! Steady pull and—HO!"

Dod remained quiet and didn't join in. He had mixed feelings. He was stirred with excitement at the prospects of discovering more about his father, but was tethered by dread, much like Sawny, of the details of the voyage. Where were they going, and why did they want *him* along?

The next few days were all a blur. Talk of the upcoming trip to the seas trumped everything else, even the fantastic Ghoul's Festival. Bonboo had cleared Sawny of any wrongdoing with the missing books when Voracio and Youk had come calling, and Commendus had been persuaded by Traygof to allow Dod the freedom to roam if accompanied, so prospects of the voyage looked good. The most difficult thing at hand was focusing on the tedious work of sifting through old records.

Commendus had gathered a substantial pile of books and documents and had instructed Dilly to charge through the material in an attempt to understand the original state of the

Code of the Kings Monument. The task was daunting. Boot and Buck struggled to keep their minds on it. The Ghoul's Festival was only days away, and the seas were awaiting their return from Raul.

Dod tried to help Sawny and Dilly, but his skills in reading the ancient writings were lacking. Not to mention, every time the room got quiet, Dod's mind drifted. He couldn't help thinking about the strange images he had seen of his father, and of a monstrous dragon, and of a frightening, flame-filled battle scene. Were they all connected? Every detail was weighed over and over.

"Why can't we get Bonboo to join us?" asked Buck, flopping down on a plush chair next to Dilly. He and Boot had just been reprimanded for their poor contributions.

"He's at the convention again today," said Dilly. "Commendus appreciates his presence. Our democracy would be little more than a dream without the strength and cooperation of major businesses. It takes money to stay free. Just look at Dreaderious: He wouldn't have troops if it weren't for the bad economic circumstances in distant lands that lure poorlings into his ranks."

"She's right," agreed Sawny from farther down the elegant table, enclosed by piles of papers. "If industry around the globe would stabilize in the underprivileged areas, war with Dreaderious would be over. The last thirty years alone have seen marked changes. The increased opportunities for work have substantially weakened Dreaderious's forces, leaving Pious a much easier job than he had years ago fighting Dreadluceous.

Boot sighed as he flipped pages, looking as if he wished there were more pictures in the book he was assigned to review.

"I think I'm ready for some heavy scrubbing," said Buck restlessly, leaving his dusty volume closed. "What are we looking for in these, anyway? Let's visit the monument and see what needs fixing. I'm done studying!"

"See! That's the trouble!" said Sawny, raising her eyes to chastise Buck. "Too many people have thought like you for the past few centuries and now the paint's all wrong. It says right here that the beams were a regal burgundy."

"So?"

"So they're brown, now," said Sawny. "People have changed the place one layer at a time. We've got to know what it once was before we can start giving orders."

"Red, brown, purple—who cares?" sulked Buck, cracking the three-inch-thick book open. "If I have to spend another day reading about stuffy, old parties and gatherings, I'm going to lose my brain. It'll turn to slosh and drip out my ears. This stuff's the worst dribble I've ever—"

"I'll trade you," shot Boot, showing off his leather-bound assignment. The ancient text was twice as thick as Buck's and took real muscles to hold.

Dod kept quiet. He had been handed an old journal with plenty of blank pages and sketches. The spot he was currently skimming had a drawing of three men standing on a large wooden box, holding up long poles with animal-faced tops.

"We can do this the right way," said Dilly motheringly. "Commendus deserves our best efforts for the next nine days. That's not too much to ask, now is it?" She smiled and looked at Boot, who instantly settled back into his book, though his eyes seemed to gloss with thoughts of where he was soon headed.

Dod read the brief text below the sketch in his book. "…three scepters for three kings," he mumbled. Something tugged at him.

"I still think nobody would care if we scrubbed the building down and called it good," grumbled Buck, feeling hopelessly outvoted. Four days of mind-numbing work was as much as he could stand. A fifth now felt unbearable.

"…with scepters in hand," whispered Dod, reading on, "the truth will stand, and all may know of that which lies hidden."

What's hidden? thought Dod, putting his hand to his chest, feeling his three keys and medallion through his shirt. The first thing that came to his mind was the secrets that Bonboo wouldn't tell—the ones he had instructed Dod to obtain once he was gone. But it didn't take long for a second thought to surface.

"Did Concealio know of The Lost City?"

"Rumors have been around forever," responded Dilly, organizing a stack of notes that proved she had paid close attention to the books she had reviewed.

Dod turned the page and studied a sketch of a kneeling man, his sword plunging into the ground. "…as one, the ties we'll cut," he read quietly, "and find the door that 'til this point must remain shut." He flipped past a number of empty pages and discovered another drawing. It was of a large, oval egg, propped up by ornately carved wooden legs and secured under a transparent sheet of shiny glass—or so it appeared in the well-drawn image.

Dod's voice grew louder as he read the words that were penned below the picture. "Within its shell lies the proof of things greater…" Dod paused, his heart pounding.

"The Dragons' Egg," said Boot, looking over at the yellowed page. Dod's hands were trembling.

"Let me see," said Dilly.

Boot took the journal from Dod and slid it in Dilly's direction.

"Concealio would mold in his grave if he knew what happened to *that* museum," said Dilly sadly.

Dod strained to recall what Dilly spoke of. Memories felt close.

"I hate looters," lamented Sawny. "It's too bad my kids will never see it."

Buck chuckled. "Can't they carve another dragon-egg stone and recreate the hall of tribute?"

Dilly gave him a shove. "It wasn't any *ordinary* dragon egg, it was *The* Dragons' Egg. Making a replica wouldn't be the same. We probably heard the story of Kray and Yark and their one egg a dozen times as kids—didn't we, Sawny?"

Sawny nodded.

Dod suddenly remembered the fable, as though someone had shared the tale with him. Kray and Yark were a pair of monstrous flying dragons that had terrorized the inhabitants of the Carsalean Sea. Their beastly attacks had struck fear into the hearts of billies and had driven many of them to unify under a great mayler who possessed the power to make the brutes obey his commands. Before their last battle, Kray had laid a mighty egg—the size of a large watermelon—and had left it upon a sandy shore near Carsigo.

Once the beasts were killed, the egg had been enshrined under glass in a guarded museum, to prevent anyone from incubating it. The large orb had been on display for hundreds of years, when in recent history, the egg-like object had been stolen and the structure burned.

Thinking about it made Dod shiver. Even though the two dragons were considered mythical, the dragon-like beast in his dreams certainly seemed real enough to fear.

"You can still tell your kids the story of Kray and Yark," said Boot, smiling at Sawny. "I'm sure I'll tell mine. It makes kids hurry to bed faster." Boot gave Dilly a sly look as he continued. "Your dad told you about Kray's eating habits, right? She was finicky. Big momma only ate disobedient children."

"You're horrible," said Dilly with a smile.

"That's what I heard," said Boot, working hard to keep a straight face.

Dilly looked at the drawing of the egg, then flipped through the empty pages that followed it. "I've always wondered why Concealio built a whole museum around the noble billies' legend. It's a shame he doesn't say more in his journal." Dilly inspected the book closer. "It's missing pages!"

Sawny popped from her seat and hurried over. After careful inspection, she began to nod. "You're right," she said, scrutinizing the manuscript from every possible angle. "It's missing a few here…and here…and right here, too."

"Maybe someone *burned* them," chuckled Buck gleefully. "Perhaps his son learned a thing or two from watching old dad fuel the fires."

Dilly rebuked him with her eyes and went back to examining the journal.

"It's The Dread," said Dod, feeling an uncomfortable wave of anxiety. "He's behind this."

"But Commendus just pulled these from the National Repository of Valuable Records. They've been locked for years."

"Valuable?" muttered Buck under his breath. He made large eyes at his hefty reading assignment and glanced at Boot and Dod. "My book's missing the valuable stuff. It's just loaded with boring details about parties and meetings and dribble like that. Did Concealio ever do anything worthwhile?"

"He most certainly did!" insisted Sawny. "Concealio built half the museums in High Gate, and added to six more, and founded eight of the ten largest libraries in Green. And that's not counting his unbelievable efforts in building the collection of books that we enjoy at Twistyard. He was anything but a book-burner!"

"And he spent most of his life fighting for peace!" plugged Dilly, grabbing at her papers. "Bonboo's great-grandfather was a hero. The more I read, the more I'm amazed. Did you know he held a meeting in the Code of the Kings Monument and tried to unite the three realms?" Dilly read from her notes. "He had possession of the Tillius sword—the one we've cherished for so long—"

"You mean the one Boot found?" asked Buck. Boot smiled and rapped his knuckles on the table lightly.

"My family kept it secure until it was *stolen*," defended Dilly, sporting an ornery eye.

"Buck's just teasing," rushed Boot.

Dilly sighed. "Anyway, did you know Concealio had our sword, and the crimson blade Sirlonk was swinging, and another one?"

"Really?" said Dod. He was interested.

"Yes," nodded Dilly. "The three swords were symbolic of or somehow tied to the three realms. So at a peace meeting, Concealio displayed one rapier for Green—of course our Tillius sword—and gave the other two away to representatives of Raul and Soosh, hoping to forge a tighter union."

"Did he make the crimson blade?" asked Boot, who had heard from Dod of its unbelievable strength.

"I don't think so," responded Dilly.

"He didn't," assured Sawny, glancing nervously at Dilly. "But he did give it back to Soosh—someone from the Mauj. They're the ones who made it. They made all three of them."

Boot grinned at Dod. "We have quite a collection. Who would have guessed we'd acquire two weapons from the Mauj?"

"Not bad," answered Dod. "Not bad at all."

CHAPTER SIXTEEN

STUCK

Shortly before lunch, a sudden rush of panic washed over Dod. He couldn't explain why. The dusty books were as boring as ever, except Concealio's diary, which he had looked over twice. Boot and Dilly were presently fighting over it and how many pages had been stripped, while Sawny had gone back to her stacks of books and notes.

"Where's the map?" asked Dod in a discrete voice, glancing at the room's open door.

Buck was the only one who heard, and he shrugged his shoulders.

"Dilly," said Dod, approaching the quarreling twosome. "Where's the map?"

"Which one?" she asked, tugging Concealio's journal from Boot's hands. "I didn't notice a map in here."

"Map to The Lost City," whispered Dod, bending down.

"Why?" asked Boot.

"I've got a bad feeling," he said, still trying to decipher what exactly was bothering him. Perhaps it was the thought of Sirlonk having stolen pages from the journal, just as he had stolen Pap's and Humberrone's volumes.

Together, the group rushed to the small guest room Dilly and Sawny had been given.

The door was ajar. Dod's heart sank.

"My bag!" exclaimed Sawny, following tightly on Dilly's heels. "I left it next to yours on the bed. Where is it?"

"Probably on the floor," said Dilly.

"Was the map inside?" exploded Dod, fearing the worst. Important things had a tendency of disappearing, as the TCC pack had back in Green Hall.

Sawny shook her head and closed the bedroom door. "I took precautions," she said, climbing on the skinny nightstand that was crammed between the bed and the wall. She reached up and carefully retrieved a painting, gently flipped it over on the bed, and popped the backing off.

A chorus of sighs followed. The map had remained safe, hidden between the wooden back of the frame and the painting.

Boot snatched the leather and rolled it up. "We've got to keep this safe," he said, clutching it as if his life depended upon it. "If someone's been rooting through your things, he's probably looking for this."

"What things?" smiled Dilly. "We hardly have anything to root through. You had us pack light, and what little we brought was mostly left in the mountains when the billies came. If Commendus hadn't given us clothing, this place would be empty."

"But my bag's missing," said Sawny with alarm, easily covering the entire room with her eyes. The quarters were much smaller than the type the girls were accustomed to being given; however, since the Global Business Convention had filled Commendus's mansion to overflowing, they were lucky to have been given a place at all. Boot, Buck, and Dod had been relegated to sleeping on the floor of a spacious broom closet.

"We can't be too careful," said Boot, tying the map's straps.

"At Commendus's house?" chuckled Dilly in disbelief. "I honestly doubt anyone's been in here. Who would dare—"

"The Dread," said Dod flatly. "He's got friends everywhere. Don't forget, Pap was poisoned within these walls."

Boot nodded and looked away.

"And whoever sent the billies after us must know we're here," continued Dod. "We've got to watch out."

Sawny cringed, then bent down and checked beneath the bed. "We're not safe anywhere, are we?" she lamented, her face turning young with concern. "The Order's growing. Who knows how many people are working for them?" She looked at Dilly with pleading eyes. "Maybe we should go home to Terraboom and forget about this stuff—at least until Sirlonk's apprehended and punished."

"Sawny!" said Dilly. "We can't!" She looked only a year or two older than Sawny, but was her senior by more than five and had an unconquerable spirit that reveled in the thoughts of real action.

"What about The Order—" began Sawny.

"We'll be sailing with Traygof soon enough," assured Dilly. "You can't get much safer than that."

Mention of boarding with Traygof and his men brought a smile to Boot's face, though Sawny's remained apprehensive.

"Don't worry. I'll protect you," said Boot. "And I'll keep this for now," he added, waving the map. "If people want it, they can face me! I'm not afraid." He puffed his chest and stuffed the leather roll into his jacket pocket that seemed to occupy half the inner lining of the sports coat he was wearing. "See," he said, grinning at Buck, "this is why I chose the light red one."

"It's pink," teased Buck. "They probably put that huge pocket in it to hold a purse."

"I've seen Commendus wear this color," defended Boot.

"Then Commendus is a pansy!" said Buck loudly. The look in his eye suggested that he was hoping his lighthearted fun with Boot would calm Sawny's nerves.

Two stern knocks hit the door, startling Buck the most, since he was leaning against it.

Boot closed his jacket and stood boldly in front of the others as he turned the handle.

"Who's a pansy?" rumbled Con, towering like a troll in the hall. He held a large flower and was dressed in a magnificent suit.

"Whoever's busy tipping his ear into private conversations is the pansy!" responded Boot, instantly agitated.

"Are you calling *me* a pansy?" boomed Con, poising to pounce. He shifted the rare bloom to his left hand and made a fist with his right.

"I don't need to say a word," jabbed Boot. "Go look in the mirror, and see for yourself!"

Con's monstrous hand plunged at Boot but was met by the oak door slamming shut. Buck had read Boot's face and sprung into action.

BOOM! BOOM! BOOM!

"YOU'RE DEAD!" shouted Con, kicking as though he fully intended on bringing the door down. A couple of loud groans followed, assumedly from Con tending his injured hand.

"Can't you two get along?" whined Dilly, suddenly joining her sister in looking concerned. She clearly didn't want Boot to throw punches with Con and seemed to fear it was inevitable.

"Put the painting back," hurried Boot in a whisper, joining Buck and Dod in leaning against the trembling door.

Sawny scrambled to return the artwork while Dilly searched the room for anything to use in cooling Con's rage.

BOOM! BOOM! BOOM!

"COME OUT, NOW!" yelled Con.

"Boot was just kidding," tried Dod through the door. "I was hoping you'd come around. I haven't had the chance to tell you the good news…"

BOOM! BOOM! BOOM!

The pounding continued, shaking the wall with such force that the framing around the door began to crack.

"I was hoping you'd join us in sailing with Traygof," shouted Dod above the assault.

BOOM! BOOM! BOOM!

"YOU'RE DEAD THIS TIME, BOOT!"

"Don't you want to sail with us?" cried Dod, feeling frantic. The door wouldn't hold much longer.

BOOM! BOOM! BOOM!

Dust was flying everywhere as the cracks widened.

"LET'S SAIL TOGETHER," yelled Dod, "ABOARD *THE AVENGER*. YOU AND ME AND TRAYGOF."

The banging stopped momentarily.

"YOU'RE A LIAR, DOD! TRAYGOF HAS ALREADY LEFT!"

BOOM! BOOM! BOOM!

"NO, REALLY," shouted Dod. "HE'S COMING BACK! I PROMISE!"

The hall went quiet.

"Maybe Con's moved on," whispered Dilly after a few minutes.

"I doubt it," said Boot, still keeping his weight against the door. "Con won't stop until he's breached through."

"Couldn't they have given you a window room," groaned Buck. "There's no escape."

"I know," agreed Boot grinningly, seeming much less bothered. "What if there were a fire?"

"Or a big, furious ox of a person blocking the exit—" began Buck when his words were interrupted.

BOOOOM!!!!!

The hit this time was different. It was so hard that the thick latch near the handle completely broke through the wall, leaving the door helplessly ajar and Dod, Boot, and Buck rubbing their backs.

We're doomed, thought Dod. And then something miraculous happened.

"What's going on?" came a familiar voice. "Isn't that the room Dilly and Sawny are staying in?"

"Ah…" stuttered Con.

"What are you doing?" pressed another, much older voice.

"That's our cue," said Boot with a fresh grin, wiping sweat from his brow. "Lady's first." He indicated toward the door and prepared to swing it open.

Sawny tried to stay back, but Dilly swooped her arm around her and forced a joint exit.

CHAPTER SIXTEEN

Out in the hall, Bowlure and Tridacello stood inches from Con, awaiting his response. Bowlure's gigantic, furry frame leaned in Con's direction, as if he were ready to pummel Con if the answer Con gave didn't please them.

"Thank you so much, Con," said Dilly, playing a strong social game. "We really appreciate you freeing us. That door certainly had us trapped—*didn't it, Boot?*"

"Yes," agreed Boot reluctantly, emerging from the room wearing a Cheshire-cat smile.

Bowlure stepped back slowly, still eyeing Con suspiciously.

"You were stuck in your own room?" pressed Tridacello with reservation, combing his fingers through the remains of his wispy white hair. It didn't make sense. How could the lockless door jam?

"We were definitely trapped," huffed Buck, moving quickly to get out, never making eye contact with Con.

Dod smiled at Bowlure, who smiled back and gave his usual, friendly nod.

"Oh! That's what the yelling was about," said Bowlure. His tone sounded like that of a father who wasn't buying his child's excuses for coming home late. "I thought a fight was breaking out. Huh. Just stuck, you say? That's strange."

Con hid his bloody knuckles under his left hand and forced a cordial chin tip.

"Well, girls, you won't need to worry about the faulty doors anymore," continued Bowlure. "We're here to aid you in carrying your things."

Dilly and Sawny looked confused.

"All of Green Hall and most of Raul Hall have come to help with the museum—just as you requested. They're raising big tents around back, creating an encampment and command post—no room indoors with the businessmen around, right?"

Dilly began to nod, still wearing a puzzled look.

"Youk had us come," he added, casually stretching his muscular, seven-foot frame. As a driadon, Bowlure was easily twice as strong as any human or tredder of his same size.

"He wants us to keep an eye out for *trouble*," said Tridacello, patting his sword and turning his attention on Dod. "He told us about your little encounter in the woods."

"Right," said Dod, straining to read Tridacello's intentions. Tridacello's face gave mixed signals. Was he sent to help protect Dod and his friends, or watch Dod, the trouble maker? It was unclear.

Bowlure broke the brief silence. "We're all glad you survived."

"Me too," agreed Dod, feeling relieved. "There's a real mess brewing with the billies."

"I'd say!" huffed Tridacello with disgust. He shifted gingerly and leaned his weight on a planter box. "I'm getting too old for this kind of thing. Billies on land? What's next?"

"I'm sure Dod knows," said Bowlure confidently, hinting at his past conversations with Dod about being psychic and aided by a swapper.

Dod held his breath. He hoped Bowlure wouldn't lead into the story of when Dod had sensed the flutters coming, since that beginning always led to Bowlure's discussion of swappers and Tridacello's ramblings of the day he had found Dod on the streets, penniless, a sad orphan. It was *that* story that Clair had heard from Tridacello and been wrongly influenced by, because it didn't fit with Dod being Pap's grandson, as Dod had so often declared.

CHAPTER SIXTEEN

"Boingy-boing!" called Dari, trotting up the hall in a bright yellow sundress. Sammywoo skipped behind her happily.

Dod sighed. He knew her arrival would change the conversation in a hurry.

"What happened here?" asked Dari, surveying the mess with raised eyebrows. She flipped her shoulder-length, straight blond hair back and forth with her hand.

"They were locked in their room," offered Bowlure, scratching at his clean-shaven face. "Strange, isn't it?"

Dari looked at Con, then Boot, then Con again. "Were you two fighting?" she asked.

"No!" snapped Con. "Does Boot look dead to you?"

Boot yawned like a lion, as if to say he couldn't possibly be less intimidated if he were being pestered by a clutch of newly-hatched chicks.

"*Well-o*," prodded Dari, kicking at the debris on the floor—Con had used a large, heavy planter-pot for the last blow. "If *this-o* isn't from a *fight-o*, than I'm chewing my *cud-y-cud* like a *cow-wow*!"

"The barn's that way, bovine!" growled Con, pointing in the direction from where she had come. "Try not to soil the halls on your way out. They're freshly scrubbed."

"You're mean!" responded Dari, frowning at Con.

"What happened to your...your hand?" asked Sammywoo, his young, innocent eyes glued to Con's bloody knuckles that were now exposed.

"You must excuse me," rushed Con snobbishly, stumbling as he hurried off. Dod could see how Con was his father's son.

"I knew it!" gloated Dari, watching him disappear around the distant corner.

"Where's this encampment?" asked Dilly, quick to change the subject. If she could keep Con from getting in trouble, he was more likely to forget about the incident and, more importantly, less likely to retaliate against Boot.

Behind Commendus's palace and a short distance from his back patios, members of Green Hall worked to set up giant tents Commendus had provided as a consolation for having his home too full to offer them bunking arrangements. Sawb and his associates sat back in the shade of towering trees and watched as Sawb's band of private tredder soldiers attended to Raul Hall's setup duties. Even though The Beast had been killed, Sawb kept the small militia at his command and rarely journeyed without them.

"See," said Dari, leading the way empty-handed. "We're staying over there." She pointed proudly at the temporary structures. Everyone else followed with armloads of clothes and things, having emptied Dilly's and Sawny's room first, then the boys' broom closet.

"It's fun to camp!" chanted Sammywoo, waving one of Dilly's sweaters in the air as he descended the patio stairs. It looked like he was announcing their arrival. "Dari likes bugs, but Valerie hates them."

"Yup," chirped Dari, bouncing along with unbounded energy.

"Oh, bugs are nice," said Dilly, pulling a motherly face for Sammywoo.

At the mention of pests, Dod was glad that the rear of Commendus's estate was significantly less infested with bugs than his lake-front fields and forests. Upon arriving the few days prior, Dod had pitied the poor soldiers standing guard by the water, not just because of their proximity to the giant snakes, but because of their proximity to the swarms of insects.

"And I hate mean guys!" added Sammywoo, scowling.

Dod looked at Boot, who grinned ear-to-ear as he watched Dilly interact with the boy.

"And sick people are gross!" jabbered Sammywoo. "If they do that one thing—you know—I want to puke." He made garbled noises with his nose plugged.

"Right," sighed Dilly. "How gross is that!"

"But worms are so cool! They squiggle around like this—" Sammywoo twisted his body as he turned in a circle at the base of the stairs. "We have lots of worms. Rot plays with worms and birds and plants and dirt—lots of dirt. My mom hates it when he makes the floor muddy with dirt. He's the messy man all right. It's his job to be messy."

"Oh," said Sawny, trying to nudge her way into the conversation. "Decaying materials help plants grow but can be tricky, too—they're more difficult to extract from household fibers than sand or small pebbles, especially when commingled with water—" Sawny looked uncomfortable.

Dari broke out laughing.

Sammywoo stared at Sawny with clueless eyes.

"Sawny's right," said Dilly in a higher voice than usual. It was her special voice she exclusively reserved for explaining things to kids and small animals. "Mud's hard to clean up, isn't it?"

Sammywoo nodded.

Once the group reached the grass, Sneaker jumped off Boot's shoulder and scurried around playfully. He was obviously glad to be let out of the closet.

STUCK

Dod looked over his shoulder at Bowlure and Tridacello, who brought up the rear. "Where's Bonboo's tent?" he asked.

"I don't think he'll be joining us down here," said Bowlure. "He's the Chief Noble Tredder. I'm sure Commendus has special accommodations for him inside."

"Oh, right," said Dod. It wasn't what he wanted to hear. He appreciated that Bonboo had put his life on the line for him and had secured his temporary freedom, but Dod still needed to talk with him. Too many questions were surfacing, the kind only Bonboo would know how to answer, and since returning to Green, Dod had only been near him twice: once briefly at the dance when Dod had given him the Farmer's Sackload and again in Commendus's Banquet Hall from five seats away, when Bonboo had been discussing matters with Youk, Traygof, and Commendus.

"You've found your friend," called Dilly to Sneaker.

"I like the black one the best," said Sammywoo. "He's bigger than the white one because he eats his oatmeal all gone. Right Dilly?"

"Eating your oatmeal is important," said Dilly, holding back laughter.

Sneaker and Thunder chased each other like two squirrels in a park until Thunder retreated into a crowd of Raul Coosings. At that point, Sneaker turned up his tail, as if unwilling to associate with such persons, and promptly returned to Boot's shoulder.

"Thanks for coming," said Dilly to Sawb and his crowd, passing near Raul Hall territory on her way to Green Hall's tents.

"It was either this or be stuck with a week of cleaning Twistyard," grumbled Joak, resting lazily against an ancient tree.

"Oh! It's this week, isn't it?" remembered Dilly.

CHAPTER SIXTEEN

Once a year, Twistyard was given a thorough scrub—every inch of stone was washed, and the metals were shined until copper looked like gold, and the drapes and rugs and counter cloths were rinsed and dried. It was a massive project where everyone was expected to participate.

"Don't work us too hard at the museum or we may be unable to entertain guests next week," said Sawb, grinning slyly at Dilly.

"That would be a pity," said Eluxa sarcastically, fixing her shiny-red lipstick. "I'm *desperately* looking forward to Dilly and Sawny joining us for the Ghoul's Festival."

"Don't worry," assured Dilly. "We won't miss it. Even Dod's been approved."

Sawb blinked. "Dod's allowed to leave Green?" he choked. "Since when? Clair said he couldn't!"

"Well, Mr. Clair's wrong," said Dilly happily, continuing past the crowd. "Commendus worked things out. Thanks for the invite."

Dod smiled and waved as he followed, enjoying the look of shock on Sawb's face.

Upon entering Green Hall's camp, the last person Dod expected to see was the first person to greet him.

"Finally!" grumbled Ingrid, thumping toward Dod with her weight on her cane. "Tell these people I need a tent set up for me and Juny. I insist on helping with the restoration. I'm skilled at fixing things. Look at this purse!" She held out a tattered bag that would have been a thrift-store throwaway. "I took this clutch from the brink of death and brought it back to its original glory. Behold it now! No matter how hard you search, you can't find a better one in any of those stuffy stores on the Pearl Strip here in

High Gate. I'm an expert at restorations. I know just what that museum needs: a new coat of paint! Perhaps yellow."

Sawny was preoccupied with greeting Pone and Sham, fifteen feet away, but when her ears caught Ingrid's words, she instantly turned around, eyes wide open. 'TELL HER NO!' mouthed Sawny to Dod, looking worried that Ingrid's 'help' would be disastrous.

"I think we have things covered," said Dod.

"Hardly!" blared Ingrid, moving in closer. Her double chin wiggled with her shaking head, like a mask that had begun to dislodge. "Have you seen the place? It's a mess! Some of the posts are a beautiful brown, while others are covered with a tacky burgundy slop. Who would paint posts burgundy?"

Dod grinned. Watching Sawny silently shout and scream behind Ingrid's back was funny, and the devil horns Pone kept holding up behind Sawny's head made it even more amusing.

"Trust me," Ingrid insisted loudly, spitting a little on Dod's face. "You need my help. I'm indisparable...I mean, indiserrenible...or no...let's see...indispensable."

Dod was grateful she hadn't eaten any garlic stew lately; her breath was tolerable for once, making it possible for him to keep seeing Sawny's reactions, despite Ingrid's close proximity.

"Maybe you could protect our camp," suggested Dod. "Besides, I bet Juny would rather remain here at the palace."

"She can stay if she wants," said Ingrid. "I trust Commendus's tredder security guards to keep her out of trouble. They're babysitting her right now."

"She's not with you?"

"No," said Ingrid, scratching at her limp, sagging curls. "I haven't seen her since I left for Lower Janice. I've been too busy attending to Higga's affairs. But yesterday, at the *Global Business Convention*..." Ingrid paused briefly and looked at Dod with eyes that pressed for him to respond.

"Wow!" said Dod. "The Global Business Convention! You're everywhere these days."

"I'm indispensable," she said arrogantly, attempting to straighten her back and prop her shoulders up. However, her efforts were thwarted by her knee that wouldn't behave, which unfortunate condition caused her to stagger forward. She only avoided a complete collapse by pouring her weight onto Dod, which nearly brought him down.

"Eeew!" came a shout from a nearby tree. Sammywoo was perched on a low branch, watching Dod's every move. "Stop dancing! That's gross! NO KISSING!"

Ingrid's squishy cheek pressed upon Dod's forehead, and when she used her cane for support and drew back, an embarrassing smudge of smelly makeup remained. Dod could feel it caked on. The whole situation was uncomfortable. Dod shifted his armload of clothes and searched for anything he could use to wipe his brow.

"NO KISSING!" yelled Sammywoo again, smiling proudly.

Dod glanced toward Sawny and saw she was giggling, and Pone and Sham were doubled over in hard laughter.

"As I was saying," continued Ingrid, undeterred by the hecklers. "While visiting the Global Business Convention, I bumped into Bonmoob and had a nice chat. He said Juny would be arriving today by carriage under supervision. Terro has requested she join Raul Hall in attending the Ghoul's Festival, and she has accepted."

"Really?"

"Naturally, I'll need to accompany her."

"How does she dare return to Raul?" asked Dod, remembering that he had heard of people who wouldn't hesitate killing her to satisfy Jungo for the wrongs Sirlonk had done in Raul.

"It's a costume party," sniffed Ingrid, rubbing her nose. "She'll blend in." She turned away momentarily, hid her head, and rumbled into her handkerchief. "Besides," she added, holding her hand to her brow, "it's not everyday that you get invited by Terro to the Ghoul's Festival. I bet you'd go if he invited you—" Ingrid paused, then looked squarely at Dod. "Wait! I heard you were locked up for murder."

"I was—" choked Dod.

"Ludicrous!" ranted Ingrid. "You're innocent, aren't you?"
Dod nodded.

"Simply ludicrous!" she wailed. She swung her thick, wooden cane in the air and smacked the ground firmly. It reminded Dod of the times she had used it to chase off soldiers.

"When will those pathetic drats believe you're not trouble?" she boomed. "You skewered The Beast, discovered its babies, and fought with Dark Hood. What more can they ask for? And what are *they* doing? Nothing! They're sitting around at Twistyard, waiting for me to feed them stew. It makes me furious! Where's their gratitude?" Ingrid staggered and took a step.

"I know," said Dod. "It's frustrating. But Bonboo and Commendus are helping me get things worked out."

"Good," huffed Ingrid. "They better!"

"I'll be fine. Don't worry," offered Dod.

Ingrid swayed. "I must sit. Please get my tent situated. We've got work to do on the museum before I leave for Raul. I haven't got long. I insist we get started right away!"

"Relax. Everything's already planned," said Dod, watching Sawny make begging hand signals. "Enjoy yourself while you're here."

"Don't be ridiculous!" blurted Ingrid. "My family's been attached to the Code of the Kings for generations. My dear kinsman was part of the ceremonies they had—he was one of the twenty-four men." Ingrid looked at Dod, then down at her worn dress and cheap necklace. "I may be a joke to you—" she began, tearing up.

"It's not like that," burst Dod, feeling like he had just uninvited her to an upcoming dance.

"I know what people say," sighed Ingrid sadly. She dabbed at her eyes with her handkerchief.

"Not me!" blurted Dod. "I enjoy having you around."

"Really?" pressed Ingrid, her face eager to believe him.

Dod nodded.

"Then let me help with the Code of the Kings Monument," she begged. "It's part of my heritage."

Dilly now joined Sawny in shaking her head. 'TELL HER NO!' mouthed Dilly, as if Sawny hadn't already gotten the message across.

"Besides," said Ingrid slowly, her voice turning sly. "You may want to use this." She dug into her tattered purse and pulled out an ancient, leather-bound book. It looked older than any of the volumes Dod and his friends had been reviewing, and the cover bore a most peculiar title: Code of the Kings.

"Wow!" said Dod, truly surprised. "That's got to be hundreds of years old!" It was far from anything he would have imagined her pulling from the wreck-of-a-purse that she dangled over her shoulder. A dead, petrified cat or a year-old sandwich was more in line with his expectations, not a valuable-looking record.

Dilly and Sawny stopped jumping around and rushed over. "Where did you get that from?" asked Sawny.

"My family," gloated Ingrid, once again trying to straighten her back and shoulders. "I haven't inherited a vast estate, or a castle, or even a fancy sword, but to me, this is priceless."

"Right," said Dod, reaching for the book.

SMACK!

Ingrid nailed Dod in the shins with her cane and shook her head disapprovingly. "It's mine!" she insisted. "Once we're at the Code of the Kings Monument, I may feel inclined to let you have a peek. The things written in here are too amazing to be viewed at a time like *this*."

Dod's eyes were watering as he stepped back. He couldn't see the book anymore, let alone the words or pictures inside; and he was wishing his impairment had come from her breath, as it had in times past, for at least then he hadn't been left with sore shins. However, through his pain and tears he found himself smiling: Ingrid was a perfect match for Traygof.

"It's nice to see you've come to be part of the restoration," said Dilly, changing songs in an instant. "We were just discussing visiting the museum this afternoon—of course not all of Green Hall—only those of us who are *supervising* the effort. I hope you'll be able to join us."

Dod wiped at his eyes and watched as Dilly and Sawny filled with envy. They had taken Ingrid's bait and were stuck with a new partner.

"That's why I'm here," said Ingrid, sliding her priceless possession back into her ratty bag. "I'll be ready to go after lunch—and after someone gets me a tent!"

Toos jogged across the grass from the patio and approached Ingrid, his hair slicked to his head and his important-man smile turned on high. "She's inside with Sabbella," he panted, readjusting a large bag that he carried on his shoulder. "Her things are right here. Where's your tent?"

"Where indeed?" asked Ingrid, turning back toward Dod.

"It's over here," said Buck, who had slipped up behind Dilly and Sawny while they were gawking at the Code of the Kings book.

Toos took a deep breath and shifted the large bag once more. It seemed he was struggling to hold it.

"Let me help you," insisted Buck, reaching for Toos's load. "I'll show you the way."

SMACK!

Ingrid clocked Buck in the shins just as she had done to Dod. "Manners!" she blared. "First you ask, then you wait! Don't go grabbing other people's things!"

Dod chuckled. "Manners?" he mumbled under his breath, hurrying off to the tent he had seen Boot enter. "Since when is it polite to hit people?"

PUSHING TROUBLE

D od entered the large tent lugging the clothes Commendus
had given him and was surprised at how nice the interior
was. The boys from Green Hall were busy situating fold-out
beds, tables, chairs, and even what appeared to be a closet or
changing room.

"Congratulations," said Toby, rushing to meet Dod the
moment he saw him. "I knew Traygof would get things fixed
for you." He rubbed his black eye that was now a light greenish-
purple and smiled excitedly.

Dod sighed, wishing he meant things were fixed for good,
though knowing he only meant fixed enough to go to the Ghoul's
Festival.

"Let me take those," insisted Hermit, following closely in
Toby's shadow and wearing a matching shiner. He pulled the pile
of things from Dod's arms before Dod could respond.

"*Thanks*," praised Dod, smirking as he thought of how
Ingrid would be clubbing the poor Greenling senseless if she
were present.

"Boot has already put dibs on your bed for you," added Hermit, leading Dod to an empty mattress. He's got you over here, right in between him and Pone. Good luck fighting off ants."

Dod glanced down at Pone's bed and noticed an open leather pouch with cookies and apples bursting its seams. "At least I'll be able to grab a midnight snack," said Dod.

"If he'd share," laughed Toby. "But I wouldn't plan on it. You know Pone."

"Right," chuckled Dod.

The two boys stood by, watching as Dod chose his blankets and pillow from a pile on the floor.

"Did you figure things out?" stuttered Toby, sounding embarrassed.

"What?" asked Dod, turning back around.

"Did Iris help you with the map?" whispered Toby, glancing nervously over his shoulder. The two boys' eyes were wide with anticipation.

"Oh," said Dod, remembering how Boot had 'filled the pipeline' with the secret news that they were leaving for Iris's house to obtain his assistance in deciphering a map. "Well, I can't say much about it," he whispered back.

"I told you!" burst Hermit, giving Toby a shove. "Boot's serious about his secrets."

"You're right," said Dod, feeling grateful that the boys seemed to understand.

"That's true," called Boot from halfway across the tent, catching Toby and Hermit off guard. They hadn't realized that he was within earshot, since he had been on the ground busily fixing something, leaving him concealed from their view by a row of cots.

Boot rose to his feet and marched over. "If Dod were to tell you what I know," he rattled, "then I'd have to tell you what Dod knows, and then the two of you wouldn't be able to sleep for weeks!"

"Really?" asked Toby uneasily.

"Big fangs, nasty breath, an unquenchable hunger for flesh—" began Boot ominously, painting a picture that seemed to remind the boys of the night they had come face-to-face with the duresser in Green Hall. Neither of them had remained in Boot's room long enough to witness the harpoon plunging into The Beast's center. Instead, they had both fled for their lives and left the battle for Boot and the other Coosings to handle.

"You've said too much already!" interjected Dod in a serious tone, playing along with Boot. He recognized the jestful glint in Boot's eye and knew Boot was working the boys over.

"They're not Pots anymore," fought Boot. "By now they've figured it out—about the map—and the stolen egg—and what we're up against. They know we're not really going to refurbish a museum—we're on a mission to put Yark Junior in his place, before other cities are destroyed. Millions of people are depending on us—these boys know it! Look in their eyes. That's why they've worn matching red shirts—to attract *him* toward *them*. What a brave thing to offer themselves as bait."

Toby and Hermit both glanced uncomfortably at their shirts, as if they were ready to rip them off.

"Boot!" exploded Dod. "Now you've done it! They can't handle the truth! Thoughts of a horrendous, blood-sucking, bone-crunching, house-toppling, fire-breathing dragon will keep them awake tonight wondering why they agreed to this plan. It's better they not know that this is the very spot where the map clearly indicates Yark's hulking son will soon attack. Remember what Iris said?"

Boot nodded, read the boys faces, and finally broke out in laughter. "We're kidding, guys," he confessed, rapping them on the shoulders. "The only blood-sucking around here is done by the resident experts."

"The businessmen?" offered Dod.

"No. But them, too," said Boot. "I was thinking of the night bugs."

"Food's here!" called someone from just outside the tent. "Who's on serving duty?"

"We're coming," responded Hermit, smiling at Boot and Dod. He pushed Toby and together they dashed off, with Hermit remarking, "Boot's funny, isn't he?"

Within seconds, the tent had emptied as the hungry boys rushed to line up. But Boot caught hold of Dod and made him wait.

"Have you felt anything?" he asked.

"Not really," said Dod. "Well...not since earlier."

"Hmmm," mumbled Boot. He patted his jacket pocket, reassuring himself that the map was safe. "I think Con took Sawny's bag," he said. "The flower routine's getting old. He probably knocked at the door, found the room was vacant, stole her bag, then went off and discovered the map wasn't inside the bag. That's when he came back to finish searching and learned we were in his way."

"He may have," agreed Dod. "He certainly wasn't happy. But you have to admit, if he had been planning on tracking Dilly down to flirt with her—"

"I know," chuckled Boot. "We ruined his day."

Buck entered the tent and jogged over. "I'm sent to tell you to come and eat quickly. We're leaving for the museum in a few minutes."

"What about Sawb?" asked Dod, looking at Boot.

"He's not going," said Buck.

"Dod's not talking about that," corrected Boot. "We were trying to figure out who stole Sawny's bag."

"Oh," said Buck in an exasperated voice. "It could have been anyone. These days, everyone's working for The Order it seems."

"Then plan on lots of unemployment," responded Boot with conviction. "I'm taking them down, even if it's the last thing I do!"

After lunch, a carriage from Commendus's barn arrived to transport Dilly and her team to the public transit. The driver got off and presented Boot with a package, saying, "I was told you were ready for your things."

"Thanks," responded Boot, hefting the large, wooden crate. It was labeled seventy-six. He opened it up and passed Dilly, Sawny, Buck, and Dod their swords that they had had the barn hands store for them. "I think it's better to err on the side of caution," noted Boot, fastening on his sheath and weapon. "Commendus can't be offended since we're now going to be out and about where his security team isn't in question."

"Out or in, I'm ready to feel safe," muttered Buck.

Dod glanced uneasily at the towering back of the castle and had a strange feeling. The beauty and grandeur of Commendus's estate didn't instill a sense of comfort and safety. Trouble lurked. Sawny's missing bag was just the tip of the iceberg. Sirlonk had begun raising an army of beasts in the front fountain until Dod had stopped him, and Pap had been murdered alongside dozens of others while visiting the castle. What dastardly act was yet pending?

Dilly nudged Dod. "Come on," she said, pressing him to hurry. As the wagon pulled away, Dod noticed why: Dr. Shelderhig was coming across the grass with Bly at his side.

The carriage ride was brief. A short distance from Discommo Manor, just past the tent city and construction site, there was a beautiful blue building with golden spires and white columns. Hundreds of people flowed in and out of the structure. Upon entering, Dod smelled the air and was instantly reminded of High Gate's unusual mode of transportation: submarines! Flashes of memories filled his mind.

High Gate was webbed with an underground matrix of waterways through which mini-subs whizzed up and down the hills. The lines were pressurized by various lakes, as well as by a giant underground stream that flowed into High Gate from the towering Hook Mountains to the north and west. The system was ingenious.

Inside the building, Dilly led the group past hundreds of people who stood below an enormous sign that mapped various routes around High Gate. "Our dock's this way," she said, pointing directly across a stadium-sized vaulted atrium toward a massive archway. It had the number sixteen posted above it. Other entrances lined the center hub, with numbers ranging from one to twenty-six. Crowds of people flowed in every direction.

"Are we almost there?" gasped Ingrid, trying to keep up with Dilly's pace. She leaned on her cane for support and lumbered along like a three-legged bear.

"Here," offered Boot, giving her his arm. "We can go slower if you'd like." Sneaker scurried to Boot's other shoulder and scowled.

Ingrid shifted her weight and stopped to breathe. "Where do all these people come from?" she muttered, shaking her head as the flow of traffic continued on around her.

Dod looked up into the domed vault and saw brilliant stacks, like chandeliers, burning smokeless flames. They lit up the room as bright as day.

"Ma'am," called someone through the crowd. A sturdy man with a white-brimmed hat approached, pushing a three-wheeled wheelchair. "We have conveyances if you'd like, ma'am," he said, pulling a lever that slid the front wheel under the seat. Once Ingrid was situated, he popped the wheel back out.

"I can push her," offered Boot.

"Nonsense," huffed Ingrid, waving her cane dangerously. "Let the man do his job. He's a professional."

Dod and Buck traded glances and awaited Boot's entry into their sore-shin club. But Ingrid situated her cane on her lap before Boot was ever initiated.

Once in corridor sixteen, the wide stone path began to descend. Around and around it spiraled downward until it leveled off five stories below ground and connected to a considerable cave. Lines of people stood alongside a two-acre lake that currently held six bus-sized subs.

"You can take her from here," said the transit officer, handing over the responsibility of Ingrid's progress to Boot. The man brushed his hat and rushed over to where a chair-bound elderly woman was approaching the daunting climb up the tunnel with only a young boy to assist her.

"Ludicrous!" blared Ingrid. "Where is he going? I'm too heavy for *you*, Boot." She tried to rise out of her seat when

Boot grabbed the rear handles and gently tipped her backward, boosting the front wheel off the ground.

"You couldn't possibly weigh more than me, Gram," beamed Boot, rolling her back and forth. "If I had my eyes closed, I'd think I was pushing Buck around. You're a lightweight."

"Stop," said Ingrid. "I insist I walk."

"Not today," said Boot excitedly. "I've always wanted to drive one of these." He darted in and out of traffic until he reached a two-hundred-foot open spot, where he proceeded to rest one foot on the chair's rear framing while using the other to push, effectively taking them both on a wild ride.

"We don't know him," said Dilly with embarrassment, slowing her pace.

"Boys!" scoffed Sawny.

Everyone at dock sixteen stared. If they hadn't been alerted by the sight of Boot's actions, they were certainly drawn by the string of calls Boot let out.

"Wu-hu-hoo!" cried Boot, as if enjoying a waterslide. "We're comin' through!"

When he reached the end of the line, he swirled Ingrid around and raced back toward Dilly, sailing proudly aboard the three-wheeler with Sneaker perched high on his shoulder.

"Wu-hu-hoo!" shouted Boot.

"SIR!" boomed a voice from the safety station that sat high above the water's edge like a crow's nest.

Boot continued. "WU-HU-HOOOO!" he hollered happily as he picked up speed. Ingrid clung tightly to the wheelchair and her cane.

"SIR IN THE PINK JACKET!" yelled the safety worker through his megaphone-like contraption. "NO RACING!"

"He said *pink*," laughed Buck gleefully, elbowing Dod in the ribs.

The reprimand momentarily distracted Boot's attention, and by the time he looked forward, it was too late to avoid disaster. A young toddler had left her mother's side and staggered right into the open space, directly in front of the wheelchair's path, making a collision nearly unstoppable.

Boot threw his weight to one side and tipped the chair precariously off course. Its front and right wheels both left the ground, and its remaining wheel screeched angrily against the stone floor as it took the full brunt of the heavy load and veered sharply toward the water.

People scattered out of the way like sheep fleeing from a lion. The reckless contraption careened in the direction of passengers who had just disembarked, rattled down a flight of five stairs, smashed through a stack of burlap sacks, and finally came to a stop at the water's edge.

"You nearly soaked me!" blared Ingrid in a gruffer than usual voice, frantically fidgeting with her curls. "I could have died!"

"Not with me driving," said Boot proudly, turning the wheelchair around. He surveyed the path they had taken and quietly whispered under his breath, "Wu-hu-hooooo."

"Inches from my demise and you're celebrating?" grumbled Ingrid. "What kind of fool celebrates his own failures? It was my cane that kept us from the water!"

When Boot's eyes finally settled on those of the gawking crowd, especially Dilly's, he took a grand bow, then waved up at the transit worker who glared at him from the safety station.

Surprisingly, people began to clap until the patter of a few hands turned to a rumble of applause.

"You've got to be kidding!" remarked Buck to Dod, shaking his head in disbelief.

"Boot's an entertainer, isn't he?" said Dod.

Boot stepped out from behind the wheelchair and gave the crowd a second bow, only to be struck in the shins by Ingrid's cane.

"Ooooo!" cringed Buck and Dod in unison.

"We need Ingrid around more often," smiled Dilly. "Someone's got to tame that boy."

Minutes later, Dod neared the dock on the far side of the cave and awaited his first ride in a sub. Prompted by a few comments he had made, Sawny explained to him the details of how the system worked. After people were safely seated within a sub, workers sealed the entrance off with levers and used a crane to push the sub into an alcove, just beyond the loading dock. Once in place, a thick door was lowered until it completely separated the alcove from the rest of the lake. Next, an unseen gate was cranked open, joining the alcove with the neighboring tunnel of rushing water. The vessel was thereafter caught by the water and carried away.

Each line had multiple stops along its course. The sub's ability to blindly exit at the appropriate time was dependent upon a properly placed metal hook on the outside of the vessel. The sub's exterior had various spots where hooks could be attached; therefore, the vessels could be adapted to stop at any number of stations along the waterway.

"So," explained Sawny, "when we reach the Pines District, a metal loop will catch hold of our hook and automatically drag us into the proper bay, which in turn will trigger the outer wall of the tunnel to close and the inner wall to rise a little. When the water within the cave begins to ripple, men will know we've arrived and they'll crank the gate open."

"Amazing," said Dod. "Subs with no drivers."

"The pressurized pipelines do all the directing," assured Sawny, flipping a stubborn curl from her face.

"It's a foolproof system," added Dilly.

"Nothing's foolproof," said Sawny, watching Boot push Ingrid's wheelchair toward the water. "Do you remember the breach they had in the Lower Hills' line?"

Dilly turned and nodded.

"A couple hundred people had to be evacuated," said Sawny. "Of course, they managed to seal off the main room, drain the line, and fix the problem in less than three days—and without any injuries. I suppose they've thought of everything by now. Traveling by sub is much safer than by horse or carriage—that's for sure."

"Good," said Dod, following Sawny across the dock toward an open hatch. A small ramp led to the sub. As Dod boarded, no one requested tickets or money, which caught him off guard. "Who do we pay?" he asked.

"You've really never ridden before, have you?" said Dilly in shock.

Dod shook his head.

"See!" insisted Buck. "I'm not the only one who hates being held under water!"

"It's free," said Boot, helping Ingrid stow the wheelchair and take a seat on the vessel. "The businesses here in High Gate pay to keep the lines running. The more people travel, the more money changes hands."

Dilly gave Boot a raised eyebrow.

"I listened to Commendus's lecture last spring on the core points of a healthy economy," defended Boot. "Who knows, maybe one day I'll be an industrialist like Bly."

"Good for you!" praised Ingrid, seemingly having forgiven Boot of his most recent infraction. She reached behind her to tap Boot's shoulder with her cane, as though knighting him. "You can't go wrong following successful people."

Inside the sub, smokeless candles hung from the ten-foot ceiling and gave off a warm glow sufficient to read by. The seats had high backs and intricate, adjustable harnesses. No sooner had Dod begun working on securing himself to his seat than the sub door was shut firmly and the vessel began to move.

This is like a ride at Disneyland, thought Dod, feeling a wave of anxious anticipation. Within moments, the sub was in place and the chamber door was being shut. A few small windows dotted the exterior walls of the sub, making it possible for Dod to see the growing darkness outside.

"Where do we end up if all the hooks break off?" asked Dod nervously, turning to Sawny who sat calmly next to him.

"Let's see," she said, looking upward. "In a lake—either Three Stone or McCoy's."

"Oh," sighed Dod. He felt the sub begin to shake as water filled the chamber. Since the door to the lake was now shut, the windows were useless, revealing only the pitch-blackness that surrounded the vessel; it was impossible to see the rising door that had separated them from the pipeline of flowing water.

"Here it comes," said Boot excitedly, wiggling in his seat.

HWOOOSH!

The sub launched into the dark tunnel and banged against the stone walls.

Buck smiled tensely.

Dod's insides jumped. "Do these things ever break?" he asked, once more turning to Sawny.

"Occasionally," she said, hiding a grin at the corners of her mouth. "You can hold your breath for fifteen minutes, can't you? It's a basic requirement to ride."

"What?" gasped Dod. He suddenly felt claustrophobic.

"She's kidding," said Buck, who sat on the other side of Dod. "These things are built tough."

"Mean," choked Dod to Sawny.

"Not as mean as leaving someone standing alone on a dance floor," whispered Sawny.

Dod went silent. He had come to think that Sawny had forgotten about the incident but now was assured that she most certainly hadn't. Her logical brain was still waiting for answers.

The sub shook side-to-side and continued to bang against the rock walls as it sailed through a bending section of the line; however, as the slope increasingly tilted downward and the path seemed to straighten out, the noises decreased to a low rumble.

Dod picked at his fingernails and distracted his mind with thoughts of home. Sawny's mention of his tardy entry to Green sent him there. It was strange to consider that his family and loved ones on Earth were paused in time while he continued daily life in Green.

But thoughts of home quickly turned to the reality of his predicament: Ruth was expecting him to give up his medallion to Mr. Brewer. Regardless of Ruth's difficult situation, Dod knew he couldn't do it. He couldn't turn his back on his friends in

Green, and he certainly wasn't willing to give up without finding out what had happened to his father. The impressions he'd had while in Twistyard's dungeon seemed to suggest that his father truly was still alive.

Yet something nagged at Dod's mind. The note he had seen in the Las Vegas trailer—the one that had referred to him as Dod—had clearly come from Sirlonk. '*Better luck next time, Dod.*' But why would Sirlonk invite him to join The Order and then seek to have people prevent him from ever returning to Green? It was contradictory.

Dod stirred in his seat.

"Look at that," whispered Buck.

Dod craned his neck to see between the seats. Buck was pointing at a man who held the *High Gate News* with outstretched arms as he inspected the front page. The bold-print title and subtitle said it all:

STRING OF CENTRAL BANK ROBBERIES!
Ten Branches, Millions Lost in Stolen Jewels!

"Ten banks!" whispered Buck. "It sounds like The Order is raising money."

"Or a few too many businessmen came to town," responded Dod. He had seen everything over the past few days while staying at Commendus's palace and had decided that many businessmen were about on par with giant mosquitoes.

"Are you talking about me?" called Boot from four seats away, ready to start another jovial conversation. He sat up straight, adjusted his seat straps, and pulled at his suit coat.

Dod nodded teasingly.

"He was just asking me why you're wearing a girl's jacket," returned Buck loudly.

Boot scowled playfully.

"You better hold on tight," warned Sawny, interrupting Dod with a nudge. "We're about to reach *the drop*." She pushed her feet against the ground, leaned back, and braced herself.

"Oh," said Dod, not wanting to be stung a second time. "You mean I shouldn't do this?" He began unbuckling his harness.

"Stop!" insisted Sawny, grabbing for his hands. "You'll die!"

Dod worked speedily to free himself. He planned on doing a dance in the walkway to prove his bravery, and he assumed it would be harmless. After all, the sub was driverless, which meant no workers to yell at him for disregarding the warning signs.

"Don't be stupid," said Sawny, pointing to the wall. 'Keep your riggings fastened at all times!' was written in such big letters that it crossed three rows.

"She's not kidding—" began Buck when the sub took a plunge forward. It felt like a giant hand had picked up the sub and tipped it vertical. Dod's loosened straps caused him to jiggle around uncomfortably as the vessel plummeted downward.

"I told you!" said Sawny.

Dod couldn't respond. His breath was gone. The freefall was anything but expected since the sub was a public mode of transportation, not a rollercoaster ride at Six Flags. He looked sideways past Sawny and saw Dilly's big smile, then beyond to Ingrid, who clung tightly to her cane with one hand and appeared to be holding her head on with the other. Her face was wrinkled with irritation. Beyond her, Boot was smiling bigger than Dod had ever seen, firmly squishing Sneaker against his chest.

"Wu-hu-hooo!" said Boot.

Minutes later, the sub returned to a reasonable slope and conversation resumed.

"The fast parts are crazy," said Buck.

"Yeah. I'd say," agreed Dod. His shaky hands were busy tightening his riggings.

"We're not going any slower now," corrected Sawny. "It just feels slower because we're on the level. The whole system's pressurized. That's why we have to sail *below* the water—the pipeline's full."

Dod looked at Sawny excitedly. "That's it!" he said.

"What?" asked Sawny.

"We're sailing below the water in…*the below ships*!"

Sawny crinkled her brow, then lit up. "Oh!" she said, slowly nodding her head.

"Below ships?" questioned Dilly.

"We'll tell you later," insisted Sawny discretely.

"THE MAP," mouthed Dod gleefully, drenched in smugness. He was pleased with himself that he had discovered a logical explanation for part of the ancient cartographer's drawings. But no sooner had he helped Dilly to understand what they were talking about than a bad feeling crept in, as if he had just pushed trouble and awakened a sleeping dragon from its lair.

CHAPTER EIGHTEEN

SMELLING RATS

The Pines District lived up to its name. As the group emerged from the three-dock station, they were surrounded by beautiful pines. Trees lined the elegant grass strips that bordered the majestic stone buildings. The landscape had the appearance of an aged college campus. Sneaker hopped from Boot's shoulder and raced back and forth exploring.

Boot borrowed the community wheelchair to push Ingrid across the wide walkways leading to the Code of the Kings Monument. In route, a stone's throw from their destination, Dod paused in front of a stunning marble structure. The building had a massive rock balcony, high up above the ground, which overlooked the surrounding woods.

"Keep coming," ordered Ingrid from her chair. "We've got work to do."

Dod ignored her. His insides were whispering something. He tried to conjure images, but none came.

"I'm sure Pap told you all about this place," said Dilly to Dod.

"Stop the chitchatting and keep moving," fussed Ingrid.

As Buck and Boot continued on, they glanced at the building uncomfortably, as though it were a haunted house.

Sawny sighed. "They should have put a commemorative post in the front."

"What happened here?" asked Dod.

"A tragedy," said Sawny. "Two of our Coosings were murdered in there—Issin and Paulic—and it's where Horsely and Bowie were injured, too."

Flashes of a moonless night darted through Dod's mind. Swords were clashing—two men were fighting—they had just exited the building—Pap was facing off against Sirlonk.

Dilly put her arm on Dod's shoulder. "Pap bested The Dread here. He beat him in a duel—up on the balcony."

"Oh," said Dod, straining to keep the images flowing. Repeatedly, he saw a hand reaching for a small bag.

Ingrid tapped at the ground with her cane and beckoned impatiently for everyone to follow. "Here I'm willing to share my family's priceless book," she blared, "and you'd rather mull around talking hearsay! I'm wasting my time! Isn't *that* the monument we're looking for?" She pointed at a large dome-shaped structure that poked out above the trees.

"It's hardly hearsay," snapped Sawny.

"Don't get me wrong," countered Ingrid, her tone softening. "I'm sad to hear your friends died in there, but since when has a lick of proof emerged that would indicate that The Dread was ever bested by anyone's sword?" She glanced at Dod and added, "No offense to Pap."

Dod did take offense, but he kept quiet.

"Pap told me the story at least twice," said Boot boldly, leaving the rear of her chair to confront her face-to-face. "It's a fact in my book!"

"Well—" stuttered Ingrid, sounding flustered. "It's just that—it seems he couldn't have bested him if The Dread is still running around and Pap's not. The Dread's an evil genius—he's unstoppable with a sword."

Boot took deep breaths as his face reddened.

Ingrid shifted in her seat and tapped her cane against the ground. "I know plenty about The Dread," she said heatedly. "He killed all five of my brothers!"

Sawny and Dilly gasped.

"They were good swordsmen," she continued, "some of the best—but not good enough."

When Boot heard Ingrid's words, his face changed.

"I'm sorry," said Dilly, tearing up. "I didn't even know you had brothers."

Ingrid sniffed. "I hate talking about The Dread. Can't someone stop him? He's taken too much from all of us!" She pulled a handkerchief from her ratty purse and buried her face into it.

"His time's up," said Boot softly. "Pap had him down, and Dod's been a step ahead of him twice now—he sees things—"

"But The Dread's so cunning," wailed Ingrid, sobbing into her cloth. "Whatever he wants, he takes…he took all five of my brothers…and for what?" Ingrid peered out from her handkerchief with angry eyes. "A stupid map to the fabled Lost City! Can you believe that?"

Dod and Boot traded awkward glances.

"The Lost City is little more than a bedtime tale," continued Ingrid, "and yet he killed my brothers so he could take our family map—the one that goes with this book." She held up her ratty bag that contained the Code of the Kings manuscript. "The map isn't worth anything to anyone but my family. It just describes the location of my early ancestors' original settlement, here below the mountains, and *they* certainly didn't have gold!"

"Oh," heaved Buck sadly.

Sneaker hopped onto Ingrid's lap and sniffed at her.

"Can't you control your pet?" fussed Ingrid, punishing Boot with her eyes once Sneaker had dodged her cane.

"Come on, boy," ordered Boot, scooping the ferret from the ground as it rushed for a second try at Ingrid's lap. "Don't bother Gram."

"That thing's gonna go for your throat one of these days," muttered Ingrid. "You should get rid of it. Weasels are dangerous!"

"He's a ferret," corrected Boot, still trying to calm Sneaker. "And as strange as it may sound, Gram, this ferret's your best defense against The Dread and his friends."

Ingrid shook her head and displayed her cane.

"Really," continued Boot. "I'm serious. He let us know when The Beast was coming—and you should have seen him the night the billies were on their way in search of...." Boot's voice trailed off.

"Billies?" said Ingrid, turning an inquisitive eye. "Here on land? What did they want?"

"We'll tell you about it sometime," hurried Dilly, moving quickly to lead the group. She changed the conversation and marched up the path to the Code of the Kings Monument.

Dod gazed at the beautiful structure. Its architecture bore signs of two generations of construction. Half the building was made of dark, roughhewn stones and the other half was adorned with lighter, smooth stones. At the front of the building, a circular tower rose fifty feet above the rest of the edifice with a giant bell situated to one side of the covered patio that crowned the top of the tower. At ground level, pointed arches framed the double-door entrances that recurred every fifty feet. The monument reminded Dod of a large cathedral, perhaps capable of holding one to two thousand people.

"There's a fix we need to include," noted Dod, pointing at the bell. It looked like someone had frozen it midair at its farthest upward point while ringing.

Sawny laughed.

"That's the security signal," said Dilly. "All of the old guard towers used to have them. See the rope? It runs down a shaft to the main level. If the locals were ever attacked, they could simply cut the line, and the bell would call neighboring swords to come to their aid."

Dod strained his eyes to see the cord that kept the bell suspended.

"If they've still got *that*," said Buck in a hopeful voice, "someone's already been working on preserving this place. There's probably not a lot left to do."

"Hardly," grumbled Ingrid, slouching in her chair. "Everyone can see all the things that need to be done! Just look at those ugly brown doors. They'd be half acceptable if they had a coat of white paint!"

With her back to Ingrid, Sawny gave Dod and Dilly raised-eyebrow glances.

"Commendus wants it authentic," said Dilly matter-of-factly. "Come along. I've got the keys. Let's see the inside."

Anxiety crept over Dod. He instinctively scratched at his upper chest, reassuring himself that his medallion and keys were safe.

"Are you getting a rash, too?" asked Ingrid, watching Dod with pensive eyes.

"No. I'm fine," said Dod uncomfortably, glancing around in search of Sneaker. The ferret had taken the lead in racing toward the building and was now out of sight.

Once the doors were opened, Dilly gasped and halted at the entrance. Four stone columns had fallen to the ground, leaving benches crushed and a row of rafters dangling in disarray.

Dod's heart leapt into his throat. Momentarily, he saw glimpses of men fighting—jumping back and forth in the hall—and one man held Sirlonk's crimson blade.

"What is it?" asked Ingrid eagerly, stuck behind Dilly, Sawny, Dod, and Buck.

"The place is breaking down," answered Buck. "It's not safe to go inside."

"That's what hundreds of years will do to a building," said Boot, nudging his way forward.

"No!" insisted Dilly, putting a hand on her sword. "Sawny and I came here last year with our dad. Someone's done this."

"Not today," noted Boot, wiping dust from the back of the door handle.

"The Order's involved," choked Dod, hearing a tumult of noise. "They're looking for something—or fighting over something…" He strained to understand the pictures and impressions that swirled in his head, and just as suddenly as they had come, they vanished.

SMELLING RATS

"Who's fighting?" begged Ingrid keenly, leaning on her cane to rise. "I can't see. Help me, Boot."

"It's nothing, Gram," responded Boot, exiting the building to give her an arm.

The hall was filled with long oak benches, like a chapel, and had brown and burgundy support posts. The pillars that had fallen were toward the center of the room, leaving the rest of the area untouched.

"What a mess!" blared Ingrid as soon as she had pushed her way in front of the others. "I'm mortified! What senseless vandalism! My grandfather's bones are shaking in the ground over this! How disgraceful! Who would allow the grandeur of such an important building to be tarnished as we now see it! I'm…well…speechless!"

The group gingerly inched into the chamber and smelled the musky air. Most of the building looked well preserved. The front was benchless and raised up a few feet—a half-circle stone stage—with a podium on the side closest to the edge, right in the center. Near the ceiling, seventy feet up, large stacks hung like elegant chandeliers, awaiting a crowd worthy of the work it would take to light them. On the walls, high above the ground, spacious windows lined the hall, providing plenty of light for daytime gatherings.

"At least the words are preserved," mumbled Ingrid, thumping her way toward the front of the room.

"Do you think it's safe?" called Buck, hanging back at the entrance.

Ingrid looked at the fallen pillars, nodded her head, then continued her course to the front, just below the stage. "KEEP EACH HIS KINGDOM STRONG FOR SUBJECTS

FIRST, THEN RULERS, BY THE UNITED WILL OF ALL MANKIND!" she roared. Her voice echoed in the empty hall and matched the large letters that were penned on the wall in bright red.

"FREEDOM! FREEDOM! FREEDOM!" yelled Boot, startling Dod who stood beside him.

Dilly and Sawny spun to face Boot with curious glances.

"Well said," called Ingrid as she took a seat on the front bench.

"I read the ceremony, too," remarked Boot.

Dilly smiled approvingly. "Keep it in mind. Concealio and his progenitors were good people, not criminals."

"That's what they've written," grinned Boot.

"It's true," said Dilly, pointing at the stage. "The twenty-four men who originally sat up there were honorable. They weren't seeking for power or glory, just freedom."

"Of course," said Boot thoughtfully. "They couldn't have ever been motivated by anything less than perfect intentions. After all, you're a descendant of one of them."

"As am I," added Sawny happily. Both sisters looked pleased with their heritage.

"And don't forget about Ingrid," said Boot, smirking broadly. "She's a descendant of one of the founders, too. Perhaps the same man."

Dilly gave Boot a shove and whispered in his ear.

"I wouldn't mind having tenacious children," he responded playfully. "Perhaps they'd get a chance to sail the seas with Traygof's stout brood he intends on raising with your cousin."

Dilly shoved him harder, this time sending him retreating behind Dod.

"Don't look at me," whispered Dod as Dilly approached. "She's not *my* cousin."

Ingrid let out a shrill cry, turning all eyes on her. The woman was swinging her cane viciously at something.

Boot and Dod rushed to her, followed closely by Dilly. Buck and Sawny lingered back, watching intently.

"RATS!" Ingrid screeched. "The floor's crawling with them!"

But by the time Dod arrived, there was only one, and it was being carried off by Sneaker.

"Don't worry," assured Boot. "We've got it covered." He scooped Sneaker from the floor and proudly displayed the rat that his pet had just killed. Its body was fatter than Sneaker's, and its yellow front teeth protruded out like a small beaver's.

"I hate rats!" said Sawny the moment she drew close enough to get a glimpse of the carcass.

"At least they're not raining down on us," said Buck. "That one would wake someone up, now wouldn't it?"

"They're all over!" whined Ingrid, fidgeting on her seat restlessly.

"Sneaker'll get 'em," assured Boot, sending his pet back to hunting. He took the fat rat and threw it out the double doors into the bushes before returning to his friends. "I'd like to see Thunder try to catch one," gloated Boot.

"Where did they go?" asked Sawny timidly.

"I don't know," said Ingrid, peering down at the floor.

Boot hopped up the two-foot ledge onto the stage and began investigating behind the podium.

"Can we look at your book, now?" asked Dilly, sitting down beside Ingrid.

"I suppose," she responded reluctantly. She reached into her purse and pulled the family heirloom out. Sawny rushed to her other side while Buck and Dod stood behind where she sat.

The small leather-bound book was so worn that parts of the cover were rubbed a grayish-white, and the thick pages on the inside were yellowed to the extent that they nearly crumbled as Ingrid carefully turned them. The content looked similar to Concealio's diary. Most of the pages had sketches and brief notes. In total, there were only twenty-two pages, each as thick as seven or eight regular pieces of paper.

"Look at this," she said, flipping carefully back to the first page. There was a drawing of a stage, and on the wall behind it, the same words which were penned in red on the wall before them. "This is how it looked in the beginning," she said, lifting the book up so Dod could easily see it. "What do you think?"

Dilly rose to her knees on the bench to follow the book.

"That's interesting," said Dod, glancing at the concise text below the drawing. It listed the responsibilities of a king, including the importance of directing education, fostering business, providing social gatherings, facilitating the creation of laws, and so forth.

"They had a stepping box beside the podium," said Dilly, quickly catching what Dod's eyes hadn't noticed.

"Oh yes," said Ingrid. "My father told me the three kings would start their meetings out by standing on the box, side-by-side, their scepters in hand, and would lead the other twenty-one men in reciting the purpose of the code, just as it's written on the wall today..."

"And then they'd each declare a cry of freedom," added Sawny, letting Ingrid know she, too, was familiar with the tales.

"Yes," said Ingrid, turning to Sawny. "Do you know what they did next?"

Sawny nodded, facing Ingrid's challenging eyes. "They posted their scepters, waved their respective men to stow their swords in the ground, and finally took their seats right up there—in three grand chairs that no longer exist. As far as I have been able to discover, someone removed the thrones at about the same time that the oak plaque was added. It must have been when Concealio remodeled this hall."

Ingrid stared at Sawny as if she had just stolen her precious book.

"The question is," continued Sawny, furrowing her brow, "why did Concealio remove the thrones? Everything else he did was adding to the original building, not changing what had been built before. He even left the bell in the guard tower."

Ingrid flipped a few pages to a sketch of three elaborately-decorated chairs, the center one being taller than the other two.

"Perhaps Concealio wasn't the only person who wanted to sit in the special seat," said Buck, answering Sawny's question.

"No, I don't think so," said Sawny. "Concealio was alone in trying to reestablish the Code of the Kings. The whole organization had long since fallen apart. No one was challenging him for the lead throne. Why remove the seats?"

"They might have been stolen," offered Dilly.

"But he'd have replaced them," countered Sawny.

Boot poked his head out from behind the podium. "Freedom," he said, pointing at the plaque. "For him it was a matter of principle. Once Concealio began his quest to reorganize the previous group, he realized that liberty for all was out of reach so long as the kings sat over there on their *special seats* and the other representatives knelt on the stone floor by their swords."

Boot's words rang true in Dod's ears. The sign on the wall clearly agreed with his line of thinking. Directly behind where the three thrones had been, a plaque now read the following:

Each – To his own – For all
With every man's scepter in hand
The pure truth at long last will stand
And all will know of that which lies hidden
Releasing the door of things forbidden

Dod read the words quietly to himself. Democracy could have been Concealio's design. It made sense.

Boot hopped off the stage and begged Ingrid's cane from her. "I'll give it right back," he insisted, returning to where he had been.

"May I see the book?" asked Sawny, reaching for Ingrid's heirloom.

"No!" snapped Ingrid. "Don't touch it!"

Ingrid carefully turned the pages and displayed the drawings. Dod's favorite was a sketch that seemed to show a man being knighted—he was kneeling upon the ground, sword down, bowing his head before a king. Another fascinating one was of three men entering a mini-sub. It made Dod wonder how old the waterways were. Perhaps Ingrid's book was younger than she thought.

"DON'T DO THAT!" shouted Ingrid, jumping to her feet faster than Dod had ever seen her move. "GIVE ME BACK MY CANE!"

Boot looked up sheepishly. He had been about to stuff the end of Ingrid's staff into a hole on the floor, directly behind the podium. "I won't let go," protested Boot. "I just want to see how far down this goes."

"NO!" shouted Ingrid, miraculously climbing onto the stage in record time, her Code of the Kings book still in hand. She grabbed her stick from Boot and scowled. "I've had this cane for over thirty years," she huffed, sounding winded from her unbelievable feat. "I'm not about to watch you drop it down some rat-infested hole."

"That's where the kings posted their scepters," said Sawny, following Dod and Dilly onto the stage. She inspected the three holes on the floor beside Boot and then looked at Ingrid as though she should change her mind and allow them to prod with her cane.

"It's *NO* to you, too," bellowed Ingrid. "Things may not be all that you think. Trust me."

Dod walked the floor where the representatives had sat in council and marveled at the intricate carvings beside each of the slits where the men had stowed their swords.

"If you were a representative," asked Boot, strolling behind Dod, "where would you sit—which symbol would you choose?"

Dod quickly took a few steps back to where a winged lion was chiseled into the stone.

"Funny," chuckled Boot. "That's the one I'd choose." He proceeded to draw his sword and bent down on one knee, preparing to slide his rapier into the slit, just as the men of so long ago had done."

"STOP! STOP, YOU FOOL!" raged Ingrid, rushing to Boot. She tipped her cane swiftly and nudged Boot's sword off course, insisting with her actions as well as her words that she most certainly didn't think it was proper to be poking or prodding anything in the monument.

"Boosap," coughed Buck, watching the scene from the front bench.

Boot knocked the stone floor twice in agreement and sheathed his sword.

"You boys are rash," insisted Ingrid, looking rattled in the head. "I'm too old to be babysitting. We were commissioned by Commendus to make this place better, not destroy it."

"Someone's already beaten us to that job," responded Boot, bouncing to his feet. He left the stage and hopped benches until he reached the center of the room where the pillars had collapsed.

"Not too close," called Dilly, her voice echoing. "We can have Commendus's builders work on that part. The rafters could come down on you."

"He's brainless as a guppy," huffed Ingrid, leaning on her cane as she hobbled to the short stairway off the stage.

Dod glanced at Sawny who was on her knees, by the posting holes, sliding her hands across the stone floor. It looked like she was searching in the dark for a lost ring.

"We should go," fussed Dilly, watching Boot with her face full of concern. "Commendus didn't expect us to find wreckage."

"Or rats!" mumbled Ingrid.

The late afternoon sun crawled out from behind a cloud and shone through the western windows, painting the front of the hall with light. The large red letters sparkled, and the polish on the plaque shined so brightly that the mysterious words it contained disappeared into the midst of a rectangular burst of light, as if a magical door had been opened and was calling Dod to walk through it.

"The door of things forbidden," whispered Dod, tingling with excitement. He rushed to the plaque and searched its edges for anything peculiar—a knob or rut—anything that could unlatch the secret door. But cold stone blocks and mortar met his probing fingers as they explored the wall around the sign. The gleaming door was as much a mirage as the pools of water which always seemed to spill across the roads near Las Vegas in the afternoon sun.

Dod turned and was startled to find Ingrid beside him.

"What are you doing?" she asked.

"Nothing," said Dod, shuffling sideways until his shadow cloaked the center of the plaque.

"Come on," whispered Ingrid. "I shared my family's book with you. What have you found?"

Dod felt uncomfortable. "I just thought this looked like a door," he confessed timidly, bracing himself for Ingrid's ridicule.

"Huh," mumbled Ingrid. "What made you think that?"

Dod stepped back out of the way so the plaque was once more fully on fire with brilliant light. "Doesn't it look like a magical door?"

"Interesting," said Ingrid. "You're a smart boy. I've been here dozens of times in my life and I've never noticed that before. What a fascinating find." She took her cane and tapped at the wood. "If it's a door, it's the thickest door I've ever encountered."

"Right," sighed Dod. "It was a stupid thought."

"No, no," whispered Ingrid, moving in so close to Dod that spit found its way onto his face. "My dad always said there was something special about this place—something unusual—something *hidden*. Wouldn't it be great if it were a chest of gold? We could split it—just the two of us. How about that? If you find something, share it with me, and I'll do the same with you."

Stepping back, Dod began to chuckle. "If you're looking for a chest of gold, I think I know someone you should meet."

"Who?" pressed Ingrid excitedly, her voice no longer a whisper.

Dilly was following Sawny off the stage and beckoned for Dod and Ingrid to exit with them.

"Traygof," said Dod. "I met him at Commendus's palace. He's invited me to sail with him."

"*The* Traygof?"

"The one and only," said Dod, standing a little taller. The more he saw how people idolized Traygof, the more he realized what a privilege it was to be invited to join the legend aboard his ship.

"*You* are going to sail with *him*?" stuttered Ingrid, leaning more on her cane than usual.

"Yup," said Dod happily. "And I told him about you. He said I should bring you along."

Ingrid gave Dod a heaving shove, like a hefty school girl might. "Stop teasing me!" she insisted.

"I'm not," said Dod.

Ingrid reached to give him a second shove when he darted out of her way, nearly causing her to topple over.

"I told him about your efforts in feeding the troops at Twistyard," explained Dod, "and he's determined he would like you to sail the seas with us—"

"Us meaning—"

"Boot and Buck are coming along, and you'd be bunking with Dilly and Sawny in the queen's suite."

"Liar," said Ingrid, hobbling after Dod who had begun to head for the stairs.

"I'm telling the truth," said Dod, looking over his shoulder. "Scout's honor."

Ingrid gave him a puzzled look.

"Trust me," assured Dod. "He wants you along."

"Goodness me," said Ingrid, inspecting her ratty purse and cheap necklace. "The queen's suite? What will I wear? I'm sure he's heard of the work I've done for Higga. I don't want to disappoint him."

"You'll be fine," said Dod. "Just be ready to cook a few meals."

"Gross!" choked Dilly from up ahead.

"He's a born hunter," praised Boot, holding up a second rat Sneaker had brought to him. "I think there may be a few more beneath this old place. The pillars appear to have come down as a result of weak footings—perhaps water damage. The floor's cracked to splinters and sagging-in where the pillars used to stand. Commendus's crew has their work cut out for them."

"Too bad," said Buck jokingly. "I was really hoping we'd be able to spend the week scrubbing and painting, but it's just not safe until the roof is fixed."

"I'd say," wheezed Ingrid, tipping her head to catch a last view of the dangling rafters. Once outside, she flopped into the wheelchair and worked on catching her breath.

When Sawny exited, she left the group momentarily to jog up to the front of the building, eastside, though no sooner had she run off than she returned wearing a victorious smile. "I discovered something," she panted gleefully. "The stage isn't authentic. It's a replica of the original one and was probably made at the same time that the extensions were being constructed. Concealio must have built it."

"Which means what?" asked Buck.

"How do you know that?" pressed Ingrid.

"The stone was quarried from the same rock," explained Sawny, "so it deceptively appears to be part of the original structure. But upon closer inspection, I discovered that the texture of the stage blocks was achieved by smooth grinding—the type performed in mills—not chiseling. And as we all know, such mills weren't around when the original building was erected, nearly a thousand years ago."

"She's my sister," praised Dilly, taking pride in Sawny's depth of knowledge.

Dod took one last look at the monument as the wide walkway turned downward into the trees. His gut was already aching to go back. Something was left behind—perhaps a chest of treasure as Ingrid had hoped—or maybe something more.

TRICKY PAST

B ack at camp, news of the monument's troubles was received with more rejoicing than Ingrid thought appropriate.

"I've never seen such lazy kids in all my life!" complained Ingrid to Juny as the two sat eating dinner. "You'd think they would prefer doing something worthwhile over wasting their time."

Juny chuckled politely. Her royal appearance wasn't dampened by the outdoor accommodations they had been given. She sat properly, straight backed, wearing a dress that seemed to suggest she had been accidentally led off course from Commendus's banquet hall to the casual setting of the encampment.

"You can't blame them for celebrating fate's gentle breeze," said Juny. "Scrubbing and painting is hardly considered fair scales against the alternative of enjoying Commendus's hospitality."

"I'd say," agreed Toby heartily, carrying a tray of desserts. He and Hermit were now both wearing different shirts, one blue and one green. Whether they had believed Boot's tale of the dragon or not, they weren't going to take any chances of being bait by wearing red.

"But it's a waste!" grumbled Ingrid. "If I were Commendus, I'd certainly find a more suitable replacement project. Sweeping patios in between games in the field and mischief around the castle certainly doesn't justify their absence from Twistyard's week of scrubbing. And did you hear—" Ingrid's double chin wiggled as she shook her head. "All of Green Hall will be accompanying Raul Hall to the Ghoul's Festival! These kids are headed from an easy week to more relaxation!"

"How nice for them," said Juny in a calm voice, smiling at Dod and Boot who sat across the picnic table from her. "It's the younger generation that enjoys the festival the most. I'm a bit apprehensive to go at all."

Boot grinned contagiously. He seemed to enjoy his lucky streak even more since it aggravated Ingrid into complaining.

"And while awaiting their departure to Raul," huffed Ingrid, "Commendus has offered to make arrangements for them to play Bollirse in Champion Stadium—just for pleasure—as though these kids don't get enough opportunities to enjoy themselves. Ludicrous! It's simply Ludicrous!"

"Commendus is a wonderful host, isn't he?" responded Juny, carefully resituating a jeweled hairpiece that had begun to slip from her silky black hair.

"We didn't choose this," chimed Dilly, who appeared to have heard enough of Ingrid's bellyaching. "We came here to help with the monument. It's not our fault the roof's caving in. Once the construction crew has made the building safe again, we'd be more than happy to come back."

TRICKY PAST

The cool evening air was unexpectedly filled with music as Bowlure approached, Rot on one side and Youk on the other.

"Springtime, if only springtime," sang the trio, "we'd be closer to our hearts and ever closer to the breeze that blows the touch of change our way; and in its tide of budding life we'd feel the tug deep down inside and want to stay, we'd want to stay."

Rot appeared shorter than usual standing beside Bowlure, but his face glowed a clever smirk as the words of the song rolled off his tongue.

"Are you part of the trio now?" asked Juny of Youk the moment the number had ended. She looked surprised.

"Only for the evening," chuckled Youk in a forced sort of voice, tipping his feathered hat cordially. "It's a fine split from the cares I've come to address."

"Are you here to play Bollirse with us?" asked Sammywoo, rushing to his father. "Dari and I get to play on Green Hall's team since they're missing some Greenlings. It's a rematch of the preseason's full-out, triple team Bollirse game. Do you want to play with us, too? We're gonna beat Sawb's team."

"Are you, now?" said Youk, scooping his son up into his arms. He gave Boot a concerned glance. "Maybe we should rethink things—"

"Play along with him," insisted Juny. "It's not everyday you get to run the field in Champion Stadium."

Youk smiled politely. "I'll see about my schedule, and we can talk later. When's the game?"

"We don't know yet," said Dari, skipping over. "Commendus just suggested it an hour ago, when he found out about the monument's problems. It's old and busted."

Before Youk could ask, Ingrid dove into a thorough description of the building's troubles, including its rat problem, and showed no sign of stopping when Dari interrupted her.

"Look what Bly gave me," she said, stepping between Ingrid and Youk. She pulled an extra-large glowing stone from her pocket and beamed gloriously. "It fits this headband," she added, demonstrating how it clicked into place on her forehead. With the sun having recently set, the stone wasn't needed yet, but appeared to glow brighter than any of the rocks Dod had seen.

"That's amazing!" praised Bowlure, looking right over the top of Rot to see it. "What'll they think of next?"

"I thought he said it was for Dilly," whispered Sammywoo in his sister's direction, though everyone could hear him just fine.

Dari shook her head. "He told us we could give it to her if we wanted to," clarified Dari. "Remember? Doctor Shelderhig said the band fit my head perfectly, and Bly agreed."

Dilly pushed her half-eaten dinner away and leaned on the table, appearing to fume as she gazed at the sparkling headlight.

"Maybe you can borrow it sometime," added Dari, peeking around Ingrid to see Dilly better. "Like…well…if you ever had to stay up all night in a dangerous jungle, with lions and tigers all around you, then I'd let you take it. Bly told us that this glowing stone lasts twice as long as the regular ones, and it only takes fifteen minutes to recharge! Pretty cool, huh?"

Sawny now joined her sister in looking jealous.

"Wow!" blurted Toos, joining Sham and Voo in leaving their plates to get a better look. "Where can you buy them?"

"Or get them for free," called Pone from his seat, his mouth full of roast beef.

"They're not free or for sale," said Dari, flipping her short blond hair. "Bly and Doctor Shelderhig are still working on them."

"My cousin could sure use one of those," said Ingrid, sulking in her seat after having been cut off by Dari. "I got a letter from Higga yesterday, and in it she said that when it gets dark, spiders the size of her hands come out to search for fresh blood." Ingrid nodded at Dari and wiggled her fingers like the legs of a spider.

"Gross!" said Dari.

"She's plucked a fair number of them off her arms, legs, and face during the long nights there in Soosh," continued Ingrid. "It sounds dreadful to be living in the deep thickets as she is. I think what she's doing for science is truly inspiring."

"Or stupid!" rumbled Dari, dishing Ingrid a disgusted look.

"Dari!" said Youk in a firm voice. "Show respect."

"But I hate spiders!" whined Dari, crinkling her nose at her father. "Anything that drinks blood is totally on my bad list. Do you remember the time Mom had a Thumbnail Tick on her neck? Who passed out? Me! Because stuff like that is way gross!"

Youk set Sammywoo down and put an arm on Dari's shoulder. "Don't you think it would be nice if you let Ingrid send your headband to Higga? That would help her know we miss her."

"It wouldn't do her any good," said Dari defensively. "Without the cool stone, it's pretty much useless."

Boot broke out in laughter.

"No. Let's give her the whole thing," said Youk, prodding her along.

"Oh," sighed Dari glumly.

"I think that's a great idea," said Dilly, rising to her feet, her face forcing an agreeable smile. "Higga deserves our support. You can hand over the light and I'll write her a nice note from us."

"How thoughtful," said Ingrid, holding out her hand toward Dari. "I'll put the package together and send it off while visiting Raul." Ingrid looked at Juny. "Terro would help us with that, wouldn't he?"

Juny nodded.

Minutes later, Ingrid caught up with Dod before he had reached the boys' tent. "Were you serious about Traygof's offer?" she asked nervously.

"Yes," said Dod. "I'm not kidding. You can ask Boot."

Ingrid glanced at Boot, who stood next to Dod wearing a mischievous face. "He's no help. He'd tease me worse than you."

Boot grinned slyly.

"Then ask Dilly or Sawny," said Dod, feeling bad that he had spent through her trust.

"I have to know the truth," mumbled Ingrid, grabbing Dod's arm tightly. "Did he really ask for me to sail on his ship?"

"Yes," assured Dod. "I promise."

Ingrid exhaled loudly. "Why does this kind of thing happen to me?" she moaned, wiping at her brow dramatically. "I finally have the chance to visit the Ghoul's Festival and—"

"Don't worry, Gram," said Boot, interrupting her show. "We're not leaving until after it's over. We'll be at the festival, too."

"That's right," beamed Ingrid. "I knew that." And without another word she returned to Juny's side.

In the tent, Boot and Dod brought bits of meat to Sneaker. The ferret was perched in a small five-foot tree that had been placed in the corner near Boot's bed. The planter-pot looked similar to the one Con had thrown at Dilly's door.

"He's missing his big perch," said Dod, "just look at his eyes."

"No," assured Boot. "He's just worn out from catching rats."

The tent went quiet for a few minutes as Sneaker ate his dinner. Dod and Boot were alone, and neither of them spoke. Dod kept thinking about the day. He hadn't said much about the flashes that had come and gone, but his mind had had a tendency of drifting back to them, especially the one about Pap. His grandfather had looked amazing with a sword. It made Dod proud to be related to him.

"What do you know of the night Pap bested The Dread?" asked Dod, breaking the silence as he took a seat on his cot.

"Not a lot," responded Boot slowly, keeping his eyes on Sneaker. "I should have been there. Pap asked me to go with him that night, but I thought I was too busy—Commendus had me doing something—I can't remember what. To be honest, I think I stayed here at the palace because one of Commendus's esteemed guests had a couple of cute daughters with him. Can you believe it? I stuck around to flirt instead of helping Pap and the others."

"Don't beat yourself up," said Dod. "We all occasionally say and do dumb things."

"I guess," shrugged Boot in a melancholy voice. "But I really should have been there. Pap knew something was going to happen. Even though he didn't talk very much about his impressions, we all knew he had a gift—a lot like you. Anyway, I'm sure that's why he went to the Chards Museum that night."

"What did Sirlonk want?" asked Dod.

"Well, I can't exactly say," offered Boot. "It wasn't announced that anything was taken."

"There was a small bag," pressed Dod, recalling the reaching hand. "Do you remember hearing anything about it? What was in it?"

Boot glanced at Dod uncomfortably. "Issin and Paulic died because I wasn't there to defend them, and Horsely was beaten really bad, and Bowie—" Boot's eyes became watery. "I let my own brother down. He was the first to confront Sirlonk—just outside of the museum. And by the time the battle was over, Bowie was stuck under a pile of logs. It's amazing he survived."

Dod studied the floor quietly.

"There you are," called Bowlure, poking his head into the spacious tent. He worked his way around the cots to Boot and Dod. "I heard something this afternoon that I thought you might want to know." Bowlure lowered his voice to a whisper. "Dungo was reportedly spotted a few days ago, heading toward the coast. Soldiers went after him but they couldn't keep up."

"So he's alive," said Dod, cracking a faint smile. He knew Dungo had done a lot of bad things and rightfully deserved punishment for his crimes. However, Dod also couldn't forget the kind things Dungo had done for him: He had protected him against criminals in Driaxom, taken a harsh beating for him, and risked his life smuggling him out of prison.

"Thanks for telling me," said Dod.

Bowlure nodded. "He's headed toward discovering the sad reality of his family's fate. I feel bad for him."

"Me too," agreed Dod. He couldn't forget Dungo's tormented face as he sat bound to the whipping post, reverently recalling Dod's small act of having given him a sandwich.

Bowlure glanced at Boot and yawned. "Say, truthfully, weren't you picking a fight with Con today?"

Boot raised his eyebrows. "It was more of the other way around," he confessed, "but I'm not scared of him."

"Fear changes faces once you've kissed death a time or two, doesn't it?" said Bowlure. "Tridacello told me how you nearly drank your life into the ground with Pap and the others who were poisoned here. It must be hard knowing you could have died with them—so close—you and Bonboo and Zerny all could have died had you joined them in toasting to a successful trip."

Boot's gaze drifted off as his brow wrinkled. "That was the worst night of my life," he mumbled, looking beyond Sneaker as if the tent's fabric had just turned into a window.

"You were *here* that night?" burst Dod, feeling a sudden pain. Why hadn't Boot ever mentioned it? How much had he spoken to Pap before the poisoning? What was Pap's final day like? So many questions hadn't been answered.

Boot nodded.

"If only Dod had been here, they wouldn't have died," added Bowlure. "His whole swapper-psychic thing would have saved the day."

Boot's shoulders sank an inch.

"But of course he couldn't have done anything," continued Bowlure. "He was fresh off the streets—just a poor orphan working for Tridacello. Nobody would have let Dod into High Gate, much less Commendus's palace. Without established family members or friends to vouch for you, this city is off limits."

Dod suddenly felt Boot's eyes turn on him.

"An orphan?" said Boot.

Dod studied the floor, his heart pounding so quickly that he wondered whether Boot and Bowlure could hear it.

"Sure," said Bowlure happily. "It's amazing to see how far Dod's come. And he wasn't with Tridacello but a couple of months. We're staring at a self-made genius—no family whatsoever. Quite a strapper! He's special to say the least. In less than a year he's gone from begging bread to fighting The Dread."

"Dod's not without connections," argued Boot. "His grandfather was *Pap*!"

"What? Who told you that?" laughed Bowlure. "Pap couldn't be his grandpa."

Dod knew he had a lot of explaining to do, but from which point could he begin? If he started at the real beginning and told of how he was an alien from Earth, transported to Green in an unexplainable way, he was sure no one would believe him, especially if he included anything about the real orphan who had died on the cliffs. Yet how could he begin at any other point and still claim to be Pap's grandson? And what about his long absence from Green, when his medallion had been stolen on Earth? He had gone back to Twistyard and told everyone he had been away visiting family.

"Who are you really?" pressed Boot, his voice beginning to strengthen as it had the time he had grabbed Dod and shaken him.

"Did *he* tell you his grandpa was Pap?" asked Bowlure.

Dod didn't need to look up to know that Bowlure was pointing at him. And had Dod looked, he wouldn't have seen much: The floor was beginning to blur as he increasingly counted spinning stars. He didn't have a good answer for either of them, and his heart was racing faster than if he were finishing a sprint.

Dod took a deep breath.

"He's in the tent over there," said a muffled voice that Dod recognized as Buck's. The words entered Dod's head more than his ears, as though he were catching things beyond his regular hearing range; and stranger still, he knew Buck was talking with Bonboo.

"I can explain," said Dod, trying to sit back up. "But since Bonboo's coming, I'll let him."

"Just tell us who you are!" demanded Boot in a rattled voice.

"He's Dod," said Bowlure. "Don't be silly."

"I'm not being silly!" thundered Boot, exploding. "He's been telling everyone for months that he's Pap's grandson! If that's a lie, what is true? He could be deep in The Order—the biggest turncoat of them all!"

"Part of The Order?" muttered Dod in a hurt voice. He couldn't blame Boot for wondering, but hated hearing it.

"The truth!" said Boot. "Was Pap your grandpa or not?"

Someone opened the tent door and walked in.

"Is Dod over there?" called Bonboo. Bowlure's large frame was blocking his view.

Dod sighed. Bonboo's timing couldn't have been better.

"He's done it again!" praised Bowlure, lighting up with excitement. "See! I'm telling you, Boot, Dod's psychic! He said Bonboo was coming, and look—here he is!"

Dod raised one hand and waved.

"Who's yelling in here?" asked Bonboo as he approached.

Bowlure pointed at Boot.

Bonboo sighed heavily as he neared the group. "I heard your question, Boot. You shouldn't need to ask."

Boot's eyes filled with shame.

"You know Dod," said Bonboo. "Of course he's Pap's grandson."

"He is?" jumped Bowlure, blinking with shock. "Wow!"

"Some things are hard to explain," continued Bonboo in his gentle voice. "Trust me. I know for a fact that Dod is Pap's blood, and he is most certainly *not* a traitor. That's why I've bet my freedom on his innocence."

"Unbelievable!" exclaimed Bowlure, reaching his furry arm over to pat Dod on the shoulder. "Pap's grandson! That's fantastic! No wonder you've surprised us. It makes more sense now."

"Sorry," offered Boot. "I don't know what got into me."

"It's my fault," rushed Bowlure. "Tridacello tells a different angle." Bowlure glanced at Dod, then Bonboo, then Dod. "You were undercover, weren't you?"

Dod smiled. It sounded like a logical explanation.

"You don't need to tell me," Bowlure quickly added, pretending to latch his lips shut. "I'm not saying a word. After all, it worked. You were onto Dungo and Sirlonk. That's why you went to live with Tridacello. Sneaky!"

Boot began to nod.

"It's definitely a complicated story," said Dod.

"More than we can tell now," agreed Bonboo, reaching into his vest pocket. He handed Dod a small envelope. "This paper and ring will stand as a show of proof for you at the portal—just in case questions arise."

"Thanks," said Dod.

"No. Thank *you*," returned Bonboo. "I haven't had a chance to adequately tell you how grateful I am for your help with the Farmer's Sackload. Your gift saved Twistyard."

"Up, up for the hero," sang Bowlure, raising a fist in the air.

Boot quietly raised a fist, too.

When Bonboo turned to go, Dod begged a favor: "Can we talk sometime?"

"Talk now—we'll leave," sprang Bowlure, stepping back. "Do you want us to guard the door?"

Boot snatched Sneaker from his perch and began to follow Bowlure when Bonboo broke in: "We'll have to sit later," he said. "Commendus is waiting for us to join the others on the back balcony. He won't start until we arrive, and I think he's probably getting impatient by now."

"Okay," said Dod, wishing to skip whatever Commendus had planned. He wanted answers, not entertainment.

GRUDGE MATCH

The next few days were filled with all sorts of activities, most of which had nothing to do with work. Commendus's fiancé, Sabbella, took the lead in orchestrating the events. Her dedication to details reminded Dod of Saluci and her annual commemorative picnic for the Zoots. No expense was spared in providing a string of first-rate parties. There was swimming at the Discommo Pool House, horse races and competitions in Long's Arena, quick-line sliding down Silver Cliff's cables, and an evening of dancing under the stars.

And just as Commendus had promised, he bought time at Champion Stadium for the two halls to conduct an epic Bollirse game. Rather than limiting each side to eighteen players, as was customary to the sport, this game was to be full-out, triple team Bollirse, a Twistyard creation that allowed all fifty Lings and fifteen Coosings from each hall to compete.

Since eight Greenlings were away on diplomatic missions for Pious, Boot labored to fill the spots for the big game. Dari, Valerie, and Sammywoo made the list first, then two of Sabbella's nieces and a young barn hand, and finally Youk and Bly. Boot had pressed to add Bowlure but had been denied by Sawb who saw the driadon as an unfair replacement for one of the vacant Greenlings.

The game was scheduled as the last event at High Gate for Dod and his friends before their exodus to Raul for the Ghoul's Festival. It was Commendus's big finale to the fun-filled week he had given his Twistyard guests. From every indication, he was trying to show the budding diplomats that his hosting skills were superior to anything they were about to encounter in Raul, despite the glaring fact that he hadn't been able to put a roof over their heads or feed them in his dining hall because of the Global Business Convention.

The opportunity to play in Champion Stadium was a spectacular treat to be relished, particularly by the Greenlings and Raulings who had never played on such an important field. Just weeks before, Green Hall's Coosings had prevailed over the notoriously powerful Lairrington Longs and won The Golden Swot—a fact Raul Hall hadn't forgotten, since Green Hall's success had ended their unbelievable six-year winning streak.

"Everyone must play fair," announced Sabbella officiously, facing the two small crowds as they sat in the nearly-empty bleachers. The mid-afternoon sun hung in the turquoise sky and seemed to anxiously watch the rivals prepare for battle.

"We're truly privileged this day," continued Sabbella, "to have the finest head judge in all of Green call the match, the well-respected Orrigo Bollirsee."

"Do you think he gave himself that name?" whispered Boot to Dod, jiggling his swot impatiently.

CHAPTER TWENTY

Dilly nudged him to be quiet as Orrigo stood and took a bow, his portly frame suggesting it had been years since he had played the game, or even left his expensive suits for a uniform.

"And a special thanks to our referees," said Sabbella, waving her hand for them to stand. Turly and three of his associates, all officers in Commendus's private security team, nodded politely.

"That's not good," whispered Buck over Boot's shoulder, emphasizing what Boot and Dod were already staring at: Turly was making eyes at Eluxa and her clique of friends.

"Typical," said Dilly, suddenly not as concerned about maintaining silence. "No wonder Eluxa kept using the tallest slide at the pool the other day—the one near the security platform. She must have heard *he* would be judging the match and wanted his eyes on her side."

"She's got mine," chuckled Pone, glancing at the creative way Eluxa had tied her red jersey up, revealing her tanned midriff.

Sawny glared at Pone.

"They're all dragon bait," muttered Hermit to Toby from the seat in front of Dod.

"Today's game is for the glory," said Sabbella, her outfit glittering in the sunlight. "As you see, the stadium is empty." She raised her hands dramatically and turned every which way, emphasizing the fanless arena. "Enjoy the afternoon, play your best, and have fun. Good luck to you all!"

Boot hopped to his feet and rallied Green Hall to line up and tip heads with Raul Hall, face to face, as a show and promise of fair play, but to his surprise, Sawb laughed at him for intending on keeping the custom without a crowd watching.

"What's the point?" chided Sawb, "No one will know the difference." He pointed his teammates toward their ladder and ordered they hurry.

Boot appeared to ignore the insult and began to lead Green Hall away when he caught a glimpse of something he hadn't expected—someone bending discretely, joining Raul Hall's exiting throng. "What's *he* doing in red?" called Boot, pouring his full attention back on Sawb.

"It beats wearing blue," sneered Sawb challengingly. "Tonnis isn't playing today, so we've opted to let Con suit up. The numbers are equal."

"But Con?" groaned Boot. "Come on, you didn't let us have Bowlure."

Sawb smiled coolly. "Con's an emeritus Coosing. It's only fair we allow him to take the spot."

Dod grabbed Boot's arm and tugged. He knew the argument wasn't worth fighting. Even though there were less than a dozen spectators, Commendus was one of them, and he certainly wouldn't choose to have his son sit in the bleachers instead of playing in the grand stadium he had just rented.

"If you want him out" taunted Sawb, glaring menacingly, "be a man and do it on the field!"

Boot gave his head-guard a tight squeeze.

"Let's go," said Dod. "The game will be more fun if Con's against us." It was a lie, but Boot swallowed it and followed Dod.

Once on the field, people scurried to take their places before the judge ordered the beginning of the game. As usual, Boot, Buck, and Pone had their squads of followers next to them, near the center, only feet from the three-foot wall that separated the field in half. Dilly and Sawny were positioned in the back on defense and were in charge of many of the weaker Greenlings, as well as Youk's kids.

Dod and Youk were given the option to roam, which meant Youk began near the front, spouting tales of his glory days gone by and trading strategy points with Boot, while Dod took a spot in the rear near the Tillius sisters.

Within minutes, the match had begun and globes whizzed back and forth across the center line. Boot eagerly made the first drive into enemy territory, pushing straight for Con's brigade, and was nearly taken out of the game within seconds by a string of powerful globes sent from Con. Commendus's son was remarkable at Bollirse. He would leave his shield on the ground, throw a globe up in the air, and use both hands on his swot to send the globe flying like it had been shot out of a gun.

But Boot wasn't easily discouraged. After being challenged so bluntly by Sawb, he seemed determined to stay his course until he had forced Con out of the game.

"Do you think Boot needs me now?" asked Sammywoo, tugging at Dilly's jersey.

Dod held back laughter. Due to Youk's concerns, Sammywoo was so well padded with layers that he couldn't hardly walk, much less run to Boot's aid against Con. He looked like a plump blueberry.

"Not yet," said Dilly sweetly. "We have work to do back here." Dilly pointed at a few globes, which had hit the ground and rolled harmlessly to the wall. "We've got to gather our supplies into piles, so we can bring more ammunition to Boot when he runs out."

"Oh!" exclaimed Sammywoo. "I can do that!" He left Dilly's side to gather globes, though once he had reached them, he struggled to bend enough to pick them up. His padding was too thick.

"Poor boy," said Dilly, watching Sammywoo. "I think someone's being overly protective."

"I wouldn't mind another layer," said Valerie in a worried tone. Her eyes were glued to the distant battle going on between Boot's group and Con's. She appeared to be having second thoughts about agreeing to play.

"You're fine!" assured Dari impatiently. "Does this hurt?" She smacked her sister squarely on the back with her swot.

"Yes!" cried Valerie, twisting quickly. "Stop! You're not supposed to hit people with your stick—you're supposed to use the ball-thingies." Her frantic movements displaced her head-guard, making her look goofy.

"Swot and globes," corrected Sawny, sounding annoyed as she returned from a visit to the other side of the backfield.

Dilly chuckled.

"We're not going to win, are we?" said Sawny, eyeing Youk's kids.

"Don't talk like that," said Dilly. "We have to win."

Orrigo froze the game momentarily as Turly helped Bly hobble from the field after being struck in the leg by one of Con's bullets. He was the first casualty.

"Cheater! Cheater! Cheater!" roared a lonely voice from the bleachers. Ingrid was shaking her cane in disgust over Bly having been dispatched so quickly from Green Hall's forces. Three seats down from her, Sabbella proudly joined Commendus in waving at Con.

"I expected more out of Bly," lamented Dod, watching the manly figure labor to get up the rope ladder.

Dilly looked slightly relieved to see him go.

"He's a greenhorn," said Sawny, "about equal with Sabbella's nieces." She pointed at two uniforms that were presently in the far rear corner, cowering, holding their swots by the wrong ends.

"Don't give up hope yet," said Dilly. "Boot's hanging tight—and look over there—Pone's moving to cross."

"He just wants to goggle at Eluxa's naked stomach," complained Sawny.

Dod smiled.

"You, too?" groaned Sawny, sounding as if her day were growing worse by the second.

"No," defended Dod. "I was just thinking of how great it would be if you tagged her there."

Sawny cracked the first grin she'd had since seeing Pone stare at Eluxa. "Maybe I will," she said firmly. "This game may not be a complete waste after all."

"It's good to have goals," added Dod, beaming from having cheered her up a notch.

Sawb made his battalion move forward, which effectively shut down Pone's attempt to get closer. But not everyone in Pone's group read the signs: The barn hand who'd joined Green Hall for the day became easy pickings when he rushed the mid-field by himself, acting as confident as if others were on his flanks.

"Rookie move," said Sawny, watching him exit.

"Totally!" agreed Dari, attempting Con's special trick. She tossed a globe in the air and hit it straight into Toos's back, only a short distance away.

"I did it!" rejoiced Dari, elated with her accomplishment. She completely ignored Toos's evil glares that followed and gave the move a second try, and a third, and a fourth, fifth, sixth, and seventh. Apparently, her first time connecting her swot with a globe was destined to be her last, but it wasn't the last time Toos would be hit in the back. Shortly after Dari's tap, Toos's attention was so distracted by the girl's repeated attempts, he naively let his eyes drift away from the frontline and missed Con's smoking globe that whizzed deep into Green Hall's territory. It thumped Toos squarely between the shoulders.

"You're out!" yelled Orrigo happily, appearing extra excited to personally call the obvious when it complimented Con. A field referee pointed to Green Hall's ladder and Toos was on his way up, but he didn't leave without first grumbling his displeasure at Dari.

"Boingy-boing!" blared Dari. "Toos's acting like his lame skills are my fault—like I'm his mentor or something. Please! He should take it up with Strat, not me." She pointed at the short row of spectators where Strat was seated beside Bly.

"He's more than justified," scolded Valerie.

"No, he's not!" said Dari. "He has an owl poop to protect him!"

"Pellet—" corrected Sawny. "And he's given that up for a rock."

"You made him lose his concentration," pressed Valerie. "It's completely *your fault!*"

Dari raised her swot threateningly at her sister, which caused Valerie to flee carelessly without looking where she was going. It was her last mistake of the game. A floating bomber from Joak, who'd just stolen into Green Hall's territory, sailed calmly through the air and tapped one of Valerie's shoes.

"That's a hit!" yelled a referee who descend upon Valerie at about the same time as the globe.

"What? Really?" exclaimed Valerie, her voice sounding overjoyed. "I thought it would hurt." As though the cares of the world had just been shed from her shoulders, she skipped to the ladder and climbed out of the pit.

"Do you still think we have a chance?" said Sawny sharply to Dilly.

"I do," nodded Dod flippantly, answering for Dilly. The game wasn't going well at all, but he was having fun. Just watching Dari was a show-and-a-half.

Boot pressed in with two other Coosings and was once more repelled by Con to the outer edges of Raul Hall territory. The battle was ferocious. Globes flew in both directions, narrowly missing players. One globe hit Boot's shield so hard that it bounced over two hundred feet before touching the ground.

"They're having all the fun," whined Dari, eyeing the frontline enviously. "When do we get to start playing?"

"Soon enough—" began Dilly, looking irritated, when Dari tripped on a globe that she had been rolling back and forth with her foot and almost knocked Dilly over. During the fall, Dari's swot smacked Dilly's head-guard, in front of her left eye, and bent the metal wires enough that they looked distractingly odd.

"On second thought," coughed Dilly, changing tones, "you can go and join Boot. He looks like he could use one more person."

"But wouldn't he get mad at me?" asked Dari, her eyes growing big. "He told us to wait back here for his orders—right?"

Dilly bent over and scooped up an armload of globes from a pile on the ground. "Here," she said, wearing a grumpy, fake smile. "Go and bring these to Boot."

Sawny rolled her eyes.

"Right-o!" exploded Dari, endeavoring to accept the task without letting go of her shield or swot. It was impossible.

"I guess I could have Dod do it—" began Dilly, appearing to read Dari's concerns.

"No! I'm steady and ready," chanted Dari, dropping her shield to the ground. She pressed the globes against herself and hunkered awkwardly to keep them from falling. "I'll be back shortly, don't worry."

"Wait!" cried Sammywoo. "Here's one more for Boot." He waddled over and proudly handed his sister a globe he had gathered, as though it were a championship ring. "Tell Boot this one's from me."

"CHARGE!" rumbled from the frontline. A wave of new attackers, led by Kwit, joined Joak in pushing deeper into Green Hall's turf, dislodging a number of cone-like bots as they marched.

"Rout the scoundrels!" cried Pone, combining his mob with Voo's and Sham's to fight the central threat.

Dari froze in her tracks.

The scrimmage lasted a few minutes with both sides taking cover behind poles. Eventually, Buck yelled to rush, at which point the opposing forces poured out upon each other. Five Raulings and five Greenlings were struck as the assailants were driven back over the wall.

"Equal numbers," mumbled Dilly. "That's not too bad."

"Right," said Dari in a less than confident voice. She continued to hunch as she left the backfield, tiptoeing toward Boot.

"Go Dari!" yelled Sammywoo, swinging his swot like he was waving a flag.

"Keep gathering," nudged Dilly in a sweet voice, directing him back to his job.

"If you want to deploy a real weapon," said Dod, smiling at the two sisters, "send Sammywoo. He could scream them into submission."

"You guys keep saying he's a noisemaker," said Dilly, watching Dari intently, "but he's not. The only night he had problems was the night he slept in your tent. The rest of the time he's been with us, and I haven't heard him say a peep. You boys must tease him into bad dreams."

"Hardly," said Dod. "We even gave him his pick of beds. He took Pone's so he could sleep close to Sneaker, but it didn't work. By the third round of screams, I was ready to put my cot in Commendus's front yard with Mama and Popslither rather than be stuck so close to him."

Dilly shivered and glanced at her Redy-Alert-Band. It was a calm, brownish-yellow.

"She's making tracks," said Sawny, looking out at Dari. Dod and Dilly joined in watching closely as she neared the midfield.

Dari kept a steady pace and only slowed when she came to the short stone wall that separated the field in half. Upon crossing into Raul Hall's territory, globes began to fly in her direction.

"I've got to admit," confessed Sawny, "Dari does what she says she's going to do. It's quite refreshing."

"And she's not easily intimidated, either," added Dilly, her eyes glued to Dari's every step.

"I think she takes after Saluci," said Sawny.

Both girls spoke favorably about Dari. Dod read their praise and assumed they were feeling guilty about sending Dari into the middle of the hottest fighting zone. Boot was positioned deep in Raul Hall territory with only two defenders anywhere near him, and despite the growing wave of opposition led by Con, Boot didn't appear ready to retreat.

Before Dari had reached the safety of the first row of poles, Youk led a team of six in rushing after his daughter, from the center, passing through the gap Joak's and Kwit's forces had just made by retreating. Instantly, Con's forces advanced into the open and began a brutal assault. Globes rained down on Youk's battalion and especially on Youk, who led by a few strides in the front.

Undeterred, Dari continued forward. Her occasional hop to one side or the other, just enough to avoid being hit, made it clear she was aware of the danger she was in.

Youk rushed with great speed until his daughter stepped behind a pole, at which point he stopped where he was and began to return fire, emptying his jung of globes on Con's crowd.

By the time Youk's forces had caught up to him, Con was no longer the biggest threat they faced. Joak's troop had been ordered to turn around and fight, and they were much closer than Con's. Things looked disastrous for Youk and his battalion. They were completely out in the open.

Suddenly, Youk yelled to retreat and took a few hardy steps, as if bent on escaping Raul Hall's territory. His mob of followers bolted over the three-foot wall to the safety and refuge of friends and didn't appear to notice that Youk had spun around and was now sprinting in the opposite direction, straight toward Con. The sight was vaguely reminiscent of the time Dod had tackled Sawb to the ground, only this time, Youk was much farther out, and Con's forces were completely loaded with ammunition.

"What's he doing?" mumbled Dilly, sounding blameworthy. "He won't be able to keep blocking those shots once he's closer."

Dod spoke the obvious. "He's trying to help his daughter."

Dari had left the shelter of the post she'd been hiding behind and had begun to hunch her way forward—a little to one side, then a little to the other—seemingly in search of Boot.

Con's forces advanced and fired on Dari, hitting her almost simultaneously with four globes, one of which was compliments of Con's two-handed move.

Dari fell to the ground and let out a howl that made Dilly and Sawny both cringe.

"She's out!" yelled Orrigo, pointing for her to exit. Though, rather than pause the game, he quickly added, "Resume play!" It was a questionable call to say the least. Dari was on the ground, and her cries made it overwhelmingly obvious that she deemed herself injured.

"What?!" rumbled Sawny. "It's an easy one. Freeze everything."

"He's a biased, pathetic, shoe-shiner," said Dilly glumly, watching as Youk changed course slightly. "If Orrigo had stopped the game, Dari's situation would have been resolved without Youk needing to risk himself anymore. But as it is, he's a father, and he's not going to retreat until she's adjusted. The whole thing's a judge-sponsored trap, that's what it is!"

"What about the referees?" asked Dod, noticing how Turly was slowly walking toward Dari. "Why aren't they speaking up?"

"Right," said Dilly sarcastically. "Question Orrigo's ruling? I don't think that would go well. They'll wait a few more seconds until Youk's been hit, then pause the game while the duo's escorted off."

"Two for one," groaned Sawny.

"Cheaters! Cheaters! Cheaters!" raged Ingrid from the stands.

Con's troop of ten didn't miss a beat in chasing after Youk. No pity, no mercy. Globes pounded against Youk's shield as he neared his daughter and knelt down to check on her.

In an instant, something caused Con to slow down and turn around. From Dod's vantage, it was hard to see what was going on. Was it Sawb approaching, giving new orders? Had a referee finally sided with logic? No! It was far more amazing than that!

A player in red was senselessly plunking the others with globes, a move that wouldn't result in any outs, but clearly annoyed Con and his troop.

"It looks like we have a friend," noted Sawny eagerly. "Who do you think it is?"

"I don't know," said Dilly, watching Con fall back to confront his traitorous teammate. "But I'd hate to be him right now."

"Sabbella did tell us to relax and have fun with today's game," chuckled Dod, staring in disbelief. The turncoat Rauling continued to throw globes, despite Con's approach.

"Maybe Dari has a twin," smiled Dilly.

"HE'S OUT!" shouted Orrigo from his sideline perch, throwing a condemning finger at Youk. "Everyone, stand still until the referees have escorted THEM off the field."

"So predictable," sighed Dilly.

"Rotten, lousy cheaters!" yelled Ingrid. "Let me judge the game. I'm not blind like Orange-o, here!" Ingrid shook her cane in the air.

As the players stood still and waited for Youk and Dari to leave, the turncoat pulled his head-guard off and pandemonium broke loose. It was Boot! He was wearing a red uniform, head-to-foot, jersey and long pants. He was the one who had hit the backs of Con's players with globes—live globes!

Boot waved his arms in the air as he explained his case to the referees, and then Con broke his swot over his leg, threw his shield to the ground, and stormed off. One-by-one, the other Raulings and Raul Coosings who had been struck filed to their rope ladder and followed Con up to the bleachers.

"I can't believe it!" exclaimed Dilly excitedly. "They're all out!"

"Eleven," counted Sawny, smiling slyly at Dod. "That's even better than your record."

"He's the best!" said Dod proudly. "Boot's incredible!"

Once it was discovered that Youk had been hit by a disqualified player, he was returned to his spot before the game resumed.

"Good job, Dari!" yelled Dilly as Youk's daughter was escorted away.

"Thanks," said Dari, walking past with her head up. She had stopped wailing and seemed okay. "I knew you and Boot were up to something!"

Minutes later, after Boot had escaped the back regions of Raul Hall's turf, he joined Dilly and Sawny for a breather.

"Where did you get the spare uniform from?" asked Dilly, eyeing Boot curiously as he pulled his blue clothes from his jung and put them on over his red ones.

"Nowhere," responded Boot, bursting with glee.

"Tonnis," guessed Sawny.

Boot smiled. "I couldn't resist trying Dod's trick."

"You pulled it off much better than I did," said Dod.

Boot shook his head nonchalantly.

"Eleven to eight," added Sawny, spelling the facts out clearly.

"Was that enough of a distraction?" huffed Youk, jogging up to the group. Dod couldn't recall having ever seen so much merriment in Youk's eyes, even when they had ridden the giant flutter together. The look reminded Dod of Josh on Christmas morning, when he had handed Dod the special crown.

"That was perfect!" praised Boot. "You can't get better than a father rushing to his daughter's aid!"

"I'd say it falls into the classic broken duck's wing strategy," gloated Youk. "Draw your opponent in with what they assume is basic nature—though I must confess, I didn't prep Dari. She rushed into the field out of courage, not my planning. I just improvised to your benefit."

Boot glanced at Dilly.

"She insisted," defended Dilly.

"That would be my Dari," said Youk proudly. "She's about as easy to hold back as the setting sun."

"We're winning!" celebrated Sammywoo, returning from his globe hunt with two in his hands. He excitedly gave one to Boot and one to his father. "Now go get Sawb."

"In a minute," said Boot, patting Sammywoo on the shoulder. "Right now it's Dilly's turn to direct an attack. I'm gonna stay back here with you for a while."

Dilly wasted no time in gathering a fresh group from the Greenlings who had been waiting in the rear—not exactly the first-round picks—and led them into Raul Hall's territory on the far right side. Sawny and Dod went along for support.

It was a short and costly run. No sooner had they begun to knock down bots than Sawb noticed their actions and sent a fresh batch of exceptional players to drive them away, which resulted in a loss of five Greenlings to only one Raul Coosing.

But Dod and Dilly didn't complain. Sawny's wish had come true. At the perfect moment, amid the chaos of globes whizzing through the air and bodies dashing from pole to pole, Sawny had been favored with the opportunity of surprising Eluxa at close range and had carried through with remarkable precision. Mission accomplished!

"Did you see where I got her?" squealed Sawny, following Dod closely. "I doubt she'll play Bollirse dressed like *that* again."

"Not against you," laughed Dod, assessing the scrimmage they were approaching. Pone had a dozen players pushing the frontline successfully, and Dilly was leading her dwindling group to join them.

Suddenly, Dod felt watched. It was a strange, gnawing feeling, as if someone were ready to pounce on him. He stopped behind a pole and glanced around.

Keep running! burst into his mind.

Dod stood still.

"Aren't you coming?" asked Sawny playfully, passing Dod to follow her sister.

"I'll catch up," he responded. The impression was getting stronger. He looked to the sky, across the empty bleachers, and around the playing field.

Nothing grabbed him as unusual. The game was continuing on. Dilly was laughing with Sawny. Buck and Boot were moving to the distant front, on the left side, followed by a small battalion. Youk had joined Pone and together they were setting out to enter enemy territory, a surge that looked more promising than the one Dilly had just led.

"What is it?" mumbled Dod to himself.

Sirlonk's cold, evil glare was somewhere nearby—watching—plotting—preparing to attack, or so Dod felt.

Dod frantically searched. Where was The Dread? How would he strike? Who was his target? Commendus and Sabbella had two guards sitting directly behind them, on security detail.

And then Dod's eyes settled on Sammywoo—he stood by himself in the distant backfield, innocently waving his swot in the air. The boy's aloneness was strangely haunting. It drew Dod to race to him so quickly that Dod's feet hardly touched the ground. Everything was dreamlike, almost in slow motion. The ongoing game faded away from reality, and Dod's attention became focused on one thing: reaching the boy in time!

CHAPTER TWENTY-ONE

WAY OUT THERE

O ut of nowhere came an arrow. Its sharp tip was destined to pierce the heart of Youk's only son.

Dod raced as the world turned fuzzy. The only sound he could hear was the thunderous flow of blood pulsing through his veins.

Without seeing the danger and currently running faster than he had ever run in his entire life, Dod left the ground in a magnificent leap, arms stretched out, shield in hand. He threw himself toward Sammywoo not knowing why, but feeling certain of his actions. Time had run out, and the boy was possibly too far away to help.

A loud crunching noise vibrated through Dod's bones as he flew past Youk's son, barely missing him.

Dod hit the ground and rolled. His head was spinning, and his vision was narrowing, as though he were peering through a revolving tunnel. He tried to get up but couldn't, not with the world growing dark. His last glimpse of Sammywoo, before blacking out, revealed a devastating truth: the boy had been struck in the chest with an arrow!

The next thing Dod knew, someone was shaking him.

"Dod, are you okay?" asked a voice. At first it was muffled. "Dod? Dod?"

"Help Sammywoo," came Dod's first words, his eyes still closed. "He's been hit."

"Where did the arrow come from?" pressed someone else firmly. It was Youk.

"I didn't see," said Dod, beginning to open his eyes. His vision had returned, but he felt nauseous.

"Of course you saw!" snapped Youk, his hand to his brow as he searched the shadowed parts of the bleachers. "Think! Quick! Which way?"

"I really don't know," staggered Dod. "It all happened too quickly."

"Near the wall—in the mid section—the high bleachers—where?" demanded Youk. "He's getting away. He could be anywhere. Give us anything you can!"

Youk's voice was more than insistent—it hung on the edge of desperate.

"We'll catch him," called Boot, rushing with a string of people toward Green Hall's ladder. "If we fan out—"

"He's escaping!" snapped Youk. "Run to the tip of the bleachers. Maybe we'll get lucky and you'll see his direction." Youk cupped his hands to his mouth and yelled at the spectators who had now clumped into a tight group around Commendus and Sabbella. "ORRIGO—WHICH WAY DID THE ARROW COME FROM? DID ANYONE SEE?"

"NO," came rumbling back from one of Commendus's security guards.

Youk took two steps toward Dod and froze. "DARI? VALERIE?" he yelled. "WHERE ARE DARI AND VALERIE? HAS ANYONE SEEN THEM?"

No one responded.

"I'm sure they're with the Greenlings that just exited," said Dilly cautiously.

"I'm not," said Youk.

Dod swallowed hard. His eyes hadn't found Sammywoo. The spot where he had been before was now empty.

"They're probably getting a drink under the bleachers," offered Dilly.

"Someone just tried to kill my son!" raged Youk, exploding. "Don't you think my daughters are in jeopardy, too?"

Tried, thought Dod, feeling hope return. If someone had only tried, that meant Sammywoo was still alive—he had miraculously survived the arrow.

"We'll help you find them," said Sawny, looking nervous. She huddled near Dilly and Dod on the ground. "Raul Hall's searching that side, and Green Hall's on this side, and—" Sawny turned to Dilly. "Where are Sawb's private guards when we need them?"

"I think they're stationed out front," said Dilly. "Remember—Sawb thought crowds would try to force their way in today to see us play, so he had them stay out there."

"They'll probably catch the shooter," burst Sawny, "or at least see him."

"I doubt it," said Youk, watching the red and blue uniforms comb the stadium. "The person who planned this…" Youk's voice trailed off as he appeared to drift into thought.

"It was The Dread," squeaked Dod. His voice was dry and scratchy, and he could taste blood.

Youk spun his eyes back on Dod. "So you saw him—" began Youk.

"No," corrected Dod. "I didn't see anyone. It was a feeling—just a hunch that something bad was about to happen."

"You ran on a hunch?" pried Youk, his eyes beating down on Dod judgingly.

"Yes," nodded Dod.

"I'm all better," said Sammywoo, emerging from behind Donshi to give Youk a hug around the waist. "I was just scared, Dad. That's why I was crying."

"You're a brave boy," said Donshi, patting Sammywoo on the head.

Youk let out a groaning sigh.

"What about the arrow?" asked Dod in disbelief. He had seen it stabbing right into Sammywoo's chest, and yet there stood the boy, not a drip of blood on him.

Youk's brow furrowed. "You stopped it," he said, bending over to pick up Dod's light-weight metal shield from the ground. It had an x-shaped hole near the center where the arrow had ripped through it. "Well, you nearly stopped it. My son's extra padding did the rest."

Sammywoo showed Dod the rip in his jersey.

"You did it again!" praised Sawny. "One more person owes you their life."

"How did you know of the attack?" asked Donshi admiringly, flashing her blue eyes toward Dod. The young-looking girl wore her heart on her sleeve, and Dod's name was currently on it.

Dod shrugged his shoulders. He couldn't explain.

"Yes," pressed Youk, unexpectedly sporting a most peculiar look. "Tell us how you knew an arrow was coming, yet didn't see it, but still managed to block the brunt of its force with your shield? You're quite a hero, now aren't you? Something like this proves you're incredible, now doesn't it?"

Dod felt uncomfortable. The air had changed. A simple 'thank you for saving my son' would have been expected. Instead, Youk's line of questioning was increasingly sounding as if he believed Dod had had something to do with the shooting—which thought was completely irrational to Dod.

"I FOUND THE WEAPON!" called Toos from a shaded spot in the bleachers. He bent over into the seating and reemerged holding a bow and quiver.

"I'M COMING," shouted Youk, darting off with Sammywoo tight on his heels.

"Can you stick with Sammywoo until we've found Dari and Valerie?" asked Dilly, assigning Donshi to continue helping Youk with his boy.

Donshi agreed, though she first congratulated Dod three more times on being "remarkable" and "magnificent" before scampering away. Apparently, unlike the rest of her teammates, Donshi had been more interested in watching Dod than the game going on around her and had, therefore, seen the whole episode unfold, right from the point where Dod had broken out into a dead run.

Once Dilly and Sawny were alone with Dod, the questions started flying.

"What really happened?" pressed Dilly.

"I don't know," confessed Dod. "I just had an impression—it seemed like Sirlonk was watching us and preparing to strike."

"In here?" said Sawny. "Are you sure it was him? I'd be leaning my guesses toward Con after the way he acted. That brute didn't appreciate being played, and from his angle, Youk and Dari were part of the trick."

"I certainly wouldn't be surprised if it were him," said Dilly. "Con was fuming. But if he were the culprit, why didn't he shoot Boot? Con hates Boot, and Boot was the real instigator of the trap. And how did he get his hands on a bow and quiver so quickly?"

"I don't know," said Sawny. She inspected Dod's face carefully and concluded: "You remind me of someone, Dod."

"Pap," said Dilly. "The more people Dod helps, the more he seems like him. I've been thinking that lately, too. Pap was always in the right place at the right time. Dod's just like him."

"Not Pap," said Sawny with a clever grin. "Someone else."

Dod smiled. He knew exactly who she meant, even though she wouldn't say.

Back at the castle, Commendus took precautions to ensure his guests were safe, so by nightfall, two dozen strapping guards were sent to watch over Green Hall's camp. He offered to send two dozen more, but Sawb insisted that his private security team was sufficient to oversee Raul Hall's protection.

Youk and his kids were housed in the castle with soldiers at their door. With the shooter still on the loose and his motives unrevealed, every defensive measure was employed by Youk to keep his family safe. It seemed like overkill to Dod until he heard what Boot had to say.

"Youk was warned," whispered Boot, sitting alone by the campfire with Dod, Dilly, Sawny, and Buck. Everyone else had gone to bed, but Boot still kept his voice down so the soldiers who held the perimeter of the camp wouldn't hear him.

"How do you know that?" responded Dilly in an equally quiet voice.

"I got it out of Bowlure," he said proudly. "He and Tridacello came here to help protect Youk and his family. Back at Twistyard, Saluci's got all kinds of people watching over her. Rumor has it that Commendus made changes and got Clair pulled off your case, Dod. Youk's your new representative to the council."

"Really?" said Dod excitedly. Anyone other than Clair sounded wonderful.

"Yup, that's the good news," said Boot.

"How was Youk warned?" asked Sawny.

"He's had notes," responded Boot.

"The good news?" gulped Dod. His gut was screaming that he didn't want to know all of the things Boot had heard, but he knew he needed to hear them anyway.

Boot raised a finger to Dod. "Youk received notes—just like me—just like you. Of course, no one can know that Bowlure told me any of this. He'd rip my legs off as a punishment if word got out."

"Notes," mumbled Dilly. "What did they say?"

"Death threats against his family." The firelight caught Boot's glee in knowing something Dilly hadn't yet heard.

"Death threats?" said Dilly stiffly. "Youk collected a pile of notes that claimed revenge against the Tillius family and he told me not to worry, but one now points at his blood and he's suddenly drenched with trouble and toting guards?"

"Let's remember, his son was shot today," said Sawny, adding perspective.

"That's true," agreed Dilly, softening back down.

"So anyway," said Boot, "Bowlure didn't clarify—I doubt he knows—but there must be more to the notes—perhaps they're asking Youk to do something—like Dod's note."

"Throw *me* under the carriage?" cringed Sawny. "Why does The Order hate me?"

"Shhhh," hushed Boot. Sawny's voice had gotten louder. "I doubt that, but I do know one more tidbit." Boot looked at Dod and smiled painfully. "Remember, you all promise not to tell—"

"We won't," assured Dilly. Sawny and Buck nodded. Dod couldn't get enough air and felt weak imagining what Boot was about to say, and his face was showing it, so Boot paused until Dod finally joined the others in nodding.

"Youk thinks you may have been a part of today's incident."

"I knew it!" exploded Dod, rising to his feet.

"Shhhh," said Dilly and Sawny in unison.

"You were," said Buck quietly. "You were the one who saved his son. We all saw it."

"That's not what he means, is it?" said Dod coldly.

Boot shook his head side-to-side. "He thinks you had someone shoot your shield in front of everyone at the game to prove you're a hero—to prove you saved his son—to prompt him to be a better witness of your kindness before the council."

Dod groaned like a sick goat. "As if I could plan something like that—" began Dod in frustration.

"And he's angry at you because he thinks you were careless," said Boot. "He thinks you were willing to risk his son's life in order to make yourself look a little better. Even with your miraculous move, Sammywoo would have been seriously injured or killed if Youk hadn't bundled him in layers of bedding before the game."

"I know!" gasped Dod. "I've got to go and tell him! He should know that I would never put anyone in a position like that—"

"Whoa, hold on," said Boot, jumping to Dod's side. "Don't go running off. Think about it. Since we've heard where he's coming from, we can act accordingly. Knowledge is power."

"Meaning what?" grumbled Dod. If he acted nice to Youk, Youk would be certain Dod had done it and was still trying to win him over, and if he acted mean to Youk, Youk would hate him as Clair had done and Dod's life would be consigned to crushing rocks in Driaxom for sure. Either way he was doomed.

"Youk's smart," said Boot. "Give the man time and he'll come to the right conclusions on his own. I wouldn't worry about it if I were you."

"I would!" said Sawny indignantly. "That's awful! How could he think such a thing? Dod's the one who saved his son! And Dod could have been hit and killed himself!"

Hearing Sawny's rage made Dod feel better. At least he wasn't the only one who found it horribly unfair.

"Still, give it time," said Boot. "Maybe he'll have more trouble while we're off at the Ghoul's Festival or sailing the seas with Traygof. Then he'll see it's not you. Besides, Youk knows what it's like to be misunderstood."

"How?" asked Dod.

"I've heard things."

"He was kicked out of Twistyard as a Coosing," said Dilly. "I'm not exactly sure why, but it had something to do with him starting the mock TCC. It was a really big deal when my great-grandpa let him come back as one of The Greats."

Buck yawned. "What time are we scheduled to enter the portal tomorrow?"

"Early," said Dilly, stretching. "I'm headed to bed. Are you coming, Sawny?"

"In a minute," she responded. "I promised to show Dod something."

Dod wondered what. She hadn't said anything to him.

"Don't worry," assured Boot one last time, turning to follow Buck to the boys' tent. "Bowlure's twice as mad as you are about it. He's certain you're psychic, and he intends on convincing Youk of it—of course, after Youk has cooled down a few notches."

Once the others were gone, Dod felt embarrassed. He had never been alone with a girl under the stars, but if he were to pick any girl to count them with, it would be Sawny.

"Have you ever seen Raul through the scope?" asked Sawny eagerly.

Dod shook his head.

"Come on—I'll show you. It's amazing!"

Sawny led Dod past the guards and up onto Commendus's patios. Toward the front of one darkened portion, a large rectangular box, the size of two giant fridges, sat upright; its metal was covered with intricate engravings of the heavens. Dod admired its beauty by the light of a glowing rock Sawny wore around her neck. Strange symbols, much like Japanese kanji, were placed beside the representations of various constellations.

"Commendus lent me his key," said Sawny, pulling a chain from her pocket. She inserted the key into a small hole and pressed down on a square block that protruded from the rest of the smooth face of the box. Surprisingly, the thick halves of the large case swung open easily and revealed a strange device inside: a sizable telescope!

"I love looking at the planets and the stars," said Sawny, "especially at a time like this. Once the moon rises, half the sky hides. Their little lights can't compete with the brightness of the moon."

"Oh," said Dod. He was impressed with how sophisticated the telescope looked. If he hadn't known where he was, he would have guessed a space lab on Earth. Though upon closer inspection, he noticed the device was entirely made of metal and glass—there was no plastic—and its appearance was clearly different than anything he had seen.

"This was originally kept beside the Portal House. The Mauj made it. You can peek deep into space with it."

"Really?" said Dod.

"Yes. Let me show you." She bent down and began to crank a number of little gears by turning knobs—first one, then another, then another. Occasionally she glanced into the scope with one eye. As she adjusted the knobs, the skyward end of the telescope moved. Finally, she stopped working the gears and turned her efforts on twisting the tube near the front eyepiece. "There," she said, looking satisfied. "Now it's in focus. Take a look."

Dod bent down and peered into the small glass tunnel. To his surprise, he beheld a beautiful planet of blues, greens, and browns, splotched with cloud cover. It looked like Earth, but the shapes of the continents were different. And to add to Dod's amazement, the planet was as visible as the moon is from Earth through a pair of high-powered binoculars.

"Wow!" exclaimed Dod.

"That's Raul," said Sawny. "Without machinery, you can't even find it. Their sun is only a twinkling speck in the sky—it's over there, just a thumbnail to the east of the tip of the Slender Fish's pointed fin."

Dod tried to see with his naked eye what she meant. Eventually, the constellation known as the Slender Fish became apparent. Its eight bright stars formed the outline of what appeared to be a long, skinny-looking trout.

"That's unbelievable!" said Dod. "Raul is a planet way out there?"

Sawny smiled.

"*The* Raul—the one we're going to in the morning?" continued Dod in disbelief. How could they walk through a portal that transported them across space—an unimaginable distance in light-years away?

"Yup," said Sawny. "We're here, and Raul's way out there. It twists your brain in knots, doesn't it? How did the Mauj create the portals? How exactly do they work? Everything I know about physics, math, and space doesn't explain what we'll experience tomorrow."

Dod stared silently at the sea of countless stars. Space travel was mind-boggling.

Sawny flipped a latch and began once more to turn knobs, directing the telescope to rotate. It veered nearly one hundred and eighty degrees before Sawny slowed its movements and fine tuned the scope. "There she is," she said happily. "Take a look at Soosh."

Dod bent down and marveled. Like Raul, Soosh was seemingly close through the glass, as if it were a moon that hovered just above Green. Its landmasses, however, were smaller, greener, and shrouded by more clouds—the planet was a blue orb with green polka dots.

"Strange, huh?" said Sawny. "Soosh is covered with big islands. It makes you wonder which one Higga's on right now."

Dod pulled back and looked into the sky. The telescope was seemingly pointing at nothing in particular, just a random patch of stars.

"You find Soosh by following the tail of the Corn Snake," declared Sawny, trying to point it out to Dod. When he struggled to see the constellation, she referred him to its likeness on the outside of the telescope box, where fifteen stars were etched into the metal in a zigzagging formation. It looked more like lightning to Dod, not a snake. But once he knew what he was searching for, the stars made sense in the heavens.

"I have a secret way of pegging the planet," shared Sawny smugly. "Once you've found the end of the snake's tail, position the bright star directly in the center of the glass, then count your toes, your nose, the ships out at sea, and finally count to three."

"What?" chuckled Dod.

"It's a verse my great-grandpa taught me," explained Sawny. "I'm sure he heard it from his father. I've read it before, too. You have ten toes, so turn the lowest knob—right down here—ten times around. Then turn the top one—up here—one time—"

"Because you only have one nose," said Dod.

Sawny smiled. "The 'ships out at sea' means straight back here—this knob. You have to turn it twenty-three times. I always remember the number because it rhymes with sea."

"Clever," agreed Dod, noticing the variety of levers and knobs on the telescope. It was a complex instrument to use.

"And for the last part, 'finally' reminds me it's this lever, right over here on the end. You crank it three times and you're there. It's like magic! After that you just focus the eyepiece."

Dod enjoyed listening to Sawny. Her voice was the most wonderful sound.

At the end of Sawny's explanation, she pivoted toward Dod and trapped him with her stare, the glow of her rock revealing even the flecks of brown in her otherwise blue eyes. "What happened at the dance?"

"Huh?" mumbled Dod, caught off guard.

"I won't tell anyone, I promise. I just have to know. How did you disappear?" Sawny was pleading for the truth.

"Well…" Dod struggled to think of what to say. Lame excuses flooded his mind.

"Please," begged Sawny, pulling a cute look. "You can trust me. I'm the tightest-lipped person you'll ever meet."

Dod looked at her lips.

"You know what I mean," she said, giving him a shove.

Dod chuckled. As an interrogator, Sawny was unusually persuasive.

"What if I share something first," offered Sawny, "something that proves I completely trust you to keep my secrets? If I did that, would you explain things to me?"

"It depends on how good your secret is," said Dod, unable to resist teasing.

Sawny punished Dod with her eyes. "Come on, pleeeease," she begged.

"Okay," said Dod. "But I have to warn you, if I tell you the full truth, you can't share any of it with anyone. Agreed?"

Sawny nodded impatiently.

"I'm not kidding, now," he added. "Bonboo's the only one who knows."

"I won't even think about slipping," insisted Sawny, biting her lip.

Dod hesitated. A shooting star burst from one corner of the sky and drew a line halfway to the opposite side before fading into the night.

"The sky nod's at our pact," said Sawny, grabbing Dod by the arm. "Some sailors won't leave port until their captain can show them a burning line like that—for good luck on their voyage."

"I doubt Traygof's men act that way," said Dod. "That one guy—"

"The one with the tri-compass?" asked Sawny.

"Yeah, he'd make them sail on time no matter what, regardless, don't you think?"

Sawny waited quietly, smirking, then nudged Dod. "Start explaining," she said, "about the dance—not the sailors."

"Weren't you going to go first?" returned Dod.

"Oh, right," said Sawny, letting go of Dod's arm. "Do you promise on your life that you won't ever mention what I'm about to reveal to you—not to anyone but me?" Sawny's face was firm and serious, though nervous.

Dod began to say yes, then stopped. "You're not going to confess that you've been out killing people, are you?"

"No!" said Sawny, glowering at Dod jestfully. "I'm serious. It's something I recently discovered, and it has—well—a few troubling implications. But I can't decide whether to even bring it up with my great-grandpa." Sawny began to fidget with the telescope, changing its coordinates. "If I mentioned it to Dilly—all the pieces and the clues—she'd be mad at me! It's proof of hard truths long since buried—or possibly burned."

"About The Lost City?" asked Dod eagerly.

"Sort of," confessed Sawny slowly. She continued to adjust the telescope as she spoke. "Years ago I studied as much as I could about our history—about the Tillius family. Most of the historical facts concerning the time period before Concealio have been muddled, at best, in the records we now have—I know that much for sure. Though, I'm confident that many of the drifting myths have a basis of real substance—a hidden bedrock—the TCC and its origins, the Code of the Kings, The Lost City, the missing portals, and—" Sawny glanced up at Dod, "even the tales of the Crazy King aren't without merit. You'll never hear Dilly say it, but it's true."

"That makes sense," said Dod, wondering where she was headed.

Sawny turned back to her tasks at the telescope, as if doing something while talking made the telling easier. "I've kept all sorts of facts buried in my head—things I've read about—little clues that have guided my opinion over the years. Just the books Ascertainy claims I stole," huffed Sawny, shaking her head. She turned back around to face Dod. "They alone have countless hints at disreputable truths—horrible things about my ancestors' shady pasts—a great distance back, though. I'm sure that's why the books were locked up. They mostly contained dribble, the kind Boot and Buck wouldn't want to read—about on par with the books Commendus had us reviewing, except Twistyard's collection was older."

"You've read a lot," said Dod. "I think The Order is afraid of you because of how hard you've searched to understand the facts and how well you've put things together. You definitely have a dangerous brain."

"Me?" grinned Sawny, glancing back at Dod. "I didn't disappear at the dance!"

"I can explain," said Dod. He felt like he had finally found someone who would believe him and not think he was insane.

"I expect you will," said Sawny, beginning to twist the eyepiece and its adjoining shaft. She quietly fiddled for about thirty seconds before stepping back. "Take a look," she said, glowing with a mixture of triumph and fear.

Dod slowly leaned toward the glass, though something inside him revealed plainly what he would see. "You've found it!" he whispered in reverent amazement. Just the sight of it made him shaky in the knees, and his eyes teared up until he couldn't see through the lens anymore. "I wondered where it was in the sky."

"What?" gasped Sawny in shock. "Are you teasing me?"

"No," said Dod. "I think our secrets are more connected than you know."

"That's impossible!" burst Sawny. "I just found it! No one—and I mean absolutely no one—knows what I'm showing you. I've broken the ancient Mauj code!" She pulled Dod back and pointed at the exterior of the box, directing him to look at various formations of stars and their adjoining squiggly and straight lines. "Everyone thinks these pictures are ancient drawings of the constellations and their respective names—words written in an unknown language. But they're wrong! These aren't names, they're coordinates! This box shows one hundred and six different constellations, and these lines next to them describe how to find them with this tool, based on the starting point of the Steady Star, the time of night, and the season of the year!"

Sawny pulled a paper from her pocket and held it up. "Do you see this? I've found dozens of places where people have sketched this same insignia into old texts, referring to Raul. As a result, people still sometimes draw or paint this picture. Everyone knows this symbol means Raul. Yet look closer. These dots are clearly the Slender Fish, and this thin line designates the tip of the pointed fin as the starting location, and this string of lines—right here—contains the directions, in code, that the Mauj would have used to explain to one another how to find Raul in Green's night sky using this instrument."

Dod's heart was pounding. She had two more pictures on her paper.

"This one's Soosh," she said, pointing to the next sketch. "I've only seen it in a few places, maybe six or seven. Last week I was singing the silly verse while reading about Soosh, just a short segment in Concealio's diary, and it dawned on me, the lines matched the numbers in the song—at least they do if you use the old style of writing, the way numbers were written on the map to The Lost City. Look here: ten down low, one up top, twenty-three deep center, and three at the end side. They overlap purposefully to give us an indication of which knobs to turn."

Dod didn't know anything about the strange, old style of writing, but he definitely felt the power of Sawny's genius.

Sawny then pointed to the last drawing. The constellation was unusual, and the insignia beside it was four times as big as the other two, with dozens of crisscrossing lines.

"I've only seen this one twice," she said. "Once in the books that were stolen from Twistyard and again on the map to The Lost City. Nothing in either location noted what it was, but I couldn't help recognizing that it seemed to follow the same pattern as the other symbols. So I checked and found this constellation—right here—it's called the Gold Miner—and after following the code beside it—which was terribly difficult, I might add—I discovered *that* planet!"

Dod stared at the telescope lens.

"We're probably the only people alive today who have seen it," continued Sawny. "Notice how small it looks. It's much, much, much farther away from here than Raul or Soosh. It's pushing the technology's limits just to put it in view at all. I'd guess in real life it's at least as big as either of the others, or possibly much bigger."

"It's big," said Dod, leaning back down to take another look. He couldn't believe it was Earth. North and South America currently faced Green and were just as easy to identify as they ever had been on maps or in pictures back home. But discovering Earth while on Green raised a multitude of questions.

"Why don't you want to show Bonboo or Dilly?" asked Dod.

"For a lot of reasons," said Sawny. "Cracking this code proves people from Soosh not only stopped here to visit, but lived here for a long time, just as the legends suggest."

"So The Lost City is real," said Dod.

"It was," agreed Sawny. "Maybe it's destroyed and long gone, who knows? I suspect my distant grandpa had a hand in its demise. I've read enough to sadly question the role of my ancestors in a multitude of treacherous things. Discovering this planet just proves to me that the hunches I've had are likely correct. It's sad."

"So what?" chuckled Dod. "I wouldn't worry about what's happened in the past."

"You're sounding like Boot, now," said Sawny. "It's more than I can easily explain. I'd have to pour a lifetime of research into your brain before you'd get it."

"Let the past stay in the past," said Dod.

"That's not all," said Sawny. "One thing that troubles me—and remember, you can't tell anyone—is that there are too many tight lines, things that connect the past with the present."

"What do you mean?"

"Secrets of old—ways to obtain power and control—doesn't it all sound familiar?" Sawny looked scared. "I know my great-grandpa keeps secrets—he's instructed you and Dilly, right?"

"A little," admitted Dod reluctantly.

"I think the original TCC was set up so a few people could rule over all of Green, Raul, and Soosh by force."

"That doesn't sound like Bonboo," said Dod frankly, seeing where Sawny was headed.

"I know, but it makes me nervous," said Sawny. "From what I've read, The Order has popped up in different forms, right from its beginnings with the TCC all the way down to the horrible reign of Doss—and now look, it's rising again! Who keeps it going? What's the thread? How does it revive? The people we're dealing with may know what the ancients did, and I don't think that's a good thing."

"What do you mean?" pressed Dod.

"The Mauj had great technologies and powers," said Sawny, pointing at the telescope. "Only a sliver of what they possessed remains with us today—the triblot fields, the portals, and other fancy gadgets like them. We can't recreate any of it. We haven't even begun to understand the science behind the technologies we possess. And yet, I believe there are still things to be found—perhaps what The Order is searching for—which could change the scales forever."

"Maybe for good," said Dod.

"I wish," said Sawny. "This planet that we're staring at—it was central to the TCC's plan, according to a diagram that was in the writings at Twistyard—or at least that's how I read it—the words and pictures were filled with symbolism."

"Oh, right," said Dod. He shivered.

"Now, here we are," muttered Sawny. "That same symbol pops up on the map to The Lost City. It's not a coincidence. If Sirlonk and the others in The Order were to discover what we know—that it represents a planet—it could possibly be the final piece they need."

Hearing that Earth was included in The Order's plan sent Dod's nerves jumping. He knew Sirlonk already had ties—he had left a message for Dod in the Las Vegas trailer—but it wasn't until Sawny spelled it out clearly that Dod felt the gravity of the situation.

Sawny took a last peek at Earth before changing the coordinates to point at Raul. "I've shared a lot," she said, closing and locking the telescope box. "You better start talking."

Dod took a seat beside Sawny on a balcony bench and sat in silence for a few minutes. Seeing Earth was beyond shocking.

"Just tell the truth," pressed Sawny, once the calm had become awkward.

"Okay," began Dod, trembling slightly, trying to push Sawny's discovery out of his mind. "The reason I disappeared from the dance is because my brother took this medallion from me." Dod pulled his medallion out of his shirt and showed Sawny the ten-point star on one side and the worn inscriptions on the other.

Sawny's face was filled with doubt, but she kept listening.

"I'm from the planet you just discovered," he said cringingly. "It's called Earth. This medallion makes it possible for me to travel from there to here and from here to there. I have no clue how, though I know it's the same way Pap did. This is his medallion. I got it after he died. While I'm wearing it, time seems to stand still on the other planet, as if everyone and everything were waiting for me to return and resume where I was. If I take it off, time starts up without me. So, while I was napping on Earth, my little brother tried to borrow this—he took it for only a minute or so before I awoke and took it back. But during that time, I disappeared from Green, leaving you dancing alone. And that's not the only time I've had it taken. Someone actually stole it from me for a while. That's why I was gone for months without any warning and missed the Bollirse games at Twistyard and Carsigo. You don't think I wanted to be away, do you?"

Sawny inspected Dod's face closely.

"I told you it would be hard to believe," said Dod, struggling to think of anything he could add that would help him prove his case. "Bonboo knows all about it. He's the one who originally explained it to me when I first came to Green. Oh, and I haven't figured out how to come and go as I choose—I'd never in a million years leave the dance hall floor with you in my arms!"

Sawny cracked a grin as Dod blushed. The words had come off his tongue without him thinking.

"If Pap's your grandfather," said Sawny, patting Dod's checkered shirt, "who's your father?"

"That's tricky," confessed Dod, grateful beyond measure that she hadn't kicked him to the curb as a liar, yet. "My name is actually Cole Richards, son of Stephen Richards."

"Coal?" giggled Sawny. "You had to dig deep to come up with that one."

"It's true," said Dod, sitting up straight. "At home they call me Cole."

A noise interrupted the night's stillness, prompting Sawny to quickly cover her glowing rock. People were coming.

"Sawny? Is that you and Dod over there?" inquired Dilly. She and Boot approached wearing swords.

"I told you they were simply trying to slip off alone," chuckled Boot the moment his glowing stone caught their guilty faces.

"NO!" insisted Sawny, jumping to her feet, her cheeks pink with embarrassment. "I just got done showing Raul and Soosh to Dod." She fidgeted with her pocket and drew out the key. "See, Commendus lent this to me. We were talking about space and the constellations."

"I've had that discussion loads of times," teased Boot.

"Really, we were looking at the planets," protested Dod, joining in the defense. "Trust me, if Sawny were trying to sneak off with someone to be *alone*, you'd need to go searching for Pone, not me."

Sawny gave Dod a crusty glance. "I don't care the least bit for Pone," she said stubbornly. "Besides, I'm way too young for courting—assuming there were boys worth the chase—which there most certainly aren't around here."

"Okay," said Dilly, snipping to the point. She lowered her voice to a whisper. "While we were off playing Bollirse or eating dinner, someone went through our things. He had to be searching for the map."

"Did they get it?" asked Dod, holding his breath as he looked to Boot. After hearing Earth was somehow connected with it, he certainly didn't want The Order to recover it.

"Please, have a little faith in me," said Boot arrogantly. "It's still safe. They won't find it."

"Good," said Dod and Sawny in unison.

CHAPTER TWENTY-TWO

THROUGH THE PORTAL

The next day, breakfast came early. Before dawn, Hermit and Toby stumbled around in the boys' tent carrying large trays of blueberry muffins. Sawb had sent one of his private guards to get the morning process going in Green Hall's camp, by blowing an obnoxious horn. Sawb wanted to make sure that the whole group would be ready to enter the portal at sunrise.

Dod hadn't slept enough to feel rested. What little of the night he had spent in his cot had been spent tossing and turning sleeplessly, wishing he could erase from Sawny's mind the things he had said and wondering all sorts of questions about the things she had said. And above all else, he couldn't get used to the idea that Earth was visible through a special telescope, some seemingly infinite distance away.

"Are you nervous about the big hug?" asked Boot, eyeing Dod cleverly as he rolled out of bed with three muffins in his hands.

"No," said Dod defensively, giving the bright, hanging candles a scowl. "Not any more than you're scared of the smoochy-smoochy-I'm-gonna-kiss-Dilly-all-over-her-face thing."

"What?" laughed Pone, losing muffin crumbs out of the corners of his mouth. He kept a blanket wrapped around him to stave off the morning chill.

"I meant *The* big hug," said Boot, smirking at Dod.

"The squeeze," said Pone. "You better eat up—the portal flattens you as thin as a sheet of paper, and I hate to be the one to tell you, bro, but you're lacking the reserves some of us are packing." Pone patted his slightly protruding gut with pride.

"Oh—right," stuttered Dod, assessing his own concave stomach. He suddenly felt nervous about going to Raul and embarrassed about ranting at Boot.

"Does it hurt?" asked Hermit, moving closer to Pone for an answer. Like most of the Greenlings and Coosings, he had never been through the portal before. Getting papers to enter Raul was extremely difficult. Only a handful of important people were allowed to use the portal.

"No," said Pone, grabbing two more muffins off Hermit's tray. "So long as you weigh at least two hundred pounds, you should be fine."

"And if you don't?" squeaked a nearby Greenling named Kurt, his young gangly figure barely pushing one hundred and thirty pounds, and that, too, if his trousers were wet.

"You may get lost in space and never arrive," said Pone. "It's a sad case indeed to die from under-eating. That's why I'm a big advocate of snacks."

"Me too," agreed Toos heartily, gazing into a little mirror as he slicked back his hair. "I've packed plenty of things for the trip."

"Didn't they tell you?" asked Boot, catching a glimpse of Toos's hefty suitcase. It bulged in the middle, but had two extra straps bracing it closed. "You're only allowed a small bag—no more than twenty pounds, no food or drinks, and no weapons. Most everything must stay here. Commendus has agreed to let us keep the tents as they are. But don't worry, Terro guarantees we'll be fed well."

Pone nodded excitedly. "The Ghoul's Festival," he chanted in a low, mystical voice. "Enter the portal of death if you dare!"

Kurt winced and his spiky brown hair began to wilt. "Maybe I'll stay back," he said gingerly.

"They're killing me," groaned Toos, measuring how large his pockets were inside the gray-and-black striped suit coat he wore. "I was planning on trading stuff. My family back home would love to get souvenirs from Raul. Do they count the things in your pockets as part of your twenty pounds?"

"Probably not," said Boot.

"I'll stay and keep watch over the tents," said Kurt insecurely. "I don't think I can handle 'the squeeze' today—my stomach's off—maybe another time."

"Pone was kidding!" assured Boot, moving in to calm his fears. "You don't have to worry. Everyone makes it across just fine. Don't tell anyone, but I'm bringing Sneaker, and he only weighs about as much as your foot. The portal's fun."

"Do people ever get lost?" asked Toby, holding a nearly-empty muffin tray. Pone still eyed the crumbs longingly. "I've heard stories about whole armies being swallowed up," said Toby anxiously.

"Stop," said Boot. "That's a crazy legend created by people who could only wish they were privileged enough to see the portal, let alone ride through the tunnel to Raul. Think about it—how many people can enter the portal at a time? I've only seen them go by twos. Does that sound like a gate that an army would pass through?"

Toby's face lightened up.

"It's just like walking through a wide doorway into another room, huh Boot?" said Toos, sounding experienced.

"A little," chuckled Boot, stepping over to give Toos's suitcase a heft. He put it on Toos's cot and began to unlatch the straps. "We've got to hurry," he said, "Sawb's bent on being prompt."

"It's way cooler than a doorway," explained Pone eagerly, wiping crumbs off his pants. He was now wearing his blanket like a cape. "Once you enter, it's like the air around you grabs hold of you and carries you to Raul. Your feet don't touch the ground for ten minutes, or maybe fifteen—what would you say, Boot?"

"I think they should all find out for themselves," said Boot, returning to Kurt's side to pat him on the back. Kurt seemed to have lodged something in his throat at Pone's mention of fifteen minutes in the air.

"If I could, I'd go back and forth all day long," said Pone. "Flying through the tunnel is the coolest thing I've ever done!"

"Didn't you say that about winning the Golden Swot?" asked Voo, coming to inspect Pone's preparations. He had his pack over one shoulder and his wavy black hair combed and ready.

"I guess I do a lot of cool things," laughed Pone. "It's fun being me."

Sawb's horn-blowing guard began making noises again. This time his bugling was followed by a warning: "TEN MINUTES!" he shouted. "LEAVE WITH SAWB OR STAY BEHIND!"

"He's serious!" said Boot, rallying the tent full of people to hustle. "We're all going. No exceptions. This is a real privilege. It may be your only chance to see Raul, and I'm certain it's your only chance to enjoy the Ghoul's Festival. Even Sawb's guards have to stay behind. If Dod hadn't saved Terro from Driaxom—"

"But Boot—" began Kurt, his face turning white.

"You'll be my tunnel pal," said Boot quickly. "Wear your pack, and I'll hold onto it. That way you won't have to worry about getting lost. I've traveled roundtrip four times. It'll be fun, trust me. We'll laugh the whole way."

Boot's offer calmed Kurt, though it did the opposite for Dod. While walking to the Portal House, located in Commendus's backyard, all Dod could think about was who he would enter with. Buck had Toos, Pone had Hermit, Voo had Toby, Sham had Donshi, Dilly had Sawny, and the list went on and on. Everyone seemed to be paired. Even Ingrid had Juny. But once the group had arrived at the building, Dod was so intrigued by what he saw that he forgot about his lack of companionship for the journey and didn't mind that he trailed in the back.

Two separate walls encircled the Portal House. The first was fifteen feet high and ten feet thick, and it had a roadway on the top. Soldiers patrolled back and forth, at the ground level and above, as if protecting Fort Knox.

The second wall was even taller—over twenty-five feet high—and it, too, had troops marching upon it.

Sawb led the group and provided the proper paperwork to the guards that kept the gates. Upon entering the inner courtyard, Dod marveled at the walls of the actual building. They were made of white stone and covered with detailed carvings of the constellations, just as the telescope box had been. The structure looked more like an ancient temple than it did a galactic transport station.

As the group filed inside, Sawny tugged at Dilly to hold back. "Notice all the symbols," she quietly said to Dod. It was the first thing she had said to him all morning. The night before had left both of them looking away from each other.

"It's got pretty pictures," huffed Ingrid, hobbling in the rear on Juny's arm, her cane thumping the ground. "Who decorated this building?"

Juny looked sick and didn't respond.

"What do you think of the carvings?" Ingrid asked Sawny.

"They're really old," she responded.

Suddenly, Juny pulled back on Ingrid's arm. "I can't do it," she said. "I can't return to Raul! Tonnis can't either! We have to go back to Twistyard. It's not safe for us to visit Raul—not yet."

"Don't worry," assured Ingrid, "I'll protect you." She raised her cane in the air.

"No!" insisted Juny. "I'm serious! They would sooner poke my eyes out and file my toes to dust than mend the bridges *my husband* has burned! If I go, I'll die in Raul!"

"But Terro promised your safety," said Ingrid. "You'll be fine. You don't have to leave his castle. We can stay put and enjoy the food and festivities. And if you send word, your family could come to visit. Wouldn't that be nice—seeing your sisters and mother?"

"No!" said Juny, planting her feet firmly. "I'm not going." She struggled to break free of Ingrid's grip.

"Please," begged Ingrid. "I must attend the Ghoul's Festival. I hear it's to die for."

"Then go with them!" protested Juny, pointing at Dod, Dilly, and Sawny. The others had already entered the building.

CHAPTER TWENTY-TWO

"But you're Terro's sister-in-law!" said Ingrid. "I want to be introduced to everyone by *you*."

"I'll show you around," offered Dilly, looking as though she felt bad for Juny.

"It wouldn't be the same," complained Ingrid gruffly, storming toward the entrance without Juny. She lumbered past Dod and nearly knocked him over with her shoulder bag.

Juny stood staring at the building. She was clothed in a beautiful, pearl-beaded dress and appeared as much like a queen as Dod could imagine. "Please call Tonnis back to me," she requested.

Ingrid seemed to ignore her as she disappeared into the Portal House.

"I'll go get him," offered Sawny, rushing forward after Ingrid. Dilly and Dod stayed back with Juny, who began crying.

"It's not that I don't want to go," said Juny. "I have a lifetime of fond memories of the Ghoul's Festival. It's remarkable fun. I just don't dare, not with all my husband's enemies on the lurk. They would kill me and Tonnis for Sirlonk's foolishness."

"I understand," said Dilly, nodding sympathetically.

"I must protect my son," said Juny, tipping her chin up. She wiped her tears away with a calm hand. "Who knows, maybe one day we could return—maybe one day Tonnis could take his rightful place in the Chantolli household. But only if he lives to see that day."

"We'll give Terro your regards," assured Dilly, beginning to move toward the entrance. The soldiers who kept the door had begun to shut it.

"He's already gone through!" said Sawny, bursting back out into the courtyard. "Raul Hall's on their way, and Green Hall's lining up. The keepers are moving us quickly today. Would you like me to send Tonnis back this afternoon?"

"Couldn't you turn him right around at the other end?" begged Juny anxiously. "I can't wait until later. He's not safe around *them*. Tell him I insist."

"The guards don't allow cross-directional traffic anymore," said Sawny. "Later today is the earliest—"

"Then I'm coming," interrupted Juny stiffly, shuffling behind Dilly and Dod.

Inside the building, smokeless torches burned solemnly. Fifteen-foot statues of people with the heads of beasts lined the corridor that led to the portal. Each held a weapon in one hand and a torch in the other. Their threatening presence made Dod apprehensive. Who were the original portal builders?

Dod looked to the ceiling and walls. Fifty-feet up, beautiful artwork depicting various aspects of the universe covered the domed vault, as though each scene had been pulled from the lens of the Hubble Space Telescope. Reds, blues, oranges, purples, and greens flooded the spectacular ceiling painting, bringing the galaxies to life.

"Youk's here," mumbled Dilly in surprise, drawing Dod's eyes back to the floor. Youk stood near the portal beside Commendus, Strat, Bowlure, and Tridacello, discussing something as he watched the Greenlings and Coosings file two-by-two through the gateway.

Dod hardly noticed the people. The portal was like a giant, slender horseshoe. Its deep-blue framing rose to twelve feet in the center, where a ten-point star interrupted the otherwise smooth archway. The contraption appeared to be made of a metallic substance and didn't have any buttons or levers on a majority of its front face, except in one small hand-sized box that was about eye-level on the left side. The center glowed a misty-green, as if it were an open doorway to a foggy swamp, yet the haze didn't enter the room.

It was amazing. Dod stared. Every fifteen to twenty seconds, a keeper dressed in a royal-red cape directed a pair of waiting people to enter. To one side of the portal, six men stood watch with spears in hand, and directly behind them, another twelve sat in chairs on a platform holding bows and quivers full of arrows.

"Dod," whispered Sawny over her shoulder. "Look!" She pointed at the star that fit snugly in the center of the archway.

Dod recognized the Raul character inscribed within it, written exactly as Sawny had shown to him the night before. *The Mauj code*, thought Dod.

Up ahead, Juny reunited with Ingrid, who had somehow moved a number of slots forward, butting deep into the crowd of Greenlings and Coosings.

"What's gotten into Ingrid lately?" Dod whispered to Dilly and Sawny as he brought up the rear.

"She's always been rude and crotchety, hasn't she?" responded Dilly, sporting the beginnings of a grin.

"It's her big worry," said Sawny softly. "Last night, on the way back from the game, she told me that she's extremely excited to sail with Traygof, but terrified of the water. She keeps dreaming she's at sea, miles from land, and the ship is attacked.

"That would be something," said Dilly excitedly. "Can you imagine fighting alongside of Traygof?"

"I'd rather not," confessed Sawny.

"I wouldn't mind," said Dilly, "but I can see how Ingrid would be concerned. She may have had sword skills in her youth, but such things are likely far from her hands at this point."

"That wasn't her big worry," said Sawny. "She's afraid that Traygof will order everyone to abandon the ship and swim miles to shore."

"Who could swim for miles?" chuckled Dilly. "That's a silly thing to worry about. Sailors hate swimming as much as the rest of us."

Youk approached wearing a fancy white suit, white gloves, and his best feathered hat, which he tipped at Dilly and Sawny before addressing Dod. "I'll be entering beside you," he said cheerfully, putting a hand on Dod's shoulder. "Are you carrying any weapons?"

"No," assured Dod. His mind was instantly jumbled with thoughts of the things he had wanted to tell Youk the night before, yet nothing came out.

"Good," said Youk, flashing a smile at the guards with spears. Two of them left their positions and made a beeline for Dod.

"Please step aside, sirs" said one soldier. "We need to check your things."

"Of course," said Youk, handing off his bag. "We're both grateful for your conscientious efforts in keeping this place safe, aren't we, Dod?"

Dod handed the men his bag as well. When the guards found them acceptable, they proceeded to pat Youk and Dod down.

"All clear," said one soldier, nodding to the three keepers.

Dod watched Dilly and Sawny step into the portal. His heart began to beat faster. He and Youk were next in line. Dod was the last of the Coosings. The others from Twistyard had already entered and were well on their way to the festival. Sawb had possibly arrived in Raul. His fifteen-minute lead put him there—or close—according to Pone's morning guesses. Dod envied Sawb.

"Wait!" said Youk. He motioned for Tridacello and Strat to go in front of him and Dod. Within seconds, they had disappeared.

"Give my best wishes to Terro for me," called Commendus, waving as Dod and Youk stepped forward. Dod braced himself for an uncomfortable amount of pressure and halted right at the line, his nose nearly touching the dimly glowing mist, while Youk continued into the portal.

"Go on!" ordered one of the keepers impatiently. "You're out of pace!"

"Don't worry," said Bowlure. "I'm right behind you. It'll be fine. Take another step."

Dod felt a tingling sensation and heard what sounded like thousands of whispering voices. Trembling, he stuck one hand into the portal and wiggled his fingers. They were invisible to his eyes, as though he had hidden them beneath a blanket.

"Are you staying or going?" called Commendus.

Dod didn't turn to look, he boldly jumped into the fog. Instantly, he was engulfed in a bright light which made it impossible to see anything, and the whispering voices turned into a mind-numbing roar. The medallion against his chest burned hot as he felt his body flying through the air. And then, only moments after jumping into the portal, everything changed! The surrounding atmosphere no longer held him, and he fell to the ground. A cold, stone floor met his knees first, then his hands. It was as if he had stumbled while jogging.

Fear overtook Dod. Why hadn't he gone to Raul? The process Pone and Boot had described was certainly different. Nothing had hugged him, and the weightlessness hadn't lasted a quarter of an hour—it had ceased nearly as soon as it had begun!

Dod blinked, trying to clear his eyes of the spots that stole his vision. In horror, he recognized the stone flooring was different than the type he had just left. But if he hadn't stayed at the Portal House in Green, where had he gone? Thoughts of Sirlonk rushed through his mind. Perhaps he had rerouted him somehow and plopped him in a dungeon.

Carefully, and after taking a deep breath of the warm, damp air, Dod lifted his head. "Sirlonk!" he said, watching a caped man step from the shadows. His walk was familiar.

"You're so funny," responded the man. "I haven't been called that in weeks."

Dod's eyes continued to adjust to the lighting, which was now infinitely dimmer than the blinding brightness he had just encountered.

"I'm so glad you made it," said the man, approaching slowly. "I was worried you'd get busy and skip out. But here you are, bowing before me in my chambers. You may arise, Dod."

Dod continued to blink.

"Help him up!" ordered the man, waving his hand. "This is the boy I spoke of."

Two people came from the sides and grabbed Dod under the arms. "He's the one who dares challenge The Dread?" muttered one. "Dared," corrected the other.

"Are you ready for hard labor?" asked the caped man, still approaching, but his face was shrouded by Dod's impaired vision.

Dod rubbed at his eyes, wishing the spots would fade faster. The glimpse he had taken of the blindingly-bright light in the portal had left him struggling to see clearly.

"What kind of labor?" grumbled Dod, racking his brain for answers. His eyes were telling him Sirlonk was approaching, but his ears were hearing a different person. Perhaps Sirlonk's voice had changed upon entering the new realm—or wherever it was that Dod had landed—or perhaps Dod's ears were just as impaired as his eyes.

"I was hoping you'd smash rocks for me," laughed the man. "I hear it keeps you sane. It's perfect for a *criminal* like you."

Dod shivered. The air didn't smell like Driaxom, yet an unexplainable wave of feelings rushed over him and, just like that, all of the horrible memories came flooding back: the smell of death, the taste of rotten, maggot-infested slop, the stabbing pain in his leg, and the constant fear of being killed by mindless brutes.

"Can you believe we came from Driaxom to this?" sighed the man.

"Terro!" exclaimed Dod, finally recognizing him.

"Welcome to my home," he responded warmly. "Sorry the buglers weren't in place. I wasn't expecting you to arrive first. I thought my son would come at the front, papers in hand, and give us a few minutes to situate your honor tribute. But alas, you're a complex ball of surprises!"

"I'm first?" questioned Dod, completely shocked. It didn't make sense. The others had left before him.

"Well, you're the first today," said Terro. "Neadrou and a few others came yesterday."

Dod glanced around. His eyes were beginning to work well enough to see his surroundings better. The room was similar to the one he had just left, though instead of having guards stand watch beside the portal with weapons in hand, a series of platforms held a gallery of unusual animals, each eyeing the gateway with interest.

One beast immediately caught Dod's attention. It was a dog that looked identical to the monstrous one which had finished off Buck's horse. Its cold glare sent chills up Dod's arms and down his spine. Five creatures were lions of some sort, two resembled hyenas, one had wings and feet like a vulture but the head and neck of a giant snake, and four seemed to be large wolves. The odd display of beasts quickly reminded Dod of the stories Boot had told of The Zoo.

"Do you like my collection?" asked Terro, noticing Dod's interest in the animals. "Trimash has done a remarkable job of training them, don't you think?"

Dod glanced at a burly tredder who sat in a comfy-looking chair, high above the beasts. He was clothed in furs, head-to-toe, and was presently chewing on a drumstick.

Terro snapped his fingers at the man. "Trimash, show my honored guest what you can do. Dod's a bit of a mayler, too."

The thick-necked man set his food on a small table beside him and rose to his feet. "Ha hoola rasha'am," he chanted, waving his hands in the air. Instantly, the animals crouched and began to growl. "Ha hoola rasha'am," he repeated. This time he waved one hand and all of the lions jumped up and surrounded the front of the portal, snarling viciously and baring their teeth.

"He's good," said Dod nervously, stepping away from the pride.

"Ha hoola rasha'am," said the mayler, pointing a crooked finger. The wolves leapt from their platforms and joined the lions, every other spot, though they looked away from the portal. One growled in Dod's direction.

"Nice trick," choked Dod, beginning to feel the unseen leashes that tethered the creatures' brains. Dod glanced at the mayler, a fair distance off, and saw what appeared to be a Soosh Mayler Belt around his waist.

"Trimash is somewhat psychic, too," said Terro matter-of-factly. "He's been taught in the craft from his boyhood. Now he lives here, in this hall, as a protector of the portal. Together with my pets, he keeps the gate."

Dod stepped closer to Terro. "Quite a job for one man," remarked Dod, glancing around the room at the ominous, tall statues. The growling beasts and dim lighting made the animal-faced sentinels look twice as threatening as the similar ones had looked back in Green's Portal House.

"I think it's a bit posh for a servant," huffed Terro, appearing slightly ruffled. "He's not entirely alone; I send guards and other keepers at the scheduled comings and goings. The rest of the time he's allowed to sit with his thoughts and my pets—and don't forget he's fed in *my house*. All of my servants eat well. The best commoner is relegated to a much lower level of living. My servants are like family to me."

"I'm sure," stammered Dod, reading the direction Terro was headed. The issue Terro had become defensive about was slavery, a condition allowed in Raul but not in Green.

Terro snapped at Trimash. "Call them to return—hold them in line—I can't talk over the noise."

"Too ca howa'am!" shouted the mayler, one hand raised to the ceiling. The lions and wolves scattered back to their respective platforms and quieted.

"Come Trimash," said Terro, "I want you to meet Dod."

Trimash descended a narrow stairway and drew close, his good eye inspecting Dod while his other—glossy and gray—seemingly stared off into the distance. Everything about Trimash gave Dod the creeps. Even the Soosh Mayler Belt around his bulging waist was devilish, adorned with small skulls.

"Tell Dod something—do your thing," pressed Terro arrogantly, and then turning to Dod he added, "I paid plenty for this one."

The huge man stood silently, then closed his eyes and breathed in deeply, as though sucking Dod's thoughts from the air.

Dod shivered. Once the man had come close, the room's wildlife had begun to tingle Dod's senses. The lions hated the vulture-snake, and the wolves hated the hyenas, and all of the creatures feared the grizzly hound. Dod couldn't help agreeing with the majority: The monstrous dog was the most terrifying.

"Anything will do," rushed Terro.

Trimash opened his eyes and gave an icy cold glare. "Death follows this boy," he said in a somber voice.

"Perhaps you sense where he's been," remarked Terro. "Did I tell you? Dod was locked in Driaxom with me. We were both wrongfully imprisoned. The whole ordeal was dreadful. I still smell the mire every time I sneeze."

Trimash cleared his throat with a deep gurgling. "He's seen death, and its fingers are ever reaching to the left and right of his shadow."

CHAPTER TWENTY-TWO

"My! That's a pleasant read for my most honored guest!" grumbled Terro, appearing annoyed. "This young man helped save my life!"

Trimash bowed his head submissively.

"Do you have anything else to say to Dod?" asked Terro in a hopeful sort of voice.

The man nodded. "Herculon doesn't like him," he said, pointing at the gigantic dog. Its eyes were glued to Dod's every move.

"That will be enough," said Terro, directing the man to return to his seat, but before Trimash had reached the stairs, he stopped and tipped his ear toward the portal.

"Hasha'ah," said the mayler. "It will only be a few seconds now. I think it's your son."

Dod glanced at the glowing gateway and suddenly realized he had a problem. "I've got to use your bathroom," begged Dod, grabbing at Terro's arm. "Could someone show me the way? Please!"

Terro raised an eyebrow, then drew one of the guards who had helped Dod to his feet. "Show Dod to his quarters," he said.

With large strides, Dod hurried along the walkway, his assigned helper at his heels. As they reached the exit, Dod could hear Terro in the distance behind him greeting Sawb. "What do you think of my costume? Isn't it funny? I'm The Dread this year."

Unlike Green's Portal House, Raul's was contained within a wing of Terro's castle, though a balcony separated it from the rest of his mansion. Outside the giant doors, four soldiers stood watch with double-tipped spears in hand and swords at their waists. They wore coats of fur to protect them against the cold wind that was blowing.

"I hear your winter at High Gate is milder than ours," remarked the guide, stepping in front of Dod to lead him. The guide tugged at his thin cloak to cover his arms better and gave a cross look to the cloudy sky. "We may get snow at the castle this year. Winter's only halfway done, and I've already seen traces of ice in the fountains six times! Why can't the cold stay in the mountains?"

Dod chuckled. The breeze felt refreshing, and all the trees within his view still had leaves. In contrast, Dod's hometown of Cedar City was, at the moment, buried in snow—a rather normal occurrence for the Christmas season.

From the balcony, Dod could see that Terro's castle was perched on the top of a hill overlooking a vast metropolis. Directly below, Raul's capital city, King's Cradle, sprawled to the north and south as far as the eye could see, bordering a long, narrow lake. In the distance, across the water to the east, Dirsitch sat at the base of a stately string of snow-capped mountains. Altogether, the two cities and their suburbs easily housed millions of people, though the buildings in King's Cradle weren't half as tall as the ones at High Gate.

"If it could just stay summer year-round," grumbled Dod's guide, "I'd be happier. All winter our vegetables struggle—except the cabbages, peas, and root crops, of course—they don't mind the cold."

Dod slowed as he passed a box that looked similar to the telescope case he had seen in Green. It, too, had strange symbols etched into its sides, though the constellations were different.

"What's this?" asked Dod, pointing at the box. Unlike the one on Commendus's patio, the one in Raul was protected by a short fence.

"Terro's!" said the man gruffly, hustling Dod away from it. "This area is off limits. The Portal and its appendages are certainly too important for a man of my station to be informed of their particulars. It's a privilege, indeed, for me to accompany Terro to the Portal Chamber at all."

"Oh," said Dod, "so you haven't spent time in Green?"

"Me?" gasped the man, his long, straight black hair blowing in the wind. "Only the Tredders with the best noble blood get such a privilege—the Chantollis, Salizars, Paykings, Lairringtons, Yoons, Jefferkeys, Hairs, and of course what's left of the Donefur clan. I'm sure it's the same in Green, isn't it? Aren't you Pap's grandson?"

Dod nodded.

"I met him once," said the man, opening a locked door for Dod. "He was peculiar. In the fifty-plus years I've worked in this castle, he's the only guest who has asked of me my name."

Dod smiled as he thought of Pap's kindness, and upon thinking of it, a glimpse of Pap's life burst through Dod's mind, leaving a clear impression: "Your name's Rughead, isn't it?" said Dod confidently.

The man stared at Dod, dumbfounded. "How did you know?" he stuttered.

"I'm psychic," said Dod happily, surprised that such a thing would pop into his mind at the right moment.

"Amazing!" muttered Rughead, pulling the door shut behind Dod. "Perhaps I don't need to tell you, then, but Terro has assigned you and your friends from Green to stay in the upper chambers of the old Donefur Wing." He led Dod to a towering staircase, three flights in one stretch. "This is where the nobles lived back in the day, before the Chantollis moved in."

The stairs creaked under Dod's feet as he climbed. Unlike Twistyard, some of Terro's castle was built of wood.

"I'd imagine the Donefur clan would be the first to line up and pat your back if you had succeeded against The Dread," said the man, almost smiling. "They hate him more than anyone else. After four centuries of war had nearly wiped them all out, he came along and caused the death of over a thousand of them. Only fourteen princes remain of their noble blood, and with their families gone—killed by The Dread—no one will marry them for fear of a similar end. Until he's dead, the Donefur men are less than shadows of their towering heritage. And to think, at one point, the Donefurs were the chiefest noble bloodline."

"Whoa," muttered Dod, feeling winded from the climb. "That's too bad. They must really dislike Sirlonk—especially if they once owned this castle—"

"Their *forefathers* owned it," interjected Rughead.

"Do they hate Sawb and Terro, too?" pressed Dod.

Rughead stopped in his tracks. "Terro's the Chief Noble Tredder of Raul!" he chided, as if the things Dod had just spoken were forbidden. "His progenitors paid the Donefurs well for these lands and built most of this castle around the old buildings. It's the Chantolli Estate! Any feelings of animosity toward Terro would be misguided and ridiculous indeed. Even if Sirlonk were proven to be The Dread, he's Terro's *half* brother—a wayward, undisciplined relative whose troubles are justly his own! Terro would end The Dread's life by a duel as fast as anyone: He was locked in Driaxom for the chance similarity of his face matching his brother's!"

"And I helped free him," said Dod boldly, sensing Rughead's mounting frustrations.

CHAPTER TWENTY-TWO

Rughead's face calmed. He stretched forth his hand and unlocked a beautiful hall. Its vaulted ceiling was covered with intricate wood carvings. "The rooms in here are for you and your friends," said the man. "If the air is too chill, feel at liberty to light the fireplaces, and should the wood burn low, make your voice heard and more will be brought."

"Thank you," said Dod, stepping inside.

Rughead turned to go, then stopped. "Terro speaks highly of you. I can't remember a time when he's been this excited to host guests from Green for the Ghoul's Festival. If you need anything, just ask."

Once Dod was alone, he inspected the main chamber. It had three grand fireplaces—one at the end and two on the sides. Couches and chairs were clumped together in multiple spots, providing comfortable seating for dozens of people. Toward the front, by the doorway through which Dod had just entered, a flight of stairs led to a balcony, which encircled the hall, allowing access to the second level of bedrooms and bathrooms.

Each room had the stuffed head of an animal above the door. Dod chose one on the main level with an elk's head. Inside, three large beds were equipped with matching pink bedspreads, and the window was half covered by flower-spotted curtains.

"Not this one," mumbled Dod to himself, walking back out into the main chamber. He tried the door below a boar's head and found it, too, was feminine: yellow sunflowers on the walls and white lacy drapes over the stained-glass window of a mother goose and her goslings.

From room to room Dod went, searching for a man cave, all the while trying to come up with a good excuse for his early arrival. Everyone was likely to bombard him with questions he couldn't answer. He knew it would be ten times worse than the probing, starlight sit-down he had just had with Sawny the night before.

Finally, after realizing all of the bedrooms on the main floor were designed for women, Dod tried the second level and found success. The first two rooms he entered were okay, but the third was perfect. It had the head of a snarling lion above the doorway, out in the hall. Inside, the furnishings were made of brown and black leather, and the walls were adorned with trophy-sized stuffed fish.

"What am I going to tell them?" moaned Dod, flopping down on the center bed. He was surprised he hadn't heard anyone enter the main chamber, yet. Above him, a chandelier made of antlers held large candles.

Dod set his backpack beside him and closed his eyes. Trimash's evil, one-eyed stare immediately came in view. 'Death follows this boy' echoed in his mind.

"Whatever!" grumbled Dod, sitting back up. Trimash's ugly face was the last thing he wanted to think about. He grabbed at his pack and unlatched it. Inside, Dod was surprised to find one of Boot's outfits—a long-sleeved shirt and pair of pants. "No wonder it felt heavier," said Dod to himself.

He looked around the room. The silence was killing him. Where were his friends? It had been at least thirty minutes since Sawb had entered—maybe longer.

Feeling uncomfortable, Dod rose to his feet and left the bedroom he'd claimed for himself and Boot and Buck. He made his way down the stairs to the entrance of the chamber. The only sound he heard was the occasional burst of wind whistling down the chimneys.

"I guess it's time to go exploring," mumbled Dod, venturing out of the guest quarters. The halls felt strange. Twistyard was never so quiet during the day. At the base of the large staircase, Dod listened for voices. When he heard none, he racked his brain for impressions. "Think about Terro's house," he whispered, hoping his mind would 'remember' a layout, or better yet, discover where his friends were.

Nothing happened. Carefully, Dod tracked his way back toward the balcony he had crossed with Rughead. And there they were! Through a large window, Dod could see his friends on the patio near the railing, looking down on the city. Terro was toward the center with his son, pointing things out, and Youk was in the back, glancing over his shoulder at the Portal Chamber doors.

Stealthily, Dod slipped out and crept across the patio. He merged into the crowd and began to hunt for Dilly and Sawny.

"Dod!" came Youk's voice, followed soon thereafter by a hand on his shoulder.

Dod's heart froze.

"Where's Bowlure?" Youk asked, reaching up to adjust his hat that had blown crooked.

Dod looked around casually, as though searching for Bowlure, hoping Youk couldn't see how stunned he was on the inside.

"Didn't he come with you?" inquired Youk.

Dod shook his head.

"But you lingered back," said Youk.

"Bowlure let me go first," responded Dod. "He said he was coming right behind me."

"Marvelous! The air smells marvelous!" sang Bowlure, stepping from the Portal Chamber happily. When the four waiting guards saw Bowlure's large hairy body trying to exit, they commanded he stand still and pointed their spears menacingly; though seconds later, Rughead popped out and the weapons were lowered.

"Ah, he's here," said Youk, and away he went with Tridacello and Strat on his heels.

Dod felt a nudge. "There it is," said Pone, pointing over the heads of others. "Dirsitch, Raul…the yummiest place ever!"

"Is food all you think of?" laughed Sawny, bouncing out from behind Pone. "We're in Raul! Look at the architecture, look at the cloud masses, and look at the leaves on the trees! There are so many things to see here that you can't see anywhere else."

Dod smiled at Sawny's enthusiasm.

"I've done all that," responded Pone slyly. "Now it's time to smell the chouyummy!" He pretended to catch a whiff of it on the breeze.

Dod couldn't believe it. Terro hadn't mentioned Dod's arrival to anyone, so his super-speedy trip across space had remained a secret—at least for now.

CHAPTER TWENTY-THREE

THE GHOUL'S FESTIVAL

Once Terro had led the group inside the castle, he assigned Pone to show the guests from Green to the upper part of the Donefur Wing and instructed him to guide them to the Great Hall after they had settled in their rooms and chosen their costumes. Pone happily took the assignment. Years before, he had spent months living in the castle as part of an internship and, therefore, knew the layout well.

"Follow me," insisted Pone, waving one hand in the air like a chief bellhop. "I'll be your guide on this tour. Please keep your hands to yourselves. Twistyard rules don't apply here." Pone glanced back over his shoulder. "I might add," he continued cautiously, peering past the Green Hall crowd, as though waiting until the throng from Raul Hall had disappeared around the corner before speaking truthfully. "The Chantollis don't like outsiders—they don't tolerate wandering—if they catch you disturbing their things, punishments are swift and harsh. We need to stay together as a group and only go where we're asked to go. Trust me, I learned the hard way."

Sham laughed. "Only half a dessert? How dreadful!"

"I'm being serious," said Pone, his face turning more sober than Dod had ever seen. "During my first week here I got curious and took a stroll, and the next thing I knew, I spent three days in the castle dungeon—and I could have been sent away for months of prison time. Their justice system is different from Green's—citizens are guilty until proven innocent and a few powerful people can do about whatever they want. When Terro or anyone else from Raul gives an order, we must comply."

"Listen to Pone," called Youk from the back of the crowd. "Don't be foolish while in Raul. For an offense, you could be cast from the castle and banned from reentry to Green—or sold into slavery for that matter. Pone's right. We must show the highest of respect for them and their customs while we're here. Don't forget, this is a different planet. We are privileged to be brief guests in their midst on their terms."

In front of Dod, Dilly jabbed at Boot with stern eyes, and Donshi and Kurt both seemed ready to go home.

"We'll be staying in the prestigious Donefur Wing," said Pone, moving down the hall. The group clustered tighter than before, as if evil lurked on the edges, ready to snatch anyone who strayed.

Toos shuffled through the mob, to get closer to Pone, and startled when he bumped into Dod. "I thought you had to stay back in Green," said Toos.

"No. Commendus worked things out for me," responded Dod.

"Where's your bag?" blared Ingrid, huffing behind Toos. "Did someone take it?"

Dod jumped to her side. "I've got mine handled," he said discretely, hoping nobody else had paid attention to her. "May I help you with yours?" Ingrid's carrying arm was sagging and her other arm clung to Juny, who held Ingrid's cane.

"Certainly," she said gruffly, dropping her bag to the ground and fetching her cane. "I can't believe how mannerless this place is. You're the first to offer. Simply ludicrous!"

As Dod picked up the bag, he noticed Tonnis walking calmly on the other side of Juny. Tonnis's confidence seemed to suggest he was ready to protect his mother from any harm. Dod couldn't help wondering what Tonnis had been thinking while Pone had commented coolly about the Chantollis.

Upon entering the Donefur Wing, Pone announced that the whole hall and its adjoining rooms were all open to their enjoyment, per Terro's decree. A chorus of sighs broke out. All of Green Hall seemed concerned about not finding themselves in the Chantolli dungeon, or worse, sold as slaves.

Dod rushed to be first up the stairs, though he soon discovered that he wasn't.

"How did your bag get here?" asked Boot pointedly, eyeing Dod with suspicion.

"I put it there," said Dod. "I was trying to save this room for us."

Buck hollered from the hall. "Where'd you go, Boot? Where's the room with your trophy fish?"

"I'M IN HERE," yelled Boot, still holding Dod with his eyes.

Buck appeared winded as he entered. "I love the growling lion," he said. "It kinda reminds me of the way that ugly dog was staring at you, Boot."

Boot's eyes let go of Dod as Boot carefully opened his pack. "Herculon wasn't interested in me," he said, reaching his hand down. "He was smelling Sneaker."

"You really brought him!" burst Buck as the black ferret hopped from Boot's bag. "Don't show anyone! We might get caught!"

"Relax," said Boot, his eyes swinging back toward Dod. "It's not like *I* packed a weapon—"

Dod and Buck both gave Boot confused glances.

"I took the knife out," said Boot, reaching for Dod's bag. "I know the guards don't usually check, but with your current condition—as an accused murderer—I figured it wouldn't be wise for you to chance it. They're really serious about stuff like that."

"Knife?" gasped Dod.

"Yeah. The one you had rolled up in your socks." Boot dug into Dod's open bag and pulled out the pants and shirt he had stowed.

"I didn't have a knife in there," said Dod. "And what are you doing rooting through my stuff? Don't you trust me?"

Boot's eyes glossed as he gazed out the window.

"He put junk in my pack, too," said Buck.

Sneaker jumped back and forth across the three beds, his nose sniffing at the air.

"Boot—I didn't put a knife in my bag!" defended Dod.

"Then who did?" asked Boot, spinning back around. "And how did your bag get here before me? I was the first up the stairs. Bonboo and I stayed in this room the last three times I visited. How did you know this is where I'd come?"

"W-what are you talking about?" stuttered Dod.

"Never mind," said Boot.

"No! Did you really take a knife out of my bag?" pressed Dod. "Youk and I were checked at the portal—it was weird, like

Youk was expecting trouble. If I'd have had a knife, I don't think I'd be here right now."

"Huh," muttered Boot.

Sneaker jumped to Boot's shoulder and stretched.

"If there was a knife," began Dod, "someone put it there—someone wanted to get me in trouble."

"It could be that," said Boot, appearing to still be thinking things through.

"What did the knife look like?" asked Dod.

"Nothing special," said Boot. "I'll show it to you when we get back to Commendus's place."

Dod sank onto his bed. Thoughts of being setup sucked the fun out of the Ghoul's Festival. Who had planted the knife?

Later, before lunch, Pone led the guests from Twistyard to an unusual room—it was a monstrous closet filled with costumes. Long rows of outfits hung in orderly fashion based on size, and baskets of wigs, hats, glasses, fake ears, horns, and other odd props were situated on shelves that lined one wall.

"Pick your person," said Pone gleefully. "And remember, you have to wear your costume for the next three days. The purpose of the Ghoul's Festival is to discover a new side of you, a side you haven't seen before."

"How fun," exclaimed Youk, hovering close to Dod. He seemed too happy to have nearly lost his son the day before.

Bowlure went straight to the largest sizes and held up his options; they were limited to a few capes and hats that could be stretched to fit his massive frame. But with Strat's creative help, a basket of fabric strips transformed Bowlure into a seven-foot mummy.

After doing his magic, Strat stood still as Bowlure helped replace the Bollirse instructor's stubble with a tie-on full beard; had it been white, he'd have been Santa, but since it was black, he looked more like an old-time prospector.

Dilly and Sawny flipped through the fanciest dresses they could find, holding them up one-by-one in front of a tall mirror before returning them. Eventually, Sawny settled on a shiny, black leather dress, bright-red lipstick, apple-red boots with three-inch heels, and a wig that replaced her light-brown curls with straight, long, raven-black hair.

She's either Eluxa's sister or a witch, thought Dod, casually inspecting the hat baskets near the two girls. He couldn't decide what to wear. Nothing struck his fancy.

"Try this on," insisted Dilly, noticing Dod hadn't committed to anything. She held a strange helmet in her hands, one with four long horns out the top and a sandpaperish, purple strap that was made to fasten below the chin.

Dod shook his head. Three days was a long time to look like a drunk football fan—the kind that wears no shirt and a big chunk of cheese on his head.

"He wants to match me—don't you, Dod?" said Sawny coyly, holding up a dark, flat-topped hat with long black hair attached. "This would work perfectly. You could be my twin brother."

Dod couldn't resist Sawny, so he tried it on. It was a snug fit, but looked much better in the mirror than he had feared it would. The hair trailed past his shoulders and poked out a little in the front, as though he had bangs. He resembled Rughead a bit.

"Perfect," said Sawny. "Put this on, too." She handed Dod a black, silky, long-sleeved shirt with shiny gold buttons down the front and near the cuffs and six-inch, white tassels draping from the shoulders.

Dod did as he was told. In a matter of minutes, he was standing beside Sawny, marveling at his transformation. His gleaming, dark leather pants and tough-guy boots matched Sawny's dress impeccably.

"Too safe," hollered Pone, approaching from behind. He was hardly recognizable. His voice and stride were all that remained of his previous self. The long cloak he had chosen came with another head, which he had dressed in a wig and glasses that matched the ones he wore on his own head. It really did appear as if he were two-headed. And he had deposited stuffing of some kind in his shirt and pants, making him seem at least a hundred pounds heavier.

"That's ridiculous!" laughed Dilly, peering at Pone from behind a pair of pink horn-rimmed glasses. She wore them low on her nose. They matched the puffy, lace dress she had finally stuck with.

"There's purpose to my madness," bragged Pone happily. "Two people mean two plates—and all of this fatness," he added, patting his protruding stomach, "leaves plenty of room to stash snacks for later. You'll be wishing you'd dressed like me when midnight rolls around."

"If I did, I'd look about the way you do now," responded Dilly, turning sideways to admire her flat stomach. It was accentuated by her dress, which shot straight out in all directions at the hip before draping to the floor, as if beneath it a stiff tutu were hidden.

"My snake'll eat your spare head for lunch," called Boot, tapping Pone on the back of his real head. The centerpiece of

Boot's outfit was a fifteen-foot stuffed snake he had draped around his waist, arms, and shoulders until its cantaloupe-sized head, with its jaws wide open, rested near Boot's head.

"Your serpent's already eaten one too many doses of poison," countered Pone, "so you definitely don't want to mess with me. I'm a toxic villain—double the trouble!"

Dod shuttered. In his mind he saw flashes of a darkened hallway, the floor lined with lifeless bodies. Someone had put large burlap sacks over their heads, covering them to their waists, so Dod couldn't tell who the people were. One corpse, however, stuck out in his mind like a blinking neon sign: it was a corpse whose feet were covered by bright-red boots.

"Are you okay?" asked Sawny.

Dod hadn't noticed he had doubled over.

"I'm fine," said Dod weakly, pulling himself back to an upright position. A million thoughts were racing through his brain. Was it the future or the past—or possibly neither?

"He's probably starving," said Pone. "Smelling all the food is driving me mad. If we don't get fed soon, I'll probably resort to eating Rone."

Dilly and Sawny both raised their eyebrows.

"My buddy, Rone," continued Pone, pointing at his second head.

Someone pranced over, hips swinging and a mess of curls flying all over the place. "How do I look?" asked a scratchy, high voice.

"Youk?" laughed Dilly.

"I'm a princess," he insisted, twirling around with the end of his flowery dress in one hand.

"Now I've seen it all," grinned Sawny.

Dod pulled a smile over his troubled face. "Saluci would be proud, I'm sure," he said, trying to act normal around Youk.

"No word of this to her!" snapped Youk, using his own voice.

"She'd think it was funny," assured Dilly. "You should try dressing up in front of your kids. They'd love it."

"Never!" said Youk, trying once more to raise his voice like a girl, but failing miserably.

"Beware of me!" grumbled Ingrid, hobbling over on her cane. "As you can see, I'm the most terrifying! I'm a nightmare! I'm the shadow that haunts your sleep!"

Dod wasn't sure what she meant. Her costume was no more than a small maroon sweater pulled over her head with the arms stretched down and tied below her chin. Juny's was the scary one. She had tucked her long hair into an old, ratty hat, put a full beard on her face and tufts of hair on her sooty hands, drawn three scars on her brow and black bags below her eyes, dressed in a dingy, splotched shirt and dirty overalls, and secured metal chains to her waist which clanked menacingly. Red streaks, like blood, dripped from her ears. If Dod hadn't noticed her earlier, picking the clothes and slipping into a changing stall, he wouldn't have known her identity. She was a perfect candidate for a haunted house.

"Can you guess who I am?" pressed Ingrid excitedly.

"Who are *you*?" choked Pone, stumbling backward the moment he caught a glimpse of Juny. She startled him.

"Death," growled Juny.

"No—for real?" asked Pone. He inspected Juny.

"Guess who I am?" nagged Ingrid, tugging at Pone's cloak. But Pone ignored her. He was mesmerized by Juny, and he wasn't alone; Dod, Dilly, Sawny, and Youk stared, too.

"I'm The Dread," rumbled Ingrid, swinging her cane like a sword. She pretended to slay Pone first, then Boot.

"But Terro's The Dread," said Donshi, wandering over wearing a princess dress and a sparkling tiara. When she got close enough to see past Pone's two heads, she stepped back. Juny seemed to frighten her.

"Classic," muttered Boot enviously, as though he were wishing to trade his snake for a rusty chain and fake blood.

"Seriously, who are you?" asked Pone.

Juny held her silence and stared with hollow, woeful eyes.

"You're all just lucky I'm feeling merciful," grunted Ingrid, spinning her bulky frame around awkwardly. "I'm unstoppable with a sword."

Juny walked away, zombielike, without ever revealing her identity.

Dilly and Sawny both offered to help Ingrid improve her costume once Death had left, but Ingrid held her ground, maintaining that what she had already put on was plenty.

Within minutes, the two-headed guide led the group to Terro's Great Hall for lunch. It was a feast to remember. Rows of tables were buried under piles of elegant foods: smoked meats, exotic fruits, bubbling soups, whole roasted pigs and goats, countless pies, heaping plates of cookies, and a seemingly unlimited supply of Raul's favorite food—beef. Six tables were devoted to displaying it and nothing else—tender steaks, long thin strips with spinach sauce, pickled cubes, ground patties, shredded meat with hot peppers, salted jerky, brown-gravy over chunks, and the list went on and on. The smells were heavenly. And though the four-story wall of windows could only let in the dim light that the stormy day had to offer, a myriad of bright stacks burned brilliantly, high above the ground, perfectly revealing the guests' colorful costumes. It was a Halloween party like none other.

Hundreds of people mulled around in the grand room, filling plates with food and enjoying one another's company.

"Eat up," said Pone. "Here in Raul, it's offensive to nibble when a spread like this is offered."

Dod chuckled, remembering how many times his mother had chided Alex for being a picky eater at Thanksgiving.

"I'm up to the task," said Toos, wearing a nesting bird on his head. "Lead the way."

Dod glanced around in search of Tonnis and wondered how he would act. The Chantolli Estate had been home to him, on and off, while his parents had been welcomed in as part of Terro's elite family; however, now that his father was known to be The Dread, things were different. Proof of the change was that Juny and Tonnis were staying in the Donefur Wing with the other guests from Green Hall, not the nicer Chantolli quarters where Sawb's fellow Coosings and Raulings were bunking.

Tonnis was dressed in a guard's uniform, standing only feet from Juny. There was no mistaking his face. He wasn't hidden behind makeup as his mother was. Instead, he was standing boldly, chin up, eyeing the strutting aristocrats as if he hadn't yet been informed that his father had disgraced the Chantolli name. It was impressive to Dod. The quiet essence of nobility in the midst of a scoffing crowd was reminiscent to Terro's posture and mannerisms while confined to Driaxom as 'The Dread.'

"Shall we?" asked Sawny, elbowing Dod. She had been standing beside him, chatting with Princess Youk.

Dod nodded happily. He was shocked that Sawny was still with him. It was a fancy party, and there were plenty of other people to associate with. Even though he had gone along with Sawny's costume choices, making him her twin, he hadn't expected she would literally treat him as part of her costume. The situation was refreshingly wonderful and a complete opposite of what he had thought. An empty wall and a cup of juice had been his anticipated buddies, not the hottest girl in the room.

Dod and Sawny passed a wide variety of disguises on their way to the food. One man wore stilts under his pants, boosting him to a height that more than exceeded the seven-foot mummy which stood in line behind Pone at the meat pie table. Accompanying the gangly giant, an elegantly dressed woman flaunted jeweled rings on every finger, a dozen bracelets on each arm, a slew of bulky necklaces, and large bat earrings made of rubies and pearls.

"Dod, what a nice choice," called Terro, sweeping through the crowd to greet him. Terro's hooded appearance, with a sword stowed at his waist, was alarmingly similar to Dod's memories of Sirlonk. The two men certainly shared blood.

"I like your costume," responded Dod. "If you looked any more like The Dread, your own guards would lock you up."

"Thank you," chuckled Terro, patting his sword. "But I think you're the one who is most likely to see my dungeons." He stepped closer.

Dod instantly felt anxious.

"Don't you know it's a crime to walk around with a girl as beautiful as this?" He smiled and pointed to Sawny, who blushed.

"She's part of my outfit," teased Dod, grateful Terro had been kidding.

"The best part," said Terro, facing Sawny. "You must be a Tillius. You look like Dilly."

Sawny bowed shyly.

"Enjoy your stay," insisted Terro, moving on to more greetings.

"You'd never guess he's Sawb's father—would you?" whispered Sawny. "At least not the way he acts."

"I know," agreed Dod, spotting Sawb in the distance tripping people. He was wearing the attire of a high-ranking general in Raul's army and seemed to be asserting his assumed authority. Joak and Kwit stood near him in different military uniforms.

Sawny and Dod piled their plates high and then joined Buck, Dilly, and Boot by the wall of windows.

"It's amazing, isn't it?" said Dilly. "Where else can you go and see so many people dressed in costumes? It's like we've been transported to a strange planet, and they're aliens!"

Sawny glanced at Dod.

"We're *all* technically aliens," said Dod. "None of us is from Raul, right?"

"That's true," said Buck, peering out from under a bushy wig. "Do you think there are other planets in space with people on them—besides Green, Raul, and Soosh?"

"Could be," said Dilly.

Dod looked out the window.

Boot swallowed his food down. "Probably," he said. "Doss was from somewhere else, wasn't he?"

"Really?" said Buck, pausing with a fork full of beef strips.

"I once read that, too," said Sawny.

"What?" choked Dilly, spinning to face her sister. "Where?"

"I-I don't remember," stuttered Sawny, looking guilty.

"How could you read something like that and not show me?" burst Dilly. "I don't believe it. You probably heard it. There are always plenty of strange explanations circling simple truths. Just look at the stories people tell of the Crazy King."

"Exactly!" said Buck. "Let's talk about those."

"That's not where I'm headed," frowned Dilly. "Even Dod's had more than his share of whispers dedicated to him."

Dod slid a little lower in his seat.

"I've heard he's the best of the best," said Dilly frankly. "And I've also heard he's as deep in The Order as Sirlonk himself. So which is he?"

Buck blinked, as if to say he recognized it was a trick question.

"He's the best of the best!" said Boot proudly, reaching over to rap Dod on the shoulder.

"Thanks," mumbled Dod.

"Well, he's certainly not deep in The Order," conceded Dilly.

"Don't forget he saved Twistyard from being sold," added Sawny defensively.

"Right. He is wonderful," agreed Dilly, seeming to wish she had used a different example. "But what I'm trying to say is that you can't believe rumors. They're always filled with the evening breeze. Good or bad, they're not reliable. Whatever you've heard about Doss is more than likely a bit tainted. I once had someone tell me he was convinced that Doss was none other than Bonboo's father! Can you believe that? Doss killed my great-grandfather's parents with the Hickopsy, and yet there are still fools who want to cling to the complete opposite. It disgusts me."

Once the feasting had slowed, entertainment began. Five troops of dancers took turns performing traditional acts, including a most unusual number which portrayed the story of creatures being slain with swords. Next, part of the hall was cleared and a circular-shaped door in the floor was slid open, revealing a sizable enclosure. A full orchestra played music while people gathered near the edges of the drop to watch burly tredders take turns wrestling giant snakes and alligators in the pit.

After the floor had been shut, a small hole in the ceiling opened up. Men dressed in blue costumes slid down ropes and began to do the most amazing gymnastic routines. Their abilities were remarkable. They could jump extremely high and do flips with ease, which feats stirred Dod's memories of the Red Devils. He wondered whether the men were tads or aided by swappers.

Finally, once the gymnasts had left, two men in suits stepped from opposite ends of the crowd and performed magic tricks. One wore white and the other black. Their closing act was a grabber. The magician in the black suit seemed to create an invisible ball between his hands, which he threw across the room at the other. As if struck, the receiving magician fell to the ground and fire instantly rose up around him.

The sight reminded Dod of Sirlonk in the pump house when he'd used the billies' tarjuice to make flames.

"Wow! Real magic!" exclaimed a young Greenling named Juck. His hair was a mess and his chin was ruby red. In one hand he held the four-horned helmet which Dilly had attempted to persuade Dod into wearing.

"He's gone!" said Hermit.

"Clever use of a trap door," whispered Sawny to Dod.

Dod mumbled in agreement, though he wasn't sure. The trick had played out flawlessly. It really did seem as if the man had been struck by something and consumed by flames.

"I wouldn't want to meet him in a dark hallway," chuckled Youk in his best princess voice. Hermit, Toby, and Juck all nodded in unison.

"I would," countered Boot, puffing his chest. "He's just an actor, and I'm the real deal. Besides, my snake would eat him for a midnight snack." Boot patted the head of his stuffed serpent.

"My protector," bowed Dilly, pulling at her dress as she curtsied.

"As always," said Boot, tipping his head respectfully.

More food and entertainment followed in waves until midnight, at which point the Green Hall crowd was gathered and counted before being escorted back to the Donefur Wing.

In the snarling-lion room, Boot fed Sneaker strips of jerky while contending with his brother over which event had been the most spectacular.

"The black magician was the top," argued Buck, pretending to make balls of fire between his hands.

"Then I guess you slept through the knife-throwing guy," countered Boot.

"What do you think, Dod?" asked Buck, looking to him to settle the matter.

"I thought they were all pretty cool," said Dod sleepily. It had been a spectacular party, and there were still two days left to enjoy.

With another early morning coming, Dod hurried his preparations for bed and drifted off to sleep with the antler chandelier gleaming brightly and the two brothers chatting in the background.

Around three in the morning, Dod awoke shivering. He had just had a horrible nightmare, but couldn't remember anything about it. A hazy, dim shaft of moonlight was all that lit the room, making visibility minimal. Buck was a snoring mountain of blankets in the bed beside Dod's, the stuffed fish on the walls looked like blobs, and the chandelier appeared to be the dangling hand of an angry tree.

When Dod's eyes reached Boot's bed, Dod froze. The bed was empty!

Carefully, Dod slipped from his covers and tiptoed around the room. Boot was gone. And stranger still, Sneaker was gone, too.

Dod slipped on his shoes, tied the laces, and opened the bedroom door. Out in the hall, a few dim candles burned a lonely sort of glow, shedding just enough light to see by. When Boot wasn't in the closest bathroom, Dod started to panic. He didn't want to face the mounting questions that plagued the back of his mind—questions about Boot. What was he up to, now?

Near the balcony, Dod surveyed the empty hall, hoping to find Boot sitting down below. No one caught his eye. Dod moved to the stairway and descended. Each step creaked ominously, as if warning Dod to return to the safety of his bed. Trouble was afoot, but driven to know the truth, Dod pressed on.

At the base of the staircase, Dod stopped in front of the main entrance and stared at the door's large brass handle. It rang a bell in his brain. Boot had touched it recently. Dod knew it, he had seen Boot grab it in the dream he had just had.

Curiosity dueled mightily against fear in Dod's mind. He couldn't recall anything else about his dream, but he knew he had awakened feeling terrified. What would happen if he left the Donefur Wing in search of Boot? Pone and Youk had warned everyone severely. Punishments in Raul were no laughing matter. Anything could be lurking in the darkened halls.

"It's not worth it," whispered Dod to himself, spinning back toward the stairs. "Boot's on his own."

Dod eagerly made his way up to the snarling-lion room and was just about to enter when a horrifying image burst into his mind. It was another glimpse of his dream—a gruesome, sick glimpse of Boot's face, lifeless, wrapped in a strange white shroud.

"He'll be fine...it's just a stupid dream," muttered Dod, beginning to shiver. The night air was chilly. The last thing Dod wanted was to go skulking around Terro's forbidden halls in the dark.

Suddenly, someone made the stairs creak.

"Boot?" whispered Dod, speeding across the balcony to greet him.

Halfway up the stairs, Dilly stood motionless.

"Where's Boot?" asked Dod.

"I thought Boot was with you," said Dilly. "Weren't you just talking with him?"

Dod shook his head.

"Isn't he bunking with you and Buck?"

"Yes," responded Dod slowly, "but he's gone."

"Oh!" groaned Dilly, clenching her hands. "I knew it! I knew Boot would go for it!"

"What?" pressed Dod, squeaking his way down to Dilly's side.

"I've been listening for him all night," complained Dilly. "My great-grandfather's father hid something in this castle a long time ago, on his way back from Soosh, and Boot thinks he can find it. Why doesn't Boot get it? He's enough just the way he is."

"Enough of what?"

"Never mind," huffed Dilly, storming down the stairs.

CHAPTER TWENTY-THREE

Dod followed her. His gut was nagging at him to race after Boot, to warn him of danger, but common sense was still winning the inner battle.

Dilly flopped onto the couch closest to the door and looked torn. "Boot keeps trying to impress me," she said, "as though some great feat will change his blood and make him good enough to marry *a Tillius*." She glanced up at Dod. "Doesn't he know I don't care? I'm not concerned about his blood—common or regal, it's produced him, and he's one-of-a-kind."

Dod instantly felt nose-deep in a conversation that he wasn't even slightly prepared for.

"Boot knows I like him, doesn't he?" asked Dilly rhetorically. She bent over and fidgeted with her dangling shoelaces, as if annoyed that her wool, shin-length nightgown didn't match her footwear.

"Yeah," muttered Dod, sounding about as stupid as he felt.

"So what's his deal?" begged Dilly, sitting up. "Every time I start thinking he likes me back, he pushes me away. It doesn't make sense. Why does it matter that I'm Chikada's daughter and Bonboo's great-granddaughter? I'm still just a person—right? I've been friends with Boot for a long time, so it's not like I don't already know Boot's family; they're poor and come from common blood. Who cares? Why does he even think about that kind of stuff, anyway? None of it matters."

Dod didn't respond. Instead, he worked diligently at appearing interested in the ugly, broccoli-shaped sculpture that was the centerpiece on the glass end-table nearby.

"Is it something else?" continued Dilly, sleepily venting her feelings. The late hour and dim lighting seemed to make the circumstance less awkward, though it had opened up a side of Dilly that Dod had never seen before.

"Maybe I've missed something," sighed Dilly. "Maybe he's hiding a secret." Dilly zeroed in on Dod. "Does Boot like someone else? You can tell me. I have to know."

Dod didn't look at her. He was new to relationship counseling, and he was only half listening since his mind was still at war, so he kept his eyes on the broccoli. Boot was possibly heading for trouble—a circumstance that would end in his death if the nightmare was right. But Dod still wasn't ready to run out and get caught. Driaxom had been awful. He didn't want to push Raul's judicial system, too. Being sold as a slave sounded dreadful.

Dod's thoughts drew him deep inside, as he quarreled with himself over whether to look for Boot or go to bed. He hardly heard Dilly's ramblings, when suddenly she sprang to her feet and exclaimed, "Eluxa!"

Dod startled forward and knocked the heavy sculpture over, causing it to crash through the glass table. Long, thick shards hit the floor.

"I knew it!" snapped Dilly. "That tramp has had her eyes on Boot since the first day she came to Green!"

Dod gave Dilly a crazy look. She had just surprised him into breaking Terro's table, and she didn't seem to notice. The sound alone had probably awakened all of Green Hall, Ingrid included.

"Why would he fall for Eluxa?" whined Dilly.

"He hasn't!" said Dod, finally opening his mouth. "He likes you. Everyone knows it. End of story."

"Really?" said Dilly, blinking sweetly.

"Yes," insisted Dod, feeling a rush of concern. "And I think he's in trouble. My gut's going nuts. What do we do?"

Dilly's eyes sparkled, as though she had just awakened. "Let's go get him."

"But this is Terro's castle—" began Dod.

"Then let's not get caught," laughed Dilly, walking toward the door happily. Dod certainly preferred this Dilly to the insecure one he had just listened to, but rushing out weaponless seemed more than rash. What if the snake bird or devil dog were on hall duty patrolling?

"Hurry up," insisted Dilly. She prodded at Dod the way she had when they'd ridden into the forest at night trailing Zerny and Sirlonk, or the time they'd followed the soldiers into the Old Pier House at Fort Castle. In her heart, Dilly clearly loved adventure, and to some extent, trouble, as much as Boot did. As far as Dod was concerned, they were two peas from the same pod.

Dod reluctantly followed Dilly out of the Donefur Wing and tried to calm his fears with logic. Terro liked him. Dod was, after all, Terro's 'most honored guest,' according to Terro's flattery in the Portal Chamber. And Dilly was Bonboo's great-granddaughter. What could possibly befall them? If they were caught sneaking around at night, things could be fixed in the morning.

But regardless of Dod's attempts, he couldn't push from his stomach the fear that he felt over the truth—the terrifying reality that something unimaginable was awaiting them.

THE FORBIDDEN ATTIC

Terro's castle corridors were dark and quiet. Some of them were pitch black. Within a few steps of the Donefur Wing, Dilly recognized the problem and went back to snatch one of the candles that burned dimly in the foyer.

"See," gloated Dilly. "We don't have to walk in the dark."

Not completely, thought Dod, assessing the dismal flame, but he didn't say anything. He just followed. His feelings were jumbled. The nightmare that had awakened him had been a bad one. He wished he could remember the details, and he wished he could get a better sense of direction. Back in Green, Dod hadn't appreciated how many times his mind had simply 'known' things, like the general layout of Twistyard or High Gate. Finding his way around in Raul was different.

"I think I know where Boot's headed," said Dilly. "He seemed really distracted when we walked past the Soldiers' Hall, don't you think?"

A glimpse of armor came to Dod's mind. "Probably," he said, plodding along slowly. He was fighting to make his feet move at all. A foreboding feeling was sapping his strength.

"Boot's silly to suppose he could find it after all these years," muttered Dilly. "It's probably been—I'd say—three hundred? Maybe more. The Chantollis have doubtless built a wall over the stash. Look at that." Dilly pointed at a darkened corridor as they walked past it. "That one's been remodeled recently. Figures of Terro and Sawb are carved into the walls. Did you see them, earlier?"

Dod shook his head. He hadn't noticed.

"I think it's funny when people do that," said Dilly. "The last thing I'd want would be a thirty-foot carving of me. Yuck!"

Dod cracked a grin. Dilly was always seeking to be the center of attention. Having people carve a wall-sized representation of her was just the kind of thing Dod would imagine her doing if she were the head ruler of the land.

"What did Bonboo's dad hide?" asked Dod as they neared the Soldiers' Hall.

"I don't know," said Dilly. "Something small—a little bag."

Dod thought of the images he had seen a few days before of Sirlonk's reaching hand, trying to take something from the Chards Museum. "Are you sure it's still here?"

"No," chuckled Dilly.

"Why did he hide it, anyway?" pressed Dod.

"The story's not fresh in my mind," confessed Dilly, "but I think he was detained here for a few days. He worried that the Chantollis would strip him of his souvenir at the Portal Chamber, so rather than give it to them, he hid it."

Dod stopped walking and took a deep breath. The Soldiers' Hall was filled with giant statues of men in battle.

"They're not real," teased Dilly playfully. "What are you worried about?"

"I don't know," said Dod, feeling stupid. They had been walking unsupervised through Terro's castle for ten minutes and hadn't seen the slightest sign of guards.

"It's the magician in black, isn't it?" taunted Dilly, tugging at Dod's arm. "I won't let him incinerate you."

Dod and Dilly wandered through the maze of crowded statues. Men were striking with their swords and spears, deflecting with their shields, and even attacking with their bare hands. Some rode horses, a few were atop flutters, and most were on foot. Here and there a soldier lay upon the ground dying. It was a dismal contrast to the happy atmosphere of Twistyard's Great Hall.

"I'd love to see *him* wrestle Con," said Dilly, pointing at a fifteen-foot man who held another large soldier above his head. "Con wouldn't reach his waist."

Slowly, the candle's faint glow surrendered to a gentle splash of moonlight. Deeper in, the hall widened, and on the far side, a wall of mostly-veiled windows allowed light to creep in through a narrow breach in the long drapes.

"He went that way," whispered Dod, shivering. He indicated that they should shift direction and head toward the distant corner.

"How do you know?" asked Dilly, giving Dod a puzzled look. Then her face relaxed. "Boot told you where he was going to search, didn't he?"

"No," said Dod, ducking under a monstrous, plunging sword. "I'm just guessing. It seems like that's the side with the ropes to draw the curtains."

"So?"

Dod slid between two statues before answering. "In my dream, Boot climbed a rope."

"Well, if you've watched it all," said Dilly, sounding a little perturbed, "you should be leading the way!"

"It's not like that," burst Dod. "I can't remember the nightmare—or at least, not very much of it. But as we walk, some things look or sound familiar. Like the moonlight over there, it made me remember Boot's hand clasping a rope."

"Oh," said Dilly, stopping to free the hem of her nightgown from a protruding metal shoelace. The statues looked so lifelike, Dod half expected Medusa to appear, but he took comfort in remembering that he had read she turned people to stone, not bronze.

"Do you recall anything else?" asked Dilly.

"Mostly how I felt," responded Dod. "There's trouble ahead."

Dilly smiled. "Isn't there always?" she said, picking up her pace.

In the corner, thick cables were situated right where Dod had forecast. Looking up, Dod could see they rose thirty feet in the air. However, two stories up, an open balcony came within inches of the rope.

"Is that where he went?" groaned Dilly, following Dod's eyes. "Are you sure?" The visible part of the loft displayed more statues, though they were smaller.

Dod's stomach was beginning to hurt with anxiety, which confirmed to him, more than anything else, that they were indeed trailing Boot. It was as if he were leading them into a nasty trap.

"Maybe you should stay here," said Dod, trying to be bold. "I'll go check for Boot."

"I'm coming," assured Dilly, and then she glanced down at her nightgown. "But you go first."

As Dod attempted to climb the rope, the gap in the drapes shut before the line held his weight. Once Dod had arrived at the balcony, Dilly situated the candle against the foot of a statue and shimmied up. With a few hardy tugs of the neighboring line, the gap in the curtains returned, once more allowing moonlight to settle in.

"Where is he?" gasped Dilly, catching her breath.

"I don't know," said Dod.

"Boot," called Dilly, marching into the dim light.

"Shhh," rushed Dod. His heart was beginning to pound faster. They were getting closer to something. He could feel it.

At the back of the terrace, where the moonlight couldn't reach, a glowing square appeared to be stuck to the ceiling, ten feet up. Its eerie image prickled the skin on Dod's arms and caused him to tremble. As though part of a horror film, Dod grabbed at Dilly and turned her head toward the sight. "He's up there," whispered Dod, having difficulty speaking. He was no longer guessing: He knew it!

The square was a small opening. Below it, a bucking-horse statue reached into the dismal light. Dod now could clearly recall Boot climbing the stallion and opening the square hole.

"We're getting close," said Dilly excitedly. She didn't seem to share Dod's dread, and within seconds, she was scaling the angry steed.

Dod followed behind her timidly, screaming inside his head. There wasn't anything to use as a weapon; everything was too big to lift. And once he was near the hole, a draft of cool, stale air brought a familiar smell to his nostrils that carried with it a feeling of doom.

"It's an attic," whispered Dilly, prodding Dod to climb up and join her.

Dod cautiously followed.

Inside the extraordinary chamber, dust-covered beams and rafters crisscrossed the vaults and dips. It was a monstrous garret that weaved back and forth, creating the beautiful, steep-pitched exterior roofline. A few small stained-glass windows lit the enclosure with an unnatural light. Chests, bags, crates, strange objects, and statues made of gold were arbitrarily placed around the floor, as if long since forgotten; and their sizes testified that some other entrance had been used to place them there.

Dilly pointed at a set of tracks in the dust and glowed with satisfaction. "You're right! Boot's up here. Isn't it fun hunting?"

Dod looked upward. The highest points of the ceiling were dozens of feet above the flooring, hidden in the shadows behind a web of beams. It was concerning. What security system did Terro employ for protecting his hidden treasures? Or possibly Terro didn't even know they existed. His past progenitors had sequestered their wealth and set booby-traps.

"Stay in Boot's steps," whispered Dod nervously, "and don't touch anything." He couldn't help thinking about the movies he'd seen of people entering tombs where the smallest wrong move had led to poisonous darts flying and large stones falling.

Dilly looked at Dod's stern face and giggled. "If anyone but Boot's been up here recently, it would have to be the magician in black." She raised her eyebrows jestfully. "Look at the tracks: They're Boot's. See the shallow drag line? Boot's been favoring his right leg ever since the fight with The Beast. He hasn't fully recovered yet."

"Let's just be careful," said Dod. Dilly's lighthearted attitude about the situation didn't erase Dod's nagging worries—nothing could. Until they had found Boot and made it back to the Donefur Wing safely, Dod was certain his apprehension would persist.

Dilly meandered around in the chamber, gleefully tracking Boot's path. The farther she went, the happier she got. "My great-grandfather's going to be shocked when we come back with the sack," smiled Dilly as she stopped near a silver unicorn. Dust had been wiped from its horn where Boot appeared to have rested his hand, and small tracks down its back seemed to indicate Sneaker had left Boot's shoulder for a quick stroll.

"What makes you think it's up here?" asked Dod, looking forward and backward. The unfinished, upper room of the castle was unbelievably long and skinny, winding back and forth in a fashion that allowed Dod and Dilly to see only a short distance in front of and behind where they stood at any given time. Yet the treasures continued from segment to segment, deposited in the midst of the matrix of support beams. If only a small handful of the chests contained gold or silver coins, the Chantollis were wealthier than the Tillius family by far.

"What?" mumbled Dilly. She hadn't heard Dod. Her eyes were gleaming with excitement as she stared at the unicorn.

"What makes you think Boot will find the sack?" repeated Dod. "Even if it's up here, somewhere, the attic goes on and on, and it's filled with good hiding places."

"We'll find it," said Dilly, patting the unicorn's neck. "This is the horned steed. Boot's following the signs. I once heard him talking about the stash with my great-grandfather. The riddle included horses of three: one reaching to fight, one wearing a blade, and one calmly eating a tree. We've found two. The third is probably up ahead."

"Who needs a tiny sack with all this gold around?" asked Dod, eyeing a beautiful statue of a dancing woman.

"Some things are more valuable than gold," responded Dilly. "The pure-sight diamonds you recovered are probably worth a thousand chests of coins." Dilly glanced around. "And besides," she said defensively, "I'm sure these objects aren't pure gold, they're plated. The Chantollis just like to be ostentatious."

Dod's worry dipped for a minute as he cracked a grin. If the Chantollis were so bent on being showy, why were their priceless gold-plated statues hidden where no one would see them? Dilly's logic was clearly twisted by her innate need to compete with the other wealthy bloodlines, especially the Chantollis.

"They could fill a dozen museums with all this stuff," teased Dod.

Dilly eyed him admonishingly.

"Sawb is extremely wealthy, isn't he?" continued Dod, rubbing it in.

"Not enough to buy a *big* ferret," snapped Dilly proudly, as if Sneaker were hers.

CREAK!

A noise came from around the bend.

"Let's be silent, now," whispered Dilly to Dod. "I want to surprise Boot. He'd never guess we'd find him up here."

Dod froze.

"Come on," said Dilly.

CREAK!

It sounded like the groan of an old timber straining to stand against a howling wind.

Dilly and Dod tiptoed forward.

CREAK! CREAK! CREAK!

The sound was more than beams settling, more than the wind shifting the roof; someone was creating it.

"He's gonna die when he sees us," whispered Dilly smugly, carefully stepping around a giant support pole. She couldn't have looked happier if she'd just beaten Sawb at a duel.

CREAK! CREAK!

Dod smelled the air and felt sick. He began to sense what was up ahead. The attic was not a safe place! Dod frantically searched for a weapon, anything he could fight with—a sword, a spear, even a stick. The only thing that caught his eye was a heaping pile of glimmering, dustless gold coins near the wide entrance to the next segment.

CREAK!

"Come on," whispered Dilly insistently. "We have to surprise him together."

Dod shook his head and silently indicated for her to come back.

Sensing Dod's apprehension, Dilly changed plans and eagerly bolted for the corner alone.

Dod tried to catch her, to save her life, but by the time his hand had grabbed her arm, she had rounded the bend and was already in trouble.

It was an ambush. Her right leg was stuck in sticky, thick webbing, and almost instantly, a line shot from the rafters and hit Dilly in the stomach.

Dilly screamed a blood-curdling cry for help.

Dod threw a hand over her mouth and continued to pull on her arm with his other, trying to free her. "Venooses attack what they hear," whispered Dod frigidly, remembering Bowlure's words from the night he'd come face-to-face with one in Bonboo's cottage.

The shadows began to move. The whole ceiling was coming to life. It was one huge web of danger, connecting the upper beams and rafters with tunnels of meshing. The space was much larger than the rest of the attic and filled with creeping spider-like venooses. The twelve-legged arachnids ranged from plate-sized babies to hog-sized mamas. Dozens of glowing red eyes hungrily peered at Dod and Dilly from out of the shadows.

"Help me!" screamed Dilly, thrashing her body like a moth in a cobweb. Her voice was muffled by Dod's hand, but still seemed to attract plenty of attention.

Dod noticed one giant, silvery-black venoos whose fangs dripped poisonous slime. It moved slowly, methodically, across the rafters, heading straight for them, and it occasionally tugged at the sticky line that it had shot at Dilly, as though it were enjoying the thrill of feeling her struggle.

CREAK! CREAK!

The scene was a nightmare, more than befitting of the terror Dod had felt when he'd awoken in the snarling-lion room. The creepy lighting was just enough for Dod and Dilly to see that they were tragically outnumbered.

CREAK!

As the shiny black bodies shuffled around, the network of webs jiggled, prompting large suspended cocoons to sway. The gently swinging cocoons caused the creaking noises. Each one dangled from a single, rope-like line. The remains of shriveled, old cocoons littered the floor. Human bones poked out of the most ancient ones. This was a chamber of death.

"Don't scream," begged Dod. He let go of Dilly's mouth and used both hands to tug, and when that didn't seem to work, he propped one leg on a neighboring post and gave a mighty pull. Dilly's nightgown crackled like the ripping of Velcro and broke free, sending Dod and Dilly to the dusty ground. But no sooner had the duo scrambled to retreat than they realized that they were surrounded. The unicorn section of the attic was now filled with the poisonous creatures as well. Two large ones had already descended to the floor and were stirring dust as they scurried for the kill, while a multitude of others haunted the rafters. Dod couldn't believe that he hadn't noticed the ceiling of webbing as he'd entered the trap.

"The gold," sputtered Dod, frantically digging his hands into the pile of coins. They felt like heavy quarters. He and Dilly began throwing them at the approaching, blood-sucking beasts, which effectively slowed their progress. But more were coming. The venooses weren't stopping. It seemed pointless to try. The mountain of wealth on the floor was quickly diminishing, and there was nothing else within reach.

Another sticky line shot from the biggest venoos and narrowly missed Dilly. "We're gonna die!" she wailed, shaking uncontrollably as she recklessly threw handfuls of coins.

A large object pounced from above and landed on Dod. He knew he was dead the moment it struck him. Fear stole his breath and caused his legs to go limp. But as he hit the floor, he realized it wasn't a foe; rather, it was a past victim.

CHAPTER TWENTY-FOUR

The cocoon was old and gray. A skeleton's face met Dod's, its hollow eye sockets seemed to gaze upon him through the thin veil of webbing. *Come and join me*, it seemed to say.

"BOOT!" cried Dod, wondering what had become of him. Which cocoon was he in? There were so many of them in the larger chamber. Was he already dead, or just wrapped?

"TURN AROUND!" screamed Dilly, petrified with fear.

Dod rose to his knees and shuddered. The two running venooses had stopped retreating from the storm of gold coins and were now just feet away, menacingly approaching. One reared up and showed off its knife-like fangs.

Dod hefted the mummified skeleton to his shoulder and gave it a heaving throw at the beasts. They instantly seized the cocoon and eagerly plunged their fangs into it.

Meanwhile, on the opposite side, the silvery-black venoos was swinging rapidly toward the floor with a whole legion of followers close behind it. By every indication, the biggest beastly spider appeared to be a determined mother, seeking flesh and blood for her young ones.

Dod looked down at the empty spot where the coins had been. Nothing remained of the pile. Dilly futilely threw her last handful of ammunition into the large chamber at the fattest spider and then recoiled.

What would Pap do? thought Dod desperately. He was out of ideas and couldn't see a scenario that would end well. Almost without question, the next thirty seconds would be his last.

Dilly screeched in torment. "IT'S GOT ME!" she wept, losing her balance. After falling to the floor, she clawed at the wooden slats. The silvery-black venoos was pulling her away with a line that it had stuck to her back.

Dod grabbed Dilly's hands in an attempt to keep her from losing ground, but to no avail. The old venoos was much bigger than all of the others—as big as a small cow—and with its strength, it was more than capable of dragging Dilly and Dod into the chamber of death; four legs pulled the line, eight legs postured strategically to keep its footing.

Time slowed and everything came into focus. Dod knew he had a shot at saving himself if he could concentrate on zapping home, but what then? If he did succeed, he'd have to live the rest of his life knowing that he had abandoned Dilly and let her die alone. And with his escape, he'd be banishing himself from the realms forever. No more Green, Raul, or Soosh. No more trying to find his father. No more helping Bonboo fight against The Order. No more dances with Sawny. Dozens of thoughts played within Dod's mind.

Dilly's screaming continued, though it was strained, now, by the way her stretched nightgown pressed upon her throat; the sticky line had attached to her gown's hearty fabric with a Frisbee-sized circular splat that seemed to cling with hooks. No amount of pulling was likely to rip it free this time.

"There must be a way!" grunted Dod, having a tug-o-war with the venoos. A pile of old cocoons weren't too far off, but still too far to reach without sacrificing Dilly. If Dod let go, he knew she'd slide across the dusty floor and be killed in an instant. And what good would the cocoons do anyway? The two venooses, which had momentarily been entertained by the one he'd thrown, were now approaching in the rear.

There really was no escape, Dod concluded, unless he could magically pull a sword from his pocket, and even then he knew he and Dilly would stand little chance at fighting their way back to the tiny entrance. One of the venooses would get them in route.

"Boot!" sobbed Dilly. "Save me, Boot! Save me!"

Dod felt his feet slip. He found himself sailing headlong toward big momma, still clinging tightly to Dilly's hands. The game was basically over. Dilly would be bitten first, and he would be second, only moments later. His meager consolation was knowing that he hadn't abandoned his friend.

Suddenly, a burst of light entered the room on the far side, followed by a large crashing sound. It was as though lightning had struck one of the windows.

The venooses cringed, and the line momentarily went limp.

Struggling to see, Dod yanked at Dilly's hands and together they scampered toward the pile of cocoons. They only made it halfway when Dilly was once more the rope in a tug-o-war. Dod pulled with all his might and strained to win.

Many of the venooses had begun to retreat, startled by the sound and light, but not the giant silvery one. She continued to tug. Her efforts successfully brought Dilly and Dod within feet of her fangs when the ground shook and a knight in shining armor burst from the graveyard of shrouded bones and severed the line.

No sooner was Dilly free than the mother of all venooses pounced on the knight who had come between her and her meal. Her fangs made a clanking sound as they struck the man's suit over and over.

The bright buster candle that the soldier had carried was now free on the floor, beginning to dim. Its flame was being choked by dust.

"Run for the door," came a faint voice from the man in the armor. He was under the belly of the venoos, struggling to squirm free.

Dod stumbled to his feet and peered over the pile of cocoons. There was an exit, and it was half open.

"Run!" yelled the knight.

Dilly seemed paralyzed.

The candle flickered, crackled, and dimmed to a glow.

With the light failing, the fleeing venooses changed direction and once more began to rally.

"Run!" ordered the knight, attempting to regain his sword. He had jabbed it at the venoos's legs, while being bombarded by prodding fangs, and had had the misfortune of getting it stuck under one of big momma's clawed feet. The creature's weight held it down.

Dilly didn't rise.

"Come on!" yelled Dod, pulling at Dilly.

Slowly, Dilly staggered with Dod's help. She was sobbing uncontrollably. Dod was acutely aware of the approaching storm of clicking fangs and scurrying legs, so he prodded her to move faster.

Into the cocoons they went, wading waist deep in some places through the crumpling remains. On either side, the mountain of wrapped skeletons rose skyward.

"Keep going!" ordered Dod, pushing Dilly into the front. He looked back toward the knight and shivered. In the dim light, Dod could see that the silvery-black venoos was now only one of the poor soldier's tormentors; others had arrived and were using their fangs to search for blood.

CHAPTER TWENTY-FOUR

"I'll catch up," said Dod, plunging back toward the fray. On the edge of the pile, Dod chose a lightweight ball of bones and webbing. "Here goes," he muttered to himself, raising his bundle in the air.

"DIE YOU PUTRID THINGS! DIE!" roared Dod, racing toward the clump of venooses. He swung the cocoon at the first arachnid he came to—a cat-sized mess of legs—and sent it flying deeper into the mob of clicking fangs.

Instantly, the spiders turned toward him. His voice and movements drew their attention.

"Die!" came a faint voice from somewhere near big momma. The giant spider reared up and plunged down with its fangs, but shortly after doing so, it rolled onto its side and began kicking its legs sporadically.

Light from a distant stained-glass window reflected gently off the knight's armor as he rose to his feet in the midst of his clamoring foes. He had plunged his sword into the center of the biggest venoos and had managed to find something vital. The old beast made a hissing sound as it lay wounded.

Seeing the large spider's distress, the other venooses quickly abandoned their chase after Dod and turned upon her, piling onto her silvery body like bees protecting their queen. Only these creatures weren't trying to help her, they were feasting upon her. It was a feeding frenzy. The smell of death turned them wild.

Dod spun and dashed back into the graveyard, followed in the rear by the knight. They made great speed, as if the waist-deep remains of hundreds of men weren't a problem.

Dod reached the other side of the debris mound first. The door was only a short distance away. Glancing side-to-side, Dod emerged from the wreckage and swiftly raced across the open attic toward the exit.

"Dilly?" called Dod, arriving at the doorway out of breath. A dimly lit room greeted him.

"Watch out!" rang in Dod's head.

He turned and raised his hands just in time to catch the front legs of a pouncing venoos. It knocked him to the ground and proceeded to stab its fangs violently at his face.

Though it wasn't anywhere near as big as the silvery-black one, its dog-sized body and twelve legs effectively fought to end Dod's life.

"Help!" screamed Dod, holding it back with all his might. The front legs of the venoos felt like smooth crowbars, its ten other legs squirmed and kicked. Webbing began to flow from the creature's abdomen. It used its rear-most legs to direct the line, tipping Dod's legs as it attempted to tie them up.

SWOOSH!

With one swift pass, the knight's sword severed the venoos in half. Instantly the beast's strength was gone and Dod was able to throw its front section away from him.

"Thanks," mumbled Dod, turning in time to see Dilly close the door. She had entered behind the man in armor.

"My hero!" said Dilly, wiping tears.

Dod blinked. He couldn't believe his eyes. Dilly was no longer sobbing, and she was hugging the knight, who moved robotically in the cold armor.

"As always, my lady," said the man, tipping his head. He reached up and pulled until his helmet came off.

"Boot!" exclaimed Dod, wondering whether the poor lighting was tricking his eyes.

"Who'd you expect would come to your rescue?" chuckled Boot in a tired voice. "It's the middle of the night."

"But I thought you were dead—" began Dod.

"Me too," responded Boot, ducking into the dimmest corner. One small window shed a purplish-blue light. "I was nearly sucked dry," he sputtered, igniting another buster candle. "That place is crawling with trouble." Boot searched the small shed-like room for additional spiders before handing the candle to Dilly and removing his armor.

"How did you know to come prepared?" asked Dod, plucking webbing from his legs. Some of it was too stubborn and required the sword's aid.

"I didn't," said Boot. "All this came from in here. Those nasty things nearly had me at the one-horned steed. If Sneaker hadn't sensed them, I'd have been a wrapped raisin by the time you came along."

"Oh, Sneaker!" groaned Dilly sadly.

"He's fine," said Boot, clanking his way over to a closed chest; half his armor was flailing mid-process. He lifted the lid, and Sneaker hopped out. The inner roof of the chest had a hole gnawed three-fourths of the way through it.

Dilly sighed and pulled an exhausted smile.

"He wanted to join me in fighting," said Boot, "but they don't make *these* for ferrets." Boot patted the last of his armor as he took it off. "Did you notice the gold coins on the ground?"

Dod nodded.

"That's where things got crazy for me," said Boot. "I dumped the coins out and crammed myself and Sneaker into that beat-up, wooden chest you just passed—the one near the door." Boot pointed as though Dod and Dilly could see through the wall into the den of venooses. "We probably spent at least two hours turtling around on the floor. The whole bottom of that box is torn up pretty bad, and it was perfectly sound when we started. Venoos fangs are stronger than I'd have ever guessed—especially the ones on that big plopper. Who would think a venoos could get that big?"

Dilly shivered.

"I owe my life to you, Dilly," said Boot softly, taking the candle from her. "That giant venoos got sick of watching the smaller ones take turns riding around on my shell, so it came along and started pounding the wood with its fangs—ripped clean through the planks in a dozen places. I only escaped because it heard you coming. It stopped inches short of killing me and Sneaker. Its weight alone could have crushed the box. Who knows where I'd be if you hadn't come along?"

Dod thought of his nightmare, the glimpse he'd seen of Boot's shrouded face, and knew right away where Boot would have been: He'd have been wrapped up and hanging from the rafters. Of course, Boot had manfully returned the favor. Dod wasn't so sure he would have done the same thing; after all, having seen the ghastly chamber of death and having narrowly escaped it, Dod was certain that no amount of money would ever persuade him to reenter the forbidden attic, even if he were allowed to wear the suit of armor.

Boot put a roll of rope on his shoulder and walked over to a strange, circular door. "Come on, Sneaker," he said.

"Is it safe?" asked Dilly timidly.

"It leads out," said Boot, smirking as he snuffed out the candle, "and as far as I'm concerned, that's better than where the other door leads."

Dod and Dilly followed Boot into the night. Even with the moon shining down, many stars still twinkled between clumps of clouds.

Boot pointed heavenward. "They call that one the 'Lazy Star,' because it doesn't move."

"Oh, it's like the Steady Star in Green," said Dilly, her hair blowing in the wind.

"Pretty much," agreed Boot. "Tells you something of their attitude, doesn't it?"

"We're definitely not in Green," said Dilly, beginning to shiver.

Dod looked behind him and noticed that the door had disappeared—it had perfectly blended into the steep roofing. Thoughts of Commendus's spring-loaded trick door to his pump house came to mind.

"It's all right," said Boot, as if sensing Dod's alarm. "There's got to be a way down or the door wouldn't have led us out here."

But as they searched, they discovered that there was no easy way off the small, porch-like portion of the roof. And upon further inspection, Boot pointed out scratch marks on the metal tiles, where claws had removed years of buildup, and suggested that whoever had frequented the attic had traveled by way of flutter.

"The Dread!" muttered Dod under his breath.

"Could have been," agreed Boot, petting Sneaker. "Sirlonk used to stay here a lot, didn't he?"

"Or Terro's not as nice as he seems!" said Dilly, walking the perimeter edge one more time, as though this round she would discover a ladder or hidden stairway. "What kind of man would keep venooses in his attic?" she added. "Terro's got to be loony—and his mayler, too. That man gives me the creeps. If anyone's been feeding the spiders, it's him."

"Yeah, no kidding," said Dod. "He probably lost his eye while delivering victims."

"I think I've got it!" burst Boot excitedly, lowering his rope. "This cord is perfect!"

Dod peered over the edge. Since the castle was perched on a hill, hundreds of feet separated them from the rocky ground below. There was no way that Boot's rope was anywhere near long enough.

Boot looked at Dilly with kidlike enthusiasm. "Dod and I will hold the line while you climb down and swing to the balcony," he suggested.

"*That* balcony?" sputtered Dilly, pointing far below them at a small, railed outcropping. She paused to think.

Dod's stomach churned at the sight. It was like looking down the face of a cliff and spying a small ledge. The three of them would barely fit on it, assuming they could survive the plunge.

"It couldn't be more than forty feet," said Boot optimistically, "and this rope's a solid fifty. You'd have ten feet of line to swing sideways with."

"But there's nothing up here to secure it to," winced Dilly.

"That's why Dod and I will hold it firm," argued Boot. "And once you've made it, I'll post it for Dod, too. He's a lightweight."

Dod glanced at Boot apprehensively.

"And then what?" asked Dilly. "We search for a giant flutter?"

"Don't be silly," chuckled Boot. "You'd never find one, and if you did, Terro would have such a storm of guards watching it that you'd get caught trying to steal the beast—" He smirked boldly. "Besides, I'm looking forward to my grand exit."

Dod and Dilly both prodded him with their eyes in the moonlight.

"Don't go back," shuttered Dod. "We were lucky to get out alive."

"Not in a million years," returned Boot. "Sneaker and I will take a swing. You know how to tie a solid knot, don't you Dod?"

Dod nodded.

"Once you've made it down, find a secure portion of the railing and tether the rope tight," ordered Boot. "I'll get down."

"But the freefall will kill you," said Dilly. "You'll drop at least forty feet. The line will break."

"Technically, it'll be more like eighty or ninety before I hit the bottom," grinned Boot. "But I won't be freefalling, I'll jump that way—" he pointed in the opposite direction of where they were headed. "The rope will pull tight quicker and swing me below. Then, when the fun's over, I'll climb up to the balcony. It's perfect, see?"

Dilly lowered her eyes.

"I've done it before in the barn back at Twistyard," explained Boot. "Really, I'll be fine. Don't worry."

"You know you're crazy, right?" said Dod.

"If you've got a better way, go ahead and share it," returned Boot. "I don't plan on being sold off as a slave. Let's get going."

Dilly went first, then Dod. Boot's strong muscles held them, even while they swung to the balcony. Next came Boot's grand departure. Dod couldn't stop worrying that his knot would slip and he'd be the reason Boot had died.

With a loud cry of "Wu-hu-hooooo!" Boot fearlessly leapt from the edge of the rooftop and sailed through the air.

Dilly closed her eyes. She couldn't watch.

Since Boot jumped in the opposite direction of the balcony, the rope stretched tight long before he hit the end of the line; and just as he had predicted, he swung harmlessly back and forth below Dod and Dilly rather than snapping free and falling to his death.

"Wu-hu-hooooo!" celebrated Boot.

Dilly peeked over the rail.

Boot waved, then whizzed up the cord like nothing had happened.

"Dod's right," said Dilly softly as she met him at the top of the rope. "You're crazy, Boot."

"You can't fool me," said Boot smugly, pulling Sneaker out of his shirt. "You like crazy."

Dilly tipped her head away playfully, as though rejecting him, but Dod caught the glimpse in her eye. She loved every ounce of Boot's craziness.

Once Boot had joined the duo, he threw the rope off the edge and prepared to kick his way into the castle through a glass door.

"Wait," said Dilly. She reached down and turned the knob. It opened with a quiet squeak.

"It's unlocked?" chuckled Boot.

Dilly eyed him. "Terro's got Venooses in his attic! What does he care if people wander in?"

"Good point," said Boot, leading the way into the darkness with Sneaker perched atop his shoulder.

"You'd have to have wings to wander up to that door," whispered Dod, stating the obvious.

Rather than going straight back to the Donefur wing, Boot strolled the dark halls, sometimes blindly, until he had located the room filled with statues. "Did you close the hatch?" he asked, turning to Dilly.

"No," she responded. "But I don't think it matters. If Terro wants to keep spiders from roaming his castle, he shouldn't raise them at all."

"It's not that," said Boot, glancing into the dim corridor. "I just don't want anyone to know where we've been. If they find the open hatch, they might search everyone at the portal."

"So?" said Dilly. "Let them search."

"Well..." Boot's voice trailed off.

"You found it, didn't you?" whispered Dod. He wished he could see Boot's face, but the lighting was too poor to see more than his silhouette.

Boot nodded.

"You couldn't have!" said Dilly.

"Shhh!" said Dod. He felt as if someone were listening to them.

"I did," said Boot, entering the Soldiers' Hall. "You don't think I spent two hours cramped in that little treasure chest for nothing, do you?"

"You were hiding from the mob of fangs," protested Dilly.

"Part of the time," said Boot. "But near the handle it had a little hole I could spy through, so I figured, since I was already up there—"

"You're teasing," said Dilly, pressing after Boot. Dod followed behind her.

"Nope."

"You found the little sack?" asked Dilly.

"Yup," said Boot proudly. He didn't seem concerned as he led the way toward the curtains.

"Then what's in it?" challenged Dilly.

"Two blue stones," responded Boot. "They look like robin eggs, only rounder."

"Show me," insisted Dilly.

Boot continued to scurry. "We've got to close the hatch before anything escapes.

Dilly stopped. "I don't want to see another venoos as long as I live!"

"You can wait by the curtains," said Boot. "We're almost there."

The moment Boot began to climb, Dod sensed something was wrong. At first he feared it was a venoos—one that had strayed from the attic—but the more he thought about it, the more he became certain it was something else. And then it hit him.

"What happened to the candle?" he asked Dilly. Boot had already climbed up into the loft.

"Maybe it burned out," suggested Dilly, joining Dod in searching the ground. In the dim light, they did a thorough sweep of the area and turned up nothing.

At a gallop, Boot reached the ropes and hurried down the line as if it were a fire pole. "We've got to get out of here," he rushed in a whisper, taking Dilly by the hand and pointing for Dod to take Dilly's other. "We'll keep to the shadows, and no talking."

"What is it?" cringed Dilly.

"Someone's been here," said Boot solemnly. "The door was shut so well I couldn't find it."

"Oh," said Dilly, sounding relieved. "I thought you were running from more venooses. You scared me."

"At this point, a loose venoos would be the least of our worries," said Boot. "We could get in serious trouble if they catch us, especially since I've got your family's heirloom." Boot let go of Dilly's hand momentarily to pull a small leather pouch from his pocket. "See," he said. "I really found it."

DEATH'S TOLL

Back in the Donefur wing, a fire burned warmly in one of the large fireplaces. It smelled like danger to Dod. Who had lit the fire?

"You'll need to burn your nightgown," whispered Boot to Dilly, patting her on the back. "It's—uh—too telling."

In the dim candlelight of the entry chamber, which now seemed bright as day compared to the places they'd just come from, proof of Dilly's encounter with a monstrous venoos was clear to see: She trailed a four-foot strand of webbing that tenaciously clung to her back.

"Oh—right," said Dilly, pulling at her nightgown. Upon inspecting her tail, she immediately disappeared into her main-floor bedroom.

Dod followed Boot into the closest bathroom to clean up. The dusty attic and piles of cocoons had left cobwebs in their hair and smudges on their faces. Even Sneaker needed a little help.

By the time the two boys exited, Dilly was seated near the fire, which now glowed brighter than before. It was fueled by her soiled nightgown. Dilly warmed her hands by the flames and smiled. "We did it," she sighed.

Boot nodded before flopping down beside her.

Dod eagerly joined Boot on the couch and anxiously waited to see what Boot's little bag contained.

"This is it," Boot whispered reverently, drawing the treasure from his pocket. The tan leather pouch was only slightly larger than a golf ball.

"Are you sure it's the real thing?" prodded Dilly. "The rooms were full of treasures."

"Positive," said Boot. "I found a statue of a silver horse stretching its neck to eat apples off a tree—"

"Oh, right," said Dilly gleefully.

"And then, while circling the trunk, it hit me—the reason the riddle says 'Don't get stumped, reach for the whole truth.' There was a hole at the base of the stump just big enough to stick my hand in—"

"And you dared?" gasped Dilly.

Dod was thinking the same thing. The attic had been crawling with venooses. How had Boot been bold enough to stick his arm out from under the shelter of the treasure chest he'd hidden under, let alone had had the nerve to plunge his hand into a hole that was likely filled with baby poisonous spiders?

"I figured death was better than not knowing," said Boot. He tipped the bag over and pointed at the Tillius insignia that was burnt into the leather. "If this isn't rightly Bonboo's, then whose is it?" grinned Boot.

Dilly hugged Boot excitedly. "My great-grandfather's going to be so surprised."

Someone stirred in a nearby room.

Boot lowered the bag down and tilted his body, protecting the bag from being viewed by anyone but Dod and Dilly. Gently, he tugged at the pouch's stiff drawstring, working its mouth until it widened enough to spill two blue stones. They looked like large marbles.

"Huh," grunted Dilly, unsuccessfully hiding her obvious disappointment.

Dod reached to touch them and felt his insides leap. Instantly, his vision blurred. A storm of images flashed through his mind. He saw Sirlonk grabbing for a similar bag, and he heard the woeful cries of the doomed souls in Driaxom, and he tasted rock dust. The air seemed to be filled with dust. And then, as though transported somewhere else, he saw a swirling black sky and felt the ground tremble. Everything around him was in commotion.

"Dod…Dod," said Dilly. She was shaking him, and he was on the floor. "Are you all right?"

"What?" mumbled Dod, gazing blearily at the ceiling.

"Did you pass out?" asked Boot, stuffing the leather pouch back into his pocket.

"I don't know," said Dod. He didn't remember falling off the couch.

"You weren't bitten, were you?" groaned Dilly.

"I don't think so," responded Dod.

Boot reached down and helped Dod up. "He's fine," said Boot reassuringly. "If a venoos had succeeded, Dod would have died up in the attic. Their poison strikes like a dagger to the heart."

Dod shivered. "I'm no good without sleep," he said, as if that had been the problem. He wasn't ready to tell Boot and Dilly what he suspected about the stones.

"Who's clanking around this early in the morning?" called a groggy voice. Ingrid emerged from her bedroom and hobbled over.

"We were just warming ourselves," said Boot, struggling to hold back a yawn.

"Oh, right, I'm sure that's all," said Ingrid sarcastically. She pointed at the broken glass table with her cane. "And I suppose none of you had anything to do with *that*."

Boot looked over his shoulder at the mess.

"I bumped into it," confessed Dod.

"When?" asked Ingrid. Her eyes narrowed until the look she gave was like the beady glare of an angry principal.

"We should all go back to sleep," said Dilly, rising to her feet. "A few more hours will make the rest of the day better."

"Where have you three been?" pressed Ingrid, stepping right in front of Dilly. "You know the rules. No one is supposed to leave this wing without Terro's express permission. If he were to hear the tiniest whisper of your escapades, you'd all be nose deep in the worst kind of trouble. This isn't Twistyard! We're guests, here." Ingrid glared threateningly down at Dilly. "*Bonboo's* protective arm doesn't reach this far!"

"Calm down," said Boot in a cool voice, carefully stuffing Sneaker behind his back. "What's gotten into you, Gram?"

"Me?" choked Ingrid. "I haven't forgotten whose castle this is! You'd do well to remember the steep consequences that can befall *rule breakers*!"

"We're fine," said Boot. "But thanks for caring."

"You could have died," snorted Ingrid. "And even now, a fate worse than death may await you if anyone finds out. You're in trouble—deep, deep, deep trouble!"

"But we didn't do anything wrong," said Dilly, beginning to look worried.

"Hardly," burst Ingrid, waddling closer to Dilly. "You've been out walking the halls. I know it. I saw you leave."

"But Ingrid—" began Dilly.

"You're all guilty!" huffed Ingrid. "Do you know, if people find out—even after you've returned to Green—you could still face harsh punishments. Green is filled with tredders from Raul. You can't imagine the far reaching consequences of your *stupid* actions. We could all be in real trouble because of you three."

"But no one needs to know," said Boot in a stern voice. His eyes challenged Ingrid's. "We're friends, right?"

Ingrid stood silently staring, as if assessing her options. Finally, after some time, she spoke. "Promise me you'll never tell a soul about your wanderings," said Ingrid. "No bragging, no hinting, no explanations. Not a word of any kind. And certainly no more *gallivanting!*"

"Why would we tell anyone?" snapped Boot. "Besides, it's no big deal."

Ingrid's eyes flared with a peculiar rage.

"Who's making noise?" called Bowlure from the second story. Youk was at his side, adjusting his costume.

"Not a word," grumbled Ingrid under her breath, and then turning to face the balcony, she changed tones. "It's too chilly to stay in bed. Of course we're out here. Would you care to join us?"

"Once I'm done wrapping," said Bowlure. "Say, where are your costumes?"

"Goodness," said Ingrid, patting the top of her head. "I'm poor at this game of charades. Were we supposed to sleep in our disguises?"

CHAPTER TWENTY-FIVE

Dilly pushed past Ingrid and made a beeline for her room.

"No," said Youk in a crackly girl's voice. "But put them on before our morning practice. You've got a few minutes, honey."

"Practice?" mumbled Dod to Boot.

Boot smiled. "You fell asleep too quickly and missed the announcement. We're scheduled to sing for our breakfast. I knew it was bad news when I saw Youk had joined Bowlure and Rot in their trio at High Gate. Now Youk's determined to have the rest of us make fools of ourselves."

Ingrid shot a stern glance at Boot and Dod as she hobbled away.

"Is it just me or is Ingrid becoming a royal pain?" remarked Boot, pulling Sneaker out from behind him the moment Youk and Bowlure weren't watching. He stuffed the ferret down his shirt and rose to his feet.

"She's cranky," said Dod, following Boot to the stairs. "But did you hear it? She finally got Bonboo's name right. I think that's the first time she hasn't called him Bonmoob."

"She's working on climbing the social ladder," whispered Boot. "It's driving me crazy. What's it to her if we were out *gallivanting*?"

"Maybe she's jealous," offered Dod, taking a good look at the snarling lion as they approached their room.

"The way I'm feeling," said Boot, "she should go out *gallivanting* by herself and take a stroll through Terro's exciting attic."

"Galli-whatting?" mumbled Buck sleepily. He rubbed at his eyes and sat up.

"Nothing," said Boot, releasing Sneaker.

By the time Green Hall was escorted to breakfast, they were all starving. Youk had sent their guide away three times, claiming a few more minutes were needed in order to perfect their special musical number for Terro. Dod felt like he could sing the whole song in his sleep if he were called upon by Youk's whiny girl voice.

In the Great Hall, seating arrangements were different than they had been the day before. Rather than an open buffet, the setting was more formal, with tables prepared for only three hundred guests. Green Hall had been assigned a pair of long tables near the entrance. They appeared to be the last vacant spots in the hall. All of the other guests had arrived earlier and were well into their meals.

"We'll sing first," insisted Youk, keeping his subjects from bolting. "Don't worry, your food's not going anywhere."

Dod looked longingly at the full plates and bowls that were placed up and down the two tables. The food smelled wonderful. Dod had been awake since the middle of the night, so it felt like he'd skipped breakfast and it was time for lunch. Boot seemed to share his same sentiments.

"I think we'd sound better if he'd just let us taste the cream pudding," lamented Boot to Dod.

Dod's stomach growled so loudly that Sawny stepped back and looked at him as though he had just passed gas.

"Gross," chuckled Boot, and then eyeing Sawny cleverly he added, "Are you sure he's your twin?"

"It was my stomach!" defended Dod. "I'm starving!"

Up ahead, Ingrid broke rank right in front of Youk. "You kids can go and sing all you want. I'm too old for crooning."

"Me too," grunted Juny, whose costume was even more dreadful and spooky than it had been the day before; additional fake blood dripped from her ears, and the soot around her eyes was more pronounced. She and Ingrid pushed past Princess

Youk. Tonnis wormed his way through the crowd and quietly set his course to follow the rebelling twosome.

"Please," begged Youk, rushing to stop them. "I told Terro we had a surprise for him. Come and join us."

Ingrid thumped her cane on the ground repeatedly. "Our breakfast is getting cold! I can't sing without eating!"

"It won't take long," insisted Youk in his regular voice, momentarily slipping from his guise. "Be polite!"

"She's losing it," whispered Boot to Dod.

Ingrid begrudgingly gave up her designs and rejoined the hungry crowd, but Juny didn't. She glared at Youk in a haunting sort of way until he waved her on.

Once she and Tonnis were nearly seated, Youk turned to the others and called out in his best girly voice, insisting everyone follow him, and he pulled at his long curls as if he were trying twice as hard to be in character to make up for his momentary lapse while confronting Ingrid. His flowery dress swayed back and forth with the swinging of his hips as he led the bunch toward Terro's table.

"I don't ever act like that, do I?" asked Sawny, pausing to examine her outfit.

Dod's eyes froze on her shiny red boots. Unexpectedly, a bitter taste plagued his mouth. "That's it. The food's poisoned," mumbled Dod.

"What?" asked Sawny. She was the only one close enough to hear him; everyone else had begun their trek across the room to sing for Terro.

"The plates of food are poisoned," said Dod, glancing nervously at Juny and Tonnis. "I've got to stop them."

Not thinking of the possible repercussions, Dod raced to Juny and grabbed at her arm, causing her first bite of food—a spoon full of cream pudding—to spill down her shaggy beard.

"What's gotten into you?" demanded Tonnis, grabbing Dod by the neck with a powerful hand. "We're not singing!"

Juny silently glared.

"The food's poisoned," stuttered Dod. Once the words had come out of his mouth, everything seemed to pause. He didn't exactly regret what he had said, but he was instantly more aware of his declaration's preposterous nature. How did he know the food was poisoned? It looked perfectly fine. Each place at the table was set in the most beautiful manner, trumping Commendus's fancy pampering.

Dod was suddenly aware of the army of waiters who stood by in fancy suits, prepared to fill requests, and the towering guards who protected the doorways. Those within earshot had expressions which turned from pleasant solemnity to discontentment.

"Poison?" rumbled Tonnis, his grip tightening around Dod's neck. "Who did it? How did they know where we would sit?"

Sawny merged on the scene about the same time as two burly guards.

"What's the problem?" asked one of the guards, taking Dod from Tonnis. His nose was unusually large and his dark eyebrows came close in the center.

"He said our food's poisoned," said Tonnis, examining his untouched plate.

"That's ridiculous," scoffed the big-nosed guard. "If yours is poisoned, there isn't a plate on this table that's safe. I personally watched the attendants put food on them, and no one's been near them since."

"Okay, I could be wrong," conceded Dod quietly, still trying to think things through.

"I can vouch for the food—it's safe," said a waiter that approached, his chin tipped up and his eyes glaring down. He looked Tonnis over disdainfully. "Go ahead and eat it," he challenged.

"I don't trust you," responded Tonnis.

"Trust? What do *you* know of trust?" grunted the waiter.

Tonnis squared his shoulders. Clearly a past conflict had grown into a grudge.

"If the food's fine, have a seat," said Juny in a stern, male voice. "Take mine." Juny rose to her feet and staggered backward, leaving her plate for the man to try.

"I will," said the waiter, rushing over to sit in her chair. "I should be the one dining with these guests…and as for *you*—" the man glared at Tonnis, "there's a different sort of place where you belong."

"Don't eat it," pled Dod. Sawny's shiny shoes had reminded him of the images he'd seen the day before, while dressing up—the images he'd seen of people laying in a row, lifeless, covered from their heads to their waists with burlap sacks.

The waiter dove into the cream pudding first. "Best I've ever tasted," he gloated, shoveling spoonfuls into his mouth.

Dod felt sick. He had made a fool of himself and pulled Juny and Tonnis into the mess.

"Let's go sing," prompted Sawny, poking Dod in the back anxiously.

Youk was eyeing the commotion from across the room where he had situated Green Hall for their special presentation, but hadn't yet begun.

"The beef and browns are to *die for*," mocked the waiter, continuing to feast while he took jabs at Tonnis. "It's too bad your foolishness guides you—*paranoid freak*!"

Dod turned to follow Sawny and found Tonnis and Juny had reconsidered their participation in the singing, though they both moved away from the table with heavy steps.

"Sorry," offered Dod. "He's a rude man."

Tonnis and Juny were silent.

"I just didn't feel good about the food," continued Dod.

Still no response from the somber twosome, and Sawny had moved ahead of them, so she didn't weigh in.

"He still may die," suggested Dod. "Some poisons are slow."

"I can only wish," muttered Tonnis coolly. "He deserves that and a little more."

"Why?" whispered Dod, dropping back a few steps to be closer to Tonnis. They were now passing between tables.

"He killed two of my friends," said Tonnis. "But since he was well connected, they gave him a flimsy punishment: five years as a waiter. It's simply pathetic."

"That is awful," said Dod, now feeling even worse than before. Plenty of eyes were watching them walk by, and most of the attention appeared to be centered on Tonnis. Judging looks of disgust and reproach were everywhere. But Juny was spared by her fantastic costume. She couldn't be identified as a woman, let alone the very wife of Sirlonk.

CHAPTER TWENTY-FIVE

"And now we're ready, Terro," announced Youk, gracefully tipping his head as Dod strolled up and joined the front row. Juny and Tonnis took their time nudging their way into the back.

The guests seated around Terro's table were mostly important-looking men, wearing expensive yet simple costumes. Raulings and Raul Coosings were seated close by. Sawb's face glowed with delight as the music began. He seemed to enjoy watching the Greenlings and Coosings squirm as they attempted to sing Raul's traditional friendship song about lilies blooming in the springtime and butterflies skirting around the edges of rainbows and little ponies.

Dod had a hard time keeping a straight face, and it wasn't just the words of the song. One peek to the side revealed his suspicions were correct: Just past Toos, Ingrid was the one singing horribly off key. And to view her face, you'd think she had begged to perform the tribute alone. With no sense of fear, she relentlessly belted each note, which booming distraction to the melody distressed Princess Youk until he appeared as if he were bearing down, his face full of wrinkles, about to lay an egg beneath his dress. His leading hand had withered in shame and now only slightly waved. If Bowlure hadn't been thundering the real tune from the rear, Ingrid's voice would have been a solo.

The song went on and on. It was eight minutes long and felt twice that because of how dreadful Ingrid sounded. Even Sawb's smirk had turned to a pained grimace by the end.

Terro didn't clap. He waved his hand at Youk without looking and muttered, "Needs practice…especially the portly one with the sweater on her head."

His guests laughed.

Ingrid lumbered away from Terro's table, huffing proudly, "I sing better when I'm not starving to death. Perhaps I'll give you an encore later—something special from Green."

"You've done enough," said Terro, rubbing his ears.

His guests laughed again. Dod could see that Terro was, indeed, a lot like his son, Sawb.

By the time Dod had reached Green Hall's assigned tables, men in suits were briskly pulling the plates off by the tray-load. A crowd had formed around someone on the ground. It was the calloused waiter. He had white foam bubbling from his mouth, and by every indication, he was dead.

"Here's the boy who said the food was poisoned," thundered the big-nosed guard. Everyone turned toward Dod and stepped back."

"I warned him," mumbled Dod, feeling a mixture of horror and relief.

Pone stood near the body, staring down at it with a glossy, pensive look.

"That would have been me," said Tonnis, pushing deeper with Boot's help.

The crowd continued to grow. Guards and guests alike struggled to see what had happened.

"How did you know it was poisoned?" asked a guard who wore a shiny rectangular badge. He took charge and moved in on Dod, while his subordinates, the big-nosed man included, forced their way to the dead man and covered his head with a burlap sack. Watching the scene made Dod shiver. Once the bag was pulled down to his waist, the waiter looked exactly like one of the corpses Dod had seen in his mind the day before.

"I—uh—just felt like the food was poisoned," stuttered Dod. He knew it was a poor answer, but the truth.

"*Felt?*" mocked the man in charge, breathing down on Dod. "You *felt* like it was poisoned? Do you really expect me to accept that explanation?"

"He's psychic," offered Boot. "Dod does stuff like this all the time. If you don't believe him, go talk with Terro about it. He's seen Dod predict the future."

Dod sighed.

"Where were you this morning?" pressed the guard.

"He was practicing his singing," responded Youk, abandoning his girl voice. "We were all together in the Donefur Wing, just as assigned."

"And before the practice?" continued the guard, still glaring at Dod suspiciously.

Dod gulped.

"He was—well—sleeping," said Youk. "Terro's confined us to stay together."

Dod's eyes settled on Ingrid's. It was like discovering a bomb in the crowd. She was staring at him firmly, as if she were trying to decide whether to turn him in or not. Her mention of Dod's nighttime wanderings would be catastrophic, especially in light of Dod's ongoing trial back in Green for the murder of Horsely.

Boot and Dilly both glanced back and forth between Dod and Ingrid, obviously worried about the same concern.

"I had nothing to do with the poisoning," said Dod in a loud voice, feeling his legs weaken. "Right now you should be detaining all of the cooks and waiters and kitchen staff. You almost killed us. Every one of those plates are probably poisoned."

"Anything for Jungo," said Tonnis, pushing past the others until he stood before the chief guard. "You know this was meant to kill me. Have the Donefurs visited lately?"

"It's not your concern," grumbled the guard crossly, appearing to take offense that Tonnis had postured his shoulders challengingly.

"It is, too, Irksum," fought Tonnis. "You, of all people, know that they want me dead for my father's crimes—bad enough that they would recklessly destroy dozens of others' lives if need be, especially if the victims weren't from Raul." Tonnis stepped closer and growled, "Don't forget Terro promised my security."

"What did I promise?" asked Terro. The crowd parted as Raul's Chief Noble Tredder approached. Sawb, Joak, and Kwit were on his heels.

"You promised *we* would be safe," responded Tonnis, instantly changing to a tone of respect, his eyes glued to the floor in submission. "Have any of the Donefurs come to visit?"

"We'll take care of this!" insisted Terro heatedly. "It's an outrage! How dare anyone try to poison guests in *my* home! I don't care for their reasons! I'll have answers before the sun sets, and whoever's responsible will be punished severely! That's my promise to you!"

"Thank you," said Tonnis, still bowing his head.

The cluster of guards hefted the dead man's body out of the Great Hall, and the crowd of spectators quickly took Terro's advice and went back to their own places—except Green Hall. They stood mingling near the empty tables, each venting their frustrations at having come so close to being poisoned.

Dod wanted to feel relieved, but he couldn't. Ingrid kept her eyes on him from a distance, which constantly reminded Dod that trouble was never more than a few wrong words away. What was Ingrid thinking? It plagued Dod so badly that he couldn't concentrate on anything else, until something unusual happened. Right in the middle of Sawny's praises, Dod watched Pone waive off a waiter who held two trays of cookies.

"No," said Pone, "I definitely don't want to eat *anything* right now!"

His words were like a clap of thunder to Dod, easily parting through the chatter of the surrounding conversations. Pone was voicing part of Dod's nightmare, the one he'd had while confined to Twistyard's dungeon, the one where a monstrous dragon had wrought havoc from the sky, the one where fire had engulfed everything in sight, the one where Boot's voice had ordered that Dod be killed.

"Are you okay?" asked Sawny.

Dod was shivering. "I don't know," he responded, pulling his eyes from the ceiling where he'd just checked for a dragon's head. His heart was racing as if he fully expected one would come crashing through the roof any minute.

"You don't look well," said Dilly, coming into view with Boot at her side. Dod cautiously inspected Boot, who appeared to be inspecting him back.

"What is it?" pressed Sawny, reaching to touch Dod's brow.

"Do you like rats?" asked Dod.

"You must be sick," responded Sawny. "I hate rats!"

"Good," said Dod.

"I hate them, too," added Dilly, "but not as much as…you know—" Dilly looked toward the ceiling.

"No kidding," said Dod. It had been hard not talking about what had happened in the attic. Now, only hours later, it all felt like a dream.

"What?" said Sawny. She clearly had been kept in the dark about their adventure. Boot hadn't told Buck, either. By the time he had awakened, people had been walking in the halls and calling for the song practice.

Ingrid startled Dod when she popped her head between Dilly and Boot. "What do we eat now?" she asked, smiling at Dod. The look on her face was welcomed. The nice Ingrid was back.

"Good question," said Dod.

"Well," grinned Ingrid, "I'm glad to have a friend like you. Foaming at the mouth doesn't look pleasant. What a miserable way to die. Poor fool! Juny told me how he disregarded your express instructions. It's fortunate she and Tonnis listened. You're quite the hero, Dod. I'm impressed. More and more I'm reminded that you're Pap's grandson."

Youk returned to the group from talking privately with Terro and announced that they would be going to Terro's food pantry to choose bottled items for breakfast, lunch, and dinner—meals they were asked to eat in the Donefur Wing.

Hours later, as the sun began to set, Terro joined the Green Hall crowd for a few minutes. He promised that they were doing their best to hunt down the perpetrator and apologized for any inconvenience it was causing. He also announced that, after much consideration, he would be immediately escorting Tonnis and Juny to the portal for reentry to Green. Things weren't deemed safe enough for them to remain in Raul.

Bowlure and Youk asked to accompany them to the Portal Chamber, to see them off, and were granted that request. Everyone else continued playing games and chatting, clumped around the fireplaces in the Donefur Wing. The visit to Raul had been demoted from an extravagant, formal party, to a cabin sleepover.

"I'd like to be going back," confessed Sawny, setting her book down to watch Tonnis exit. "I'm done with the Ghoul's Festival."

"Me too," said Dilly. "But you know how it is—unscheduled jumps through the portal are frowned upon."

"At least we'll be returning tomorrow night," said Dod. He couldn't get out of Raul fast enough. With giant venooses in the attic, the world of Raul seemed like the right place to encounter a massively destructive dragon, which event Dod was hoping to avoid.

"Babies," teased Boot, stretching out with his legs to the fire. "Enjoy the stay. It may be your last."

"I'm fine if it is," said Buck. "Seeing that guy bubbling really got me thinking. People are crazy here in Raul. It's no wonder this world produced the likes of Sirlonk."

"He's really from Soosh," corrected Boot. "Right, Dod?"

Dod nodded while warming his hands by the fire. "Sort of. His father was from here, but his mother was from Soosh, so he was raised in Soosh. At least that's what Terro told me."

"They're crazy there, too," sputtered Buck. "I like Green."

"You're gone a couple of days and you're already homesick," laughed Boot. "Raul's a nice place. If it were warmer and we had more time, you'd change your mind. Dirsitch is pretty *sweet*." Boot dug his hand into the mouth of his stuffed snake—he was no longer wearing it, but had it beside him—and drew out a long block of chouyummy. "Anyone for a piece?"

Once Boot had begun splitting portions, Pone and Toos magically appeared, having deserted their game of cards in the middle, leaving Kurt, Voo, and Sham all complaining.

"Where'd you get it from?" asked Pone, eyeing the treat suspiciously. After the morning poisoning, Pone's eating habits had become more restrained. He looked twice before stuffing things into his mouth.

"There was more than beef and beans in the pantry," chuckled Boot. "I loaded up."

"Thanks," said Toos, smiling slyly as he tried to steal Sawny's seat while she was reaching for chouyummy.

Dilly sent him sideways with a quick kick.

"She's lethal," warned Boot. "And after the day she's had, I wouldn't mess with her." Boot grinned at Dilly and Dod. They had all three agreed not to talk about the attic with Sawny and Buck until they had safely made it back to Green, and even then, only with great discretion.

When Youk and Bowlure returned, they didn't come back alone. Trimash was with them, decked in furs, as he had been before, and trailing him was his beastly hound, Herculon.

"One quick announcement," called Youk, standing at the entrance beside Trimash. "Do you see this wonderful puppy? It will be roaming the halls tonight, keeping us safe. You need not fear."

A chorus of gasps followed.

"Not *in* the Donefur Wing," clarified Youk. "Out here."

Sighs of relief overtook the room.

Youk and Bowlure entered the chamber and went upstairs, but the door remained open.

Dod stared at Trimash, who had fixed his one good eye on him. The mayler spun his hand in the air, as if calling Dod.

"I think he wants to talk with you," said Buck, nudging Dod with his foot.

"*You* go talk with him," returned Dod. "I'm staying here."

"I'll go with you," offered Boot, hopping to his feet. He left his snake on the couch and let everyone know it was saving his place.

Reluctantly, Dod gave in to Boot and walked toward the door. The closer he got, the more he could hear Herculon's thoughts. *Can I attack now?* it seemed to say. *Where's my prey?*

Trimash somberly touched the top of his grizzly hound's head. *You may hunt tonight,* he seemed to tell the dog with his mind. Up close, Dod could see that the horrible creature was bigger than a lion.

"I said death follows you," grumbled the mayler in a low, haunting voice. "Its fingers are still reaching. More will die."

"Life follows him, too," said Boot defiantly, puffing his chest like a nobleman. "We'd all be dead from poison if it weren't for Dod. If you want to hocus-pocus a prediction, go and figure out who tried to kill us."

The beastly hound's eyes narrowed. *Can I attack him and crush his throat?* it seemed to say. Its mouth was gaping open, showing it had two rows of sharp teeth, the likes of which Dod had never seen before.

Trimash glared at Boot and inhaled as if he were sucking Boot's soul right out. The tiny skulls around Trimash's mayler belt began to tremble. "You speak boldly for one who hides the truth," he finally said, his voice growing raspy.

"You're hardly one to talk," snapped Boot. "I know plenty about the deaths you've caused. Predictions go both ways. Maybe I'm psychic. I think you prefer dungeons of webbing over dungeons of stone for your victims. Do you want to talk anymore?"

Herculon began to growl from the very rear of his throat. *Can I kill them now?* it seemed to say. *They've made you mad. Let me eat them.*

Trimash touched his hound on the head again. *Not that one,* he seemed to tell the beast. *The Order has need of him.*

What? thought Dod, trying to decipher whether the 'one' he meant was him or Boot.

Trimash instantly spun his good eye on Dod. He appeared to recognize that his privacy had been breached. "Ha-ku, ha-kuwon," he grumbled, raising one hand in the air. "We will go, now. The halls will be safe tonight."

Dod shivered. The whole circumstance was creepy. Even once the door had been closed, Dod could still momentarily feel the beastly dog's thoughts as it walked away.

CHAPTER TWENTY-SIX

UNFAIRLY CONFINED

All night long Dod tossed and turned. Trimash and his ugly hound plagued Dod's dreams. They were everywhere; sitting in the Donefur Wing foyer, walking the halls of the castle, visiting the Portal Chamber, and then back to sitting in the Donefur Wing foyer. Dod couldn't stop thinking about them. He would awaken and try to redirect his thoughts only to find himself once more dreaming that they were close by, spying on him, with Trimash attempting to read his mind. The man's glossy, dead eye was always the trigger that would cause Dod to startle out of slumber.

In the morning, Dod discovered the reason for his sleepless night.

"Who do they think they are?" raged Boot, waking Dod and Buck up with his stomping. "We're victims, not criminals! And Youk expressly promised us that we wouldn't have to deal with that *thing!*"

"What's happening?" asked Buck, keeping his covers pulled high. Morning light was gently creeping in through the window, a sign that the sun would soon rise.

"Trimash!" spat Boot, making a fist. "That man and his creature are sitting in front of the door downstairs, ordering all of us to stay in our bedrooms. Can you believe it? He says we must be interrogated."

"Why?" asked Dod.

"I guess the poisoning," muttered Boot in a less than convincing manner.

"Is that *all* they're looking for?" pressed Buck.

"What's that supposed to mean," flared Boot angrily, spinning to face Buck.

"You know what I mean!" returned Buck. "I'm not stupid!" He glanced at Dod, too. "You and Dod and Dilly were acting weird yesterday. Something's up. I know it, I just don't know what. You guys did something, or took something—"

"Buck!" said Boot.

"It's true, isn't it?"

Boot turned away momentarily, then slowly turned back toward Buck. "You can't tell a soul, but we found the Tillius stash—the one Bonboo's father hid."

"I knew it!" exploded Buck, throwing his covers off like a crazy man. "The three of you went roaming the halls, and now we're all doomed to become slaves." He began panting nervously. "Did you take it?"

"Of course we took it!" said Boot.

"You had to take it," moaned Buck, smacking his own head. "You couldn't just leave it! You had to take it! Now they'll say we were trying to steal from them—as if breaking their rules wasn't enough! I'll never see Green again. This nightmare won't end."

"But you're technically not even involved," said Boot.

"It doesn't matter," despaired Buck, wringing his hands. "They'll search our room and blame us equally."

"Not if I tell them I did it alone," responded Boot. "Besides, we don't know what they're looking for. Perhaps they're just making sure we didn't help with the poisoning."

"Oh," groaned Dod. "That's the part that scares me. If they hear we were out yesterday morning, they'll think we contaminated the food. It could cost us our necks."

Dod's heart began to beat faster. He knew what he had to do, but he didn't want to do it.

"Don't worry," said Boot, seeming to wish he had stayed silent. "I'll take care of everything. Let me do the talking."

"Put the stash in my things," mumbled Dod, frantically pulling his clothes on.

"What? No!" gasped Boot, looking shocked. "It's too risky."

"Terro owes me," said Dod. "If the bag becomes an issue, I'll face up to it alone and get Terro to help me out." Dod didn't tell, but he knew he had a way to escape if the worst case scenario happened, assuming he could get his medallion to work in Raul as it had in Green.

Boot's brow furrowed. "I don't know," he said guiltily, beginning to reach his hand into his pocket. "Are you sure?"

"Terro would be dead without me," said Dod. "That should be worth something to him." The more Dod talked, the more he almost believed his own words. "And my bag's bigger, too. It has a funny seam at the bottom. If I stuff it in the corner, it might not catch their eyes.

"Oh, yeah," said Boot. "I saw that when taking the knife out." Boot handed Dod the little pouch.

Instantly, two loud knocks hit the door, startling all three boys.

"Open up," said a voice that Dod recognized as Terro's.

Dod fumbled the small stash and stuffed it in his pants pocket.

"Hi, Terro," said Boot, masterfully faking a calm composure. "What's going on this morning? Are you bringing us breakfast?"

Terro frowned a little. "I wish," he said. He was flanked by three stuffy-looking aristocrats, two guards, and Trimash. In addition, someone was approaching them from behind.

"What's she doing up here?" asked one of the guards, pointing at Ingrid. It was the chief guard who had interrogated Dod the day before.

"You've got to go back to your room," ordered Terro.

"But I can't stay down there alone," shuddered Ingrid, wearing her costume crookedly, as if she'd tied the sweater on her head in a hurry. "Not with your dog in the hall. It's too dreadful without Juny. You must let me accompany you. This is ludicrous!" Ingrid thumped her cane against the ground.

"No!" said Terro bluntly. "We're done talking with you. If we have further questions, we'll come calling."

"At least let me stay up here with Boot and Dod," begged Ingrid. "Please, your dog scares me. I'll be quiet as a roach, I promise."

"No!" repeated Terro.

"But I have skills," offered Ingrid, sounding desperate. "I know things. I can help you. Trust me."

Everyone stared. Dod's heart felt like it was going to jump out of his chest. Was she about to drop the bomb?

"What do you think, Trimash?" asked Terro. "Is she useful?"

The mayler scratched at his fur cap and approached Ingrid. He smelled her hair first, then her hands, then her cane. "Let her stay," he grumbled hoarsely.

"Fine," sighed Terro.

Ingrid straightened her back officiously and raised her chin.

"What can we help you with?" asked Boot.

"We're here to search your room," said the chief guard. "If you have anything to hide, now would be the time to bring it forth. Your sentencing would reflect your willingness to cooperate."

Boot glanced at Dod.

"Search," said Dod, pulling his closed bag from the floor. He set it on the bed and opened it up. "Have you found the person who tried to poison us?"

Dod was shocked with the answer.

"Yes," said Terro.

"You did?" choked Buck.

Terro nodded. "It appears that Tonnis was correct in asserting that the Donefurs were involved."

"Someone gave them what they deserved!" rattled Ingrid excitedly, pushing her way past the aristocrats and into the bedroom. "They tried to pickle us and found that murder is a game two can play—or I suppose more than two—five or six—"

"Nine," corrected one of the aristocrats, brushing lint from his sleeve. "Two Donefur princes were found dead, here in the castle, run through with a sword. They had vials of poison in their coats—"

"*Their* deaths may have been justified," burst another aristocrat, tweaking his glasses, "but the seven others weren't! We must respect their honorable rights. Their kin will demand justice!"

"Others?" asked Boot.

"Seven Donefur princes were spending the night at the Old Manor House," said Terro. "It's just a stone's throw away, down in the valley. By several eye-witness reports, one cloaked man defeated them all in a swordfight, a little after midnight."

"Wow!" blurted Boot.

"He showed no mercy," rattled the last aristocrat. "People say it was The Dread. But of course, since that doesn't seem reasonable, the next logical possibility would be one of his friends."

"Or family," groaned Terro. "You don't have to hide your intentions in front of them. Everyone knows you're considering me and my son as suspects, which thoughts are certainly at the height of stupidity. We were with guests here at the castle until past one, and the poison wasn't aimed at us—it was aimed at them!" Terro pointed directly at Boot.

"I shouldn't be wearing this costume," mumbled Ingrid, grabbing at her sweater. "It's a bad time to be posing as The Dread."

Terro looked at Ingrid and raised an eyebrow crossly. He was no longer wearing the disguise he had worn the other two days—the one that had looked remarkably similar to The Dread—though he seemed to curse Ingrid with his glare for reminding the three aristocrats that he had done so before.

"If we find proof of a connection, wherever it may be, we'll press for judgment," said the aristocrat with glasses. "The

Donefurs are all but gone. Their dynasty is in ruins, now. People will be shouting in the streets about this. It's an outrage!"

Trimash took a loud breath and gazed coldly at Dod. "I've said it before, death follows *that* boy." He tipped his head toward Dod.

"I was here all night," defended Dod. "We all were. You know that."

The guards meticulously searched the luggage, then the bedding and beds, then the furniture and stuffed fish. Coming up empty, they inspected Boot's clothes first, followed by Buck's. Dod strained to keep from shaking. The anticipation was killing him. He knew that they were about to see the loot that Boot had taken from the attic. What would follow?

Cringing, Dod dug his hands into his pockets and put the contents on a tray.

"What's this?" asked the chief guard, scooping up the little pouch.

"Interesting," said Ingrid, shoving her way closer. She pushed down with her cane and drove it squarely into the chief guard's big toe, causing him to yelp in pain and drop the leather pouch back onto the tray.

"WOMAN! THAT'S IT!" yelled the guard. "You've got to leave!"

"I thought you wanted an explanation," responded Ingrid, picking up the precious treasure.

"We do," said the aristocrat with glasses. "From him!"

Dod swallowed hard.

"He may not wish to be truthful with you," offered Ingrid. "This is embarrassing for him."

Boot seemed to be holding his breath, and Buck had turned away.

"I doubt you know what he's put in there," raged the injured guard.

"Trust me," defended Ingrid. She handed the pouch to Terro and glanced at the tray. "Just as I suspected."

"What?" huffed the chief guard.

"Do you see this ring and note?" Ingrid held them up. Dod had completely forgotten about them. "I'm feeling confident," insisted Ingrid, "that this note is from Bonboo, Chief Noble Tredder of Green, testifying of this boy's good character and promising his own life as a guarantee. And look, this ring is Bonboo's."

"So what's in the bag?" asked the injured guard. "We can see the note and ring."

One of the aristocrats took and opened the note and began skimming its contents.

"I was just getting to that," huffed Ingrid. "Since Bonboo's put his life on the line, he's also sent Dod off with a pair of ooblies—two blue stones—meant to remind Dod that if he steps out of line, even a little, his whole family will be punished." Ingrid made a slicing noise.

"Preposterous!" said the chief guard.

Terro tipped the bag upside down and inspected the insignia. "This bears the mark of a Tillius," he nodded, and then he carefully opened it up. Out popped the two stones.

"She's right!" exclaimed one of the aristocrats.

"I have skills," gloated Ingrid.

Dod and Boot stared at her, dumbfounded.

"You're cleared for now," said Terro, handing Dod back his things. "I'm terribly sorry for the string of uncomfortable events. This visit was intended to be my way of thanking you."

"It's all right," muttered Dod, feeling grateful that he wasn't being hauled off to face Herculon.

Terro sighed. "Breakfast will be delivered shortly—still in bottles, straight from my pantry. Sawb and his friends will be coming by to serve it, and they'll eat first from the items you choose—as a show of trust. I really am sorry about the poisoning. This sort of thing has never happened in *my* house."

Ingrid hobbled to Dod's bed and sat down.

"What are you doing?" asked one of the aristocrats, giving her a stiff reprimand. "We still have rooms to check."

"I'm satisfied to wait here," said Ingrid. "When the dog's gone, I'll return to my room."

"Come along," chided the chief guard, still hobbling. "They want your help. You asked to play your part. Now it's your duty."

By the look in the man's eye, had Ingrid begged to continue on, he would have been lobbying for her to stay behind. Whichever action she did, didn't seem to matter to him, so long as it was the opposite of what Ingrid wanted.

Ingrid sulked her way out the door and shut it behind her.

"That was close," whispered Boot, grinning ear-to-ear. He seemed to enjoy having narrowly escaped trouble.

"Too close," said Dod, holding the special pouch in his hand. "How did Ingrid know about this? Did you show it to her?"

"Not directly," responded Boot, "but I guess she might have caught a glimpse of it yesterday morning. She could have been peeking at us before she emerged from her bedroom. That's probably why she was so cranky. She assumed we had been off looting Terro's treasures."

"They're not really ooblies, are they?" asked Buck. His face hadn't yet regained its color.

"I've never heard of an ooblie," said Boot. "Ingrid probably made it up. She's a pretty good story teller."

"And really observant," added Dod. "If I weren't me, I wouldn't have known that my note was from Bonboo, proving that he's my guarantor. I had actually forgotten all about the note until she brought it up. It was a good direction to go in."

"No kidding," said Boot. "People here still respect Bonboo. His trust in you is probably what saved us—well—that and Ingrid's ability to spin a good tale."

"She warned them she had skills," smiled Buck, beginning to loosen up.

"Where's Sneaker?" asked Dod, suddenly realizing that he hadn't seen the ferret all morning.

Boot raised his eyebrows. "He's protecting the towels in the bathroom closet. I was preparing a little prank when Trimash ordered me back to my room."

"Prank on whom?" asked Buck, already seeming to know the answer.

"One of my favorite brothers," said Boot.

All day long, the Donefur Wing was buzzing with chatter. Trimash and Herculon sat outside the door, as ordered, and prevented anyone from leaving. Around the fireplaces, clumps of Greenlings and Coosing tried to play games or read to pass the time, but few succeeded because of their heightened anxiety. No one could believe what had happened.

After the thorough morning search, Youk, Bowlure, Strat, and Pone had been taken away for further questioning. Everyone else had been informed that their planned return to Green had been cancelled. Going home was out of the question until Raul's

Head Judiciary Panel had agreed to let them go, which wasn't anticipated to be anytime soon. Three to four weeks had been given as an estimate. And by decree of the three aristocrats, whose judgment superseded Terro's in the matter, all of the Donefur Wing crowd were to be held as criminals until proven innocent.

"It's just not fair," lamented Sawny, pushing her mushy peaches around with a spoon.

"I know," agreed Buck, plugging his nose and swallowing. "How can they call this dinner?"

"That's not what I meant," said Sawny. "We're innocent! It's not our fault that someone copied Sirlonk."

Dilly sat beside her on the couch, sipping the last of the juice from the bottom of her bowl of peaches. "Who could have done it?" asked Dilly. "The Donefur princes were known for their swordplay. How could anyone defeat seven of them at the same time?"

"Traygof could," said Buck glumly.

Everyone groaned.

For hours, Buck, Boot, and Dilly had whined incessantly about being detained, because of the sad reality that it would cause them to miss their once-in-a-lifetime chance to sail the seas with Traygof.

"Don't even start," said Sawny. "My head's killing me."

"If he were here," grinned Boot, "we'd get out in a flippy. Traygof would explain things—how we have a strict deadline to meet—and they'd let us go."

Sawny rolled her eyes. "He's not that influential in Raul," she said.

"He is, too!" burst Toos, hopping into the conversation. He had been on the edges, listening.

"Since when?" challenged Sawny.

"Everyone knows Traygof," said Toos. "The man's victories are too big to stay in Green."

"And you know this how?" pressed Sawny.

"I just do!" exploded Toos furiously.

"Whatever," said Sawny, turning her back on him. "If they let us go soon enough, I'll make sure I ask Traygof what connections he has in Raul."

Toos seemed to lose his mind. He took his bowl of peaches and dumped it over Sawny's head.

Screeching in horror, Sawny jumped up wiping juice from her face. "What's your problem?"

Instantly, Dod had Toos on the floor, pinned. He wanted to pummel him with his fists, but held back. "Never treat a lady like that!" growled Dod.

Toos's eyes glared back angrily. "We're locked up because of *you!*" he sputtered. "You killed Horsely, and now you've caused problems here in Raul! We'll probably be sold as slaves thanks to you! Go ahead and punch me if it makes you feel better. Everyone's watching."

Dod released him. All of the conversations in the room had quieted.

"That's not true!" defended Sawny, pulling peaches from her hair. "What's gotten into you, Toos?"

"It is true!" said Toos. "Dod's part of The Order. I know it!"

Dod felt a growing tide of negative judgment from his Green Hall friends.

Sawny shook her head. "You've lost it. Dod just saved us from being poisoned."

"He made it *look* that way!" fought Toos. "Don't you see? It's convenient how he was the only one who knew the food was bad. He keeps pretending to be a hero—so everyone will think he's great—so everyone will think he's *Pap's grandson*. But he's not. Just ask Tridacello where Dod's from. He'll tell you, Dod's nothing more than an orphan! And with no family, what do you think he was really doing when he went home to visit? Think about it!"

"You don't know anything," said Boot, rising to his feet.

"Oh, yeah," rumbled Toos. "Why do you think Bowlure and Youk and Strat came along? They weren't invited—no papers from Terro. The only way they were let into Raul was with special exemptions. They're here to keep an eye on *him!*" Toos pointed at Dod.

Boot silently walked over to Toos and whispered in his ear.

"But Boot—" began Toos.

Boot shook his head and whispered again.

"Ludicrous!" called Ingrid, thumping her way down the stairs. "How many idiots do we have in this room?"

Boot continued to whisper, his hand firmly on Toos's shoulder.

"I know an idiot when I hear one," huffed Ingrid. "A jealous idiot. Let's all stop fighting. Raul's got their own problems that don't involve any of us. Hopefully they'll get things worked out and we'll be on our way soon. I've got appointments to keep, seas to sail." She seemed unwilling to believe that her trip with Traygof had been ruined.

"Sorry, Sawny," offered Toos begrudgingly, making his way to the stairs. Without another word, he went up to his bedroom and shut the door.

"If anyone else wants to be rude and tell lies," announced Boot authoritatively, eyeing the crowd down, "you can plan on packing up once we get back to Twistyard. As the Head Coosing, I won't tolerate it!"

Sawny dashed to rinse out her hair and change her clothes, while Boot returned to his spot on the couch and Dod took a seat on the floor next to the fireplace.

Dod didn't say anything, though a thousand speeches went through his mind. He wanted to gather everyone together and spill the beans about his situation—let them all know the truth once and for all—but he knew it wouldn't work. Most of them wouldn't believe him, they'd gravitate toward Toos's more sensible explanation.

At length, the door creaked open. Youk, Bowlure, Strat, and Pone, entered the room with somber faces.

"Please, everyone," announced Youk, "go and get your things. We've been summoned to report for our first round of assessments. The Head Judiciary Panel has gathered here at Terro's castle. They plan on splitting us up. Some of us may be asked to spend time in a—well—more securely guarded location. Don't fear. Let's cooperate and show a little faith in the integrity of their system. Accidents like this happen. I'm sure, in time, they'll recognize the truth, and we'll all be set free."

"Unless we're dead," muttered Buck. "This is the worst vacation ever!"

In the Great Hall, Boot wore a particularly worried face. Dod knew why. Boot had Sneaker in his bag. If the luggage were searched a second time, the ferret would be discovered and Boot would be charged with smuggling an animal into Raul without a permit. The exact penalty for such a crime was unclear, however, given the strange circumstances, anything horrible was possible.

As a minimum, the ferret would be gone for good—most likely it would become a gift to Sawb, who had long since loathed Boot for his bigger ferret.

Like a line of soldiers standing ready, every member of Green Hall stood with their bag of belongings in front of them. Donshi and a few other younger Greenlings were crying. Trimash and his grizzly hound waited for instructions and watched, along side of Terro and Sawb, as the Head Judiciary Panel members walked up and down the row.

The special group was composed of eight people. Three of them were the aristocrats that had participated in the morning search. They all wore long black robes and golden tassels on their shoulders.

"I'm sure you know why we're here tonight," announced the tallest one, scowling. His pale face and sunken eyes appeared ghostly, and his demeanor was that of an undertaker, or possibly the grim reaper himself.

"At least tell them," ordered Terro in an uncertain voice. "They're my guests."

"Fine," snapped the tall man, shooting a cross look at Terro.

Dod glanced over and noticed that they had taken Bowlure and put him in the corner, away from everyone else, and had assigned armed guards to stand near him.

The tall man cleared his throat and stepped forward toward Dod. "Do you see the heavens?" The man pointed at the wall of dark windows. All eyes obediently looked, though they couldn't see much beyond the glare. "Everything out there is in perfect order," he said. "Every star, every planet, every constellation. That's how we expect things here in Raul—perfect order!"

A loud gasp shot from Donshi, who couldn't hold back her sobs. Sawny was attempting to console her, gently patting her shoulder, however, it wasn't working. The girl clearly believed she was about to be sold as a slave, or worse.

"I am Boorish Salizar, Chief Judge and commanding official of the Head Judiciary Panel. Because of Terro's close affiliation with this circumstance, it is by unanimous vote that we, the Head Judiciary Panel, take full control of this matter."

Terro grimaced, then tipped his chin proudly.

Boorish straightened his back and scowled up and down the line before continuing, as if asserting his superiority. "You are brought before us today because of crimes which were committed in this castle and its surrounding grounds. One man was poisoned to death and nine nobles of *extraordinary blood* were ruthlessly cut down. These events have details which appear to suggest a cause and effect relationship. Some people among us have even drawn a dark conclusion as to the true origins of this disaster. If indeed The Dread's associates are involved, we shall make this case an example! Green must stop dumping such persons into our society!"

Dod found it odd that Boorish and his fellow panel members would come to such an irrational conclusion, since Raul and Soosh had raised and fostered The Dread and shipped him off to Green with a shiny badge of royalty, as the only brother of their Chief Noble Tredder.

"You are brought before us now," said Boorish, "for a primary sentencing. Trimash is not without abilities. He will pull from among you the most problematic souls, which we shall escort to the dungeons for further examination, and the rest of you will be returned to the Donefur Wing. Know this, we apologize for such measures, as you can imagine we only want the best for those of you who are, indeed, innocent. If we had a better way, we would use it. But as it is, our honorable citizenry are waiting anxiously for extraordinary answers. We can't disappoint."

Dod groaned. He knew he was on his way to the dungeon. Trimash hated him. He had spoken ill of him since the moment Dod had entered Raul.

"Come, Trimash," called Boorish, pulling at his long black robe. "Bring your dog and do your job. We need suspects."

Dod inched forward to watch.

Trimash approached the end of the line where Dilly stood. He pushed Herculon forward and called out, "Haku! Rasha'am!"

The beastly dog began to drool and sniff. Slime from its gaping mouth dripped to the floor and crossed Dilly's shoes.

Next was Sawny. She closed her eyes and stood like a tin soldier as the dog's monstrous face smelled her neck. When Herculon tried to move on, as if not satisfied, Trimash nudged the dog back, calling, "Roshonk! Roshonk!"

Following Sawny, Donshi and three other crying Greenlings were subjected to a terrifying search. Each one trembled and whimpered. All the while, Trimash stood staring at them with his one good eye.

The closer Herculon came toward Dod, the more Dod seemed to hear the beasts thoughts. It was excited to hunt. It kept asking to attack. It had no idea what it was looking for. Trimash was using his hound to appear official before the panel. Dod was certain of it.

Glancing around the room, Dod counted guards and weighed options. There were twenty-six armed men and a number of others. It was pointless to fight. They were trained warriors, and many more were likely stationed close by.

Sawb stood beside Terro with a smug look on his face. He didn't seem the slightest bit concerned. Behind the two royals, the dark wall of windows reflected the horrible scene. Dod began to wish that a dragon would make its appearance. He wanted one to come crashing through the glass and gobble up Trimash and his stupid dog. But the dragon wasn't coming fast enough. Time was running out. It was nearly Boot's turn. Herculon would definitely smell Sneaker in his bag. What would Boot do?

"Check them carefully," called Boorish, seeming annoyed that so many people had been passed.

"So far I've identified two possibles," responded Trimash slowly in a hoarse voice. "I just haven't pulled them out, yet. I first need a clean read of the others."

"Splendid," said Boorish, clasping his hands together. His long, twiddling fingers looked like the legs of a spider, entrapping its victim with silk line.

Dod glared at him. And then an idea burst upon his mind. It was worth a shot.

"Sir!" said Dod, stepping completely forward. "Would you like to solve this mystery?"

"I am!" responded Boorish indignantly.

"Well, I can see you are using the best you have," admitted Dod, faking boldness. Inside, he was shaking.

"We have our ways," said Boorish. "Step back."

Dod nodded politely, but remained in place. "Wouldn't you like to use a greater technology—one that could draw the very thoughts from their minds?"

The Head Judiciary Panel members' eyes lit up, including Boorish's.

"I have such a technology," claimed Dod, pulling the best Ingridish tale he could create. "And I am willing to help you on certain conditions."

"Preposterous!" scoffed Boorish, still clearly interested but unwilling to expose himself to being tricked.

"I can prove it," said Dod. "Using my technology, I can draw the most intricate of thoughts from a mind—the very pathway to places only that person has been."

"Do you suppose we're that gullible?" rumbled Boorish, swirling his robe like a cape as he turned to his peers.

"No, sir," said Dod in the most polite voice he could muster. His knees were now shaking. He had made the mistake of glancing to his side. Trimash appeared terribly distraught, and Herculon was feeding off of Trimash's anger. Both man and beast were glaring coldly at Dod, as if they couldn't wait for their chance to 'interrogate him' in the dungeon.

"Terro knows I can do it," said Dod. "Don't you, Terro?"

All eyes turned on him.

"Well—he's somewhat clairvoyant," stuttered Terro. "I'll give him that much."

"Meaning you witnessed what?" asked Boorish pointedly. "We need specifics on this *technology*."

"I—well—" Terro's voice became quiet. It appeared that he hadn't told very many people of his visit to Driaxom, and the more he beat around the bush, the more clear it became that he didn't plan on the Head Judiciary Panel members finding out. "I may have seen that boy do a mind trick or two while visiting my good friend, Commendus. They revere Dod as something special in Green."

"He knew my name without asking," offered Rughead, stepping from the crowd of guards.

"That's a simple deception," laughed Boorish. "He merely inquired of another."

"But he couldn't have, noble sir," responded Rughead. "I met him at the portal and was with him every second up to that point. It's his first visit, and I'm a nobody."

"Perhaps a good guess," countered the aristocrat with glasses, clearly trying to discover the truth.

"My name's Rughead, noble sir," said the man sheepishly.

"How unusual," said Boorish, beginning to smile in a morose way as his sunken eyes zeroed in on Dod. "What's my father's, father's, mother's, only brother's pony's name?"

"Who cares?" chuckled Dod. "If he had one, it's dead."

Everyone in the Head Judiciary Panel laughed except Boorish.

Dod quickly dug his hand into his pocket and drew out the ring Bonboo had given him. "Here's part of the secret," he said, displaying it well, before slipping it onto his right pointer finger. *My precious, precious*, he thought, but he didn't say it.

"Ooooh," rumbled guards and judges alike.

"I'm serious," snapped Boorish mockingly. "Now that you're wearing your *magical* ring, tell us all, what's my father's, mother's, father's, only brother's pony's name?"

"Didn't you mean your father's, father's, mother's, only brother's pony's name?" retorted Dod.

"That's what I just said!" huffed Boorish.

"No, you didn't!" rumbled Ingrid, hobbling from the line-up, six down from Dod. "You said your father's, mother's, father's, only brother's pony's name, not the other way around. Which is it? Do you even know?" Ingrid glared pressingly.

"I most certainly do!" barked Boorish, grabbing anxiously at the sides of his robe, as though pulling a vest tight. "From the start I asked, and I do repeat, what's the name of my mother's, father's, father's, only brother's pony's name?"

"That's not what you said," interrupted Terro, leaving his son's side and moving in to challenge Boorish. "Your questions are too ridiculous. Let Dod propose his terms."

Boorish's face had gone from pale to flush in a matter of moments.

"I second the motion," said the aristocrat with glasses. "Let's vote."

Terro and seven of the eight Head Judiciary Panel members raised their hands.

"Suit yourselves, fools," sputtered Boorish, moving from the center to stand with the guards.

"Now tell us, Dod," began Terro, hiding a gleeful smirk. "How do you propose convincing us that you can see other people's thoughts so clearly.

Dod looked at the floor. He had hoped that Terro would have told everyone how Dod had saved him from Driaxom by knowing that a box would be waiting and that Dungo would be asked to drag it out to the pavilion.

"Maybe I could write something on a paper," offered the aristocrat with glasses. "If you could read my mind, you could tell me what I wrote."

Dod gulped. He had dug himself in too deep.

"I'd be satisfied if he could speak our mother's first names," suggested another member of the panel. "Mine is an ear-turner."

"It's all a trick," grunted Boorish, looking at the wall of windows. "He just wants to convince us, if he can, that they deserve to return to Green." Boorish pointed at the night sky.

"I think I have a way," said Dod, feeling a surge of courage. "I've just thought of a terribly difficult thing to draw from someone's mind. A matter of fact, I would ask for two minds. It would take an unbelievable amount of gleaning to do what I propose. This ring will need to work twice as hard."

The room went silent. Even Herculon's breathing quieted.

Dod stepped closer to Terro. "I sense you have a mechanism whereby you are able to peer deep into space—is this not correct?"

"I do," said Terro, holding out his hands as if Dod had done enough. "You've read my mind."

"Fools," grumbled Boorish.

"And Boorish," called Dod, "Have you not used this machine?"

Boorish turned. "Of course I've used it, I'm an expert! We Salizars have our privileges."

"Perfect," said Dod. "Is it a simple contraption? Can anyone find their way in the night sky? Could Rughead replace you and teach me how to use it?"

"Most certainly not!" insisted Boorish resentfully. "Anyone could touch it, but only a master could find a prize."

"And just so we're clear," added Dod, "as an expert, how different would you say your night sky is from Green's?"

"Apples and horses," responded Boorish. "Do you understand space?"

"Not really," admitted Dod. "It's all a mystery to me. But it's not to you. So I propose my test. I'll take from your mind and Terro's the detailed information necessary to use your special contraption to find Green in the night sky."

Gasps erupted. Whispers followed.

"You can't do it," said Boorish. "It's impossible!"

"Perhaps for Trimash," chuckled Dod, "But not for me. I have this." Dod held up his hand and pointed at the simple ring. "However, once I've passed your test, I fully expect you'll allow me to use this ring to clear my friends for departure, assuming they're innocent."

Some of the panel members looked concerned and Boorish's mouth was beginning to object.

"After that," said Dod, raising his voice, "I shall have Trimash wear the ring to help him further divine my innocence…and I suppose, I could let him borrow it to aid you in your ongoing investigation."

Boorish's mouth went closed. Dod knew what he was thinking. It didn't take any psychic abilities. Assuming the ring worked, Boorish intended on wearing it, and likely for more reasons than clearing suspects. But Boorish would have to fight, because all of the aristocrats, and Terro and his son, seemed to have the same look in their eyes.

"We have a plan," said Terro excitedly.

"I second the motion," rushed the aristocrat with glasses. "Shall we take a vote?"

Nine hands shot up. It was unanimous. If Dod could read their minds and determine how to use the fancy telescope, well enough to find Green in the night sky, he would be given the authority to clear his friends for home.

The plan was set, but would it work?

THE LONELY CELL

"Come," said Dod, waving his arm. "I must read your minds near the portal. The ring has greater powers there."

"The portal?" said Boorish, pausing in his steps.

"Feel free to bring all the guards you want," added Dod, "I have no intention of sneaking away. Besides, you and Terro are the ones who need to stand near the portal for me to do my best work."

Terro began to nod. "As you know, Boorish, my equipment is on the patio beside the Portal Chamber. He'll need to go there, anyway, to prove his point."

"How convenient," said Dod.

When Boorish didn't move, Dod chummed the water with more bait. "You really should order all of these guards to come along. Once I'm done with the ring, it would be wise of you to inspect your guards' deepest thoughts. Even if they didn't participate in the poisoning or swordplay, who's to say their motives are in your favor?" Dod waved his hand in the air, displaying the ring. "You should check their loyalties."

With that thought in mind, the panel members instructed Trimash and Herculon to lead in the front and the soldiers to carry up the rear. In haste, they all made way to the special chamber.

It was the shortest walk Dod had taken in the castle, or so it felt. He was so busy going over his plan in his mind that he scarcely noticed where he was until he was standing before the glowing portal. Eight guards were there, filling in for Trimash, keeping watch and helping approved persons enter. At the moment, they were directing someone to move forward. It was Neadrou.

Dod couldn't believe it. He hadn't seen the man the whole time he'd been at the festival, yet now he remembered having heard from Terro that Neadrou had arrived in Raul the day before Green Hall's entry.

"Neadrou!" yelled Youk, from behind Dod in the crowd.

He spoke too late. Neadrou was gone in a flash. The man's deafness to his niece's husband reminded Dod, all to well, of the time that Neadrou hadn't recognized him at Carsigo.

"I don't recall Neadrou at the banquets," said Dod, turning to Terro.

"He wasn't," responded Terro. "The Lairringtons had him over in Dirsitch for their holiday festivities."

"Oh," said Dod, beginning to feel a sudden wave of anxiety. Boorish was speaking with the portal guards, who tipped their heads and then backed away, leaving Boorish alone, directly in front of the portal.

"I'm ready to have you pick my brain," said Boorish mockingly. "Good luck."

Terro joined Boorish in standing close to the greenish glow.

Dod glanced to the side and watched Trimash climb the stairs to his usual seat. Herculon growled his superiority as he passed the other animals that crouched in their stations. *I was chosen to hunt*, it seemed to say. *Bow to me or die.*

To the side of the portal, set back a fair distance, another portal was visible. Its misty face glowed a light yellow instead of green. "Soosh," whispered Dod to himself. He had been so distressed at the time of his entry to Raul that he hadn't noticed the other portal door. It was set out of the way, as if it weren't used very often.

"Having second thoughts?" ridiculed Boorish. "Even Trimash can't read beneath my skull."

Dod sighed as he glanced at the ten-point star that was positioned in the middle of the doorway's arch. "I just need a paper and something to write with," responded Dod, feeling confident once more. "Let's see...I need an assistant....Sawny, you could be my scribe."

Sawny trembled as she cut through the whispering mob.

"Does anyone have paper?"

The aristocrat with glasses produced a fancy leather notebook and pen.

"All right," said Dod, pushing himself to act official. "Everyone, please step back. I must be able to focus on their thoughts. It's such a pain hearing so many of you at the same time. Stop troubling me with your fears, especially you guards in the back. I'm sure Boorish will understand. He's wise."

Boorish shot a mean glare toward the soldiers.

"What's your plan?" whispered Sawny into Dod's ear, rattling the pen against the paper.

"The Mauj code," responded Dod. "Look up there."

Sawny's eyes went to the ten-point star. Rather than having the symbol for Raul inscribed within it, as the one on Green's side had had, this star displayed a new symbol.

"I don't know Raul's sky," muttered Sawny in horror. "I've never seen that marking before."

"That's okay," said Dod, beginning to feel nauseous. "The code is the same, isn't it?" He held his breath. Everything was riding on her answer.

Sawny looked back at the portal. Slowly, she began to nod. Wheels were clearly turning in her brain. "The numbers and positions appear to be written in the same manner," she said.

"Good," whispered Dod. "Let's put them down on paper. I think the starting point has got to be the Lazy Star, don't you?"

"Starting point for what?" panicked Sawny, suddenly looking nervous again. "Don't you know where *that* constellation is?"

"Constellation?" gasped Dod, glancing back toward the portal.

"If you don't know the constellation," groaned Sawny quietly, "what are we doing?"

Dod saw what she meant. He had forgotten that the symbols for Green and Soosh had contained within them a constellation and key star from which to start. It was the Mauj code which had been etched beside the constellations on Commendus's telescope box that had used the Steady Star as a beginning point. "Can't you find that constellation?" asked Dod.

"Not unless I had instructions," complained Sawny. "You didn't plan on us spending all night randomly searching the sky for that configuration, did you? It wouldn't look good."

Dod bit his lip as Sawny continued.

"Without locating that key star—the one right there, at the top of the constellation, the code we've got in front of us is meaningless. It doesn't matter that I can read it. We can't use it if we don't have a starting point."

Dod took a deep breath. "The box on Terro's patio shows constellations. I think it has codes next to them, too, just like Commendus's. Once we get outside, I'll keep everyone occupied while you find and write the code for that one."

"And you're sure that the base starting point for their sky is the Lazy Star?" asked Sawny.

"It must be," responded Dod. "Boot said it's the only one that doesn't move."

Boorish stomped his foot. "I don't see any writing," he boomed. "You're stuck, aren't you?"

"Hardly," said Dod. "I'm busy mastering the particulars of a subject you've studied all of your life. This should be interesting."

Boorish furrowed his brow, as though stubbornly holding back his knowledge.

"Resistance is futile," said Dod, waving his ringed hand in the air; and then turning to Sawny, he whispered, "Don't worry. If this doesn't work, we can use plan B." He didn't have a plan B, but he felt certain he'd think of one if Sawny couldn't find Green.

"Hasha'am!" blared Trimash from above, and two lions settled their growling.

Sawny began to write. Her face gradually shifted from terrified to intrigued. Each part of the symbol was a puzzle. Dod repeatedly whispered into her ear, as if directing her scribbling, though in truth, the things Dod said had nothing to do with finding a planet in the sky. Instead, he noted the obvious—that Terro's hair looked unusually messy, and that the room smelled like rotten eggs, and that Boorish had stepped in fresh animal poop.

Boorish and Terro keenly watched Dod and Sawny. The more Sawny wrote, the more Dod's two subjects displayed signs of discomfort.

"You're searching for our knowledge of the stars—nothing more, right?" asked Terro.

"Sort of," responded Dod, enjoying their distress.

"You've had enough time!" growled Boorish, moving away from the portal. "Show us Green!"

Dod glanced at Sawny, who nodded cautiously.

"My observation station is just outside," said Terro. "Let's go back the way we came."

Within moments, Dod and Sawny were standing behind the little fence that surrounded the telescope. Terro had just opened its casing, and Boorish had peered into the glass to ensure that the telescope was currently facing nothing in particular. All of the panel members huddled beyond the fence wearing expectant faces.

"Here's a glowing rock to read your notes by," offered the aristocrat with spectacles, reaching over the fence. Dod took the stone and handed it to Sawny, who had already begun searching the telescope's outer case for the critical constellation.

Smelling the night air, Dod casually looked up into the moonless sky. It was perfect for stargazing. With Boot's guidance, Dod had easily found the Lazy Star before, but now it was hidden. Which one was it? Dozens of twinkling dots seemed like perfect candidates. Its apparent disappearance was troubling. Without the star, Dod knew Sawny wouldn't be able to proceed, even if she located the constellation's Mauj code on the box.

"We're all waiting!" said Boorish impatiently. "Get on with your show. It's chilly out."

"Right," said Dod, racking his brain. He knew he needed to stall for Sawny, and he needed to find the Lazy Star. "What you're all about to witness is truly amazing," he said, pulling an uncomfortable grin and still glancing skyward in hopes of discovering the missing star. "I have successfully sucked the information I need, and I am confident that each and every one of you will be more than satisfied that *this ring* is no ordinary ring!" Dod held his hand up for emphasis. "It has the capacity to greatly enhance natural psychic abilities. I'm sure Trimash is eager to put it on." Dod smiled at Trimash, who stood behind the panel members glowering.

"Prove your abilities," said Boorish, leaning on the fence. "We're all watching. Show us Green."

"I'm getting to that," responded Dod. "But let me first establish my case. It's not easy being psychic. There are all sorts of things that can distract the mind. I personally hate knowing so much. And with this ring—well—let's just say it's a little too easy to discover *too much*." Dod forced his eyes upon Boorish, as if he had discerned things which Boorish would want to keep secret.

Boorish took a few steps back.

"Knowledge is good," said the aristocrat with spectacles. "You can never have too much of it."

"I've heard people say that before," sighed Dod, shaking his head. He then proceeded to make up a story about a prince who had sought to know everything and had inadvertently stumbled upon the details of his own death.

"That wouldn't be bad," protested the aristocrat with glasses.

"Actually, it was," responded Dod, tapping at his chin and pacing as he thought of an ending that would fit. "Once the man knew the specifics of his own horrible downfall, it plagued him night and day. Finally, he gave up his kingdom and sailed away to a distant land in hopes of escaping fate. But alas, it didn't work. Instead, he unwittingly led himself right to the very demise he had hoped to avoid. So, in his case, knowing too much was a problem — it's what killed him!"

A few people nodded.

"Fate always wins in the end," said Trimash gravely.

Dod shivered. He could tell some of the spectators were losing interest and becoming annoyed by the cool breeze. Glancing anxiously over his shoulder, Dod saw Sawny scribbling ferociously. It was a good sign.

"He's a fraud," called one of the guards. "It's all a trick. Let's go back to the Great Hall."

Dod focused his attention on him. "If I were purporting to be reading minds concerning the heavens, and I merely taught my assistant a well-known thing — let's say, for example, the location of the Lazy Star — you could all think that I was nothing more than a flimsy conman. Probably half of you know where the Lazy Star is, don't you?" Dod paused and watched. "Well, don't you?"

Multiple men in the group nodded knowingly as Sawny took her place at Dod's side, her face beaming with satisfaction.

"You," said Dod, selecting a sturdy-shouldered panel member who had just nudged his neighbor and pointed. "Would you please show my assistant where the Lazy Star is. She's from Green and hasn't ever seen it."

The man nodded and identified the gleaming spot in the sky, explaining that he had always remembered its location by knowing its position in the Fishhook constellation.

"Thank you," said Dod. "You've proven my first point. I could choose at random and likely find a man with that sort of knowledge. But let me ask you this—" Dod dramatically spun to face the fancy telescope. "How many of you could use this device to locate Green—a planet that is so far from here, it's not visible with the naked eye?"

Terro and Boorish were the only two people who raised their hands.

The crowd seemed pleased. Dod was shocked. He hadn't realized that he had chosen the only two men. He had assumed that multiple nobles would have possessed the knowledge. Terro had been a given, since the telescope was his, but the only reason Dod had chosen Boorish was because of the way Boorish had referred to the heavens.

"As you can see," announced Dod, "I'm about to do the impossible, I'm about to teach my assistant how to find home."

With that explanation, Dod and Sawny stepped up to the telescope. Dod held the light for Sawny and leaned in as she worked the intricate contraption. From time to time, he whispered and moved his hands as if directing her. It was all a show. Once Sawny knew the location of the Lazy Star and had the Mauj code for finding the mysterious constellation, she was off and running, systematically turning knobs.

"There it is," whispered Sawny, pointing at the distant horizon. "Only half of the constellation is visible right now. But we've got our star. It's the one poking out above the mountains, just up from Dirsitch. That's our starting point for finding Green."

"No wonder Boorish said we couldn't find it," grinned Dod. "He assumed that even if I could pull the information from his mind, we wouldn't be able to locate our beginning point this early in the evening."

Dod stood and momentarily spoke to the crowd. "My assistant is learning very quickly. She's remarkable. I'd like to thank Terro and Boorish for being so kind as to provide us with the necessary information to find Green. Isn't this exciting?"

Terro tipped his head, and Boorish frowned.

Dod went back to Sawny's side and returned to his role as mentor.

Finally, after an extensive amount of knob turning, Sawny counted to seven, carefully twisting the last knob on her list. "I think this should do it," she whispered excitedly.

"I'm crossing my fingers," said Dod, putting his eye to the scope.

There was nothing to see.

"I probably need to focus it a little," whispered Sawny, appearing to sense Dod's concern. She put her eye up to the glass and began to adjust the tube near the eyepiece. "We're off somehow."

It wasn't what Dod wanted to hear.

"Have you found it?" asked Boorish smugly, as if he recognized that they were toppling into trouble.

Dod looked at the device. Maybe it was broken.

"Time for plan B," said Sawny nervously. "I failed."

"Let's first recheck your notes," returned Dod. "Maybe we missed something." He put his finger on the page where Sawny had sketched the marking they'd seen in the Portal Chamber. "Are you sure about each of these steps?"

Sawny began at the beginning, muttering, "This has to be the top front knob, sixteen turns, and this one's the third down, four turns, and this one's the back big one, three turns, and this one's the front and center one, six turns, and this one's…you're right!" Sawny looked like she would pucker up and kiss Dod for joy. "It's *seventeen* turns, not seven!" She eagerly reached over and began counting out ten more turns of the last knob.

"Is it better?" she asked. Dod was staring into the glass.

"Much better," he responded gleefully. "You're amazing, Sawny!"

Green was just as visible through the telescope as Raul had been from Commendus's patio. Its stunning image was breathtaking. Much like Earth, it had continents that were various degrees of greens and browns, and it had large oceans and seas that were a spectrum of blues. Cloud cover splotched some areas.

"Let me see," nudged Sawny, excitedly moving in. She peered into the telescope and gasped. "I can't believe how big the Ankle Weed Desert is."

Dod had noticed a sizeable spot on one continent, but hadn't recognized what it was.

"Green is by far the most beautiful planet, isn't it?" sighed Sawny.

It instantly struck Dod that Sawny had never seen her own planet. Aside from maps that displayed landmasses, she had been blind to how it looked from space — no movies, no pictures, not even a single painting. Raul nobles hadn't been open to allowing very many people to peer into space with their telescope, especially visitors from Green.

"Have you found it?" asked Terro, entering the gated area.

CHAPTER TWENTY-SEVEN

"Take a look for yourself," beamed Dod.

"He's done it!" exploded Terro the moment his eye approached the glass.

Boorish and the other Head Judiciary Panel members filed by, one-by-one, to inspect the proof of Dod's abilities. Though when others asked to take a peek, they were denied.

"We must get on with the process," insisted Terro, closing and locking the telescope case. "Portal monitors in Green will be expecting arrivals for only a short while. Hurry back to the chamber. Dod has some mind reading to do."

Conversations erupted throughout the crowd and continued into the Portal Chamber. Everyone seemed astonished. The panel members kept their word and allowed Dod to use his powers to detect guilt, though the group's demeanor had changed completely, as if the prospects of getting to use the ring for other purposes wiped away any need for interrogation of Dod's friends. Even Boorish smiled as he watched Dod clear dozens of people for entry to Green.

The process was easy. Dod requested for people to stand at the portal in pairs, and once he had checked their minds for guilt, he waved them on and they were allowed to march into the greenish haze. Bowlure and Youk went first. Dod specifically put them at the front, for he knew that Bowlure was being judged unfairly because he was a Driadon, and Dod hadn't forgotten that Youk was his personal representative to the council back in Green.

Next, he had Dilly and Sawny depart, then Boot and Buck, and then he let individuals line up of their own accord.

The procedure was simple enough that within a short time, only a handful of people from Green Hall remained. Sensing a few panel members were growing concerned, Dod made his readings more interesting, to give him credibility.

"Next," called Dod, watching Pone and Toos step forward. Pone smiled comfortably, though Toos wore a troubled face. If Dod were going to seek revenge on Toos for the awful things he'd said earlier, now was the perfect time.

"Let's see," said Dod, slowing his speech. "These two are interesting. I'm guessing Trimash would have pulled them out of the lineup for being troubled souls."

"Guards," said Boorish happily. "Take them to the dungeons."

"Wait!" burst Dod. "Like I was saying, I can see how Trimash would sense mischief, but it's not what you think. Neither of them had anything to do with the crimes."

Toos staggered sideways and had to be supported upright by Pone. It appeared he was in the process of fainting.

"That one," said Dod, pointing at Toos, "is keeping a secret that makes him seem guilty. But it's nothing to worry about. He's simply green with jealously. He's jealous of Terro and his mansion, and of Sawb's position as the only son of the Chief Noble Tredder of Raul, and he's even terribly jealous of this whole panel of noble judges. He desperately wishes to be like all of you, but he recognizes he never will. He simply doesn't have the blood."

Terro and his associates nodded, clearly pleased that Toos had been envious of them.

"And that one," said Dod, holding back a chuckle as he pointed at Pone. "He's got a hidden story. Beneath his eyes he's trying to keep quiet about a crime he's committed."

Boorish waited anxiously, his fingers twiddling.

"It's actually funny," said Dod. "Now I see it clearly, this is the person who clogged the upstairs bathroom, third door down. He's horribly ashamed to admit that he used too much paper."

"It happens," mumbled Terro, shaking his head at Pone forgivingly.

Pone broke out in laughter. "I'm sorry," he said loudly. "You caught me. The food was too good. What can I say?"

Bidding farewell, Pone saluted Terro and tipped his head before dragging a weakened Toos into the portal.

As the numbers continued to dwindle, Dod attached specific details to every person—little things that he knew would keep the mood light in the room, despite the glaring fact that he was providing no suspects. If he could think of anything funny, he added it. Juck was teased for his love of superheroes, Toby and Hermit were reminded that dragons weren't real, and Sham was scolded for having only mouthed the words at Terro's morning banquet.

Mentioning the failed presentation turned most of the eyes in the room from Sham to the last remaining person in line: Ingrid. Terro couldn't help chuckling as he pointed at her and whispered to a few of the panel members who hadn't been present for her performance.

Dod strained to think of what to say. He wanted to play off of the truth enough that it would draw the desired look of recognition; and with Ingrid, if he misspoke her thoughts, he knew there was a reasonable likelihood she would feel the need to correct him, which wouldn't help her case or his. Fortunately, Dod had just seen something worth noting. While waiting, toward the back of the lineup, Ingrid had been approached by Trimash, and they had traded sticks. Ingrid had not seemed ready to give up her cane for a fur-covered staff, but looking the man over, she had done it anyway.

"Ingrid, please step forward," called Dod, making a show with his hands.

She hobbled to the portal's edge jabbing and dragging the staff, as if she hadn't mastered how exactly to hold it right. Her approach was humorous.

"I see a lot of things when I look at you," said Dod, waving his hands for emphasis. It was his last reading. He knew it had to be good. "You are deeply conflicted," he said.

"Not as conflicted as you," she snapped, her eyes turning unusually cross. "I don't need a fancy ring to tell everyone a thing or two about *your* history, Dod. I know all about your family, and everything else. In a place like this, it must feel good telling people Pap's your grandfather. Isn't it nice? He was the kind of man that could take a stroll, day or night, and not worry."

Dod knew what she was saying: She was referencing Dod's nighttime gallivanting and Toos's comments that had created such a stir in the Donefur Wing, as though she were ready to drop the bombs if he dared read her mind and reveal anything embarrassing.

"As I was saying," announced Dod, giving Ingrid a friendly eye, "I can see that you feel conflicted inside about your most recent trade. Don't be. A fur stick suits you. It makes you look at least ten years younger."

"Or ten pounds lighter," laughed Sawb.

Dod waved his hand. "You're cleared," he said, feeling bad that her singing and weight had been mocked.

"Thank you for the visit, Terro," she offered, tipping her head cordially at Raul's Chief Noble Tredder before entering the portal.

No sooner had she disappeared into the murky-green mist than a shout rang out. It was someone who had burst from the other portal, dressed in a Raul military uniform. "War has begun in Soosh!" yelled the man. "It's a level ten disaster. Where's Terro?"

"I'm right here," said Terro, stepping from the crowd to greet the man.

"It's a ten, sir," announced the man, standing at attention. "We've arranged ten day intervals on your mark, as of this present time. They will wait to receive your messenger before attempting to send anyone else. If they lag their return at all, they understand you will reseal the portal."

"Thank you," said Terro, heading straight for the portal to Soosh. He pulled an item from his pocket, did something with his fingers, and then put his right hand against the small control box. The yellowish glow dissipated and the archway became empty, revealing the backdrop of the room.

"Barbarians," said Boorish calmly, chatting with the other panel members. "It's good we can shut the door and keep them out. I wonder, some days, why we ever open it up. What's in Soosh, anyway? Sickness, poverty, and trouble!"

Dod felt Trimash's anger.

Herculon began to growl. *Let me eat him, master,* it seemed to say. *The man has made you angry. I'll bring him to you by his throat.*

"Go and report," commanded Terro, nodding to the young soldier who had just come from Soosh.

"Wait!" said Boorish. His eyes were aglow with a plan. "It's time for Dod to allow us to use the ring, so let's keep this man here for inspection."

Dod instantly felt anxious. Now was the real moment to dread. He knew he needed to hand off the ring, but feared its lack of usefulness would complicate his departure. And the crowd was no longer laughing; they were all sobered by the news of war in Soosh.

"It's time, Dod," said Boorish, holding out his hand. "We've been more than generous."

"I agree," admitted Dod, taking the ring off. "Trimash, would you please come and take my place?"

"Stay put for now, Trimash," called Terro quickly. "Boorish is right. We'd like to test this technology out first."

Boorish's brow furrowed when he saw Terro reaching for the ring, too. "I would like to propose that we, the Head Judiciary Panel of Raul, be in charge of the ring for now," said Boorish. "One man alone shouldn't control its powers."

"But Dod's *my* guest," barked Terro. "He's agreed to let *me* borrow it in order to aid us in this investigation."

"You're too close to the crime," scoffed Boorish angrily. "We, the panel, have already determined that much. Besides, as you said, Dod's your guest, and by his devices we've allowed all of our prime suspects to go free. If you were to evaluate Dod, we'd never know the truth. You'd protect him, and send a guilty man home!"

"How absurd!" raged Terro. "I take offense that you would even suggest such a thing! If Dod's guilty, he'd pay with his life just as quickly from my sentencing as he'd pay from yours! He's my guest, nothing more!"

Dod felt like running for the portal. The arguing was making things worse. If it were discovered that the ring was a sham, the consequences would be swift and unfriendly.

"I call for a vote," said Boorish, raising his hand. Seven others shot up.

"Outrageous!" moaned Terro.

Boorish turned his frustrated eyes on Dod. "Give me the ring!"

"Fine," said Dod, slowly moving toward Boorish. "But I really think you should have Trimash wear the ring—or choose one of your other psychics, someone with vast experience in the art."

"I'll decide who will wear it!" snapped Boorish. "It's *my* turn to pick *your* brain!"

"I'm all right with that," said Dod, handing the ring to Boorish. "But just so you know, the ring was made by the Mauj—much like the portals—and was only intended to be worn by people who already possess a great degree of natural ability. When others try it on, there are harsh consequences."

"So you say," grumbled Boorish, gleaming brightly at his prize.

"Some people would even suggest it's cursed," said Dod, "but of course, I'm sure you're not afraid of losing an eye."

Boorish glanced at Trimash, then back to Dod. "What do you mean?"

"Well," said Dod. "To the untrained, that ring may cause physical blindness, or the withering of an arm, or complete insanity. Many psychics try such mechanisms as this before they're ready, hoping to leap forward in their abilities, and sadly discover that they've caused for themselves great suffering. Haven't you noticed the trend? Often people with special gifts look like *him*—" Dod pointed at Trimash. "They're missing something or other."

Terro's peculiar mayler held his peace, quietly watching the struggle from his perch, with his glossy, dead eye seemingly warning casual dabblers in the art of the supernatural that extrasensory enhancers weren't meant to be toyed with.

Terro's face softened toward Dod, then turned on Boorish. "I'm sure you'll be fine, Boorish. Try it on! Dod doesn't have all day. The people in Green are waiting for him. If he's guilty of a crime, we must send word by way of a messenger, and if he's not, let's give him our thanks and allow him to pass."

"Perhaps Trimash should test the ring," offered the aristocrat with glasses, his attention glued to the ring as though he fully expected it to sprout fangs and bite.

"If you're all insisting," rushed Boorish, shrugging his shoulders. "I suppose I could give my consent to allow Trimash the first turn." He held the ring out in his flat palm, nowhere near his fingers, and seemed like he couldn't rid himself of it fast enough. By every indication, he intended on never touching it again.

"Take your spot," said Trimash in a low and ominous voice, sliding the ring onto his pinky finger.

Dod approached the portal.

"Tooka howa'am," thundered Trimash. The beasts in the room began to growl. "Tooka wa, tooka wa, tooka wa," chanted Trimash, raising his hands and wiggling his fingers. Soldiers and nobles alike kept their peace out of respect for the man's powers.

Near the glowing mist, Dod could faintly hear endless whispering voices, as if a multitude of people were just out of view.

Trimash took a deep breath, closed his good eye, and began humming. The sound of his voice matched the growling of his pets. "I see many things," muttered Trimash, "many dark things."

"Well," sputtered Dod, making a last effort to avoid the dungeon. "Don't get caught in a *web* of trivial paths. With that ring on your finger, you're far too powerful to miss the important truths that lay scattered around like *hidden treasures*."

"Tell us the dark things," said Boorish. "Has Dod helped with these crimes? Did he allow the guilty to go free?"

"Many dark things," said Trimash, sounding less forceful than he had the first time. "Death is always near him—but he isn't the one you're seeking. Let him go."

"Just like that?" gagged Boorish. "Perhaps you should look a little deeper. Did you know, he's charged with murder in Green?"

"I have spoken!" thundered Trimash in a forceful voice.

"But Trimash—" began Boorish, when all of the animals started howling and roaring.

"Good luck, Dod," yelled Terro, raising his voice to be heard over the fray. "Tell everyone hello from me, and let Bonboo know my son and his friends will be returning to Twistyard in a week or so."

"Okay," nodded Dod.

"Oh, and tell them that the portal to Soosh is closed until we give further notice," added Terro.

"I will," promised Dod. He turned toward the greenish glow, closed his eyes tightly, and jumped. Just as before, he was enveloped in a blindingly-bright light, heard the roar of a million voices, and felt his medallion burn against his chest. Within seconds, he stumbled out of the portal.

"You made it!" cheered Dilly and Sawny in unison.

Dod blinked until he could see. Boot, Buck, Youk, and Bowlure were also waiting beside the girls.

"That was amazing!" said Youk. "Sawny's been telling us of how you studied up on the stars while in the Donefur Wing, just in case the nobles turned cross. What a brilliant plan! I never would have thought of that. Great job!"

"Anything to help out," stuttered Dod happily, catching Sawny's "*you-owe-me*" look.

"You must have used some of your psychic powers, too," insisted Bowlure. "That trick was unbelievable."

"I had a wonderful assistant," praised Dod. "She did most of the work."

Sawny smiled as she pushed a curl from her face.

Before leaving the Portal House, Dod informed the authorities about Soosh. It sparked a conversation that continued all the way back to Green Hall's camp. Sawny explained that Terro had shut down the portal to Soosh using a Blood Lock. Both sides of each portal had them. They were set up by the Mauj to ensure a respected family in the area would take care of the door. Only that family's blood could activate the portal's controls. In Raul, the doors responded to Chantolli blood, in Green it was Tillius blood, and in Soosh the bloodline had ended, so their door was permanently open on their side.

Boot listened with one arm around Dilly's shoulder and the other around Sawny's. "It just proves what I've said all along," grinned Boot. "You've got good blood, ladies. Even the Mauj trusted your forefathers."

"And Sirlonk's, too," said Buck slyly, carrying Boot's bag for him.

Dilly crinkled her nose at Buck.

The following day, all of Green Hall made a grand exit from Commendus's estate and set their sights on Twistyard at the dropping of the triblot barrier. Their visit to Terro's castle in Raul had left them feeling a greater level of appreciation for Bonboo's hospitality.

Back in Green Hall, Boot took Dod aside and informed him about the tight timeline they would need to keep in order to make it to Fisher before *The Avenger* was scheduled to set sail. Dod just smiled and nodded. Buck and Boot were excited beyond measure about their rare opportunity.

As the evening sky turned dark, Dod lay on his bed thinking. He had had an unusual feeling press upon the back of his mind since the moment he had stepped foot in the castle. For some reason, he felt compelled to visit Twistyard's dungeon and see the cell where he had been detained. It was as if he had left something important down there, perhaps a clue about his father.

Boot called out a reminder of their early morning departure as Dod crossed the bedroom. When Dod didn't respond, Boot caught him in the backside with a rolled-up pair of socks.

"What?" said Dod.

"We're leaving early tomorrow," returned Boot, as if Dod hadn't already heard him say it a million times. "I don't care how tired you are. If Buck and I have to, we'll tie you up and haul you off to Fisher like a bag of gear. Don't stay out too late."

"I won't," assured Dod. "I'll be right back. It's Buck you should be working on. He's not done packing."

Buck shot Dod a jestful glance from the floor before throwing a small ball of twine at him, but this time Dod was ready and caught it in the air.

"Never mess with a Jedi," gloated Dod. Boot and Buck gave him strange looks as he spun and exited the room.

Dod found himself nervously squishing the ball of twine in his hand as he walked the halls. He dreaded seeing the bars that had held him, yet almost instinctively his legs were carrying him there.

As Dod descended the winding staircase to the unfriendliest part of the basement, memories flooded his mind of the horrible experience he had had. It made him shiver. Since that point, everything had improved. Bonboo was fully behind him, Youk was his representative instead of Clair, and Commendus was optimistic that the murder charges would be dropped—he had personally noted to Dod, while bidding him farewell, that Dod's willingness to help Traygof would not go unnoticed by the council assigned to his trial.

As Dod neared the cells, he was surprised to find two soldiers standing watch. It made him wonder who was currently behind bars.

"You're back," said one of the guards. It was Upton, the drat who had persisted that Bonboo wouldn't help Dod.

"Yes—sort of," said Dod awkwardly, shoving the string into his pocket with one hand while fidgeting with the glowing rock around his neck with the other. He had intended on finding the place dark and vacant.

"Well, Dod, you're welcome around us anytime," said Upton cheerfully, tugging at his pointed little beard.

Dod looked the barrel-chested man over curiously.

"You were right," Upton whispered. "I went to Zerny's place and caught him out back training birds. I'm sorry I didn't believe you before. Everyone was saying you'd killed him along with Horsely."

"Rumors rarely tell the truth," responded Dod. He paused, not knowing what to say next.

"Can I help you?" asked Upton.

"Oh, it's kind of a dumb thing—" began Dod. "I just wanted to see the cell I stayed in."

CHAPTER TWENTY-SEVEN

"You can look," said Upton, "but it's not empty. We caught a man who seemed suspicious, and as it turns out, Voracio was able to identify him as a notorious villain. He's the one who stole The Dragons' Egg and destroyed the museum. Soldiers from High Gate will be arriving tomorrow to pick him up."

Dod was intrigued. What did the man look like?

As Dod rounded the corner, his heart sank.

It was Abbot!

CHAPTER TWENTY-EIGHT

TORN APART

In the lonely cell where Dod had sat fearing the worst, Abbot now crouched, facing the back wall, muttering to himself.

"He's got scars all over his legs and back," said Upton to Dod. "The man has spent time in Driaxom, that's for sure. And I suppose that's where he left his mind. Since his arrest last week, I don't think he's said a single thing that has made any sense."

"I've heard Driaxom can do that," muttered Dod, assessing his options, trying to find a way to free Abbot. If Bonboo were around, he'd speak with him, but since he was preoccupied at High Gate, it wasn't an option.

"It's puzzling to think of how this nut ever escaped in the first place," mused Upton, looking at Abbot. "He doesn't seem like much, does he?"

"Nope," said Dod, glancing at a large ring of keys on the far wall, opposite the cells. "He must be full of surprises. Maybe he has magical powers."

"Perhaps," agreed Upton.

A distant bell rang. Dod recognized the sound. It was the signal that the guards were about to change positions.

"We've got to go," said Upton.

"Right, I understand," mumbled Dod. "It's too bad. I was hoping to stay a little longer."

Upton hesitated. His face showed he felt conflicted.

"But rules are rules," said Dod. "You couldn't let me sit here for a while, could you?"

Upton didn't respond.

"Please," said Dod.

"I suppose I could tell the next shift that you're down here," offered Upton.

"Would you?" said Dod.

Upton agreed before sauntering around the corner.

No sooner had the guards left the dungeon than Dod found himself grabbing for the keys. A plan had crossed his mind, though it was risky, especially considering Abbot's fragile condition.

"Quick, Abbot," said Dod, opening the cell door.

The man kept crouching, facing the rear wall.

"Abbot, you've got to come now!" insisted Dod, trembling as he entered the enclosure. When he put his hand on Abbot's shoulder, the man turned.

"Dod?" whispered Abbot. "You're alive." The man's eyes were clear. He was having one of his rare moments.

"Quick," mumbled Dod, grabbing the man by the arm. "You've got to do exactly what I say."

Abbot nodded and let Dod lead him away. Together they rushed through the darkened corridor until they came to a short statue. It wasn't much to hide behind, but it was Abbot's only shot at freedom.

"Stay here until the new guards pass," said Dod. "Be as invisible as you can. Once they've moved on, hurry up to the roof. They'll come looking for you when they find your cell's empty."

The frail man nodded.

"Do you understand?"

"Yes, thank you, sir," whispered Abbot. "But what about you?"

"I think I'll be okay," said Dod with reservation. He carefully knelt down beside the man and looked into his big eyes. "I need you to take care of things while I'm gone. Tomorrow I'll be leaving with Boot and the others for a trip out to sea. Can you keep watch for me from the rooftop? Pay attention to everything. I think Sirlonk is still around."

"Out to sea?" wheezed Abbot.

"Yes, we'll be helping Traygof."

"Out to sea, sea, sea," muttered Abbot. "I didn't do it. I didn't do it. I didn't do it."

"Stay with me," begged Dod. "You need to be silent." He rubbed the man's shoulder. "I'm your friend, Pap's your friend. We're friends. We know you didn't do it."

Abbot stumbled out of his chant. "Don't go, sir," he whispered. "The Carsalean Sea is dangerous now. She would be big—too big."

"Who?" pressed Dod.

"Tooshi-wanna, Tooshi-wanna," mumbled Abbot, bending his fingers into claws.

"Who's Tooshi-wanna?" asked Dod, feeling frantic. He could hear the fresh guards coming down the stairs.

"Tooshi-wanna," mumbled Abbot.

"Shhhh!" ordered Dod, tapping on the man's shoulder. "I'm your friend, Pap's your friend."

The man quieted. "Don't go to sea, sir."

"I'll be careful," said Dod. "Now be silent—and run like a shadow once they've passed. Do you understand?"

Abbot nodded as he slunk into an odd position near the small statue, hiding his frail frame better than Dod had hoped.

With his heart pounding, Dod dashed back to the dungeon, carefully hung the large ring of keys back on the wall, hurried into the cell, and pulled the door shut.

"No!" groaned Dod. The door of bars was ancient and needed the key for it to lock. Without the key, the door wouldn't even close all the way.

Frantically, Dod left the cell and fetched the keys. He was about to lock himself inside when a better idea crossed his mind. He took the ball of twine from his pocket, looped part of it around the hook on the wall, and pulled a double line forty feet over to the jail cell. Once he'd locked himself in, he attached one end of the twine to the large key ring with a weak knot and began pulling the other end of the line. The keys rattled as they slid across the stone floor and up the wall to the hook.

"That was something, wasn't it?" came a muffled voice from around the corner. The guards were arriving.

Taking a deep breath, Dod gently tugged at the line. The large metal ring flopped over and was instantly snagged by the hook, leaving the keys dangling as they had been before.

Next, Dod pulled the line tight until the knot slipped off.

"I never would have guessed that," laughed one guard.

Dod quickly retrieved the string and stuffed it into his pocket.

"Help!" yelled Dod, rattling the bars. "You've got to help me, please!"

"What's wrong?" grumbled one man as two drat soldiers rounded the corner. The first was tall and round with mean, beady eyes, and the other was short and skinny.

"He's done it!" ranted Dod, shaking the door. "One moment I was out there, and now, look at this: I'm locked in here, and he's gone! It's as if he's a ghost or a demon!"

"Dod?" said the skinny soldier, his face lighting up with recognition. "What happened? Where's the crazy man?"

"He's gone," stammered Dod, as though winded from a struggle. "He could be anywhere. Didn't you pass him in the hall?"

Both men shook their heads.

"There's only one way out of the dungeon," said Dod. "You must have seen him! How could you let him escape?"

The two guards blinked with apparent shock.

"Quick, get me out!" ordered Dod. "I don't like being locked in a ghost's cell. There's dark magic at work."

"Magic?" mumbled the skinny soldier, reaching for the keys. "Upton informed us that you were down here....But—what happened to our prisoner?"

"He's escaping!" burst Dod. "That's what I'm trying to tell you! The last time I saw him, he was heading up the hall you just came down. How could you have let him get away?"

"We didn't!" grumbled the heavy soldier. "*I* certainly would have noticed if he were in the hall. He's got to be down here, hiding in the dungeon somewhere. Your trick won't work, boy. We'll catch him, and both of you can do some explaining."

"Huh?" choked Dod.

"You let him out and got in yourself, but we'll find him. He's still down here. I'm certain of that." The heavy drat pulled a handkerchief from his pocket and wiped his mouth. "Had we seen him passing us, we would have stopped him."

"No! He's not down here!" insisted Dod, shaking the door. "He's running free. You've got to race after him. He's getting away! Who knows what harm he'll cause?"

"We'll see about that," grumbled the portly soldier. From his jacket pocket he drew a buster candle and struck it against the wall, doubling the light in the room. "I'll find him," he said, turning to his smaller companion, "and you—keep an eye on the boy." The large drat soldier huffed as he ventured deeper into the empty dungeon in search of Abbot. A few minutes later, he returned, scratching his head. "All of the cells are empty," he muttered. "Where'd he go?"

"You let him get away!" scolded Dod. "Why didn't you listen to me? I told you he was escaping up the hall."

"But that's impossible," said the heavy soldier.

"Not if he had *powers*," offered the smaller guard cautiously.

"Of course!" blurted Dod. "How else do you think I got trapped? We've all been beat."

The two drat soldiers looked at each other, then at Dod.

"I think we should let Dod go," said the smaller man. "I heard at dinner he's scheduled to sail with Traygof."

"Well," grumbled the larger man, wiping his brow nervously, "only if he promises to stop saying *we* allowed the prisoner to escape. This could look really bad for us."

"I won't say a word," offered Dod. "The two of you can figure out what happened. My lips are sealed."

"Remember, complete silence," muttered the heavy soldier, unlocking the door.

Dod raced back to Green Hall without slowing down. His feet felt as light as air. Abbot was free.

In the morning, just as promised, Boot roused Dod and Buck before the sun had begun to rise. And upon leaving the bedroom, Dod discovered that Boot wasn't alone in his enthusiasm. Dilly and Sawny were dressed for the day in matching outfits.

"Are you ready?" asked Dilly excitedly.

"I guess," said Dod. His sleep had been poor. After Abbot's mention of the dangers at sea, all Dod could think about was the dragon that had plagued his dreams.

"I'm feelin' like feastin' on the briny breeze," rumbled Boot, stomping gleefully like a captain. Sneaker was perched on his shoulder. "Pull the anchor! Post our sails! Bring me that horizon!"

"Hoi, sir! I'm on it!" snapped Buck, pretending to pull a rope.

Sawny broke in. "Quick question," she said. "Is the map safe?"

Boot stopped his play and lowered his voice. "I've stashed it along with the *ooblies*."

Dilly giggled. She and Sawny had found Boot's telling of Ingrid's performance a bit humorous, especially Ingrid's creation of the word 'ooblies.'

"We'll eventually give them to my great-grandfather, right?" pressed Dilly.

"Obviously," said Boot. "Along with the Tillius sword and Miz's mayler belt."

Dilly had a guilty look. She clearly enjoyed having those two items safely stowed in Boot's hidden compartment in the floor of the big closet.

CHAPTER TWENTY-EIGHT

Before leaving Green Hall, Boot woke The Triplets and had them help carry luggage to the carriage that was parked in front of the castle. On the way down, Boot informed Pone, Voo, and Sham of their roles as the head Coosings in charge while he was away. Voo and Sham nodded in agreement while Pone kept breaking in, trying to convince Boot that he needed to come along.

Dod felt bad for Pone, but he knew Boot was wise to have him oversee Green Hall in Boot's absence. With Bonboo away from Twistyard and Sirlonk on the loose, a seasoned Coosing at the helm was necessary to ensure the safety of the other Coosings and Greenlings.

The ride to Fisher took all day, winding up through Janice Pass and down to the south-eastern shore of the Gulf of Blue. Dod felt uneasy in the wagon. It was Bonboo's plush twelve-seater, the one that had nearly gone over the edge of Drop's Cliff near Twistyard. And to make matters worse, Jibb was driving, per Voracio's orders. However, Upton and a battalion of sixty drat soldiers rode alongside the wagon, which made Dod feel safer. They were headed to Fisher to rotate drat guards with a number of new recruits who were supposed to be arriving.

By the time that the wagon rolled into Fisher, the sun had set and stars were twinkling. Fog shrouded the boats in the bay, though the groaning sounds of the docked ships revealed they were close.

Driving the wagon, Jibb followed the soldiers into a small military base that was located in the center of town, just a short distance from the harbor, and informed his passengers that they could stay the night in tents.

"Aren't we going to join Traygof?" asked Ingrid in a weary voice, staggering from the carriage.

"Not until tomorrow," responded Dilly, stretching her neck. The fourteen-hour ride had been taxing on everyone.

Dod smelled the air. He was instantly reminded of the crazy night he'd spent running around Fort Castle with Dilly. "Are there any gizzlers around here?" he asked.

"Could be," said Boot cautiously, "but not nearly as many as they have up north."

Dilly glanced uncomfortably at the Redy-Alert-Band on her wrist. It was presently a brownish-yellow. "No snakes," she sighed with relief.

The next day, after eating piles of greasy hash browns and eggs, Dod and his friends boarded an open-back wagon and rode the short distance to the wharf. Three of Traygof's men were standing beside a small boat that was tethered to the dock. A half-mile from shore, *The Avenger* sat calmly awaiting the tide.

"You've come to join us!" said one man, picking something out of his thick beard. "I kinda thought you'd yellow-belly outta the job." He eyed Dod up and down.

"Then you don't know Dod, do you?" responded Boot eagerly, nearly skipping for joy. "He doesn't back down from a challenge."

"Are you Traygof?" asked Ingrid, thumping along with a new cane. She'd given up on her fur-covered staff while still at High Gate.

All three bearded men broke out in laughter.

"No," said one man, missing half his front teeth. "He's not so handsome as me. Were you hopin' to catch a glimpse whilst you're saying goodbye to your son?"

"I don't have kids!" grunted Ingrid. "I'm coming along. Be useful and fetch my bags from the wagon! Those four big ones are mine."

The three sailors all winced. "Says who?"

"Traygof invited me," responded Ingrid, tapping at her cheap necklace as if it were a string of rare diamonds.

"He told us to bring them," said Boot, pointing at Juny and Ingrid.

"They'll be staying in the queen's suite with us," added Dilly.

"Four at once," sighed one man, scratching at his graying beard. "Traygof's lost his freshy mind. There's no telling who we might face. The seas are dangerous—trust me, girls!"

"Good!" nodded Dilly, showing herself to the small boat beside them.

Ingrid looked out at the water and held back.

Within minutes, everyone but Ingrid was loaded. The ship was pushing its limits. Boot forced his row in the boat to squeeze together, barely creating enough room for one more person.

"I'll wait here for your return," said Ingrid, stepping back to a nearby bench. "Tell Traygof I haven't forgotten. I'm honored he's invited me. The water doesn't look scary at all."

"Come on," called Boot. One seaman was in the process of untying the line.

"No. I'll catch the next one," insisted Ingrid timidly. Her eyes were glued to the water.

"Hurry!" ordered Boot.

Ingrid stubbornly turned her head.

"She doesn't care for the water," whispered Juny. "It might take her a few minutes to adjust her mind. The last time she sailed was a bad experience. Someone had her seated alone on the outer deck with the wind raging, and she almost fell overboard."

"Oh—that's right!" said Dod, remembering how much Ingrid had complained at Fort Castle. "She lost her papers, too, didn't she?"

Juny nodded. "She needs to collect her courage."

"Fine by me," grumbled the sailor with the graying beard, using his oar to shove off the dock. "She can collect her courage while she waits for the next transport."

The boat rocked sluggishly as it rose and fell with the small waves. Dod felt like he had eaten a swarm of butterflies for breakfast. What mission lay ahead of them and why had Traygof wanted him? As the seamen rowed heartily, Dod searched his brain, but nothing came.

Once the little boat was beside *The Avenger*, Dod realized that Traygof's ship was monstrous. From the waterline, the bulwarks and rail were at least three to four stories up; and from stem to stern, the ship was longer than two football fields. It looked like a giant Spanish galleon, with a foremast and mainmast and two other smaller masts. A crow's nest sat atop the mainmast.

"Down lines hoi!" yelled someone from above. Two cables descended from derricks that had just swung out over the water.

"Where's the ladder?" asked Buck.

"Stay put," ordered the sailor with the graying beard. He dug into the front of the small boat and drew out four ropes that connected to the hull in various spots. The ropes were about ten feet long and joined together into one thick cord. A metal loop was secured to the end of the cord. Near the rear of the boat, a sailor dug around and drew out a similar set of ropes. The metal loops were then attached to the cables that had been lowered down.

"Up lines hoi, hoi!" called the sailor beside Buck.

Instantly, the cables pulled tight and began to lift the small boat from the water. Once the boat had risen just above the bulwarks and rail, a second set of pulleys drew the cables in along the derricks, landing the boat into a fitted framework.

"Welcome aboard," said Acor, standing on the deck in front of a bustling multitude of sailors. He wore a three-piece suit, complete with a fancy vest, and a white hat that resembled Youk's. His bushy beard was gone. Smiling, Acor reached into the front of his vest and drew out his special gadget. It looked like a pocket watch. "Two hours and counting," he said, tucking it away carefully. "Please, come and stow your things. I'll have Skip and Par accompany you."

Dod stared in disbelief. The ride off the water had been unexpected, and the number of crewmen was shocking. Hundreds of tredders were going about their tasks: mopping decks, recoiling ropes, opening and closing hatches, mending sails, and sharpening swords. Though many of the sailors looked like pirates with full beards and tattoos, many others could have been taken from the best of Pious's forces. All of them appeared to be strong soldiers.

"Wow!" exclaimed Dilly.

"*The Avenger*," muttered Boot happily.

Two crewmen approached and stood on either side of a little stairway that made disembarking to the deck simple.

"I'm Skip," said the man to the left, running his hand across his bushy beard while nodding his bald head. His broad chest pulled the buttons tight on his white-and-red striped shirt. "I'll lead the way to the queen's suite. It's second to the top level of the sterncastle. Ladies, come this way."

Dilly, Sawny, and Juny rose and followed after the man, and trailing them, five younger sailors carried their bags.

Once the women were gone, Par announced himself less enthusiastically and pointed toward the front of the ship. "Your quarters are in the forecastle, sirs, just below the top deck." The man's thin, tall body and tanned face reminded Dod of a younger Tridacello.

"Yes!" exploded Boot, patting Sneaker on the head. "We'll have the best views of the horizon!"

Dod took his bag and brought up the rear. The whole situation was beyond belief. With so many able-bodied men on board, it didn't make sense why Traygof would care whether Dod joined them or not.

The bunking accommodations were nicer than Dod had imagined. He and the Dolsur brothers had been given a spacious room with large circular windows, vaulted ceilings, oak furniture, elegant hanging stacks, and a private bathroom. A sizable round table with tall legs sat beneath the front windows, and beside it, dozens of rolled maps and charts were neatly stowed in fancy brass urns.

"This is the life," sighed Boot, sprawling out on one of the beds. "When we're sailing, we'll be able to see our destination before everyone else."

"I'm surprised they let us stay in here," added Buck, tugging at the handle of a locked closet door. "This place seems like the captain's suite."

"Maybe it is," said Dod.

"Who cares," chuckled Boot, "just so long as he doesn't have any dead bodies in here."

Buck raised his eyebrows.

CHAPTER TWENTY-EIGHT

"We're talking about Traygof," defended Boot. "I'm sure his sword has ended plenty of foes."

"But he wouldn't keep them in his closets," said Buck.

"Unless he's feeding a swarm of venooses," chirped Dod, giving Boot a knowing glance.

Boot shivered and rubbed his arms. "Thinking about it gives me the creeps. It must have been Sirlonk's private death chamber."

Two knocks hit the door. "You have visitors, sirs," said Par.

All three boys hurried to let their guests in.

"You've got see our room!" exploded Dilly. "It's amazing!"

"Ours isn't bad, either," smiled Buck, stepping back to allow Dilly and Sawny a better view.

"Wow!" said Sawny. "The captain's quarters!" Her eyes quickly settled on the maps. The next two hours were spent examining the world of Green on paper. Sawny's knowledge made the drawings and charts come to life. Every ocean, sea, and landmass had a story to tell, and Dod loved hearing them from her.

At length, a loud bell rang.

"He's arrived!" called Par from just outside the door.

Exiting the room, Dod quickly saw what the commotion was about. Traygof circled the ship three times on the back of a flutter and then directed the beast to land.

"Flutters, too," sighed Boot, as if he'd just awakened and found he was in heaven.

Descending the stairs to the main deck, Dod watched Acor pull his gadget from his vest pocket and tap on it in front of Traygof.

"Then raise the anchor!" yelled Traygof. "Up with the sails! Catch the wind, men! Let us be off!" Traygof slung a bag over his shoulder and handed the reigns of the flutter to a large sailor who led the beast down a ramp into the ship's belly.

Hundreds of men began pulling ropes while chanting. It was a magical moment. The sun's noon rays caught the white sails and made them sparkle like pearls.

"Am I just dreaming?" muttered Dilly.

Across the way, Juny was a small dot, standing on the balcony just outside of the queen's suite. Ingrid wasn't beside her.

"Do you think Ingrid arrived?" asked Dod.

"I'd imagine," said Dilly. "We have three of her bags."

"Your friend chose not to join us," interrupted Skip, tipping his head down respectfully like a butler. "I hope that's all right."

Boot began to chuckle. "Juny's torn from her constant companion. I wonder how freedom feels for her?"

"Probably pretty good," grinned Buck, smelling the light breeze. "After the past few months of Ingrid's garlic stews, that poor woman deserves a breath of fresh air!"

CHAPTER TWENTY-NINE

THE SHRINE

Once all of the sails were flying, *The Avenger* cut across the Gulf of Blue with great speed, as if it weren't touching the water.

Dod and his friends followed Skip and Par around the ship. To their surprise, they bumped into someone they hadn't expected to see. It was Con, dressed in military attire and sporting a clever grin. He had arrived three days before and had claimed to be Dod's dearest friend and private security guard. Accordingly, Con had been accommodated below deck somewhere near the kitchen and had been introduced to many of the crewmembers. Con's face beamed with enjoyment.

Dod greeted him cordially and held his breath as he watched Boot and Con tip heads. Clearly, neither of them had forgotten about the recent Bollirse game at Champion Stadium, but both of them seemed to recognize that fighting aboard Traygof's ship was not advisable.

Dod grinned inside as he walked away from Con. When Commendus had suggested that Dod's help with Traygof wouldn't go unnoticed, he had also clearly meant that he appreciated his son being able to sail with Dod aboard *The Avenger*. Perhaps the murder charges would be dropped. Regardless, Dod was just grateful that Con hadn't been asked to share a bedroom with Boot.

After being shown around, Dod and his friends were summoned to Traygof's quarters for a meeting. The commander's room was up above the queen's suite.

"I'm glad you came," said Traygof, addressing Dod specifically. His eyes only briefly acknowledged that Dod wasn't alone.

Dod took a deep breath and tried to act calm.

"Commendus has asked that I retrieve a special item for him," said Traygof, drawing a rolled scroll from his jacket. "Of course he's sent men out looking for it before, but they've all come back empty....It's hidden."

"What is it?" asked Boot.

Traygof glanced his way, then back to Dod. "We must find an ancient scepter which was originally held by the chiefest nobles in Raul."

"Raul's Code of the Kings scepter," blurted Sawny.

"Precisely," said Traygof. "It may not sound very important, but Commendus intends on doing more than honor the Code of the Kings Monument as a memory of things past...he intends on reestablishing its order. Rising tensions between Green and Raul have begun to jeopardize the democracy we love so much. And now, well, with war breaking out in Soosh, the reinstatement of that brotherhood could be an invaluable tool in aiding our diplomats. We all want peace and democracy to prevail. This scepter could be the very key to our maintaining it."

"Why *that* scepter?" asked Sawny, watching intently as Traygof began to unroll the scroll on a table.

"Two reasons," said Traygof. "The first is simple. Green's original scepter is safely kept at High Gate under great security, and Soosh's is protected by their ruling authorities as well. Raul's, on the other hand, was stolen by billies hundreds of years ago, here in Green and, therefore, is not held by its rightful owners."

"Okay," nodded Sawny.

"The second reason is more complex," continued Traygof. "The staff was used by early nobles in Raul as a key of sorts, so without the exact original, some treasures have been kept hidden in their historic Dome of Surprises Building....The very whereabouts of the correct vaults to break open in search of the governmental stashes is long since lost, leaving the vast wealth inaccessible—concealed from their view within Raul's largest bank."

Buck yawned.

"That building has rooms that could hold this ship!" blared Traygof, slamming his fist on the table. "It's five times as large as any bank in Green! Can you imagine them trying to find the government's coffers that are sprinkled amidst the wealthy nobles' vaults? Which is which? They can't tell. It's driven them mad for centuries. Yet, by simply inserting the staff into each room's master keyhole, the various vaults would be opened and the wealth would be usable....Think of how much more your friends from Raul would like you then—with all that money to help them maintain peace."

"I see," said Boot. "If Commendus proposes the creation of the panel without the scepter, Raul's officials would snobbishly turn up their noses at it; but with the scepter, they'd be so grateful for the return of their wealth that they'd happily comply."

"Exactly," said Traygof. "Now you can see why Commendus wants the scepter."

"So, why do you need Dod?" asked Sawny, moving closer to the table. Her eyes were already examining the map that Traygof had unrolled.

"Well, quite frankly young lady, because Humberrone is otherwise preoccupied right now."

"Don't you mean dead?" said Buck.

"No," insisted Traygof, scratching at his beard. "He's quite alive. Who told you he was dead?"

"Everyone," stuttered Buck.

"Well, they're all wrong," muttered Traygof, turning to zero in on Dod. "That's why I'm glad you've come aboard my ship." Traygof patted Dod on the shoulder. "I've heard plenty about your *special* abilities. Perhaps you'll be able to sense where the billies hid the scepter. Take a good look at the map. Reportedly, this very parchment was used by the men who carried away the king's staff. They had thought to take a ransom, but died before such means could be obtained." Traygof pointed. "Look, they made special notes next to these seven islands. I suspect we should start with them."

"Great," said Boot. "A treasure hunt."

Sawny turned the map toward her and bent over it. "Wait," she said gleefully. "Don't waste your time. I know where they've hidden the scepter."

"What do you mean?" choked Traygof.

"It's not on any of *those* islands," confirmed Sawny, sliding her finger across the patch that Traygof had just identified. "It's closer to home—perhaps two days out to sea, or maybe one day aboard your ship. The notes they've made are clues. See, look at this." Sawny pointed at the first island. "Why would they mention bundles of gloriantha flowers? And then here, next to this one, they've written *blocks of salt*, as if penning a shopping list. We've got fruit here, oysters here, tuna here, an alligator here, and a horse over here. It's common knowledge that the islands haven't had many horses. I doubt they were trying to purchase these items."

"Oh!" groaned Traygof. "You've got to be kidding me!" His eyes indicated that he was following Sawny's logic. Everyone else waited for her to explain.

"These clues point to one location," smiled Sawny. "The Shrine of Boodwana."

"What?" asked Dilly.

"But it can't be," mumbled Traygof.

"According to billie legend," said Sawny, "young Boodwana sought to become the greatest mayler of all time, so he started with a ceremonial cleansing. He rubbed salt all over his body, washed in pure water, and anointed himself with a crown of gloriantha flowers. Next, he spent two months eating nothing but fresh fruit, fish, and oysters, to purge his inner system. Finally, he tamed the only horse he'd ever seen and rode it to the top of the highest peak of his island, only to be thrown off when a strange alligator emerged from the rocks and spooked his horse."

"You're brilliant!" praised Dod. "It all fits!"

"But it can't be hidden on *that* island," said Traygof. "I have acquaintances there. They told me they knew nothing of the scepter. They wouldn't lie to me."

"Maybe they feared you would take what's been given to the shrine," responded Sawny. "Once they've offered a gift into the pit, billies don't plan on *anyone* retrieving it."

"You're talking about Tripeak Island," said Boot, "the one where billies give presents to Kray and Yark."

"The Shrine of Boodwana," repeated Sawny. "After the alligator fled from Boodwana's sword, the young man knelt down and bowed his head—"

"And that's when Kray and Yark flew to meet him," rushed Boot. "I love this story. As children, Buck and I heard it dozens of times."

"Dad never mentioned Bood-whatever—" said Buck.

"Boodwana," chirped Sawny. "He was the mayler."

"*The* mayler?" asked Buck.

"Yes," smiled Sawny. "Once Boodwana gained power over the dragons, he stopped the beasts from assaulting the billies' islands and turned their rage on the billies' worst foes."

"Our forefathers," mumbled Dilly, "or, at least, hypothetically speaking. But it's all mythical. I don't think there is any real proof of the billies ever uniting as a people, much less under the leadership of a dragon-taming mayler."

"Every land has its strange myths," sighed Traygof, staring intently at the map. "And myths do have a tendency of creating unusual practices....I suppose we're off to check the Shrine of Boodwana for our scepter. It may have been offered as a gift to the fabled dragons."

The next morning, Boot woke Dod and Buck in a hurry. "We're heading into battle!" he said, shaking their beds. "Quick! Get up!"

"Stop!" whined Buck. "A few more hours."

"No! I'm serious," insisted Boot. "Look who's coming our way. It's not Pious. I've seen drawings of this ship. We need to get ready. Things are about to turn intense."

Dod and Buck both humored Boot by staggering to the round windows.

"Oh no!" groaned Dod. In the distance, a large ship was surrounded by six to ten other smaller vessels. They were heading straight for *The Avenger*. And worst of all, Dod knew he had seen the biggest one before. It was Dreaderious's *Magellan*. Memories of Dod's awful entry into Green flooded his mind.

"See! I told you!" said Boot, rummaging through his things.

"It's the *Magellan*," groaned Dod. "We'll soon be facing Dreaderious's fleet."

Out on the upper deck, Dod, Boot, and Buck were greeted by Traygof who was standing near the stem, gazing at the approaching ships. He had given orders to keep pressing full speed ahead. Beside him, a hulking brute held two rags—one white and one blue—which he used to communicate Traygof's orders to Acor, who stood at the helm atop the sterncastle.

The lower deck was bustling. In the dim morning light, hundreds of sailors worked the sails and prepared weaponry.

"We've got a bit of unfriendly company approaching," remarked Traygof. "You may want to stay indoors for a while."

"Give us swords and we'll fight beside you," offered Boot boldly. "We're not afraid of Dreaderious."

Buck and Dod wore less than convincing faces.

Traygof smiled and tapped his sword. "I have a little surprise that goes beyond steel. Shall we give them a show?"

"Yes sir!" responded Boot.

Traygof stepped from the stem and moved across the upper bow. "Do we have pressure?" he shouted to his men below.

"Fair, sir!" announced Par, who seemed to be overseeing the efforts of sixty men. Three large I-shaped contraptions were being handled. Like a teeter-totter, they each had a fulcrum in the center. Ten men would press down on one side, lifting the other, and then men on the opposite end would press down. Metal poles plunged into the deck and rose out as the men worked. It was as if they were pumping water.

"On my mark," called Traygof. "We'll keep it short—let's say, to the count of twenty. Are you ready?"

"Hoi!" shouted Par excitedly, signaling for his men to stop pumping. "Stations—Are we ready?"

Someone from out of sight called "Loaded, sir!"

Par nodded at Traygof.

"Move to the front, men," said Traygof, displaying a boyish glint in his eyes. He pointed for Dod to approach the foremost rail at the stem. "This is why I don't think you'll need your swords today."

Dod looked out across the dark water. The ships were still a few miles away, keeping a straight course toward *The Avenger*.

"FIRE!" yelled Traygof.

Instantly, flames shot hundreds of feet from both sides of the bow in tight streams. Within seconds, the sea raged with flames to the right and left of the stem of the ship. *The Avenger* cut up the center, leaving two trails of burning water in its wake.

"*The Avenger*'s ballast is mostly tarjuice," chuckled Traygof. "When you add a little pressure, it's quite impressive, isn't it?"

Boot, Buck, and Dod all stared at the flaming water with awestruck faces.

In the distance, the *Magellan* and its little fleet slowly changed directions and began heading due north instead of east.

"Acor wants to know your plans," said the sailor with the rags. "Shall we stay our course for Tripeak Island or pursue Dreaderious?"

"We have our orders from Commendus," responded Traygof. "Our time is short. He's counting on us. We must continue on. Perhaps another day we'll join with Pious and give him chase."

"Wow," muttered Boot under his breath, nudging Dod in the side. "Did you see that?"

"It keeps burning on top of the water," stuttered Buck.

"Oil docs that," said Dod.

Boot and Buck gave him strange looks.

Traygof scratched at his bushy beard. "I'll have my men bring you breakfast in your quarters," he remarked, sniffing the morning air as if nothing had happened. "Rest up. By evening we'll earn our keep. Checking the shrine won't be easy. Tripeak Island is crawling with billies. The mission will require a certain amount of stealth on our part."

"Yes sir!" said Boot. "You can count on us."

"I know," smiled Traygof, strolling to the stairs. He tipped his hat and descended into the scurrying mob of sailors.

All day long, Boot, Buck, and Dod took turns recounting the morning's show. Dilly was green with jealousy. She couldn't believe that she had slept through the whole encounter. And Sawny was disappointed that she hadn't witnessed the *Magellan*, since she had read two books about the boat's remarkable capabilities.

Dod wondered what Dreaderious was up to. Usually he stayed far from the mainland, avoiding any contact with Pious's troops. Was he working with Sirlonk? Perhaps Dungo had joined them. Glimpsing the *Magellan* had caused a whole gamut of worries to cross Dod's mind, despite the fact that the ship had quickly retreated from Traygof's display of power. Was Pious all right? In the barn at Twistyard, Sirlonk had claimed Pious was in trouble. Perhaps the ninety-plus dashers of billies hadn't been found by Pious, or they had joined Dreaderious, or Sirlonk had stolen more jewels to pay them with and was currently getting the hundred thousand billie warriors ready to attack High Gate.

Such thoughts plagued Dod's otherwise relaxing day. The weather and sea couldn't have been nicer, and Con kept his distance from Boot, spending most of his time beside Acor at the helm. *The Avenger* moved so quickly through the water that by mid-afternoon, the sailor on watch in the crow's nest called land in view, and by evening, Tripeak Island was plain to see, directly in front of the setting sun. It was covered in lush greenery. A light line of smoke emerged from the highest point of the landmass, an old volcano.

"It should be called Onepeak Island," joked Boot, sitting on the deck between Dod and Sawny. "Where are the other two?"

"In the sea," responded Sawny matter-of-factly, sipping the last of her lemonade.

"Yikes," said Buck. "Volcanoes make me nervous."

"She's gonna blow!" teased Dilly, coming up from behind. "Watch out for flying lava!"

"It's not *that* kind of volcano," said Sawny. "At its worst, the core opened up and swallowed two of the three peaks, but nothing shot out. Now there's a giant cauldron in the center of the island."

"Cool," said Dod, pretending he was fine. His insides were screaming. It was as if he were sitting on the deck of a ship that was circling one of the islands in *Jurassic Park*, and everyone around him was merrily commenting on its beauty and tranquility.

"Check out Juny," whispered Dilly, bending closer to the conversation. "I think Traygof's putting the moves on her. Ingrid's gonna lose her man."

"And Sirlonk's gonna lose his woman," said Boot smugly.

"It'll probably end in a swordfight," said Dod, looking over his shoulder at the twosome. "Traygof's the only man who dares flirt with her."

"I would if I were interested," challenged Boot.

"She's married!" scoffed Dilly, shoving Boot out of his chair. "Besides, she's as old as your mother!"

"But not as wrinkly," said Boot with a clever eye. "Time's been kind to her. If we didn't know her son, we'd think she was a lot younger. She and Sirlonk have fared well."

"What are you trying to say?" pressed Dilly pointedly.

Boot immediately changed gears. "Nothing, really. All of that doesn't matter. She could be as young as us and it wouldn't turn my head—not with *you* around."

Dilly smiled and stole Boot's seat. "Good answer," she said. "Can you fetch me a drink?"

Boot stood to comply but was stopped in his tracks by Par. "We're about as close to the island as we dare go with *The Avenger*. Any closer and we'll attract too much attention. Traygof has asked that I help you find small swords for the journey. He's ready to leave when you are."

Dilly popped to her feet. "Hoi, hoi," she said, nudging Sawny to rise.

Sawny slunk down deeper into her chair. "I think I'll stay with the ship," she responded. "The shrine's halfway up the hillside, and the sun's setting fast. It'll be dark before you hit the beach."

Par wiped sweat from his suntanned brow. "Traygof wants all of you to go along," he said. "The billies won't be as concerned if they see your young faces. Skip and I will keep the boat safe while you accompany Traygof to the shrine for a peek."

"You've only seen it in books," added Dilly. "Aren't you curious?"

Sawny squirmed. "I've got a bad feeling," she confessed. "Billies don't usually let tredders go near the shrine. What will they think of us sneaking up there at night?"

"We're going with *Traygof*," said Boot excitedly. "Come on. It'll be fun. What could go wrong?"

Dod felt nervous too, but he kept quiet.

All the way to the island, Par and Skip reminisced about past mishaps that had ended poorly. Some friends had tripped overboard during storms and been lost at sea. Others had fallen prey to a wandering derrick or coil of rope. One story was particularly tragic—six of their shipmates had been accidentally fed to a pit of alligators by billies who had mistaken them for thieves.

In the distance, *The Avenger* sailed away. It was scheduled to come back after dark with its lights hidden, but watching it leave created a sense of panic and abandonment that Dod hadn't expected. It was a strange, foreboding feeling.

Once the little boat rolled into the shallows, Dod followed everyone out before the waves tipped it upside down. Par and Skip pulled the small craft onto the empty beach and situated it just above the tide line. The sun had set and the sky was turning dark.

Traygof drew glowing-stone necklaces from his pack and passed them out. "Watch the tree line," he cautioned Par and Skip. "I doubt we've landed unnoticed."

Leaving his men behind, Traygof led Boot, Buck, Dod, Dilly, and Sawny up the beach in search of the trailhead to the shrine. Earlier they'd seen it clearly through noculars from the deck of *The Avenger*, but now it had become lost in the wall of greenery that separated the beach from the rest of the island.

"If things turn bad," muttered Traygof, "get back to the ship. And if you're captured, ask to see Jamba One Arm. Tell them Traygof sent you to deliver a message."

"What message?" asked Buck.

"Well," staggered Traygof. "If they find Jamba, inform him that I want you back on the mainland....He'll probably help."

"*Probably?*" squeaked Sawny.

"They'd most likely let you go and search for him on your own," said Traygof. "That would give you the chance to head for the beach. Billies aren't as bad as most people think. Aside from their general hatred toward tredders, I'd say they're almost decent....Look, here's the trail."

A wide pathway dug into the forest. It was smooth, as if thousands of feet had polished the dirt and stones. Distant voices—talking, singing, chanting—floated down the hillside. People were close. The smell of smoke and burnt pork wafted on the night breeze.

As the group journeyed up the steep trail, Dod lagged in the rear. He felt like running and hiding. The bushes and trees seemed to have eyes that watched his every move.

Eventually, Traygof stopped. "We're approaching the crossover," he whispered. "Let me do the talking."

Up ahead, the front of a small thatched-roof shack was lit by two burning torches. Four huge men stood talking in the dim light. They were dressed in worn, dirty outfits and had full beards.

Dod struggled to swallow his fear. The last time he'd seen billies, they had tried to kill him, and they had nearly succeeded with Buck, and they had killed Buck's horse.

"Hoi, hoi," called Traygof.

"Who goes there?" rumbled one hulking billie. All four drew their swords.

"We come in peace, my friends," said Traygof in a smooth voice. "I have gifts for your service and dedication. Jamba One Arm told me you'd be here."

"Who?" growled the billies.

"Jamba One Arm…of the Inner Circle."

Grunts followed, and the swords stayed ready.

"Here, my good men," said Traygof, holding out a small pouch. "I've sailed the seas and brought gifts for the shrine, to bid us good luck on our journeys. But, I suppose I can spare this much." Traygof stepped into the light and dumped the contents of the pouch into his hand. It was four gold coins.

The men reached for the money as Boot and Buck stepped into the light.

"Tredders!" roared one guard.

"We're all tredders," laughed Traygof, seemingly not intimidated by their weapons. He lifted up his beard so they could see his tredder ring. "These kids have never seen the shrine. Let us pass."

The men inspected the coins.

"I've got this, as well," offered Traygof, pulling a bottle of wine from his pack. "It's light. If you share it, it'll only warm your watch through the night....Chilly, isn't it?"

Slowly, the men softened. "We'd let you pass," said one billie, "but up there—" He pointed at the dark, steep hillside. "They won't take kindly to your visit."

"Aye," agreed another. "It's best if ya be headin' back the way ya comed. No sense in losin' your lives tonight." He looked at Dilly and Sawny with a sinister eye. "Such pretty girls."

"We'll take our chances," said Traygof, puffing his chest much the way Boot often did. "Drink up and don't worry. We won't tell a soul that you let us pass. And if we're caught, it's our trouble."

The billies looked at each other and finally sheathed their blades. Three of them kept their watch while one guard led the way into the rickety shack. The back wall was mostly missing, revealing a zip-line of sorts.

"Hold on tight," instructed the billie, pointing at a wooden rod that resembled a pogo stick. It had a short, cross pole lashed to the bottom where one person could stand, and at the top of the rod was a small wooden wheel with a deep groove down its center, which fit the cable snuggly. A length of twine was attached to the rod, making it possible to pull the contraption back up the cable once it had reached the other side.

"All right, then," said Traygof. He pointed at Boot and indicated for him to go first. "Keep quiet."

Boot fearlessly climbed aboard the pole and jiggled it forward. The zip-line made a hissing sound as the wheel ran its course. Boot's glowing stone held Dod's eyes. The crack in the mountainside was about fifty feet wide.

"How do we get back?" asked Sawny tensely, noting that gravity was key to crossing the chasm.

"There's a second line up above, right?" responded Traygof, turning to the guard.

"Just like this one," said the billie, demonstrating how to pull the stick back to the little hut. "But you won't need it. The men on duty at the shrine will catch you and march you over the top and down to the city....You shouldn't be going, especially you girls." The large, hairy man eyed Dilly and Sawny. "These two can stay with me."

Sawny stepped closer to Traygof.

"That won't be necessary," assured Traygof, nudging Sawny to go next. "We'll be careful."

Dod followed Sawny. The line swayed and bounced as he sailed over the deep crack. On the other side, the receiving hut sat on the edge of two cliffs; one ran parallel to the beach, making the escape boat inaccessible without returning back over the chasm.

"See," chirped Traygof the moment he'd crossed, "I told you billies weren't bad." He took the lead and marched forward up a trail that got increasingly steeper. At times, slats of wood severed the path, forming stairs, making the slope passable. Finally, near the top of the hillside, the dense foliage and trees opened up and leveled off. Out on the bluff, dozens of torches burned brightly near a two-columned stone platform.

"That's it!" huffed Boot, gasping for breath. "The pit must be near the altar."

"It is," wheezed Sawny. "Books show it's right beneath it.... But, what about the guards?"

A small battalion of billies stood watch. Dod counted thirteen men. Perhaps others were out of view.

"Stay here in the shadows," ordered Traygof, fluffing his beard. "I'll work on a distraction, and once the men have left their posts, you can move in and search the shrine."

"What if they take you?" asked Dilly.

Traygof chortled as he patted his hidden sword. "Best of luck to them," he responded confidently. "If they're *all* hauling me away, it's your cue—and don't drag your heels. You've got to search the cave thoroughly. Don't worry about me."

Dod watched Traygof swagger down the trail as if he fully intended on being greeted with a hero's welcome. It was inspiring. He seemed fearless. It made Dod wonder if Humberrone had acted similarly. After all, they were both legends.

Boot reached beneath his cloak and drew the sword he'd stowed on his back. "It's probably time to be ready," he said, inspecting the blade.

Dod recognized the look in Boot's eyes. He didn't trust billies.

"Do you think we'll need swords?" asked Buck apprehensively, drawing his.

"No—probably not," said Boot.

"Good," added Dilly, swinging her blade in the air. "These weapons are shorter than I'd choose."

"But not bad for hiding," explained Boot. "The guards down below didn't even suspect a thing."

"Not with the gold Traygof was dishing," said Sawny, peering out from behind a patch of bushes.

Dod watched Traygof. Once he had reached the shrine, the guards circled around him. It seemed as if he were telling them something. He kept raising his arms and pointing toward the top of the hill.

"Is it working?" asked Buck, stepping a little deeper into the undergrowth.

"I don't know," said Boot, turning his full attention on the scene that was playing out in the distance. The people's voices were growing louder, but not clearer.

Eventually one sound answered their questions: It was the clanking of metal. Traygof had drawn his sword and was fighting against the mob.

"Let's go!" said Boot.

"Wait!" snapped Dilly, grabbing him by the arm. "Traygof told us to stay here until he had led them away."

"But he's outnumbered!" responded Boot. "We've got to go and help him!"

Sawny moved from the bushes and looked toward the fight.

"He'd be mad if we ruined his plan," said Dod, watching how the mob of activity was beginning to shift away from the shrine. "If the billies saw us too, they'd never leave the shrine unattended."

"Dod's right," agreed Sawny anxiously. "Look! They're following Traygof."

As the minutes passed, all of the men on watch moved away from their posts and joined the crowd that was slowly migrating toward the nearby ridgeline. Swords continued to clank. Traygof was hidden in the midst of his foes.

Keeping to the thickets beside the trail, Boot led his friends to advance on the unprotected Shrine of Boodwana. It was amazing to behold at night. The large stone platform was suspended ten feet in the air by two thick columns. It spanned fifteen feet across. Between the posts was a cave entrance. A row of torches flickered ominously within the cavern, revealing sprawling piles of small trinkets—mostly miniature carvings of people and animals. Dod couldn't believe how many billies had contributed to the sea of woodwork.

"How would we ever know if it's buried in there?" gasped Dilly, eyeing the mountains of gifts.

"We search," whispered Boot. "Buck—you stand guard. Let us know if the billies are coming."

Buck nodded.

With sword in hand, Dod hurried to join in probing. His heart was pounding with concern. Entering the cave was like venturing into a lion's den knowing that the lion was likely to return any minute.

"It would be near the back," said Sawny uneasily. "This memorial cave was young when the scepter went missing."

Dod waded through knee-deep carvings of fish, deer, people, dogs, alligators, and everything else imaginable. The farther he went, the more the cave smelled like rotten wood and the figures crumbled under his feet. Beyond the last torch, large spider webs hung down from the ceiling like layers of curtains, catching an array of nightlife. Hand-sized spiders patrolled the webs. They were nothing compared to the venooses Dod had seen in Terro's attic, but they still made him shiver. "Now Dari should lend *me* her glowing headband," muttered Dod, venturing into the shadowy back regions of the cave.

"Take a look at this!" called Boot, holding up a torch he'd taken from the entrance.

Dod ran to join him. On the rearmost wall of the cave, eight feet up, three hooks protruded from the stone. Above them was penned in black, 'Death to Raul!'

"Someone's beaten us to the staff!" groaned Dilly, standing beside Boot. "It must have been kept there."

"That's what it looks like," responded Boot. "Maybe The Dread has it. He's cozy with billies."

"Buck's whistling!" shouted Sawny from the middle of the cave. She hadn't ventured past the torches and into the spider webs.

Boot spun around. "Let's get out of here!" he ordered.

Dod turned to follow Dilly and Boot when an image flashed through his mind. The ground was shaking. "Maybe it just fell," mumbled Dod to himself. He postponed his retreat and frantically shuffled back and forth through the rotting wood below the hooks.

Nothing stuck out.

"Hurry!" yelled Boot over his shoulder. The light around Dod had dimmed to the glow of his stone necklace. Boot and Dilly were now running for the exit.

Dod hastened his search, kicking and stomping and tearing with all of his might. Below the loose material, thousands of small carvings had decomposed and coalesced into a foot-thick layer of matter that resembled firm dirt. At first Dod had thought it was the floor of the cave, but upon stabbing his short blade downward, he had discovered the bedrock.

"It's got to be here," mumbled Dod, freeing large chunks of debris. He worked like a crazed maniac. Every second counted. Billies were likely approaching.

Suddenly, Dod's foot hit something. Dropping to his knees, Dod let go of his weapon and plunged both hands into the stiff pulp, clawing and tearing the debris from the stone. Buried against the rock, two things were found: a sheathed sword and the scepter!

With the legs of a fresh gazelle, Dod raced to get out. He was thrilled to have found the king's staff but terrified to know that trouble was coming and possibly awaiting him at the entrance. Both feelings pressed adrenaline.

Cautiously emerging from the cave, Dod saw Boot and Buck wrestling on the ground with a billie guard. The man's hands were tied behind his back, and Dilly's handkerchief was in his mouth. Boot was in the process of binding his legs at the ankles.

Dod heaved a heavy sigh.

"You found it!" exclaimed Sawny, dashing over to greet him.

"Right where you said it would be," praised Dod, holding the staff up. He handed it to Sawny and began the task of attaching the dirty sheath to his belt.

"On three," huffed Boot, counting with Buck. They moved the bulky man to the cave and tied him to one of the torch posts.

"Where was it?" asked Boot, excitedly rushing to inspect the scepter once the guard was secured.

"Below the hooks," said Dod. "It must have fallen during an earthquake."

"Or eruption," noted Dilly.

The captured guard thrashed back and forth.

"Time to go," said Boot, taking the scepter from Sawny and leading away from the shrine. "Any sign of Traygof?"

"Did I hear my name?" called a winded voice. Traygof jogged out of the shadows. He had blood splotched on his face, clothes, and hands.

"Are you all right?" gasped Dilly.

"Just a little tired," said Traygof, pulling his glowing-rock necklace out of his shirt. "They insisted on the hard way."

Boot held the staff up. "Is this what you wanted?"

"Hoi!" chanted Traygof excitedly, reaching for the prize. "This grime'll come off with a good scrubbing. Great work! You've saved the Democracy!"

Speeding down the dark, steep trail, Dod couldn't help wondering whether they were being pursued. Traygof ran in the front, holding the scepter, chatting with Boot and Buck about the fun they could have at sea, while Dilly and Sawny followed behind them, and Dod brought up the rear. The night air was calm. Voices carried through the dense forest in an almost mystical manner, as if the trees themselves were alive. Perhaps they were talking about the battle Traygof had just endured.

At the upper zip-line shack, no one stood guard, and the thatched roof was sagging in disarray. But the contraption necessary for crossing appeared stable.

"Follow quick behind me," ordered Traygof. "I'll go first, just in case we've got eyes awaiting our arrival on the other side—and Dod, you should be next. If danger lurks, I'd appreciate a little help." Traygof hugged the pole with his legs and held the scepter in one hand and his sword in the other. The shack groaned as Traygof rolled away.

As soon as the contraption had been retrieved, Boot rushed after Traygof, his sword drawn as well, clearly hoping to fight side-by-side with the legend. Dod didn't mind trading spots. Boot was more qualified to fend off billies.

Buck and Dilly followed thereafter, each appearing to share some of Boot's enthusiasm.

As Dod drew the contraption back for Sawny, something dreadful happened. The croaking frogs and chirping crickets were suddenly overpowered by a roaring explosion of screaming voices. Dod handed Sawny the twine and peeked out the front door of the hut to see what was happening. To his horror, the whole hillside was coming to life with a surge of moving bodies. A few of them held torches. Some were dashing down the trail, others were pressing straight through the thick foliage. It was an army of angry billies.

"We've got to go!" yelled Dod. "Let's jump double! Quick!"

Climbing aboard, Sawny and Dod eagerly bounced the contraption to nudge it off the platform. Unfortunately, a loud cracking noise followed. The thick beam around which the cable had been tied was now broken down the center, leaving the rope nearly ready to break free.

"We're gonna die!" wailed Sawny, beginning to cry. The approaching army was shaking the ground with their galloping feet, and two flaming arrows had just struck the roof of the hut.

"I won't let that happen!" assured Dod, faking his best courage. In truth, he was petrified.

Almost in slow motion, Dod reached up and forced the knot over to the short part of the beam that looked sturdy, then wrapped the remaining tail of the rope once around a neighboring pole.

"There's not enough to tie it off!" screamed Sawny through her tears. Three more flaming arrows struck the hut.

"Then I'll hold it for you!" yelled Dod, grabbing Sawny by the hand. "Trust me, you can do this!"

Sawny shuddered as Dod helped her to the edge. "You're going to be all right," he assured, letting go of her to return to the short piece of rope that kept the knot from falling off the broken beam.

Sawny hugged the pole, closed her eyes, and pushed off. Instantly the knot began to slip toward the break.

Dod threw his full weight against the cord and held it firmly. He could feel the fibers of the rope tearing into his soft palms. He squeezed tighter. Sawny's life was in his hands. She was sailing over the deep ravine and would die if he failed. Every second felt like a thousand. The knot was still slipping. Dod squeezed tighter. He was so bent on saving Sawny, he hardly felt the heat that was nearing his flesh. Within seconds, the whole shack would be engulfed in flames.

Dod watched Sawny's glowing rock with great earnestness and at last was rewarded with the knowledge that she had made it safely across. No sooner did the pressure lift than Dod's strength gave out. He fell to the floor and watched the knot slip from the beam and whip out into the dark chasm.

With no escape route, Dod closed his eyes. He wished the fire would speed up and eat him quickly. Surviving long enough to be tortured by billies wasn't an appealing thought. As the ground shook, Dod burrowed deep within himself, preparing for death, and then remembered his only hope—his medallion!

PRICELESS

The thatched roof and walls of the hut began to burn hotter and hotter. Black smoke was everywhere. Dod crawled to the cliff's edge and gasped a breath. Arrows had hit the shack across the chasm, leaving it ablaze as well. His friends were nowhere in sight.

Flaming pieces of the roof rained down from above. The fire was now louder than the army of billies. It crackled and sizzled. Dod was trapped. His clothes felt as if they were about to ignite. He did his best to cover his head and neck. The heat was painful. Burning to death was worse than he had imagined.

Focusing all of his inner strength, Dod pushed to leave Green. If he couldn't make it to Earth, he at least wanted to die. The flames were unbearable.

Suddenly, Dod felt his body floating, and all of the pain was gone. The roaring fire was no more than a ringing in his ears.

I'm dead, thought Dod, trying to open his eyes. A bright light made it impossible for him to see anything, but shortly thereafter, it dawned on him: The gentle warmth on his face was coming from the south, through his bedroom window. It was the winter sun peeking out from behind a cluster of storm clouds. He wasn't dead, and he wasn't floating—he was laying on his bed in Cedar City.

Rolling over, Dod gazed around his ragged bedroom. It was the most beautiful sight he'd seen in ages. It didn't matter that the walls had cracks and the furniture was secondhand. It was Earth! The medallion had taken him all the way across space, back home to his tiny room in the duplex.

"Oh!" sighed Dod, beyond relieved. He sniffed the air. His clothes smelled like fabric softener, but his skin reeked like bonfire smoke.

"Never again," he mumbled, pulling the medallion off. After resting on his bed for a while, as if he had just finished a marathon, he staggered to his feet and draped the medallion and chain over the crown Josh had given him for Christmas. "Someone else can be the king of Green," he said.

SPLAT! SPLAT!

The bedroom window was assaulted with snowballs. Dod walked to the pane and looked down. "I'm coming," he mouthed, waving at Josh, Alex, and Ruth. Despite feeling drained, he wanted to run out and hug his brothers, and he wanted to join them in building a snow fort, even if his coat and gloves were currently being used by Ruth.

In the kitchen, Dod found that Aunt Hilda had draped Pap's old coat over a chair and had left his gloves on the table. A note read 'Cole, now you have no excuse.'

"Cole," whispered Dod, sliding the coat on. He liked his name.

CHAPTER THIRTY

Out in the yard, Josh greeted Cole with a snowball to the head. "We're halfway done," he reported proudly, showing off a three-foot wall. Alex peered out from behind it.

"Nice of you to join us," grunted Ruth, pushing a large snowball toward the fort.

Cole smiled at Ruth. He felt at peace knowing he had made up his mind. The next day he would give up the medallion and save Ruth's aunt from Mr. Brewer.

Josh grabbed a large stick and hopped on top of the wall. "Keep it rolling," he ordered to Ruth, pointing at the spot where he envisioned the addition.

"I'm not lifting this alone," laughed Ruth. Josh was indicating that he expected her to begin a second level.

"I'll help," grinned Cole, moving into position.

Ruth looked at him. "I didn't know you had a fireplace."

"We don't," said Josh, squirming in his puffy coat. "Stop your talking and start lifting. We have work to do."

Ruth raised her eyebrows inquisitively at Cole. "Why do you smell like smoke?"

"It's nothing," said Cole, grunting as he helped heave the snowball into place.

"Your hair's scorched!" burst Ruth, pulling her gloves off to inspect the top of Cole's head. She drew her hands back and rubbed her fingers together. Small ashes of burnt hair turned to dust and sprinkled the ground.

"Is it that noticeable?" laughed Cole. He hadn't thought of looking in the mirror. He was alive and felt okay. After his close encounter with death, what did it matter if his hair was singed?

"You went back to Green without me!" exclaimed Josh, jumping off the little wall. He pointed his stick at Cole as if he were brandishing a fine sword.

"I had to," said Cole. "But don't worry, I saved the Democracy."

"How?" insisted Josh.

Cole began at the beginning and explained the places he'd been and the things he'd done, and eventually he got to the part about helping Traygof to obtain the special scepter. The more he told, the more Ruth's face grew concerned.

"What about tomorrow?" she finally asked in an anxious voice.

"I'll go with you," said Cole.

"Where?" demanded Josh.

"Can we come, too?" asked Alex. "Please. I want to meet Traygof."

"We're not headed to Green," said Cole. "We have somewhere else we have to be—right, Ruth?"

Ruth cautiously nodded. "Keep smoothing the wall," she said, turning to Josh and Alex. "Cole and I will roll more balls." She then grabbed Cole by the arm and hauled him off to the corner of the yard. "What really happened to your hair?" she demanded. Cole recognized that the look on her face was only one step from tears.

"I'm sick of hiding the truth," said Cole, pulling his gloves off and running his hands through his charred hair. "Believe it or not, you just heard what happened. Green's a real place, and Raul is, too. And Sawny's just as real as you and me—only she's way out there somewhere." Cole pointed into the cloudy sky. "But it doesn't matter. I'll give Mr. Brewer the stupid medallion tomorrow. You'll get what you want. Your aunt will be fine. Everyone will be happy."

"Your hands!" gasped Ruth.

Cole pulled them down. His hands were red and puffy. A few blisters had formed. One of his fingers showed a ring line. "My Coosing ring," muttered Cole, rubbing the white band of skin. He teared up.

"How can Green be real?" whispered Ruth.

"I don't know," responded Cole, taking a deep breath. "It just is. Why do you think Mr. Brewer is making such a big deal out of the medallion? He knows where it leads."

Ruth stepped back. "Will you really give it up tomorrow?"

"I guess," groaned Cole. "I already told you. In Green, I'm stuck. I was lucky to get out. My friends are running for their lives as we speak. If they're quick, they might be rowing in search of *The Avenger*. Either way…" Cole shook his head. "It's over for me. At least I helped them get the scepter they needed."

Ruth eyed Cole suspiciously and grabbed for his hands. She turned them over. "You have a rope burn!" she blurted in shock. Her eyes glossed with deep thoughts. "You saved Sawny, didn't you? Green's real. You're not just telling stories…"

"She's real," lamented Cole sadly.

The next morning, Cole awoke while his room was still dark. He didn't need to look at his clock to know that it was almost five. His gut told him. He had agreed to meet Ruth on the front porch at five-thirty. As far as Doralee knew, he and Ruth were going to meet Ruth's aunt and spend the day together. It was mostly true. Cole would be back by bedtime.

Glimmering in the dim light, Cole's medallion sat undisturbed. It was somewhat surprising for Cole to see it was still there. He had half expected Ruth or Josh to have stolen it.

Climbing from bed, Cole counted the hours. Sixteen. Green was currently enjoying mid-afternoon. He took a deep breath and slid the medallion back around his neck. It felt strange—different somehow.

Breakfast was cold pancakes and hash browns. He almost used the microwave, but changed his mind when he thought of needing to peel Josh off. If Josh knew Cole were planning on giving up his path to Green, he'd stop him. No doubt about it. Josh wouldn't understand.

At five-twenty-five, Ruth tapped quietly at the front door. Cole opened it up. He was in the process of putting Pap's coat on. It was almost a mile to the bus stop.

"Are you ready?" asked Ruth.

Cole pulled on the chain around his neck and showed her that he had the medallion. "Let's do it," he said.

Together, they hurried to the bus stop and caught an early morning ride to Las Vegas. Neither of them said much on the way down. Most of Ruth's comments revolved around the snow levels. In Cedar City, a solid foot lay on the ground. Saint George had only a skiff on the north-facing hillsides, and Las Vegas was snow free.

It was still early when they arrived. The city appeared to be sleeping. Casinos and stores looked mostly vacant.

"We could have slept in," remarked Ruth. "Everyone else did."

"Not my mom," assured Cole. "If we'd have waited to catch a later bus, she'd have been asking questions—and Hilda, too—and Alex and Josh! They wouldn't have let us leave without them."

CHAPTER THIRTY

"You're lucky," said Ruth, heading down the sidewalk toward the Circus Circus casino. "You have a lot of people who care about you. I'd give anything to be loved like that."

Cole felt uncomfortable. "I'm sure your dad loves you," he mumbled. Girls' feelings weren't something he knew how to address.

"If he does, he doesn't show it," said Ruth, pushing her straight brown hair out of her face. The wind was blowing lightly. "But it's okay," she continued. "I'm used to it, now."

Close to Circus Circus, Cole noted the huge construction projects. Old casinos were being remodeled and new ones were being built. The bad economy had slowed things down and left most of the sites temporarily dormant, or so they looked.

"I bet he'll try to meet us in there," said Cole, pointing at a maze of metal beams and scaffolding.

"What?" choked Ruth.

"Mr. Brewer," said Cole.

"Right," agreed Ruth.

Just past Circus Circus, Cole and Ruth entered a McDonald's to kill time and wait for Mr. Brewer's call. Ruth ordered a chocolate shake and offered to share it. Cole declined. His stomach was feeling restless.

They made small talk for hours. Three times they walked around Circus Circus, and after each jaunt, they migrated back to the McDonald's. When Ruth ordered her third shake—strawberry—Cole finally agreed to taste it. He sucked nearly the whole thing down and left her with a pile of foam at the bottom. It felt better on his nervous stomach than he had thought it would.

"Thanks," said Cole, almost grinning.

Ruth's phone rang.

With a trembling hand, Ruth took the call. "Yes," she said. "We brought it. He's right here with me. Just tell us where. We're at the McDonald's. Right. I saw that…" Ruth stared at the ceiling. "No! We're alone! I promise! Just don't hurt her…"

Cole shuffled his feet back and forth. He wished he and Boot could approach Mr. Brewer in a dark alley with their swords at their waists. Or better yet, he and Traygof. No guns, just swords.

"We're coming," said Ruth, rising to her feet. She hung up and looked at Cole. "He promised he would let my aunt go if we do exactly what he asks. He just wants the medallion."

"Then let's go give it to him," said Cole. He wished he could give him something else, like a knuckle sandwich.

Just as Cole had suspected, Mr. Brewer had asked Ruth to go to one of the nearby construction sites. He had directed her to enter at a certain point and pass into the center. Once there, she would receive another call.

The metal beams crisscrossed above their heads as they walked. Both Cole and Ruth kept an eye out for Mr. Brewer. At the predetermined point, Ruth's phone rang. Mr. Brewer had eyes on them. He directed them to cut through the site, cross a street, and enter another construction site. He also informed Ruth that he had men watching for any signs of a police tail. He would only meet with them if he were completely convinced that they weren't being followed.

On the way to the second location, Cole and Ruth passed a line of cement trucks. A deep foundation was being poured. Dozens of workers manned the cranes and directed the flow of cement into place.

"Can't we have Mr. Brewer meet us over here?" asked Cole, wishing to stay near the bustling traffic. They were headed to a much more secluded spot.

"Nope," said Ruth. "He wants us alone. If we even appear to have anyone following us, he'll call it off and kill my aunt. He even had me turn off my phone. I'm supposed to switch it back on when we find the red bucket."

"Red bucket?" mumbled Cole. His gut was beginning to sense trouble. If they showed up alone with the medallion, what guarantee did they have that Mr. Brewer would keep his word?

"What if I stay here?" asked Cole. "You could bring him and your aunt to me."

"You're kidding, right?" pressed Ruth, picking up her pace. "We have to do exactly what he says."

"Or what?"

"Or he'll kill my aunt!" said Ruth in an exasperated voice. "You can't back out on me now!"

"I'm not trying to back out," defended Cole. "I've just got a weird feeling about this."

"Stop worrying," huffed Ruth. "How bad could he be? He was your science teacher."

"Worst ever!" rumbled Cole. "Besides, we're not talking about him giving me an F, we're talking about him pulling out a glock and giving me two to the head and one to the heart."

"He just wants the medallion."

"Right," grumbled Cole. "If this guy is connected to The Order in Green—and I think he is—then he's not going to let us leave while we're still breathing. It's like we've double-crossed the mafia."

"Don't say that," chided Ruth.

"Six feet under," muttered Cole, hurrying his pace to keep up.

Deep within the next abandoned site, a red bucket lay upside down. Ruth took a tense breath and turned her cell phone back on. It immediately rang.

"We're going as fast as we can," said Ruth into the phone. She paused in silence for about thirty seconds. "Okay," she said. "It doesn't matter to us. No one's tracking my cell!" Ruth hung up and tipped the red bucket over. A cheap-looking phone lay on the ground. She traded hers for the poor replacement and put the bucket back the way it had been.

Within seconds, the new phone began to ring. It played the same eerie tune as the phone in *Jurassic Park*—the one that got eaten by a dinosaur. Cole took it to be a bad omen.

Mr. Brewer instructed Ruth to cut through the site and enter a building. Once inside, she was to make her way to the covered parking garage on the opposite end.

"Isn't this a lot of work for a simple trade?" pressed Cole. His gut had gone from anxious to ill in a matter of minutes.

"He thinks we're being sneaky," responded Ruth.

"We should be!" said Cole, stopping dead in his tracks. "Think about it. Why is he so cautious?"

"Please!" begged Ruth. "Let's just do this! It'll all be over soon!"

"That's what I'm afraid of," groaned Cole, giving in to her persuasions.

In the garage, most of the stalls were empty. "What now?" asked Cole.

The ground shook. From the second level, two SUVs with tinted windows raced down and rounded the corner. Their tires squealed as they approached. The second vehicle stopped beside Ruth as the first sped away. Two large men hopped out.

"Weapons?" asked one man, holding a gun with a silencer.

Cole and Ruth shook their heads, though it didn't stop the men from frisking them thoroughly before shoving them into the Escalade. Cole recognized both of the men from his last visit to Las Vegas. They had been in the trailer the day he'd reclaimed his medallion.

"No clever stuff," huffed the man with the gun. He had a skull tattoo on his arm. Seeing the mark reminded Cole that it was the same man who had been in charge of the people in the trailer.

"Where's Brewer?" asked Ruth in a quavering voice. Her face seemed to show regret for having not listened to Cole.

"None of your business," snapped the pirate-like man. He leaned forward and shoved the driver. "Slow down. We're supposed to look normal. Frank's driving the decoy."

Ruth glanced at Cole.

From the back seat, a gangly man with alcohol on his breath cleared his throat. "Where are their blindfolds?"

"They don't need 'em," chuckled the driver. "Booze don't care this time, right boss?"

The man with the skull tattoo nodded. His black gloves made a quiet squeaking noise as he squeezed the handle of his gun.

The vehicle entered the freeway and headed to the outskirts of town where the bustling city was replaced with lonely warehouses. Christmas break was still in full sway. With skill, the driver navigated skinny access roads between buildings, showing he knew right where he was going. Eventually, he pulled into the open bay of a metal fabrication plant. The tall door closed as soon as he entered.

"Time for some fun," mocked the driver.

Ruth and Cole were led through the dark factory at gunpoint and forced to climb a metal cage of winding stairs to the roof. Outside, Mr. Brewer and three other men stood near the far edge. A lady was with them.

"Naomi," whispered Ruth.

Cole glanced side to side. The sprawling tar roof was dotted with ventilation hoods and air conditioners. Beyond the building, no one was in sight—not even a delivery truck. It was baffling. So many large warehouses, so few people. Cole couldn't help thinking that in the middle of the Nevada desert he would have had more eyes watching him. At least out there, a few lizards or crows would have noticed the trouble that was unfolding.

"Keep moving," charged the man with the tattoo. He pressed his gun against Cole's back.

Walking slowly, Cole had a burst of flashes. He saw Naomi thrown over the edge of the building and Ruth shot in both legs. The premonition was disheartening. What could he do? Two men with guns were currently escorting him to his death. If either of them pulled the trigger, no one would know. The place was deserted, and they had silencers.

"Cole," called Mr. Brewer in an evil, calm voice. "You've been a bad boy. Look at all the problems you've caused. I think you owe me an apology."

Cole continued to plod toward him, but didn't respond.

Mr. Brewer pulled his phone from his pocket and made a call. It was quick. Instantly, a loud clanking noise filled the air, like the sound of a blender on its highest speed with a box of screws and bolts inside.

"Take a look!" ordered Mr. Brewer. He pointed for Cole to walk to the edge. Fifty feet below, a giant dumpster was groaning; within, scrap metal swirled around. It was being shredded.

"It would be sad if your friends slipped off the roof and landed in there, now wouldn't it?" said Mr. Brewer. "You better give me back the medallion and answer my questions! Do you understand?"

The man certainly didn't look like a teacher anymore. His face was dark, distorted with anger and greed. It rivaled those of the other men who stood by, ready to do his bidding.

"I understand," growled Cole, pretending to stretch. He grabbed the back of his neck, pulled the medallion off by its chain, and dangled it over the edge. "BACK UP OR I'M DROPPING IT!" yelled Cole.

"Whoa!" snapped Mr. Brewer. "Let's stay calm. You don't want to destroy it." He pulled his phone from his pocket.

"SET YOUR PHONE DOWN!" added Cole. "IF YOU BREATHE WRONG, THIS MEDALLION IS GONE!"

"Okay! Okay!" said Mr. Brewer, dropping his phone. "Let's be rational. You don't want your friends to die, do you? Hand me the necklace and no one gets shot."

"LIAR!" shouted Cole. "I'M NOT THAT STUPID! WE'RE DOING THINGS MY WAY, NOW! Here's what you're going to do, you're going to let these two ladies go. You don't need them, you have me. They're going to walk over there to the fire-escape ladder and climb down to the ground—all while I'm watching. Got it? And if anyone tries anything, your precious trinket is toast!"

The men with guns looked to Mr. Brewer for orders.

"Okay," said Mr. Brewer, cautiously wiping sweat from his brow. "We can let them go. But while they're walking, I want answers."

"THIS IS *MY* SHOW!" yelled Cole, bursting with frustration. "We'll talk once they've gone behind that blue building over there.

Mr. Brewer cringed. The blue warehouse was in the distance, across a dry riverbed and field. Cars couldn't follow them. They'd have to drive the long way around if they changed plans and pursued.

"Be reasonable—" began Mr. Brewer when Cole let the chain slip through his fingers, leaving the medallion dangling precariously over the metal-shredding machine.

"I'VE HAD ENOUGH!" shouted Cole. "DON'T MAKE ME MAD!"

"Go!" ordered Mr. Brewer, releasing Ruth and Naomi. "But if I see the cops, he's dead." Three guns continued to point at Cole.

Ruth glanced anxiously at Cole as she walked away. Her eyes seemed to apologize for getting him into trouble.

The next ten minutes were tense. Mr. Brewer kept asking questions. Cole repeatedly shook his head and refused to answer. It was a stalemate. Mr. Brewer's men had guns, Cole had the medallion.

Every second was murder on Cole's stomach. The shake he'd had wasn't mixing well with the stress he felt. His blood pounded mercilessly in his ears. It reminded him of the time he'd passed out in third grade while attempting to do a math problem on the board—but worse.

CHAPTER THIRTY

Eventually, Ruth and Naomi disappeared behind the blue building. It was time to act. "Let me climb down the ladder and I'll leave this on the ground," suggested Cole feebly. His courageous yelling was over. He knew he lacked a winning hand.

"Nope," said Mr. Brewer. "Give it to me, and we'll talk."

Cole groaned. There was no easy out.

"I'll tell you what," said Cole, straining to muster a voice. He slipped the medallion and chain into one hand, then pretended to shift it back and forth, leaving a small part of the chain showing. "Let's play a game. After all, this is Las Vegas." He tried to chuckle, but not much came out. "Pick a hand," he offered, timidly approaching Mr. Brewer.

The men with guns smiled, like a posse of farmers who'd just outsmarted a fox near their chicken coop. Their postures loosened as they drew close.

"Which one?" asked Cole, trying to sound like Josh or Alex. The younger the better. He hoped to catch the men off guard. Inside he was sweating bullets.

"It's in that one," said Mr. Brewer, pointing to Cole's right hand.

"Are you sure?" pressed Cole, holding both hands up for inspection.

"Positive," said Mr. Brewer.

Cole clenched his fist around the necklace, making his fingers look gnarled, pulled a horrified face, and let out a shrill cry. It was blood curdling. It wrenched his gut and burnt his throat to do it. "IT'S EATING MY HAND!" he yelled, shaking his arm as if he were trying to let go. "GET IT OFF OF ME! HELP!"

The men startled, Mr. Brewer included.

Then, doubling over, Cole used his anxiety to produce a fountain. Pink slime went everywhere, compliments of Ruth's shake. It splashed across Mr. Brewer's leg and onto the ground.

"HELP ME!" raged Cole, shaking his crumpled hand. He staggered side to side while screaming, faking that he was in the most excruciating pain. It was the best acting Cole had ever done. He wobbled his way over to a ventilation hood and banged his body against it, trembling and shouting. "TAKE IT! TAKE IT! HELP ME!" he pled.

Over and over he threw himself against the protruding duct, as if the medallion had taken control of his body. On the fourth hit, the bird guard popped out. Quick as a flash, Cole jumped down the hole. He didn't care where it led. Anywhere was better than on the rooftop with three guns pointed at his head.

No sooner was he out of their view than a feeling of power washed over him. *I'm going back to Green!* he thought, and just like that, the small air duct no longer held him. Instead, he was lying face down in a pile of ashes with a warm sea breeze blowing against his back.

"Priceless," mumbled Dod, slowly rising to his knees. The medallion had worked!

IMPOSSIBLE

Glancing around, Dod happily found that the fire was out and the billies were gone. In front of him, the deep ravine had sheer cliff walls that dropped hundreds of feet. The volcanic rock appeared to have split during an earthquake and moved apart. The crack continued all the way down to the sea on one side and up to the top of the hill on the other. Now there was no way to cross it—the billies had burned all four shacks to the ground. Nothing remained of the two zip lines.

With his heart still racing, Dod searched the hillside for movement. When he saw none, he turned his attention to the sea. There wasn't a ship in sight. Traygof and his crew had sailed away without him, which only made sense considering the circumstance. They had likely assumed he was dead. Anyone else would have been.

Feeling exhausted, Dod crawled into the nearest thicket and laid down. "Wow," he sighed, taking his medallion off. After the stressful morning he'd had on Earth, hiding in Tripeak Island's foliage was comparatively wonderful.

IMPOSSIBLE

The sun crept across the sky while Dod rested. He didn't dare go exploring until he'd let a few hours pass with the medallion beside him on the ground. As he waited, he inspected the old sword he'd recovered from the shrine. Its casing was tarnished with grime from sitting beneath the wood for hundreds of years. Carefully, Dod took a stick and scraped the debris from the lip of the sheath until he could draw the sword out. To his surprise, the blade had survived beautifully. It was a dazzling white metal, the likes of which he hadn't seen before; and etched into its side in shiny black lettering was a curious phrase: *'Chantolli, Power for All.'*

"Chantolli?" muttered Dod. He instantly thought of Sirlonk. Regardless, the people who had taken it clearly didn't like the Chantollis. They'd written *'Death to Raul'* on the wall of the cave.

Dod gave the sword a swing. It was perfectly balanced. And then it dawned on him. "This is the third sword!" he gasped, remembering his conversation with his friends. "The Mauj made it. Now we have all three…the Tillius blade for Green, the crimson blade for Soosh, and the Chantolli blade for Raul!"

With a new desire to stay in Green, Dod rose to his feet and looked around. How could he get back to the mainland? He thought of searching for Jamba One Arm, but pushed the idea away since Traygof's connection hadn't gotten him anywhere with the guards he'd confronted at the shrine. Dod's next thought was to head for the beach, but that idea was also whisked away when he remembered about the cliff he'd seen at the lower shack. Without the zip lines to help him cross the chasm, the beach was an impossible option. So, as the afternoon sun began to stretch the palm-tree shadows, Dod put his medallion back on, sheathed his glimmering white sword, and began his ascent up the steep hillside.

Not daring to risk being seen by billies, Dod stayed off trails and kept his movements quiet. In the deep thickets, the shrine wasn't visible until Dod was already high above it, nearly to the ridgeline. Down below, dozens of men kept watch over the cave, and others came and went using the wide trail that rolled over the top. It made Dod curious. What billie city lay on the other side? If the slopes were anything like they were on the seaside, the city couldn't be big. Yet the traffic was steady.

Once Dod crested the top, he had to take a seat. What he saw was alarming. Just as Sawny had indicated, the whole center of the island was gone, leaving the remaining landmass in the shape of a donut; inside the watery center, a massive fleet of ships lay still.

"The billies' dashers!" groaned Dod. They were hidden. All of Pious's searching wouldn't find them. How the large ships had entered the bay in the first place was a bit of a mystery, since the only entrance was a long, winding, narrow waterway with three low-hanging bridges crossing over it. Dod's only conclusion was that the bridges had been temporarily removed in order for such bulky vessels to have been pulled up the channel. It was a masterful way to hide the fleet. Tripeak Island was billie territory. No one ventured among them, so the secret bay of ships would remain hidden.

Beyond the narrow channel, seaward, Dod could see part of a small cove. A few ships were docked. Traygof had kept *The Avenger* away from the island for fear of drawing attention, and Dod suspected the ships in the cove were just the type of vessels Traygof had worked to avoid. Their presence near the entrance to the hidden bay was likely a great deterrent to curious outsiders. It was brilliant. Sirlonk and Murdore were raising an army in Pious's backyard. Over a hundred thousand men were waiting for battle, concealed from view only one or two days from the mainland, and more were likely coming. Billie voices rose up on the breeze. It was a floating metropolis that dwarfed the real city, whose inhabitants lived in little huts along the hillside near the water's edge.

"I've got to warn Pious," whispered Dod. He knew where all of the money had gone from the High Gate bank robberies—Sirlonk had been keeping his men fed and happy.

Cautiously, Dod worked his way through the thickets near the ridgeline. His plan was to approach the outer cove stealthily and see if any trade ships docked alongside the billies. From their vantage, the hidden bay would be kept from their eyes by the winding channel, so it seemed plausible that non-billie ships would be allowed to visit for commerce, so long as they didn't venture inland. After all, trade was necessary if such a massive body of people were being fed. The cauldron wasn't large enough to provide a sufficient supply of fish for the men anchored there, and the neighboring city certainly didn't grow enough fruit or vegetables for the legions.

Once Dod had managed to cross the trail that led to the Shrine of Boodwana, the rest of the day was comparatively safe traveling. The lush vegetation kept him hidden from view as he hiked near the ridgeline. And by the time he was descending toward the billies, darkness had come. The whole bay twinkled with lights. It was deceptively beautiful, and the aromas that floated on the night breeze made Dod's stomach rumble. Thousands of men were enjoying roasted fish, pork, poultry, and beef. It was a mixture of torturous smells for someone who had lost his meager lunch and currently had no plans for dinner.

In the darkness, Dod skirted around the edges of the billie city and continued his course toward the channel that led to the open sea. Gruff voices sang songs about war and love. Hearing them made Dod feel like he was sneaking through the depths of a headhunter's jungle. Their tunes praised violence and carnage.

With careful steps, Dod occasionally veered close to the huts in search of food. He was starving, and the long hike wasn't helping. From the hilltop, the sea hadn't looked so far away. Ultimately, his snooping paid off. Beside one thatched shack, a large roasted goose sat cooling on a wooden table. It was unattended. Dod swiped a leg and hurried into the forest. The meat was better than Thanksgiving turkey. It had been seasoned appropriately with his hunger, making each bite taste heavenly.

Having stolen his dinner, Dod picked up his pace and rushed to get away from the huts. But before he had gone far, a strange feeling stopped him. It was as if he were being summoned. Someone needed his help. It was a woman. Dod could sense her pain and desperation. She was near, detained, and crying.

Dod finished his meal and sat in a thick bush. He couldn't decide what to do. Even if he could find the woman in need, his efforts to help her would likely mean confronting billies, which was the last thing he wanted to do. If he were forced to run, they'd catch him for sure, since he was worn down from hiking and their legs would be fresh.

Determined to avoid trouble, Dod tried to push the feelings from his mind. But memories of Pap overwhelmed him. Pap would never leave someone in need. Thoughts of Pap's goodness rallied Dod to action. Nervously, he ventured on tiptoe into a cluster of huts that seemed to draw his attention, and to his surprise, he heard whimpering. The woeful sounds weren't half as loud as the laughing that came from a communal fire pit a sort distance away.

Dod followed his ears and discovered a woman—early thirties—who was tied to a tree. Her clothes were torn, her feet were bare, and her long brown hair was matted to her head and dirty face. She was bound hand-and-foot. Dod cautiously approached, putting his finger to his mouth. If the men around the fire pit were to turn, they'd see him.

When the woman's eyes met Dod's, she stopped crying. Dod recognized her, even though he'd never seen her before. It was Yarni, Commendus's wife. She wasn't dead, though she had clearly been taken captive by the billies, just as Commendus had suspected.

Once the woman seemed to understand that Dod wouldn't hurt her, Dod drew his sword and quietly cut her ropes. The blade was sharp and easily did the job.

Taking the woman by the hand, Dod led her into the forest. "I've come to free you," whispered Dod, "but we've got to hurry. Can you run?"

"I'll try," said Yarni in a frail voice.

Together, Dod and Yarni raced through the thickets toward the channel that meandered to the coast. The billies would eventually find the woman was missing, and they'd search for her. If they had dogs, the night wouldn't go well. Dod couldn't push from his mind the pack of dogs that the billies had used to pursue him and his friends when they'd camped above The Goose Egg. Knowing how important Yarni was, Dod recognized that the island would likely be crawling with searchers by morning.

"We've got to reach the water," panted Dod. "They'll have hounds tracking us. We can throw them off if we swim part of the way."

Yarni followed Dod into the marsh by the bay. As they neared the water, luck struck. Dod tripped over a small boat that had been hidden under a pile of cut swamp grass. It looked like a two-man kayak. One long double-sided paddle lay beside it. Dod handed Yarni the paddle and began to slide the boat toward the water. Once the brackish sludge was knee deep, they climbed into the boat and began paddling. It was risky business leaving the foliage and venturing out where they might be easily spotted, but with the moon still down, it seemed worth a shot, especially considering Dod's tired legs and Yarni's fragile condition.

In the distance, dogs began barking.

"They're coming," whispered Dod. He was glad that they had hit the open water. At least the dogs wouldn't tree them.

"Do you know who I am?" asked the woman in a soft voice.

Dod turned to respond. "Yarni," he said.

The woman looked surprised. "How could you tell? I'm a dreadful sight! It's a wonder they planned on me marrying one of them."

Dod paddled as hard as he could. The narrow channel was close. Once inside, they'd look less conspicuous.

"They said they'd feed me better if I'd consent," yawned the emaciated woman. "But I'd die first."

"I'm sorry," offered Dod. "Billies are mean."

The dogs in the distance were getting quieter.

"Are you all that my husband sent?" asked Yarni after a few moments of silence.

"He thinks you're dead," confessed Dod frankly, breathing heavily. Dod had gotten into a rhythm that made the light boat glide quickly across the smooth water. At the moment, paddling was as much as he could concentrate on. Dip, pull. Dip, pull. Dip, pull. Dip, pull. The rhythm was everything. His arms were burning, but it didn't matter. So long as he kept his pace steady, the boat would continue to speed away from trouble.

Yarni stopped talking as they entered the slender waterway. It wasn't a stream. No current helped push the little vessel to the sea. Instead, the water became increasingly choppy. Both sides of the canal had wide trails that hugged the water's edge; beyond them, steep, wooded hillsides rose up.

Dod put his head down and kept paddling. Darkness was on their side. He hoped the people they would pass wouldn't notice them. Unlike the bay full of lit ships, most of the channel was void of any light. It was the twinkling stars that helped Dod differentiate water from land. He tried to keep to the center. Since the way was narrow, land was always closer than he wanted.

"Thank you," whispered Yarni.

Dod nodded. He was out of breath, but filled with hope. Now the barking dogs were too far off to hear. Into the darkness they went. When they passed the first bridge, Dod noticed how it hung within ten feet of the water. The second and third bridges hung similarly, though Dod didn't look directly at them. Upon approaching, billie voices and torches necessitated he and Yarni keep their heads down. No one followed. Perhaps if they were trying to paddle up the canal, things would have been different. Especially at the last bridge. It was well lit, and billie soldiers with weapons marched back and forth, letting visitors know that they weren't welcome.

CHAPTER THIRTY-ONE

In the cove, waves rocked the boat more than they had before. Dod fought against the swells. The distant eastern stars near the horizon were becoming faint as the sky began to lighten. The moon was on its way up. Shortly, it would pull its head from the dark sea and take its place in the sky.

"Which ship awaits us?" asked Yarni. She hadn't spoken for over an hour. Dod had begun to think she was asleep.

"None," he groaned. There were five large vessels anchored beside the island. They all looked like billie dashers. Dod had paddled the boat beyond the heavy waves near the shore and was now catching his breath as they floated aimlessly.

"You mean none of *these*," she corrected. There was a stately manner about her speech that reminded Dod she was Commendus's wife.

"No, I really do mean *none*," disclosed Dod sadly. "I arrived aboard *The Avenger* and came to shore with Traygof, but when we fought with the billies, I got separated, and they sailed away without me."

"Oh," said Yarni curtly. "Then why did you save me?"

"You looked tied up," chuckled Dod, wishing Bowlure were around to get a laugh out of his joke. He was trying to stay positive amidst the reality that they were now sitting ducks.

"Obviously," said Yarni. "But who told you I was there?"

"I stumbled upon you," responded Dod. "I just figured you'd rather take your chances with *me* than...marry one of *them*." Dod broke out in laughter. The first rays of moonlight had caught Yarni's face and shown how appalling her hair was.

"No laughing!" said Yarni. "I don't usually look dreadful! Back in Soosh, my friends would die to see me like this." She reminded Dod of an older version of Ruth.

"I'm not laughing at *you*," lied Dod, attempting to act like a gentleman. "I just think it's humorous that we're stuck."

"That's not funny."

"I know," sighed Dod. He'd been mulling over what to do for several minutes and had already decided their course, even though it wasn't a great option.

"Here's my plan," confessed Dod. "The ship over there is sitting higher out of the water than the others, so that's the one we'll board."

"What?" gasped Yarni. "Billies won't have us—not unless we're tied to a pole and scrubbing their decks. Do you know what they'd do to us?"

"I can guess," said Dod. "That's why we won't tell them we're boarding. It'll be our little secret. Soon enough, they'll sail away, and we can sneak off at the next port."

"What makes you so certain they're not planning on staying a while?"

Dod pointed. "It's sitting high in the water. They must have already taken the cargo out. Besides, it's the biggest, which means there will be more places to hide. If we stay out here, we'll get caught when the sun rises, and if we row to shore, who knows what sort of mischief will happen. They're mad that you're missing."

Yarni smiled. "I hope the ugly one gets punished for my disappearance. He was told to kill me, but thought I'd like to be his wife instead. Disgusting, right? Anyway, I'm guessing The Dread will rip him senseless when he finds out. Murdore's gonna pay."

"You were taken by The Dread?" asked Dod. The story had just gotten more interesting.

"No. But he was behind it," explained Yarni. "I was tricked away from the castle by an old lady, and the next thing I knew, I was bound and gagged and headed to sea."

"And you've seen Murdore?" pressed Dod.

"Sure. He would come around daily, testing to see if I'd changed my mind, as if I cared that The Dread had put him in charge of all those billies. He's still an ugly man—inside and out! I can't stand him! I'd rather drown than be his wife!"

"Good," smiled Dod. They were nearing the front of the dasher he'd chosen. "You've lowered your expectations to about the right level. I can't promise anything but this—you won't be marrying Murdore in the morning, and if things go well, you might even make it back to your current husband."

Beneath the bow of the ship, a stiff rope hung down and disappeared into the water. At the stern of the ship, an identical rope hung down. The two anchored lines kept the dasher from drifting.

Dod pointed upward. "I'll check it out," he whispered. "Hold onto the rope while I'm gone so you don't sail away."

In a flash, Dod zipped up the thick line and discovered a small compartment where the rope was stowed while at sea. From the deck above, men would crank a wheel that would raise the anchor and wrap the rope around a wooden pole. But the space was large enough to hold two stowaways as well. It was a perfect place to hide.

Returning to Yarni, Dod shared the good news, then swamped the little boat until it sank below the waves—to cover their tracks. Rising from the water, Dod followed Yarni up the rope, allowing her to push off of his shoulders every so far, enabling her to make the climb. It was a grueling string of tasks which sapped the rest of Dod's strength, leaving him grateful for sleep.

A few short hours later, Yarni shook Dod. "Wake up," she whispered. The boat was rocking back and forth and settling deeper into the water, as if a giant were climbing aboard. The deck above was hopping with activity and conversations. Billies were calling orders and rushing around. Their feet shook the planks above Dod and Yarni.

"Up with the anchor!" yelled someone close by. Instantly, the pole in the center of the compartment began to turn, drawing the rope from the water.

"You were right," said Yarni. "We're leaving."

Dod smiled. He didn't even mind that seawater was flying everywhere. It was a minor downside to stealing a ride in the anchor's hold.

Within minutes, the ship began to move. It headed into the moonlit sea with purpose, clearly posting all of its sails to harness the night breeze. Dod stuck his head forward and took a deep breath. It smelled like freedom.

"Where do you think we're going?" asked Yarni, working her hands through her hair for the hundredth time. It still had a few stubborn snarls.

"I don't know," said Dod. "Maybe they've spotted *The Avenger* close by. Wouldn't that be awesome? We could trade ships and sail home."

Yarni gave Dod a strange look. "You're a funny boy," she said.

Dod watched the horizon with interest. In the distance, something stuck out above the water. Was it another island or a ship? Dod couldn't tell by moonlight, but he kept watching. Eventually, it became clear that the break in the seafront was four ships, and a few minutes later, their shadows took rigid forms. They weren't dashers. It was fabulous news. They were likely merchant vessels or part of Pious's fleet. If the ships could just sail close enough, Dod was ready to jump out.

Suddenly, a high-pitched whistle blew and the dasher wobbled. From deep within the belly of the boat came a groan. The whistle blew again. This time Dod sensed what was happening. He couldn't believe it. He didn't want to believe it. It seemed impossible. But he recognized the circumstance. It was like he'd seen a movie and was now just becoming aware that he was watching it over again.

"This is bad," said Dod, shivering. His wet clothes felt cold.

"They look friendly," noted Yarni, glancing at the approaching quartet.

The whistle blew again. This time the whole ship teetered back and forth and plopped up and down in the water. Something large had just left the cargo hold, and Dod knew what it was.

"D-dragon," stuttered Yarni.

A humongous beast swooped in front of the dasher and glided out over the water, heading straight for the nearing ships. Its wingspan dwarfed a giant flutter's like a hawk would a sparrow.

"This isn't happening," groaned Dod.

"It's a *real* dragon!" said Yarni.

The beast flew toward the closest vessel and hit its center mast with its long, thorny tail. Almost instantly, a barrage of flaming arrows launched from the dasher toward the injured ship. The dragon circled its prey as if surveying the fire. The sails and deck were ablaze. Dod could see people jumping overboard. Whatever actions were being taken to hit the dragon with arrows or stones weren't working. The dragon's wings fanned the flames into a roaring inferno.

Shifting course, the three trailing vessels spread out. Dod watched as five flutters launched from their decks. Like attack pilots, the men on flutters dove at the dragon and tried to make a hit with their weapons. Perhaps arrows pelted the dragon. Dod couldn't tell. But nothing caused the gigantic beast to falter. Instead, swirling agilely in the air like a falcon, it pursued the flutters and tore them out of the sky with its teeth.

"I've got to stop it," said Dod, realizing that he had his hand on the hilt of his sword.

"Stop *that*?" burst Yarni, blinking. "Are you kidding?" The scene in front of her eyes was horrific. She clearly thought he was crazy.

Dod couldn't idly watch anymore. The dragon had finished off the aerial-assault squad and had gone back to sinking the first ship. It circled upward into the sky and then dove. Its body pounded the flaming deck and tore the bow from the hull, leaving the remaining craft in burning ruins atop the water.

"If you feel this boat going down, make sure you jump," said Dod, leaning out of the front hole.

"You're leaving me?" said Yarni, shaking.

"I've got to stop the dragon," said Dod somberly. He didn't say, but based on the horrible dreams he'd had, he feared he knew who the mayler was—the one controlling the dragon. He'd heard the person calling orders in his nightmares. It was a familiar voice, someone who Dod hoped was just misguided—tricked into The Order as Horsely had been—and who would possibly turn against The Order, regardless of the cost, if only Dod could convince him.

As Dod climbed to the upper deck, he thought of Pap and wondered whether he had known that the dragons' egg had not only been stolen, but had produced a beast. Pap had clearly been aware of the circumstance. Abbot's rescue from Driaxom testified of that much.

Dod arrived on deck just in time to see a mob of billie warriors launching another round of flaming arrows from the lower deck, this time at a different ship. The arrow tips appeared to be wrapped in rags. Each warrior would take an arrow, dip the tip into a flaming cauldron of tarjuice, move to the rail, and fire. Most of the shots hit their mark. The second vessel was beginning to burn. The dragon circled above it and seemed to wait for orders.

In the commotion, no one noticed Dod's quiet arrival, even the three billies who manned the helm a short distance away. Dod looked down at the burning pot of tarjuice. It dangled from a matrix of chains, which kept it suspended a safe distance above the wooden floor. Two sturdy derricks held the chains.

Almost instinctively, Dod made his way across the upper deck to a rope that steadied the foremast. Hand-over-hand, he climbed out over the lower deck and scurried up toward the crow's nest. From his lofty vantage, he could easily see the despair of the second burning ship. The dragon was destroying it. Its tail had just knocked down the mainmast and plowed a hole into the ship's side.

"Let's see how billies like a taste of their own medicine," said Dod, drawing his sword. He began to slice ropes that kept the dasher's foremast sails flying. By the time he'd descended to the middle of the thick post, the giant blanket of white had folded over itself, and its tip had plopped right into the cauldron of tarjuice, sending flames soaring.

Like ants scurrying, billie warriors fled the growing fire. Dod narrowly escaped its swirling heat by swinging to the lower deck. Within seconds, one of the derricks that had helped suspend the tarjuice began to sway. Its rope-pulley system had been caught in the flames and was now compromised. It teetered, reeled, and then its front dropped five feet, tipping the pot over. Flaming liquid poured onto the deck.

Through the blaze, Dod could see a caped man standing atop the upper deck on the rear of the ship. His back was to the commotion. He waved his gloved hands in the air and kept his focus on the dragon that continued its assault. Dod's heart sank. He had hoped his dream was wrong. He had hoped he wouldn't recognize the mayler. But not so. By the way the man stood and moved, Dod knew who he was.

"BOOT!" shouted Dod, racing to get around the flames. He passed billies who were futilely attempting to put the fire out. None of them seemed to have noticed that he had caused it. The opposing vessels were far enough away, it wasn't reasonable that a foe had boarded their ship.

The closer Dod got to Boot, the more Dod's senses began to tingle. He could feel the interaction between Boot and the dragon. Boot seemed to be exerting a great amount of focus to keep the beast obeying his commands. *Leave the burning ship*, he seemed to tell the dragon. *That's enough. Now you must stop. Hunt the other two! Crush them with your tail! Don't let them escape!*

NO! thought Dod. *Keep flying over the burning ship. You like to watch it.*

The dragon appeared conflicted. *I want to swim*, it seemed to say. The large creature circled the flames and glided toward the water.

Dod had passed the fire and was nearing the stairway to the mayler.

HUNT THE OTHER SHIPS! Boot seemed to command. And then, waving his hands in the air, he shouted "TOOSHI-WANNA! TOOSHI-WANNA! TOOSHI-WANNA!"

Dod shivered when he heard the mayler's voice. It was Boot's. He suddenly thought of Abbot's warning to beware of Sir Boot.

The dragon rose higher and began to fly toward one of the fleeing ships.

SWIM! thought Dod, hurrying to confront Boot. *SWIM! SWIM!*

The beast slowed its pace.

"What?" gasped the mayler, spinning around.

"Boot?" choked Dod. The man standing before him was Boot's mirror image, but older.

"GUARDS!" raged the mayler. "KILL THE BOY!"

Dod lunged forward with his blade. He knew the man. It was Boot's grandpa, the one Boot had been named after, the one Boot had mentioned with shame—Boot Bellious Dolsur the first.

The mayler dodged Dod's blade and drew his own. "How do you know my name?" he rushed, one eye still glancing toward the dragon.

"You look like your grandson," responded Dod.

The man choked a laugh. "Please! He's weak!"

Dod lunged at him again. This time the mayler deflected the blow and returned it with a burst of rage. He was good with a sword. If it hadn't been for the training Dod had received from Jack Parry and The Guys, Dod would have died. The mayler's blade narrowly missed cutting Dod's head off.

"GUARDS!" yelled the mayler again. He looked nervously toward the dragon. It had landed in the water, midway between the dasher and the enemies' retreating ships, and it seemed to be enjoying itself.

DIVE! Thought Dod, commanding the dragon to play. The dragon disappeared beneath the moonlit waves.

Boot's grandfather glared at Dod. He was furious. He swung his weapon with such force that it knocked Dod's blade out of his hands. But in so doing, the mayler's blade broke off at the hilt. Forged by the Mauj, Dod's sword was stronger.

Time seemed to slow down as Dod weighed his options. His weapon had slid across the floor and fallen off the upper deck. Billie warriors were rushing the stairs. Any minute he'd be overwhelmed by attackers. What more could he do to damage their efforts?

In a seemingly vain move, Dod tackled Boot's grandpa at the waist.

The man didn't fall. He was built solid. It was like slamming into the trunk of a seasoned tree. The mayler's grappling-hook hands seized around Dod and violently threw him across the upper deck. "You stupid boy!" raged the mayler, beating one fist upon his puffed chest. "I'll rip your head off with my bare hands! Do you really think you can beat me?"

Dod wiped his bleeding brow with his sleeve and coughed. "Yes!" he said triumphantly, holding up part of the man's precious mayler belt. He tossed it over the rail into the water. "Call your pet now."

"NO!" cried the mayler, looking for the dragon. The beast emerged from the water and flew right over the dasher. "TOOSHI-WANNA! TOOSHI-WANNA! TOOSHI-WANNA!" screamed the mayler, waving his gloved hands in the air.

Dod could feel the broken leash. The dragon didn't even turn. It sailed right past the ship and soared into the air, heading west.

"Fetch my flutter!" bellowed Boot's grandfather, knocking billies over as he thundered his way down the stairs.

Dod didn't waste any time. He rolled his bruised body to the edge of the upper deck and surveyed the scene. The whole ship was in flames. Tarjuice had dripped into the massive cargo hold and had consumed much of the hull. Any minute, the vessel would start taking on water. Billie warriors were grabbing loose planks and jumping overboard to avoid being burned. The few men who had begun coming up the stairs to get Dod had turned around and were now following the mayler down a second stairway into the stern of the ship.

A flaming rope broke free from the rearmost mast. It had been a securing line which had steadied the post. Now it lay against the wall. Dod grabbed the top of the rope, near the knot, and climbed halfway down to the lower deck, then jumped beyond the flaming portion. He scooped the white sword from the floor, stuffed it into its sheath, and dove over the burning edge of the dasher.

Plunging into the sea, Dod rose with the waves and swam toward the front of the ship. Looking skyward, he watched a flutter head west. "Good luck catching your dragon," chuckled Dod.

Upon reaching the bow, Dod saw Yarni still peering out of the anchor's hold, just as he'd left her. He yelled for her to jump.

She hesitated. The dasher began to tip sideways. It was sinking. Steam hissed from its center.

Dod continued to yell words of encouragement, but nothing could coax her off the boat. Finally, without warning, the rear of the ship sank into the water and the bow popped up, tipping the vessel completely vertical. It only stood upright for a moment before it sunk straight down. Dod took a deep breath. He was so close to the plunging hull that he could almost touch it. No sooner had the wood submerged than a wave pulled Dod under, forcing him to follow the ship down. Dod didn't fight it. He swam ferociously with the suction and caught hold of Yarni's arm, then pulled upward against the current. By the time he reached the surface, his lungs were burning for air.

Yarni was unconscious but breathing. Dod tipped her on her back and floated toward a piece of debris. It wasn't large enough to climb upon, yet it helped Dod keep himself and Yarni afloat. They bobbed up and down, waiting for Pious's ships to return in search of survivors.

Since the dragon had flown off and the billies' dasher had sunk, it was only a short while before both of the ships came back. Happily, Dod waved to them and was rescued.

To Dod's surprise, the captain of the *Muddy Toad* greeted him by name. It was General Faller, the lead officer he had dealt with at Carsigo.

"You've saved the day again!" exclaimed Faller. "You sabotaged their ship, didn't you?"

Dod nodded tiredly.

"And who's this?" asked the general. Yarni was leaning against Dod for support.

"Yarni Discommo," responded Dod.

"Oh! Yarni—of course!" General Faller quickly saluted her and tipped his head. "The lighting's poor, isn't it."

Once the general had heard of Dod's heroics, he insisted that the *Muddy Toad* sail straight for Fisher, while the other ship sail back to Fort Castle to report the news to Pious of the billies' hidden bay and the dragon.

Dod was surprised to find that most of the sailors had been fearing a dragon for months. Rumors had spread that a mayler, much like the legendary Boodwana, had tamed a dragon and had been rallying the billies to follow him. What they'd just witnessed was confirmation of everything they'd already feared.

As Dod drifted off to sleep in the captain's quarters—in General Faller's bed—a thought crossed his mind. He'd heard Boot's grandfather once before. It was at the Old Pier House, at Fort Castle. He was the visitor that had joined the wayward soldiers in getting food for a beast. Dod knew it was him, but Dod was too tired to think of how or why Boot's grandpa had been there. For now things were perfect. Dod was in a cozy bed and headed for the mainland.

CHAPTER THIRTY-TWO

SNEAKER'S DISCOVERY

It was lunchtime before Dod awoke. General Faller's bed was soft and warm, and the thick shutters did a great job of keeping the morning light out. Stretching and yawning, Dod emerged from the captain's suite feeling more refreshed than he'd felt in weeks. His stomach bubbled with excitement over the idea of returning to Twistyard. What would his friends think? It would be like he had come back from the dead. And Boot would die when he heard how Dod had fought with his grandpa and sunk his ship.

Yarni sat at a table on the open deck, taking in the breeze. "Thanks for saving my life *twice*," she said as Dod approached. "I was out of it last night."

"Why wouldn't you jump?" teased Dod.

Yarni rolled her eyes.

"It's the hero!" boomed General Faller, strolling up to rap Dod on the shoulder. His massive frame blocked the sun. "Neadrou was right about you. He said you were full of surprises...and well...I'm surprised. You rescued Commendus's wife, found the billie dashers, and chased away a dragon. Not to mention, aren't you the reason their ship sank?"

Dod smiled as he nodded. "But Yarni and I would have drowned without you, so that makes *you* the hero, sir," responded Dod.

General Faller chuckled. "We were happy to fish you out," he said. "By tomorrow morning, we should make port. I'll have some of my men escort you to Twistyard."

"We'll go, sir," offered a few sailors who stood nearby. They eyed Dod with the same look he'd seen Toos give Traygof.

Dod liked being respected. It felt much better than being seen as a criminal. And since he had single-handedly saved Yarni, he was certain that Commendus would fully support him in getting the murder charges worked out.

The *Muddy Toad* moved quickly through the water, catching the breeze in its sails. It wasn't quite as fast as *The Avenger*, but by early the next day, Dod and Yarni were being rowed to shore. And just as General Faller had promised, an entourage of sailors forthwith escorted them to Twistyard.

Darkness had long since cloaked the castle by the time they arrived. Dod thanked the tredder sailors and left them with the drat guards that were encamped in the courtyard. As he led Yarni away, he heard Faller's men begin to tell the guards of how Dod had fought a dragon. It put a smile on Dod's sleepy face to think of all the ways they would likely embellish that story.

Outside of the Great Hall, piles of rocks sat beside each door. *I wonder who died,* thought Dod, and then it hit him—they were likely in remembrance of *his* death.

Since it was well past midnight, Dod showed Yarni to Green Hall instead of bothering Youk or Voracio for accommodations.

He knocked on the door leading to the girls' rooms. His heart was thumping. He wasn't sure what to say, and it had crossed his mind that Dilly and Sawny were likely at High Gate delivering the scepter to Commendus.

Dilly answered and immediately broke into tears. She leapt forward and grabbed Dod in a hug, exclaiming to Sawny that Dod was alive. It was only moments before Boot, Buck, and others joined Sawny in surrounding Dod. They had spent the day talking about his life and had begun plans for a memorial service.

"I'm not *that* easy to kill," remarked Dod, feeling grateful for their friendship. Sawny was giving him an especially favorable eye, and Boot kept rapping him on the back. Dod's friends were so glad to see him that it took them several minutes to notice Yarni. Once they had, Dod simply informed them that he had found her while escaping the island. Most of Dod's explanations were greatly abbreviated. He didn't even mention the dragon. With all of Green Hall present, it wasn't the right setting to reveal things about his medallion, or Boot's corrupt grandpa, or the hidden bay filled with dashers. The truth had to be truncated. Fortunately, with the late hour drawing yawns from most of the Greenlings and Coosings, well wishes were accepted quickly and everyone sauntered off to their rooms before too many questions had been asked.

Boot and Buck, of course, pushed for more information while Dod readied himself for bed, but knowing Dilly and Sawny would want to hear the stories too, Dod assured them that they would get every juicy detail later, and he let things end there, claiming he was too tired to stay up.

Strangely, despite their enthusiasm, Boot and Buck fell asleep within minutes, while Dod lay awake. He couldn't push from his mind the feeling of concern he'd gotten when he'd heard that Ingrid had accompanied Juny to deliver the special scepter to Commendus. Yarni's abduction story had forever changed Dod's view of older women. Could Ingrid be a traitor? Maybe. She was certainly cranky and rude at times. Perhaps she'd allowed her hunger for attention to lead her into The Order. It bothered Dod that he couldn't get on the phone and call Commendus. Either the scepter had arrived or it hadn't.

In the morning, Dod awoke to the sound of singing in the hall. It was a song about Kray and Yark. Clearly, someone was spreading news about his encounter.

"You didn't tell me you saw a *dragon*!" exploded Boot, rushing into the room.

"I was saving that story for today," mumbled Dod, rubbing his eyes.

"How could you hold back about a *dragon*?" pressed Boot excitedly. "Yarni told us she thinks its from the egg that was stolen. Can you believe it? The stories about Kray and Yark must be true. No wonder the billies love their shrine so much."

"Yup," said Dod.

"But how could they control it?" mused Boot. "Do you think a mayler would have any luck with a creature like that?"

Dod looked at Boot. "Shut the door for a minute," he said. Dod rose to his feet and went to the closet to dress.

"What is it?" asked Boot.

"There was a mayler who worked the dragon," confessed Dod. "It was your grandpa."

Boot stood in silence.

"I'm sorry to tell you," said Dod. He went on to explain about his confrontation with the billies and Boot's grandpa, and how he'd watched Boot's grandpa fly away on a flutter, chasing after the dragon.

"I'm not surprised," shrugged Boot. "Years ago when everyone said he was dead, I let them know I didn't believe it—not after the things I saw him do in Driaxom. Someone that dark and cold can't die easy. It'll take a lot to send him where he belongs—" Boot tipped his head at Dod. "And I suppose the two of us are just the people to send him there."

Dod took the Chantolli Sword and sheath from his charred belt and put it on. "Take a look at this," he said, drawing the blade out. "It's the third sword."

"You found it!" smiled Boot. "Now we have all three."

Buck entered the bedroom and called out for Boot and Dod. "They're getting the horses ready," he announced, searching until he found them. "You'll both need to eat breakfast on the hoof. We can't miss the dropping of the triblot barrier. Yarni's been gone long enough." Buck's grin grew until it touched both ears. "Won't Commendus be surprised?" he said. "I can't wait to see his face when we escort her in."

"I can't wait to see Sabbella's," chuckled Boot. "She'll probably swallow one of her finches."

On the way to High Gate, Dod took the opportunity to explain almost everything to Boot, Buck, Dilly, and Sawny about what had happened on the island, though he couldn't bring himself to tell them how his medallion had been the key to his escape. Instead, he skipped straight to the part about him crawling into the thickets to hide. Sawny gave him a knowing look, as if to say she recognized that there was more to his story and she hoped he'd tell it to her later.

To keep their conversation private, Dod and his friends rode a short distance behind Yarni and the battalion of tredder sailors who insisted on escorting her to Commendus. Boot proudly wore the crimson blade Commendus had awarded to Dod, and Dilly sat taller with the Tillius blade at her side. They figured it would be fitting to display the kingly weapons while receiving commendations from Commendus for recovering the scepter and saving his wife.

As they neared High Gate, the subject of Concealio and the Code of the Kings resurfaced. Dilly praised the idea of reinstituting the brotherhood but added that she hoped Commendus would be broadminded enough to include women as well as men in the group. She clearly envisioned herself holding the Tillius scepter and wearing the Tillius sword as the head representative from Green to the three-realm council. It made Dod chuckle. Commendus obviously planned on being the chief leader from Green.

Sawny appeared to be deep in thought. Eventually she joined the conversation. "Traygof said that Raul's scepter was a key, right?"

"That's what he said," chirped Boot. He and Sneaker seemed to enjoy riding on Grubber alone. They'd been doubling with Buck since Buck's horse had been killed, but upon returning from the sea, Traygof had purchased a fine stallion for Buck before rushing to join Pious at Fort Castle.

"Well," said Sawny. "Maybe that's what Concealio was referring to on the plaque."

"Treasures?" questioned Buck excitedly, nudging his white stallion to drop back toward Sawny. "How did Concealio know about Raul's vaults?"

"No. That's not what I meant," grinned Sawny. "On the front wall of the monument, he's got that saying—the one that replaced the three chairs. Didn't it say something about a door being opened when the scepters were in hand?"

"I remember that," said Dod. His gut told him she was onto something.

"If we could just get all three scepters," sighed Sawny, "wouldn't it be nice to try them out? Who knows what Concealio may have hidden—possibly more clues. I'm starting to think our map to The Lost City is more than a map to The Lost City. It's a map to something hidden within The Lost City."

"Treasures!" repeated Buck. "Rooms filled with gold."

Sawny looked at Buck and rolled her eyes. "A few days aboard *The Avenger* was too much for you. No more sailing!"

"It's not that," responded Buck defensively. "If dragons are real, who knows which legends are true. They're probably all true! The Lost City is filled with gold—mountains of it. Can you imagine what we could buy?"

"I wouldn't waste my time on such things," said Sawny, prodding her horse to speed up beside Dilly's.

"That's because you Tillius girls already have everything," called Buck. "If you had more money, what would you buy, Dod?"

"A house for *your mother*!" responded Sawny, speaking up for Dod. She was reminding Buck how Dod had selflessly given up all of Pap's gold coins to him and his brothers.

"Thanks again," said Boot, turning to Dod. "Bowy's helping Mom find a place. He sent a letter to Twistyard saying that they've narrowed it down to three choices. Once she's moved in, you'll have to come with us to see it. I still can't believe you did that. It's the nicest thing anyone's ever done for her."

"Yeah, thanks," added Buck sincerely.

"It's okay," said Dod, feeling a little guilty. If he could have used the money to have helped his own family, he wouldn't have given it to them—not with his mom pulling extra shifts at the diner to make ends meet. To Dod, the coins had felt like play money, not real gold. What did he need money for in Green anyway? If he could have, he would have happily traded Pap's whole bag of coins to have been able to bring home a few thousand dollars to Earth.

Up ahead, the bells began ringing. The triblot field was coming down. Their timing couldn't have been better. Dilly sped up so she could enter beside Yarni.

"Typical Dilly," laughed Sawny to Dod. They lagged back and watched her. Dilly's voice rose above the others, proudly informing the officers on duty that she had just returned from sailing the seas with Traygof.

"Is she really your sister?" teased Dod.

Sawny smiled shyly.

The blocks of construction in front of Commendus's estate were as busy as Dod had ever seen them. In some places, deep foundations were being dug—even deeper than the old ones. Workers were everywhere, and their tent city covered all of the land directly beside the fence that enclosed Discommo Manor. Dod surveyed the endless commotion. He couldn't help thinking of Sirlonk and his determination to find The Lost City, even if it meant destroying all of High Gate.

In the distance, a strange thing caught Dod's eyes. He blinked twice and wished he had a pair of binoculars. There was a tethered horse that was laden down with a gigantic bag on its back. The load looked extremely similar to the one he'd seen Sirlonk riding off with when he and Buck had confronted Sirlonk in the master barn back at Twistyard, weeks before. Was it a corpse? Maybe Sirlonk was overseeing the site and killing workers who slowed his progress. It was probably nothing, but Dod still wanted to check it out.

Dod pulled on Shooter's reigns and brought the horse to a stop.

"Aren't you coming?" asked Sawny.

"I'll be there in a minute," said Dod. "Go on without me."

Sawny looked forward nervously. "Can't you come now?" she pled.

Dod quickly realized why. The others had sped up and were halfway to Commendus's castle, leaving Sawny to ride beside the lake by herself. Soldiers no longer guarded the water's edge for escaping baby duressers.

"Please," begged Sawny, pushing hair from her face.

Dod tapped Shooter forward. "I'm coming," he said, "so long as you promise not to slap me if a nut *accidentally* hits the water."

"It wasn't an accident!" smiled Sawny. She looked at Dod's cheeks and seemed to be recalling the marks she'd given him the night he'd teased her beside the lake.

Inside the castle, Commendus greeted the group with a curious look, then nearly passed out when Yarni stepped forward. Sabbella stormed off as if Commendus had been leading her along with lies. No one hugged. But given the circumstance, where Commendus had approached with Sabbella dripping off his arm, it only made sense that Yarni didn't rush to show affection. Dod felt bad for her. She'd endured a horrendous experience and had returned home to find her husband contently moving on with his life.

A curt thank you was all Dod got before Commendus whisked Yarni away to speak privately. However, lunch sweetened the disappointment. With the business convention over, the castle was back to its regular level of service, meaning, Dod was able to join Buck and Boot in eating as much as they wanted. Dod had three slices of blueberry cream pie before stopping.

The only businessman left in the banquet hall was Dilly's favorite person—Bly! He sat across the room at a table with Dr. Shelderhig and Newmi. Dilly made sure Dod and Boot didn't venture over, as they jokingly threatened they would. She said she was having a good day and didn't want it spoiled. Unlike some visits to the palace, she didn't have to worry about Con, since Acor had taken a liking to him and had invited him to stay aboard *The Avenger* for a spell.

While waiting to speak further with Commendus, Dilly tried to track down the whereabouts of Ingrid, Juny, and Bonboo, but was told by one of her favorite waiters that he hadn't seen Juny and Ingrid, and Bonboo had left for Raul two days before.

Dod didn't like hearing that Bonboo was gone. He had felt frustrated that Traygof had sailed away without telling him about Humberrone, and as a result, Dod had hoped, even more than before, to have had a face-to-face with Bonboo. Where was Humberrone? Why hadn't Bonboo mentioned he was his father? Dod knew he was alive. He could feel him, just as much as he could feel his fingers and toes. After freeing Yarni from bondage and facing a dragon, Dod felt like he was ready for any challenge. It didn't matter where Humberrone was or what trouble he was in. Dod wanted to find him.

When Commendus finally made time to speak with the group, he met them in a quiet room and looked different than Dod had ever seen him. His face was red and puffy, as if he'd been crying nonstop since the moment he'd walked away from them four hours before, and his voice quivered. "Thank you for saving Yarni," he humbly said. "I was an idiot to believe my sources when they informed me she was dead. Everything is political to some people."

"You couldn't have known," offered Dilly. "Dod was lucky to have found her."

"I really am grateful," he said wearily, glancing at Dod. "I owe you. You're a hero, just like your grandfather."

"And he's the one who discovered the scepter, too," added Sawny.

Commendus sighed. He appeared to have just remembered his heavy agenda regarding his lofty plans to recreate the Code of the Kings. "Where is it?" he asked. "Is Traygof coming?"

"Juny and Ingrid should have arrived yesterday!" said Boot, keeping Sneaker hidden beneath his shirt. "Haven't you seen them?"

"No," said Commendus flatly. He looked so emotionally drained that it seemed as though nothing could alarm him.

"They had the scepter!" burst Boot. "They promised they'd come straight here! Where could they be?"

Commendus shrugged his shoulders. "I'm terribly sorry," he said. "I'm not feeling well. Perhaps you can speak with Turly. They may have given it to him." Without another word, Commendus staggered from the room and was gone.

"It's been stolen!" groaned Dilly. "The Dread's taken it!"

"Or Turly has it," offered Sawny unconvincingly.

CHAPTER THIRTY-TWO

The group rushed to find Commendus's Chief Security Officer. Just as they'd feared, Turly hadn't seen Ingrid or Juny, and worse still, he had additional news that almost certainly proved the scepter had been taken: He had received word from Raul that one of the reasons war had broken out in Soosh, according to the messenger who had declared the sad tidings, was because Soosh's special scepter had vanished, and various clans of noble tredders had claimed the others had stolen it as a sign of their right to rule. Its disappearance from their Assembly Building had been the last straw.

Leaving Turly, the group bolted for their horses. Boot proposed they rush to the museum where Green's scepter was kept and warn the security officials there. His eyes showed he was ready to fight. The Dread was on the move. Even Sneaker appeared to sense it—he shifted back and forth between Boot's shoulders and sniffed the air cautiously.

As Shooter trotted through the construction site, Dod remembered what he'd seen. "Boot, hold up!" he called. "Sirlonk may be here in the tent city."

"He could be anywhere!" shouted Boot in frustration. It was clear he was in torment. They'd miraculously obtained the scepter only to have it taken by The Dread. And Boot had personally told Traygof he'd make sure the scepter reached Commendus quickly. If it hadn't been for the memorial service preparations at Twistyard, he would have delivered it himself, but given the circumstance, he had trusted Ingrid and Juny to make the delivery. Now he seemed trapped in a slump of regret.

"I saw something earlier," said Dod. "Can we give it a couple of minutes?"

Boot glanced anxiously around at the sea of organized chaos. "If he's stolen two of the three scepters, he'll be headed for the third, assuming it's not already gone. We should go now."

"Please," begged Dod. "We have to check something out. I've got a feeling."

Boot consented begrudgingly.

Dod led the group through the maze of tents and people to the spot where he'd seen the tethered horse with the unusual cargo. It was gone. Dod frantically looked around. There was no sign of the horse. Tredders and drats came and went in an almost constant flow. Thousands of people were working at the site in shifts, and the tent city was used by them around the clock for eating and sleeping.

"It was right here," said Dod, pointing to a post.

"What?" pressed Boot impatiently.

"Sirlonk's stuff—I think."

Sneaker hopped off of Boot's shoulder and scurried around on the ground, stretching his legs.

"Come on, Sneaker!" shouted Boot. "We're leaving!"

Sneaker ignored Boot and darted in and out of the neighboring tents.

"We're wasting time," complained Dilly. "We might catch him at the museum if we hurry. He's probably taken Ingrid and Juny as hostages."

"That doesn't sound like his style," muttered Buck.

"Juny's his wife!" exploded Boot. "I'm such an idiot! She's got to be helping him. Why did I trust them? Juny has likely overpowered Ingrid and run off to meet her husband."

"I don't think so," said Sawny. "Juny looked sincerely happy on *The Avenger* with Traygof. I think she's had a change of heart.

I doubt she cares two bits for Sirlonk anymore. She was planning on getting back together with Traygof after he gets done chasing Dreaderious with Pious—or, at least, that's what she said in the queen's suite. Of course, Traygof's list of things to do may be longer now that the dashers were discovered—"

"And there's a dragon!" added Buck, as if wishing he were back on *The Avenger*. Dod knew that Boot and Buck hadn't had their fill of sailing, but with Dod's presumed death, they had sobered enough to return to Twistyard with the girls.

Farther down the row, Sneaker emerged from a tent and ran in circles. He was right in the way of foot traffic. People kept narrowly missing him.

"Get over here, Sneaker!" yelled Boot. "You're gonna get trampled!"

The ferret didn't come.

"Get over here!" he yelled again.

Still no response.

Finally, Boot slid off of his horse and angrily stomped toward the ferret. "We've got to go!" he ordered.

Sneaker darted under the leather tail of the closest canopy tent and disappeared.

Dod jumped down to join Boot in retrieving his pet. The tent Sneaker had chosen was mostly empty. It had a few wooden chairs surrounding a three-legged table.

"Come on!" scolded Boot, chasing the ferret into a corner. Dod was right behind him.

But Sneaker wasn't done running. When Boot reached to scoop him up, the ferret ducked under the lip of the back lining.

"What's gotten into him?" asked Dilly, meeting Boot and Dod at the door of the tent as they exited empty-handed.

"He's feeding off of Boot's anger," said Sawny, still seated on her horse.

"I'm not angry!" huffed Boot, and then he paused. "Not at him anyway. It's just frustrating that I let my guard down. Now Traygof will never trust me to help him. I've got to get that scepter back!"

"Sneaker," said Dilly in a smooth, motherly voice. "Come on, boy. Daddy's not mad at you."

The ferret remained hidden.

"I'll go get him," said Dod, sliding between the exterior of the tent and the next one. He squeezed through the narrow space and pressed toward the rear, when Sneaker emerged holding a wig in his mouth, as if he'd just killed it. Dod stared. He recognized the ugly curls.

"Do you need my help?" called Dilly.

"You've got to see this!" exploded Dod, gaping dumbfounded. The pieces were coming together. Boot and Dilly pushed after Dod, and Dod followed Sneaker who turned and pranced away with his prize.

Directly behind the large canopy was a smaller tent with no doors. To enter, Dod had to pull up two stakes and slide under. Sneaker had discovered a storage chamber, and in it was only one thing—the hefty bag that Dod had seen on the back of Sirlonk's horse.

"He's found it!" said Dod excitedly. "This is Sirlonk's!"

Boot and Dilly joined him. Sneaker was proudly sitting upon the bulging bag. Dod unlaced the top and tugged at the sides until the mouth opened. Inside was a very large costume!

"This can't be," stuttered Boot. He looked shocked and confused.

"What? How?" said Dilly in horror.

"Bonboo said it before," whispered Dod. "He's a master of disguise."

"But...no...this isn't—" Boot began to pull a huge, padded bodysuit from the bag.

"Ingrid?" gasped Dilly.

"He's traded places with her?" mumbled Boot.

"Or he's been *her* from the start," said Dod. "Think about it. She's always looked a bit odd, and who do you think killed all of those people in Raul? Doesn't that sound like something The Dread would do, especially if they had just barely tried to poison his wife and son?"

"But it can't be!" insisted Dilly. "I introduced her to so many people."

"You told me she was Higga's cousin," said Boot to Dilly.

"Well, she said she was," defended Dilly. "Besides, you're the one who went with her to Higga's house—"

"She had the key!" insisted Boot. "I saw her letter from Higga and assumed it was genuine."

"When Terro was stuck in Driaxom, Sawb still got letters," reminded Dod. "Sirlonk's good at faking mail."

All of the times Ingrid's voice had lowered when she'd gotten mad or excited, all of the times she'd fidgeted with her face and hair, all of the times she'd surprised them with something—a rare book or a way out of trouble—it all made more sense. She was Sirlonk. It was no wonder why Ingrid hadn't wanted Boot to push her in the wheelchair—she recognized he would likely detect that she didn't weigh as much as she looked. And the time she had entered the dock at Fort Castle without papers, they hadn't blown off a ship as she had defended, she hadn't had any authorization in the first place! It all fit. Sirlonk had been pulling a big scam, moving freely at Twistyard and High Gate, rubbing shoulders with important people, and getting introduced by none other than Dilly and Boot.

"I think I'm gonna be sick," mumbled Dilly, turning pale.

Boot appeared to be scanning his mind for all of the interactions he had had with Ingrid. His face grew more and more concerned by the second. "I called her Grandma," he winced. "If that was Sirlonk—"

"Oh, it was," assured Dod. "Can't you feel it? He's been playing us. That's how he knew so much about our circumstance when I spoke with him in the pump house."

"He's been using us," grumbled Dilly.

Boot's face instantly lit up. "We'll catch him!" he declared happily, stuffing the costume back into the bag. He had to fight with Sneaker to get the wig, but he eventually prevailed. "When Ingrid shows up and plays her game of hobbling and huffing and whining, we'll quietly pull guards into the mix and then reveal her! Sirlonk's going down for the crimes he's done. He'll be off to Driaxom, and everyone will know he's been parading around as a girl. It'll be great." Boot smiled broadly. "It'll be better than great."

CHAPTER THIRTY-THREE

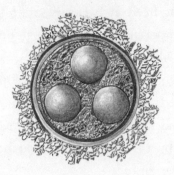

REVEALING SECRETS

Once the costume had been stowed properly to make it look untouched, Boot made Dilly and Dod promise that they wouldn't tell a soul of their findings—except, of course, Sawny and Buck. In order for the trap to work, Sirlonk would have to reappear as Ingrid.

But for good measure, Boot still led the way to the museum where Green's scepter was kept. Dod could see in Boot's eyes he was serious about catching Sirlonk. The crimson blade Boot wore at his waist seemed to boost his confidence.

"Museum of Antiquities," mumbled Dod. He walked between Sawny and Dilly to the little brick building that reportedly held Green's scepter. Boot and Buck strode in the front with steps that left Dod and the Tillius sisters lagging.

"Do you think it's still here?" asked Sawny.

Dod shook his head. "I bet he's already taken it."

"But why?" said Dilly. "He's got the one that's a key to the treasures in Raul."

"The Code of the Kings Monument," responded Sawny. "It's like I was saying earlier, I think the three staffs work together to open a door in the hall. Concealio's hidden something there. And now that we know more about our *elderly foe*, think back. She was adamant that we not poke anything into the scepter holders. Do you remember how quickly she jumped when Boot started to prod at one of them with her cane?"

Dilly giggled as Dod opened the door for them. "It was a strange sight to see her hop up on the stage like that," she said.

"And for what?" asked Dod rhetorically. "To save her special cane? I don't think so. She had no problem letting Trimash take it as a trade for his ugly, fur-covered staff."

"That's how he got it!" exploded Sawny. "It had to have been Soosh's scepter! The Order must have obtained it for Sirlonk and had Trimash wrap it in furs so Sirlonk would be able to smuggle it out of Raul."

"Shhhh," whispered Dilly, "he's well connected." She looked forward toward a domed room which held six guards. Boot and Buck were already talking with one of them.

Dod smelled the air. It was thick with the aroma of fresh paint.

"It's still here," said Boot quietly, catching Dilly's arm in the entry foyer. "Sirlonk will probably come soon. The sun will be setting in an hour. I warned the men, but they laughed. They said they just barely had their forces doubled today because of Soosh's missing scepter. Now there are six more soldiers in the viewing chamber."

"Twelve men," said Sawny. "That's only a start. Do they know who they're dealing with?"

"We should stick around," said Dilly eagerly, looking down at her special Tillius sword with excitement.

Sawny disagreed. "Let's go back to Commendus's palace and convince him to send a battalion of guards. They'd do a better job than we would."

Boot smiled at Sawny. "We can do both," he said. "You can ride back and tell him we need reinforcements, and we'll hide in the shrubs nearby."

"Can't we wait in here with the soldiers?" asked Buck.

"Not with this smell," insisted Dilly, wrinkling her nose.

"If you think we've got it bad," chuckled Boot, "the six soldiers in the viewing chamber must be dying. That's where they've been painting."

Dod had a funny feeling. "Did you see the scepter?" he nervously inquired.

Boot read Dod's face. Without another word, the whole group stripped their weapons off, per the requirements, and plowed across the domed section of the building to the stinky viewing chamber. Within, six guards stood near a covered box. Tarps were draped all over the room. It was currently useless as an open museum. All of the displayed items were blanketed to protect them against the white paint that had recently been applied.

Dilly smiled and used her charm until the tredder men on duty finally consented to pull the coverings off of the largest glass case. To everyone's astonishment, the scepter was gone!

Minutes later, Grubber and Song set a galloping pace toward the Code of the Kings Monument, with Buck, Sawny, and Dod nudging their horses to follow close behind them. It was a race to the finish line. The Dread, almost certainly, had all three scepters;

and based on Ingrid's actions, he seemed convinced that a prize lay in store for whomever used them first.

Upon entering the Pines District, they galloped up the empty walkway. It was a quiet evening. No one was around. The only sounds were the horses' hooves against the stone path and the mild breeze that occasionally whistled in the pines.

"Do you remember how Ingrid told us her brothers were killed by The Dread?" called Boot over his shoulder, slowing down. He had reached the place where she had mentioned it. "I'm sure she was trying to take the map from us. It proves the map is valuable." Boot smiled gleefully. "The Order must be putting pressure on Sirlonk to get it back."

"When you say '*she*,' you mean '*he*,' right?" smirked Sawny. Dilly had just teased Boot about pushing Sirlonk as Ingrid in the wheelchair.

Boot rolled his eyes and led on.

Dod looked over at the Chards Museum as they passed it. "Ooblies," he muttered, wondering whether Sirlonk had created the term. Either way, Sirlonk had known about them—he had accurately described the contents of the pouch without looking inside. Dod wondered what the blue stones were. He was almost certain that another similar pouch had been at the center of the fight Pap had waged against The Dread at the Chards Museum.

"I forgot—no keys," said Dilly as the group dismounted near the Code of the Kings Monument. An unpleasant smell wafted in the air from a pile of burlap sacks that held garbage.

"We don't need them," responded Boot. "It's open. The construction workers must have forgotten to shut it all the way."

"And they forgot to haul off the trash, too," declared Dilly, plugging her nose.

"Workers have to eat," said Boot, glancing at the pile of bags. Chicken bones and corn cobs were falling out. "Judging from that mound, Commendus is serious about getting this place fixed up. He's hired an army."

Dod surveyed the sight. A rat scurried from the trash pile and entered the monument through a slit where a door was slightly ajar. It looked like someone had forced his way into the building, leaving the door unable to close properly. Sneaker hopped from Boot's shoulder and raced after the rat.

"Maybe we should wait outside until the soldiers get here," offered Sawny. "The sun's already down."

"They'll take forever," argued Boot. "The lanky one told us that before soldiers could be sent, he had to first go and report the missing scepter to High Gate's central command post. That could easily be hours. I'm not waiting." Boot readily marched after Sneaker who had already entered the structure.

"Hold up," called Dilly, hurrying to accompany him.

Buck stayed near the horses. "I'll keep a watch out here," he said.

Sawny inched closer to Dod. "They're crazy," she whispered. "What if Sirlonk's in there?"

Boot and Dilly swung the door open wide.

"What happened?" gasped Dilly.

Sawny and Dod hurried over. The inside of the hall was more broken than before, though in different spots. The four stone posts which had littered the cracked floor were now standing firmly, holding up the rafters, and below them, new benches shined with a glow of freshly waxed wood. But toward the front of the hall, two areas were completely wrecked. Seven posts had fallen, leaving thirteen benches destroyed and the roof compromised. It was questionable how safe the structure was.

"Maybe Sirlonk's tearing the place down, piece by piece, in search of something," said Boot, entering the hall. He fearlessly went straight to the rubble and began inspecting it.

"The air's dusty," noted Sawny. "The posts probably collapsed today."

Dod followed Sawny to the stage. She bent down and examined the three holes where the scepters would go.

"What do you think?" asked Dod.

"He's been here," sighed Sawny disappointedly. "I wonder what he found."

"How do you know?" pressed Dod.

Sawny pointed at a faint golden scratch near the center hole. "He tried the staffs," she said. Then, sadly reading the plaque on the back wall, Sawny emphasized the words "*every man's scepter in hand*," as if bemoaning that she didn't have one.

"*Every* man's scepter?" repeated Dod. "Only kings have scepters."

"But Concealio wanted democracy," said Sawny. "He wanted his people to share in the responsibilities of liberty. That's why he sought to reinstate the Code of the Kings. He wanted twenty-four men to help lead the realms, not one or three."

"You're right!" said Dod, feeling a burst of inspiration. It made the tips of his toes tingle to consider the logic that was flowing through his brain. "What scepter does every man have?"

"I don't know," said Sawny. She appeared to sense Dod's excitement.

"What does it take to stay free?" hinted Dod.

Boot and Dilly approached.

Dod stepped back and counted the slits in the stone—the ones next to the engravings. "Didn't you say that the kings would post their scepters and then sit in puffy chairs?"

"I'm not sure how puffy they were," responded Sawny, "but they sat in chairs, and their men knelt on the floor."

"Exactly!" boomed Dod. "Concealio changed things! That's not what he intended. If we had his writings, perhaps books that have been lost, or pages from books—"

"His diary pages!" snapped Dilly.

Dod nodded. "If we knew what he had intended," continued Dod, speaking faster, "I suspect we'd find that the kings' scepters were meant to be retired as symbols of things in the past—things that didn't work—a system that only led to destruction!" Dod pointed at the ruined parts of the hall. "Maybe that's what happened when Sirlonk tried to use them."

Sawny's eyes lit up.

"Concealio rebuilt this stage!" she said. "He could have installed triggers that would cause the beams to collapse if the scepters were ever inserted. One of the books I read at Commendus's house was written by Concealio's son. It had a sketch that showed wax or clay over the holes."

"*Ingrid* sure didn't want me putting her cane into one," added Boot. "She had probably already tried it out earlier in the week."

"And it caused the first collapse," said Dod.

"Then what does the plaque mean?" pressed Dilly. "Every man's scepter…"

Dod reached down and drew his sword. "Liberty comes at a price that every free man must be willing to pay. By our voices we vote our opinions, and if the majority is overruled by a dictatorship, let every man take up his *scepter*." Dod waved his white blade in the air, displaying the words, "*Chantolli, Power for All.*"

"Swords," mumbled Sawny gleefully.

"Count the slits in the stone," said Dod. "There aren't twenty-one, there are twenty-four! In Concealio's plan, even the head representatives from each realm were to kneel side-by-side with the other men and stow their swords, too!"

Dod took a deep breath, pointed the sword at the ground, and plunged it into the slit that had the Chantolli insignia carved into the stone beside it.

A groaning sound bellowed from beneath the stage.

"It's releasing the door of things forbidden," said Sawny excitedly. "Quick, Dilly, use the Tillius sword."

Dilly and Boot studied the carvings on the floor.

"It's right there," said Sawny.

Dilly drew her family's blade and plunged it into the Tillius slit. The ground groaned again, this time making a snapping sound, as if taut ropes were being severed.

From the back of the hall, Buck whistled. "We've got company approaching," he hollered. "I can hear their horses. They may be soldiers, but I doubt it. Sneaker's out here doing circles."

"Use your sword!" begged Sawny, looking to Boot.

"Which hole?" he responded. "What's the sign for Chards?"

Sawny, Dilly, Boot, and Dod all hurried up and down the half circle of carvings on the floor in search of the right one. Since the scepters had seemed to have caused the posts to collapse, they didn't want to randomly guess or try all of the other slots. It was too dangerous.

Dod's eyes finally landed on one simple carving near the end of the row. He recognized it. He'd seen it once before. His heart beat within him, telling him that it was the right one. Yet when he considered where he'd previously seen the mark, he felt hesitant to suggest that they try it.

"Dod?" pressed Sawny urgently. "Have you found it?"

"Sneaker's going nuts," called Buck from the doorway. "We should go and hide before they get here."

"Lead our horses into the forest," yelled Boot. "We're coming."

Dod trembled. "I think this is the insignia for Chards," he said, pointing at a circle which had three smaller circles engraved within it. The mark looked exactly like the one Josh had drawn on the crown he'd given to Dod for Christmas.

Boot bent on one knee beside Dod, took the crimson blade in both hands, and thrust it into the slit.

The floor began to shake, and the large stone upon which the front plaque was fastened began to slide backward, revealing a hidden compartment.

"It's working!" cried Sawny.

Boot jumped off the stage, grabbed three burlap sacks from the first pew, and flew back to the crimson blade in time to draw it out of the floor the moment the massive stone had stopped moving. Dod and Dilly sheathed their swords as well.

"It won't be gold," assured Sawny, moving gingerly with the others to the opening.

Boot waved the burlap sacks. "I'm ready just in case," he said breathlessly.

The treasure was a pile of fifteen books. They looked old like the one Ingrid had shown to them. Sawny dusted the first one off. In big letters were written *TCC* across the top, and in smaller letters were written three names down the front. TCC didn't stand for True Climbers Club, or not according to the book Sawny held. The letters stood for *Tillius*, *Chantolli*, and *Chards*. Sawny flipped to the first page. A dedication was given by the author: *In honor of the greatest scientist, Rea Bonboo Chards. May his legacy be forever remembered.*

Dod grabbed the next book. It didn't display a title, but the thick leather front had ten round circles imprinted into it. They looked like ooblies. Dod carefully turned the pages. There were detailed maps that showed what had occupied the land before the birth of the Ankle Weed Desert, and there were drawings of a terrible storm or explosion. Dod hungered to sit down and read every page. It seemed to be a compilation of accounts, as if someone had gathered parts of journals or records.

Boot and Dilly both reached for the next book. It was entitled, *Visits to The Lost City*. And beneath it was one called, *The Zoots*.

Suddenly, a distant clanking noise brought the foursome back to reality. Buck had warned of approaching danger. They didn't have time to flip through books, they had to grab them and run!

Boot stuffed the whole pile into one of the burlap sacks and threw it over his shoulder. "Let's go!" he said, tugging at Dilly who kept inspecting the empty compartment.

More clanking sounded.

At the open doorway, Boot paused to peek around the corner. He instantly dropped the sack and ran from the building yelling. Sawny put the bag over her shoulder as Dod and Dilly warily stole a glimpse of what had provoked Boot. Two men in uniforms were dueling against Buck, who seemed to be losing ground. Boot was rushing to his aid with the crimson blade in hand. Behind the two soldiers were three more on horseback, watching the duel.

"It's the soldiers—they've begun to arrive," said Dilly. "Why are they fighting with Buck? There must be a misunderstanding."

Dod had a bad feeling. "They're here too quickly," he muttered. "Stay inside." Dod took a deep breath and slowly walked out the door. He hoped his presence and stride would make the men fear there were others coming, possibly many more. It was a bluff, and it didn't work.

The three horsemen dismounted and drew their swords. They clearly intended on staying to fight.

Adrenaline raced as Dod continued to walk forward. He approached Buck, who had fallen a distance behind Boot and was attending to a wounded arm.

Boot was currently punishing the two soldiers who had injured his brother. With each powerful swing or jab of his sword, he seemed to show that he had enough rage to handle them and the three others as well. Dod earnestly hoped he did. All of the soldiers were large tredders.

"Are you okay?" asked Dod, keeping one eye out for the horsemen. They lingered near their steeds.

"It's deep," muttered Buck through gritted teeth. He was using his right hand and mouth to tighten a knot that held a ripped piece of shirt around the wound on his left arm. The creamy-brown color of his crude bandage was being dyed plum red. "At least it's not my fighting arm," he growled. "These traitors won't stop. They're scheduled to give Sirlonk something."

Dod suddenly recognized the largest horseman. It was General Oosh. He was the commanding officer who had listened to Ingrid's preposterous story about a two-hundred-year-old heirloom pet and had seemingly fallen for the tale and been tricked into letting them pass. In retrospect, Dod knew it had been a show, just like Ingrid's performance.

"The big one's high up," said Buck angrily, noting Dod's stare. "Our whole democracy's falling apart. The Order's buying people left and right."

"DO YOU SURRENDER?" shouted Boot, drawing Dod's eyes back to the conflict. Boot had disarmed and injured both contenders and was now following them as they retreated toward General Oosh.

"Brave words," called the general. "It would be a pity to kill you and your friends. Perhaps we can reach an arrangement."

"I don't bargain with traitors!" insisted Boot, stopping to glance over his shoulder at Buck and Dod.

"That's the wrong answer," said General Oosh. "We can't have you tell anyone of our affiliations. I'm a respected man. You might convince good people into believing bad things."

Holding their swords, Buck and Dod moved in behind Boot. Dod was anxious. Not only was he worried about his dueling ability, he sensed additional trouble.

"Throw down your weapons!" ordered the general.

Boot stretched his neck casually. "That would be a stupid way to fight," he said. "What kind of training do you have, anyway?"

A short distance behind the general, the men who had limped away from Boot mounted their horses and drew bows and quivers from their supplies. It was like they planned on bringing guns to a knife fight. Dod felt the odds fading as arrows were pointed at Boot.

"Would you care to reconsider?" chuckled General Oosh.

Options raced through Dod's mind. He concluded they should flee into the trees. Without shields, it would be difficult to block arrows while confronting the three men with drawn swords. The general wasn't preparing for a duel, he was preparing for an execution.

Out of the neighboring thicket came Sirlonk aboard a beautiful horse. "Dod!" he exclaimed. "You're alive! I'm so glad to see you!"

"Enough acting!" burst Dod. "Your men are about to kill us."

"They overheard our conversation!" explained General Oosh. "We didn't notice *that one* for the trees—" He pointed at Buck. "He was eavesdropping. And when we took appropriate measures, these two came to his aid."

"He was tethering their horses," corrected Sirlonk, pulling his hood off. "Besides, *they* shouldn't be punished for *your* stupidity." He glared at the general. "Don't you know, these boys are my friends—right, Dod?"

"Friends don't try to kill each other," responded Dod.

"I don't want *you* dead!" huffed Sirlonk. "On the contrary. I want you very much alive. The Order needs you."

"LIAR!" yelled Dod. He'd had enough. He wasn't sure where his courage came from, but without thinking, he moved toward The Dread, tauntingly waving the Chantolli sword.

"Nice blade," grinned Sirlonk.

"Whether I'm here or at home, your men won't stop," fumed Dod. "You've given them orders! I know it! *'Better luck next time, Dod.'* Sound familiar? Don't play stupid with me."

"Oh, right," said Sirlonk. "At home....Well...things change, you know. A little reading can be very enlightening. I'm glad you're still breathing. Besides, it's your fault, too. You wear your grandfather's necklace *all* the time. It makes altering orders more difficult. Without constant communication, fools often go trotting into contradictory behaviors." He shot General Oosh a scorching glare. "Especially the sort of help that is *so far* away." Sirlonk smiled at Dod and looked skyward at the first dim star that was beginning to appear in the evening sky.

Dod quickly felt his chest for his medallion. It was still there.

"I'll tell you what," said Sirlonk, "if you'll remove the necklace, I'll fix things for you back home. I'll call everyone off right now. It'll be my gift to you."

"I'm not that stupid," said Dod.

"Just for a minute," said Sirlonk, seeming to grab Dod with his eyes. "Trust me this once. You can move closer to your friends if you'd like. I'm not *all* bad. You should know that by now."

Dod glanced over his shoulder at Boot and Buck. Both had looks of horror, as if they fully believed Dod was already somehow involved in The Order.

"Go on," said Sirlonk. "Set it on the ground. And if anyone moves toward you, scoop it up. You have nothing to lose and everything to gain. We're friends, Dod. Let's make things better for your family."

Butterflies danced in Dod's stomach as he drew his medallion from his neck. He was midway between Sirlonk and Boot. At the moment, he trusted neither of them—Sirlonk because he was The Dread and Boot because he hated traitors. But Sirlonk had made a good point. What did Dod have to lose in giving Sirlonk a shot at calling off the thugs on Earth? The very idea that he could do it was intriguing. How would he communicate with them?

Dod carefully set his medallion on the stone walkway and kept his hand inches from it.

"Dod? What are you doing?" demanded Boot.

"He's listening to reason," smiled Sirlonk, reaching blindly into one of his saddlebags. He pulled out a purse-sized leather pouch, unbuckled the lip, and began to write on something. It looked like he was drafting a letter.

"Dod!" thundered Boot agitatedly. "You've already been working with The Order, haven't you? I knew it! *You're* the rat!"

Dod didn't dare turn. He kept his eyes on his medallion and Sirlonk, and he hoped Boot wouldn't rush over and stab him in the back.

"Funny thing for *you* to say," quipped Sirlonk, keeping his head down as he worked. "Have you told Buck and Dod *your* little secret?"

"Boot tells me everything," defended Buck with reservation.

"Do they know what you did—all the people *you* killed?"

Dod instantly felt ill. It was like he'd just awakened from a dream to find that he himself was a murderer. Boot was his best friend, not a villain.

"Tell him he's lying!" said Buck.

Boot remained silent.

"Tell him!" he begged.

Sirlonk chuckled with delight. "I thought you'd want to keep *that* story to yourself." He stopped writing and proceeded to turn knobs. The thing in his bag was some sort of machine.

"What is he talking about?" asked Dod, still focusing on his medallion. He could see Boot's face in his mind. Boot was staring hollowly off into space as he had done in the tent in Commendus's backyard.

"He wouldn't do it!" insisted Buck. "He didn't! He couldn't have! He's not part of The Order! He'd never join you!"

"Pathetic fool," said Sirlonk to Buck as he closed the lip of his bag. "Open your eyes. It's a new world. Help your brothers embrace their destiny."

Boot still remained silent.

"Well, that's it, Dod," said Sirlonk. "Everyone should fall back into line, now. Your family's safe."

Dod snatched his medallion from the ground, put it back on, and spun to face Boot. "Did you kill my grandpa?" he pressed, marching toward him with his sword in hand.

"That's ridiculous," scoffed Buck.

"No it's not!" raged Dod. "He did it! He poisoned my grandpa! That's why he was so concerned when X wrote him letters that said '*Cheers, Boot.*' He was the one who offered the toast instead of Commendus! When X started sending notes, he knew his secret was out. That's why he got upset every time I brought up my grandpa's death. He was trying to cover up the truth." Dod shook his head and felt tears welling up in his eyes. His steps slowed and his sword sagged. He had wanted revenge against Pap's true murderer, but now that it was his best friend, he didn't know what he wanted. "Why'd you do it, Boot?" he groaned. "Why'd you poison 'em?"

Tears were streaming down Boot's face. He threw the crimson blade to the ground and staggered forward. "I'm sorry, Dod," he mumbled. He bent down on one knee and bowed his head. "Do what you need to do. I understand." Boot's words were garbled by his tears.

"Why?" pressed Dod. "Why did you kill them—why did you kill Pap?" His anger was rising. There was no excuse. The blood in his head was pounding like tribal drums.

"You should punish him!" snapped Sirlonk sternly. "Take his ears, and make him promise his allegiance to you! A living slave is better than a dead one."

Dod blinked away tears and looked down at his hands. He was clenching the Chantolli blade so tightly that the blood had mostly drained from his fingers, making them match the white sword. He was angry and frustrated, and his insides felt like they were exploding with fury.

"CUT HIS EARS OFF!" ordered Sirlonk, as if his thunderous voice would force Dod's rage to blossom.

Boot didn't flinch, and Buck stood back in shock, seeming to have disappeared within himself.

"DO IT!" yelled Sirlonk. "JUNGO! JUNGO! JUNGO!"

General Oosh and his men began to chant, too, following Sirlonk's lead. "JUNGO! JUNGO! JUNGO!" they cried.

"Please don't!" sobbed Dilly, rushing from the monument. Sawny was on her heels, carrying the burlap sack. "Don't hurt him, Dod."

Trembling, Dod sheathed his sword. "I don't hate you, Boot," he said, beginning to cry. "I just don't understand."

"It was all a stupid prank," muttered Boot, still looking down in shame.

The girls stopped near the pile of garbage. Something large was emerging from the woods.

"I was mad that they were leaving me behind," continued Boot. "So I thought I'd pull a prank. I had help. A friend gave me the powder to put in their drinks. It was only supposed to make them a little sick. Nothing serious."

"Grab the girls!" ordered Sirlonk.

Dod looked in time to see Dungo leap from the forest and take hold of Dilly and Sawny. His four arms easily contained them. Dod had forgotten how large he was.

"Dungo?" called Dod.

Boot slid and recovered his sword.

"Dey have books," reported Dungo.

"You found them!" burst Sirlonk greedily. "I knew they were in the rubble. The scepters worked!"

"Give them back!" said Dilly, struggling futilely to break free.

"Sirlonk killed your family," shouted Dod to Dungo. "They're all dead."

"Don't listen to him," said Sirlonk. "I already told you. Pious is the man responsible for their deaths. The Democracy doesn't have a place for freaks like you."

"HE'S LYING!" shouted Dod.

"Me?" scoffed Sirlonk. "Dungo knows better. He's my *most trusted* associate."

It was getting dark, so Dungo's face was hard to see. Dod strained to know which way he was leaning in the fight.

"Now, Dod," said Sirlonk. "It's time for you to choose. I need a price for my services. But since I'm a reasonable man, I'll let you pick between Sawny and Buck. One of them lives, the other dies. Prove your loyalty to me. Let's seal this friendship."

Dod couldn't believe his ears.

"Personally, I'd kill Buck if I were you," added Sirlonk. "Sawny's become useful."

Boot sprung from the ground and ran at Sirlonk with the crimson blade in hand. In the dim light, his sword's luminescence made his blade more visible than everything else. "This is for Pap!" he raged angrily, taking a swipe at Sirlonk. "You knew it was poison! You had Horsely give it to me, didn't you? It wasn't warsing powder at all. No matter what dose I gave, they still would have died—"

"Stop being a baby," chided Sirlonk, deflecting Boot's blows. "It's long over." He slid off his horse nonchalantly and positioned himself for a duel.

"But Horsely had me believing that *I* messed up," raged Boot. "He had me thinking that *I* overdosed them—"

"Oh please!" said Sirlonk, twirling his sword in the air. "What does it matter? They're dead! Besides, you can't tell me you haven't enjoyed the benefits of The Order. The past few months have been kind to you."

Boot lunged at Sirlonk and jabbed ferociously. He then dove, rolled, and swiped again. Around and around Boot went, engaging Sirlonk in a battle the likes of which Dod had never seen before. Boot's moves were even more incredible than they had been the night he'd fought the billies, only this time, his opponent was able to hold his ground.

"You can't beat me," laughed Sirlonk. "I'm The Dread! I'm unstoppable! Give me your best. Don't hold back. I love it when you're mad, you fight better—and I must say, Boot, you're one of the best."

Boot pressed at Sirlonk with such force that it made Sirlonk stumble backward, and as he did, Boot struck his left arm. "That's for my brother!" he raged, diving for the kill.

Sirlonk nearly flew from the ground to avoid Boot's attack, though once he'd retreated to a safe distance, he rubbed his wounded arm and moved it slowly. "Oosh," he called. "Dod's made his decision. Kill Buck!"

Without thinking, Dod tackled Buck to the ground. Two arrows flew by.

Oosh and his uninjured soldiers moved in.

"We can take them," said Dod, feeling a burst of confidence. A heavy load had been lifted when he'd heard Boot mention the warsing powder. Clearly Boot hadn't meant any harm, and as for Horsely, Dod had already experienced how evil he'd become. If The Order had said to kill Pap, the Horsely Dod had faced wouldn't have thought twice about trading poison for warsing powder; and he'd have only seen it as an advantage if he could double the crime by enslaving Boot with guilt.

When the soldiers attacked, Dod plunged forward. "You're all cowards!" he yelled. "Death to traitors!"

Darkness was quickly settling in. Dilly and Sawny were now no more than a part of the large blob that remained near the garbage pile. In the heart of the fray with the soldiers was safety from the men with arrows. Dod knew they wouldn't chance a shot near General Oosh with such poor lighting, so he and Buck pressed closer to their attackers and fought valiantly with their swords.

Together, Buck and Dod attempted to hold the three men, but the soldiers' blows seemed much heavier against Buck than Dod. The reprimand they had just received from Sirlonk had set them on a course to lightly injure Dod while killing Buck.

Slowly, the battle moved as Buck and Dod lost ground, though Dod took comfort in knowing that they were headed away from the men with arrows. Eventually, they neared Boot and Sirlonk, until Dod's back was against Boot's.

"I'm so sorry," huffed Boot over his shoulder to Dod. "I loved Pap like he was my own father."

"Too sappy!" mocked Sirlonk, pressing in on Boot. "Let me find you a skirt!"

Dod saw a glimpse. Sirlonk was positioning to drive past Boot in order to personally kill Buck. The move was coming. Dod knew he had to do something, but what?

The night air began to fill with chirping crickets, and suddenly Dod felt the answer. His senses were tingling. There were rats in the monument. He could feel their numbers. From so far away they were stubborn and wouldn't come. Dod pressed with his mind—calling them, begging them. *Come! Fight!*

Back and forth the duel continued. Buck seemed to be tiring. He was facing two men while Dod had half of one. The soldier who was clanking swords with Dod had stopped jabbing inward, likely out of fear that he would strike something vital and face Sirlonk's twisted wrath.

Dod continued to plead with the rats. *COME! FIGHT!* He could feel them climbing through the walls, gnawing on the beams, and scurrying across the rafters. If only they were closer. If only they would obey. And then a burst of inspiration shot through his mind.

CHEW THE ROPE! he mentally shouted, pushing the rats to attack the line that kept the emergency bell loaded. *CHEW! CHEW! CHEW!* Dod exerted all of his inward efforts. He could feel Sirlonk's approach and his gleeful anticipation. Sirlonk's dark heart was brimming with delight in his next move. He couldn't wait to plunge his sword into Buck's back. Dod knew it.

Suddenly, the heavy bell atop the circular tower began ringing, and just below it, a number of torches began burning. The sound was heavenly music to Dod. "THE TROOPS ARE HERE!" he shouted happily. "I KNEW THEY'D COME IN TIME!"

REVEALING SECRETS

Sirlonk took a few steps back and waved his gloved hand in the air. Dod could feel him calling his horse. "We'll finish this later," he cackled, swinging aboard. "HURRY DUNGO!" he shouted loudly. "BRING MY BOOKS BEFORE THE TROOPS TAKE THEM!"

General Oosh and his men fled.

"You're a dead man!" yelled Boot, tiredly shaking his sword in the air.

With a burlap sack tucked against his chest, Dungo scampered to join Sirlonk, though he slowed in front of Dod. For a brief moment, they locked eyes. "Enjoy your garbage," he grunted.

Within seconds, the mob of villains was gone.

"That was too close," muttered Buck, taking a seat on the ground. He laid back panting heavily.

"I almost had him," gloated Boot, gasping nearly as much as Buck.

With the lit tower in the backdrop, Dod could see Dilly and Sawny. They were a hugging silhouette.

Dod approached Boot and patted his shoulder. "We're still friends, right?"

Boot dropped his sword and gave Dod a hug. "I'm so sorry—" he began.

"I know," said Dod, taking deep breaths. "It's all right. You need to forget about it. I have. Horsely's to blame, and The Order's to blame, and maybe Sirlonk's to blame—but you're not. Let's let it end here. No one else needs to know."

Out of the darkness came Sneaker. He jumped to Boot's shoulder and sniffed at Dod's hair, then licked Boot's sweaty cheek.

"We should check on the girls," said Buck in a quavering voice, crawling to his knees. "They haven't left the garbage pile. Do you think Dilly's lost her nose?"

"Probably," said Boot in an equally compromised tone, wiping tears from his face. Both brothers seemed grateful beyond measure that Dod could get past the poisoning.

By the junk pile, Dilly and Sawny were sobbing and hugging when Boot, Buck, and Dod hobbled up. The light from the top of the tower lit the immediate area surrounding the building, including the mound beside the girls.

"You're alive!" exploded Dilly, changing over to hug Boot.

"I thought we were all dead," whimpered Sawny. "If someone hadn't cut the rope—"

"The troops had perfect timing," responded Buck, sounding like a new man. He'd just survived Sirlonk's death sentence.

"What troops?" said Sawny.

Everyone but Dod looked around as if they expected to see men coming from the opposite side of the building.

"*I* did it," confessed Dod. "Lately I've discovered, when I'm near a Soosh Mayler Belt, I can sometimes…well…get animals to move. So tonight, when Sirlonk came close, his belt helped me recruit a few rats to chew the line."

"I love rats!" mumbled Sawny blearily, half crying and half laughing.

Still in Dilly's arms, Boot looked at Dod. "You made the mice rain down in the barn at Twistyard, didn't you?"

Dod smiled. "I can't figure that one out," he said. "There was no mayler belt."

"I was wearing one," said Dilly, beginning to gain control of herself. "For good luck, remember?"

"Oh yeah," nodded Dod.

Dilly zeroed in on Boot with penetrating eyes. "You had me worried! Why were they yelling *Jungo*, Boot? Why were they trying to make Dod hurt you?"

Boot sighed, as if he were about to tell Dilly the truth.

"They wanted a show, so we gave them a show," responded Dod. "You knew we weren't really going to hurt each other, right? We're best friends."

"Dod's a great actor, isn't he?" added Buck.

"I told you," said Sawny, eyeing her sister before jumping to give Dod a hug.

"Did you keep back any of the books?" prodded Buck.

"How could we?" said Dilly. "Dungo's huge. I thought for sure he was going to suffocate us and add our bodies to the garbage."

"That's it!" burst Dod, leaving Sawny's arms to rush to the trash pile. He quickly circled the edge and inspected the top bags. "Here it is!" he said excitedly, picking up a burlap sack. He opened it up and showed his friends. The old books were inside.

"Impossible!" exploded Boot.

"I'll take out the trash," laughed Dilly, grabbing for the sack.

"Dungo's not bad," explained Dod. "He's just stuck. I bet Sirlonk's gonna kill him for this one."

With the bell slowing down and no one coming, Buck showed them to their horses and explained how he'd been spotted while tying them off. He also said that General Oosh had mentioned a present for Sirlonk, something that his men in Driaxom had obtained.

"I hope it's an Ankle Weed," said Boot, mounting Grubber.

"I hope it's two or three," added Dod.

CHAPTER THIRY-FOUR

HAPPY NEW YEAR

B ack at Commendus's palace, the books were immediately taken and stored in a room that was guarded by two dozen of Commendus's best men. Dod and Boot had wanted to hide them and tell no one. But Sawny, Dilly, and Buck had convinced them otherwise, reminding them that Sirlonk would be more prone to kill them if they were the ones keeping the books. So instead, they had given Commendus the records and had gotten him to promise them that they could have free access to the books while staying at the castle. It was a fair compromise.

Commendus had looked only slightly better than he had earlier, but his sense of duty had improved. Upon meeting with the group, his first words had been the announcement that Dod's murder charges had been dropped. The news was expected, yet still wonderful. Dod had forgotten how nice it was to breathe as a free man.

Just before retiring to their bedrooms, Boot's face grew cheery. "None of us mentioned Ingrid to Sirlonk," he whispered, glancing a short distance away at the crowd of guards who stood watch. "We can still catch him with our trap! I bet Ingrid and Juny will show up in the next few days bearing the scepter and hoping to 'help us' with the records. We'll be waiting."

Buck smiled sleepily. "I'll be glad when The Dread's dead," he muttered. "I can't stand him."

"Me too," agreed Dod.

"At least he's decided *I'm* a keeper," teased Sawny proudly.

"You are in *my* book," said Dod, drowsily speaking without thinking. Once he had realized his words, his cheeks flushed.

As Dod lay in bed, he tried to put things together. "Are you still awake, Boot?" he asked. The lights were out, and Buck was snoring.

"Yeah," responded Boot.

"Do you think Humberrone is dead?" asked Dod.

"No," said Boot. "Traygof mentioned he was detained. That means he's still alive, somewhere out there in Soosh."

"Soosh?" mumbled Dod. "Why do you say he's there?"

Boot paused. "He just is."

Dod thought about the images he'd seen of his father in a jungle. Soosh made sense. "I guess I'll be going to Soosh," he whispered to himself, feeling his mind drift off.

All night, questions came and went through Dod's mind. Why were Sirlonk's feet red, and how had he known about the ooblies? Who had told Youk that the Dolsur brothers were going fishing with Dod, or the billies that Dod and his friends would be camping with the map? What had happened to the TCC pack and the special Twistyard books? Who had shot an arrow at Sammywoo, or put a knife in Dod's bag? Where was

The Lost City, why was it so important to The Order, and what connection did it have with Earth?

The list went on and on. And knowing that Sirlonk had friends at Twistyard and had hidden behind the guise of being Ingrid made Dod dream all sorts of things about the people around him. Even his best friend, Boot, took center stage a few times, forcing Dod to face the reality that Boot kept secrets from him—perhaps countless things. Poisoning Pap and the others at High Gate was just one of them.

In the early morning hours before the sun had risen, Dod startled out of sleep. A name was on his lips. Rea Bonboo Chards. Countless puzzles and clues played in Dod's head. How did everything fit together?

Dod was so excited to read the precious books, he struggled to stay in bed. Perhaps some of his questions could be answered by the old records, and others could be answered by Bonboo, just as soon as he returned from Raul. But for the moment, it was dark outside, and his friends were asleep.

As he lay pondering, Josh crossed his mind. Had he visited Green? How had he known about the three kings and the symbol for Chards?

Suddenly, Dod found his face pressed against the dusty metal of the ventilation duct in Las Vegas. Crumpled in an awkward position, Cole lay still. His heart was pounding. He had taken his medallion off for a few hours while on Tripeak Island—had it been long enough? Where were the men with guns?

Cole didn't move for ten minutes. He lay listening for voices. Eventually, his legs began to tingle and cramp. Staying as quiet as possible, Cole slid backward and pushed his way out of the duct. To his relief, the rooftop was empty and the metal-grinding machine was off. No one was around. The late afternoon sun warmed his face.

"I've got to call home," he said, hurrying down the fire escape. He raced across the empty field he'd seen Ruth and Naomi pass through and bolted into the first open establishment. It was a gas station. Three guys stood by the drinks with their pants hanging low, joking about rainbow shoelaces and bubblegum. Cole walked up to them and begged a call.

When Aunt Hilda answered, Cole didn't explain the details, but he told her he was okay and insisted they leave the house and meet him at a neighbor's. He would be there in a few hours.

The next three days were a jumble of crazy experiences. The police couldn't find any proof of the alleged hostage circumstance, and therefore, took Cole's, Ruth's, and Naomi's testimonies and said they would get back to them later. Their tones said never.

While Cole's family, Ruth, and Naomi stayed with neighbors, Naomi paid to have top-of-the-line security systems installed in her house and both sides of the duplex. She said it was the least she could do to repay Cole for saving her life. It made returning home on New Year's Day almost bearable.

Thoughts of the men with guns wouldn't leave Cole's mind. What would stop them from coming and stealing Josh or Alex? The FBI was too busy to listen. They said they would get involved if he or his family members were taken hostage or killed. But that was the sticker: An obvious crime had to have already been committed for them to lend help. No one had the resources to prevent a crime! It made each day maddening. Cole felt like he'd never feel safe again. And since Naomi had told his mother and Aunt Hilda about her experience, they were both worried, too.

When the second of January arrived, Cole and his brothers didn't return to school. It was too soon. They stayed home and spent the day chatting. It was the first chance Cole had had to talk with his brothers alone. He told them all about his most recent adventures in Green, including his discovery of the scepter. When he got to the part about the symbol for Chards, Cole held the crown Josh had given him and pointed at the scribble Josh had drawn with permanent black marker. "How did you know about *this*?" he asked Josh.

Josh stared at the floor. "Promise you won't get mad?" he said.

"I won't get mad," agreed Cole. "Just tell me the truth. How did you know about the symbol and the three kings?"

Josh sighed. "I opened your letter from Dad," he confessed. "He said we're the descendants of one of the three kings—the one from Soosh."

"Rea Bonboo Chards?" burst Cole.

"I don't know," said Josh. "But our family sign is the big circle with the little circles inside it."

The doorbell rang. Alex ran to hide in a bottom cupboard as Josh rushed to see who it was. Cole followed Josh, his heart in his throat.

"It's another present for you," groaned Josh jealously. "You get all the good stuff!"

"Naomi's just trying to thank me," said Cole.

"She can tell *me* thank you if she wants," snapped Josh. "I'm not afraid of guns. Nothing scares me."

The package was sizable and heavy. Cole's name was on the label. Not wanting Josh to hover over him, Cole hefted the package up to his room, shut the door, and leaned his back against the door so Josh couldn't barge in. Banging ensued as Cole cut the top of the box open.

"What?" gasped Cole. He couldn't contain his shock. The entire box was filled with hundred-dollar bills, stacked and wrapped in ten-thousand-dollar packets. Cole counted the money twice. "One million dollars!" he muttered under his breath. Josh was still banging against the other side of the door. "Ruth's dad must be really, really rich."

Smelling the money on his hands, Cole carefully opened the envelope that had sat atop the brick of bills and pulled the note out. There were only five words on the page:

Welcome to The Order, Dod!

Book 4

THE ADVENTURES OF DOD

SECRETS OF THE CURSED

Feeling The Order's pull, Cole battles over what to do next, but when someone in his own home drops shocking news, his course becomes crystal clear: He must face his fears and fight for his family.

With armies gathering, dark forces rising, and a dragon roaming the skies, the world of Green is poised to topple into chaos. The Order's power and influence seem limitless and their tactics underhanded. Nevertheless, Dod and his Twistyard friends push forward, determined to prevail. As they unravel secrets, they gain power to fight back in creative ways. Will their plans work? Will their books and maps and discoveries be enough to stop the tide of evil? Can they keep their loved ones safe while thwarting The Order's progress? Only time will tell. If you dare read on, follow the clues to the truth.

Thanks for being part of the adventure!

We would really love to have you come and visit us at **www.TheAdventuresofDod.com** for free downloads: free e-books, free audio-books, free maps, free comics, and more! It's the site for all things Dod related. Make sure you tell your friends that they can read book one for free if they download an e-version of it from our website. We hope everyone gets a chance to enjoy the series.

Questions for Discussion

1. Cole was asked to give up something he valued in order to save someone else. What was it? Have you ever had to give up something you wanted in order to make someone else happy? How did it make you feel? What did Bonboo do for Dod? Why do you think he did it? Can other people trust you the way Bonboo trusts Dod?

2. Sawny loves to learn new things from reading books. Because of her curiosity, she often discovers the answers to difficult questions. What kinds of books do you like to read? Can you think of a time when you were able to teach a friend something that you learned from reading a book? How does it feel when you know the answer to someone's question?

3. In chapter 12 it states, "Buck was scared—truly terrified— but he wasn't going to let his fears stop him from helping his brother." What would you be willing to do for someone you love? Do you have any friends or family members who are serving or have served in the military? What kinds of sacrifices have they made for us?

4. In chapter 5 Youk says, "Many a wise man has been tricked by the foolish assumptions of a carefully played show." What do you think he means? What does it mean to be deceived? Consider the advertisements you see each day. How might they contain deception?

5. Boot spoke of his mother's stubbornness. When addressing this characteristic, Dilly lamented, "...you can't force a chick to hatch." What does Dilly mean? Is it sometimes hard to

wait for the things we want? How do you act if you don't get what you want?

6. In chapter 8 Boot explains to Dod, "I know people are sometimes driven to do dumb things and are stuck thinking there's no way out. But they're wrong. You can always choose—every moment... everyday... every minute." Why do you think Boot said this? Has anyone ever tried to get you to do something you didn't want to do? What are some ways to say no?

7. While confined to a prison cell in the basement of Twistyard, Dod "couldn't help feeling happy" as he thought about the possibility that his father was still alive. What brings you happiness? How can you change your mood from a bad one to a good one? What difference can a good attitude make?

8. Within the Code of the Kings monument the words are written, "KEEP EACH KINGDOM STRONG FOR SUBJECTS FIRST, THEN RULERS, BY THE UNITED WILL OF ALL MANKIND." Does our country have a similar creed? What protects your rights as a citizen? What does it mean to have a democracy? What differences can you see between Green's government and Raul's? Which do you prefer? What kind of a government do we have?

9. Boot and his mother had hard feelings toward Boot's grandfather, Boot Bellious Dolsur III, because of things he had supposedly done. Boot said, "I'd have changed my name years ago if it weren't for my father. His legacy is worth remembering." What does it mean to have a legacy? Can you think of something about your parents or grandparents that you are proud of? How do you want to be remembered?

"Breakfast!"
"Wait. That looks like a dragon egg to me."

"Don't be silly. Everyone knows dragons aren't real!"

The Adventures of Dod

"Why do you think they call ME The Dread?"

The Adventures of Dod

"And to think they said Soosh was dangerous!"

The Adventures of Dod

"Don't worry. This is going to hurt a lot!"

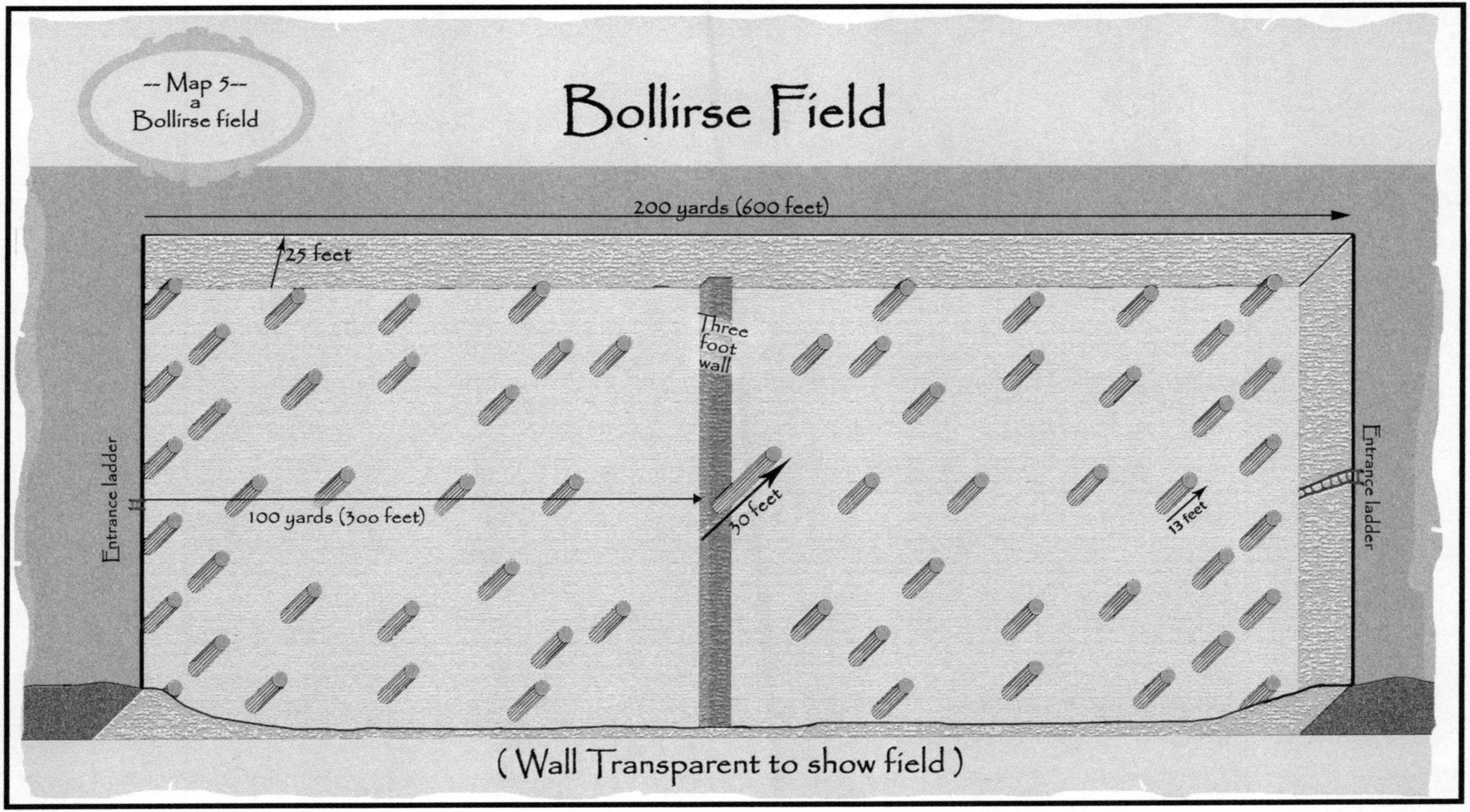

--- Map 5 ---
a
Bollirse field

Bollirse Field

Entrance ladder

25 feet

100 yards (300 feet)

Three foot wall

30 feet

200 yards (600 feet)

13 feet

Entrance ladder

(Wall Transparent to show field)

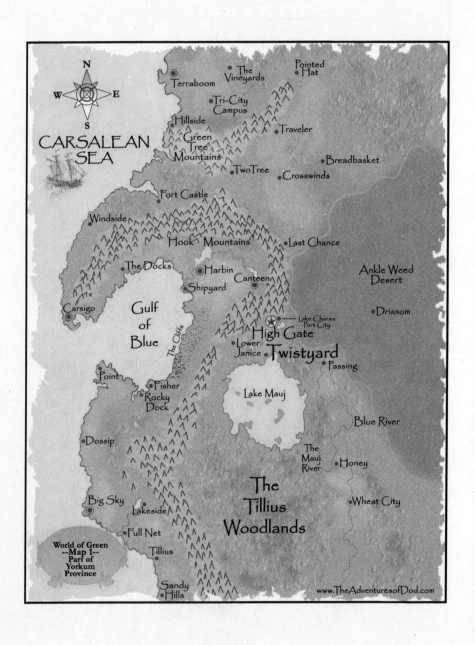

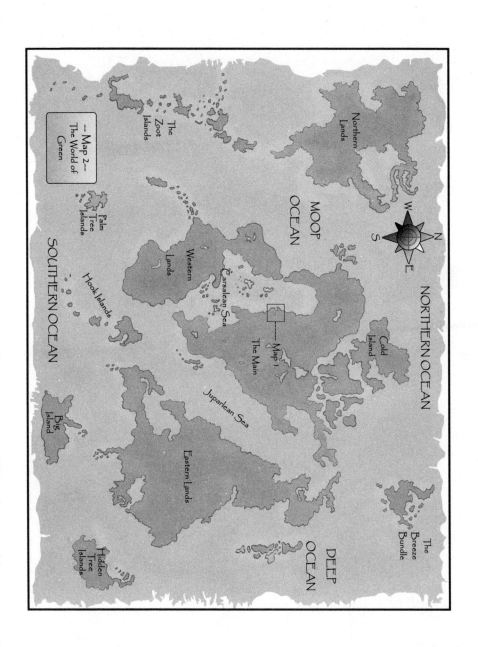

-- Map 2 --
The World of
Green

The
Zoot
Islands

Northern
Lands

MOOP
OCEAN

NORTHERN OCEAN

Palm
Tree
Islands

Western
Lands

Carsalean Sea

Map 1

The Main

Cold
Island

SOUTHERN OCEAN

Hook Islands

Juparlean Sea

Big
Island

Eastern
Lands

DEEP
OCEAN

The
Breeze
Bundle

Hidden
Tree
Islands

N
W
S
E

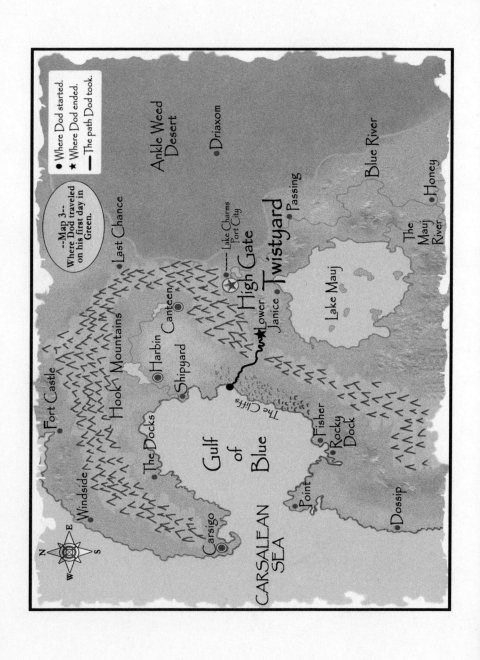

- • Where Dod started.
- ★ Where Dod ended.
- — The path Dod took.

--Map 3--
Where Dod traveled
on his first day in
Green.

Ankle Weed
Desert

• Driaxom

Blue River

Honey

The
Mauj
River

Last Chance

Passing

Lake Charms
Port City

High Gate

Twistyard

Lake Mauj

Hook Mountains

Harbin

Canteen

Shipyard

Lower
Janice

The Cliffs

Fort Castle

The Docks

Fisher

Rocky
Dock

Windside

Gulf
of
Blue

Point

Dossip

Carsigo

CARSALEAN
SEA

N
E
W
S

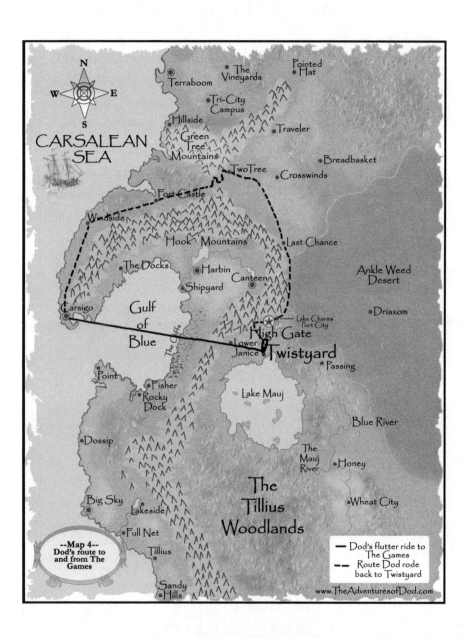

About the Author

Thomas R. Williams lives in Utah with his wife and thirteen kids. He regularly visits Green to help oversee the destruction of The Order before time runs out. His children constantly amaze him with the things they put together from clues they've found in the Dod series.

Recently, after a close brush with death nearly claimed the life of a family member, Thomas's kids remarked, "If Dad died, that would be the worst, because then we'd never find out the secrets and how the series ends!" From countless emails, the author recognizes that his kids are not alone in their desire to know the full truth. Fortunately, Thomas says his health is moderately good and should hold up just fine.

To learn more about the crazy author of this seven-book series, or to have a few laughs, go to www.TheAdventuresofDod.com. Also, you can email the author at Tom@TheAdventuresofDod.com.

6 10563 10156 6

PORTRAIT OF AUTHOR